SHADOW OF THE SCORPION

NEAL ASHER

SHADOW OF THE SCORPION

TOR

First published in the United States of America 2008 by Night Shade Books, NY

This edition first published 2009 by Tor
an imprint of Pan Macmillan Ltd
Pan Macmillan, 20 New Wharf Road, London N1 9RR
Basingstoke and Oxford
Associated companies throughout the world
www.panmacmillan.com

ISBN 978-0-230-73859-1 HB
ISBN 978-0-230-73896-6 TPB

A CIP catalogue record for this book is available from
the British Library.

Typeset by Setsystems Ltd, Saffron Walden, Essex
Printed and bound in the UK by CPI Mackays, Chatham ME5 8TD

Visit **www.panmacmillan.com** to read more about all our books
and to buy them. You will also find features, author interviews and
news of any author events, and you can sign up for e-newsletters
so that you're always first to hear about our new releases.

For the Island of Crete, where the scorpions are small, the measures large, and the sun ever shining

Acknowledgements

Thanks to those who first published this book in America: Jeremy Lassen and Jason Williams of Night Shade Books. Thanks also to my agent Simon Kavanagh for striking a deal with Macmillan for this book and for his unflinching support of my previous Night Shade Book, *Prador Moon*. My best wishes to those whose work at Macmillan brings this book to the shelves: Peter Lavery, Julie Crisp, Chloe Healy, Steve Rawlings, and many others besides – if I've missed you out, demand beer from me. And as always, ευχαριστώ πολύ Caroline.

1

Sitting on an outcrop, Ian Cormac stared at the words and figures displayed on his palmtop, but could not equate them to anything he knew. A world had been bombed into oblivion and the death toll was a figure that could be read, but which it was impossible to extract real sense from. Though the battle lines had not shifted substantially for twelve years, and such a cataclysmic event was unusual, it was not a story that could hold a young boy's attention for long.

Ian's attention wandered, and he gazed back down at the rock-nibblers swarming over the massive fossil – like beetles over a decaying corpse. Slowly, cutting away and removing the intervening stone with small diamond saws and ceramal manipulators, they were revealing the intact remains of – he cleared the recent story from his palmtop screen and returned to an earlier page – an *Ed-mon-to-saurus*. To one side his mother Hannah sat with her legs crossed, monitoring the excavation on a laptop open where the name implied. She was clad in a pair of his dad's Sparkind combat trousers, enviroboots and a sky-blue sleeveless top, her fair hair tied back from her smudged face. She was very old – he counted it out in his head – nearly six times his own age, but she looked like an elf-girl since the new treatments had cleared the last of the old anti-geris from her system. While he watched she made some adjustments on the laptop's touch-screen, then transferred her attention to the line of nibblers entering a large crate set to one side. In there, he knew, they were depositing the slivers of stone they had removed, all wrapped in plasmel and all numbered so that their position in relation to the skeleton could be recalled. On the side of the crate were stencilled the letters FGP, standing for Fossil Gene Project.

'Why do you want to keep the stone?' he asked.

With some exasperation Hannah glanced up at him. 'Because, Ian, its structure can tell us much about the process of decay and fossilization. In some instances it is possible to track the process back through time and then partially reconstruct the past.'

He listened carefully to the reply, then glanced down at the text the speech converter had placed across his screen. It was nice to see that he understood every individual word, though putting them all together he was not entirely sure he grasped all of her meaning, and he suspected she had, out of impatience, not given him a full answer. It was all something to do with fossilized genes, though of course it was impossible for genes to survive a process millions of years long. She'd once said something about molecular memory, pattern transfer, crystallization . . . He still couldn't quite grasp the intricacies of his mother's work, but was glad to know that many a lot older than him couldn't either.

Anyway, he felt she hadn't really answered the real drive of his question. It struck him, at the precocious age of eight, that collecting up all the stone like this was a waste of *resources*. There was a *war on*, and a *war effort*, and it seemed odd to him that his mother had been allowed to continue her work when Prador dread-noughts could arrive in the Solar System at any time and convert it into a *radioactive graveyard*.

Ian raised his attention from his mother, focused briefly on the gravcar they'd flown out here in, then gazed out across the rugged landscape of Hell Creek. People had been digging up dino-saur bones here for centuries, and finding an intact skeleton like this one was really something. He grudgingly supposed that not everything should stop for the war.

Now returning his attention to his palmtop, he began again flicking through the news services to pick up the latest about a conflict that had started thirty-seven years before he was born. Though the Prador bombardment of one world was the main story, he searched elsewhere for news from another particular sector of the Polity and found that after the Hessick Campaign the Prador had suffered heavy losses at a world called Patience. He felt a glow of pride. That was where his father was fighting. Moving on, he then as usual returned to reading about the exploits of General Jebel U-cap Krong. What a name! Jebel Up-close-and-personal Krong; a guy who, during the early years of the war, had liked to take out Prador by sticking gecko mines to their shells.

'Why did you call me Ian?' he abruptly asked, peering down at his mother.

She glanced up, still with a hint of exasperation in her expression. 'You're named after your grandfather.'

Boring.

Ian checked the meaning of the name on his palmtop and discovered his name to merely be a Scottish version of the name John, which meant 'beloved of God' or some such archaic nonsense. He decided then to check on his family name. There was a lot of stuff about kings and ravens, which sounded really good until he came across the literal translation of Cormac as 'son of defilement'. He wasn't entirely sure what that meant, and with those kings and ravens at the forefront of his mind, he didn't bother to pursue it.

'I'd rather be called just Cormac,' he said.

As soon as he had started attending school people began referring to him just as Cormac, and even then he had decided he preferred his second name to his first.

His mother focused on him again. 'You and Dax are both "Cormac", Ian – it's what is called a surname.'

True enough, but she had chosen to retain her own surname of Lagrange and had passed it on to her other son Alex.

'It's what they call me at school,' he insisted.

3

'What you may be called at school is not necessarily the best choice . . .'

'I want to be called Cormac.'

This seemed to amuse her no end.

'Why certainly, young Cormac.'

He winced. He didn't really want that prefix. He also understood that she was humouring him, expecting him to forget about this name-change. But he didn't want to. Suddenly it seemed to take on a great importance to him, seemed to define him more than the bland name 'Ian'. Returning his attention to his screen he researched it further, and even remained firm about his decision upon finding out what 'defilement' meant.

After a little while his mother said, 'That's enough for now, I think,' and folding her laptop she stood up. 'Another month and we should be able to move the bones.'

Cormac frowned. When he was old enough, he certainly would not become an archaeologist and would not spend his time digging up bones. Maybe he would join the medical wing of ECS like Dax, or maybe the Sparkind like his father, or maybe he would be able to join Krong's force, the Avalonians. Then after a moment he reconsidered, understanding the immaturity of his choices. Only little boys wanted to be soldiers.

'Come on little warrior, let's go get ourselves some lunch!'

Cormac closed up his palmtop, then leapt from the rock. He was going to walk but it was so easy to run down the slope. In a moment he was charging towards her, something bubbling up inside his chest and coming out of his mouth as a battle cry. As she caught him, he pressed his palmtop against her stomach.

'Blam!'

'I take it I've been U-capped,' she observed, swinging him round, then dumping him on his feet.

'He's blown up loads more Prador!' Ian informed her.

She gave him a wry look. 'There's nothing good about killing,' she observed.

'Crab paste!' he exclaimed.

'I think I'm going to have to check what news services you're using, Ian.'

'Cormac,' he reminded her.

She grimaced. 'Yes, Cormac – it slipped my mind.'

He held her hand as they walked down to the gravcar. It was okay to do that here, where only the AI who kept watch over all these bones could see them. Shortly they climbed into the car and were airborne.

He considered for a moment what to say, then asked, 'Isn't the Fossil Gene Project a waste of resources?'

'Research of any kind is never a waste, even in the most dire circumstances,' she replied, then allowed him a moment to check on his p-top the meaning of 'dire'. 'However, though our funding here has been much reduced because of the war, we are allowed to continue because our research might have some war application.'

'Make dinosaurs to fight the Prador,' he suggested, this idea immediately turning into a lurid fantasy. Imagine Jebel riding a T-rex into battle against the crabs!

'No, I'm talking about the possible uses of some coding sequences in the creation of certain viruses.'

'Oh, biological warfare,' he said, disappointed. 'Aren't they difficult to off that way?'

'They are difficult to "off" in many ways, excepting Jebel's particular speciality.'

Abruptly she turned the car so it tilted over, swinging round in a wide circle, and peered past him towards the ground. He looked in the same direction and saw something down there, perambulating across the green. It appeared big, its metal back segmented. As they flew above it, it raised its front end off the ground and waved its antennae at them, then raised one armoured claw as if to snip them out of the sky. A giant iron scorpion.

'What's that?' he asked, supposing it some excavating machine controlled by the AI.

With a frown his mother replied, 'War drone,' then put the gravcar back on course and took them away. Cormac tried to stand and look back, but his mother grabbed his shoulder and pulled him down.

'Behave yourself or I'll put the child safeties back on.'

A war drone!

Ian Cormac behaved himself.

The campsite beside the lake was mostly occupied by those here for the fishing. Their own accommodation was a bubble house of the kind used by many who were conducting a slow exploration of Earth. You bought the house and outfitted it as you wished, but rented the big AG lifter to take you from location to location. While they had been away, some more bubble houses had arrived and one other was in the process of departing – the enormous lifter closing its great earwig claws around the compact residence while the service pipes, cables and optics retracted into their posts. As his mother brought the gravcar down, the lifter took that house into the sky, drifting slowly out over the lake on AG. This time, rather than land the gravcar beside the house she took it into the carport, and upon landing there sent the instruction for the floor clamp to engage.

'Are we going?' he asked.

'We certainly are,' his mother replied.

As they clambered out of the car he peered at some damage on his door and wondered when that had happened, and if he might be blamed. Then he hurried after his mother when she shouted for him.

Two hours later Cormac was playing with his cybernetic dinosaur when an AG lifter arrived for their home. As he abandoned his toy and walked over to the sloping windows to watch the process, he heard a strange intermittent sound. He tentatively identified it as sobbing, but even then he could not be sure, because it was drowned out by the racket of service disengagement and the sounds of the lifter's clamps clonking into place around the house. Soon their home was airborne and, gazing beyond the campsite, he was sure he saw the war drone again, heading in. A hand closed on his shoulder. He looked up at his mother, who now wore an old-style pair of sunglasses.

'Why are we going?' he asked.

'I've done enough here for now – the project won't need me for a while,' she replied. Turning to gaze down at him, she added, 'Cormac,' and the name seemed laden with meaning at that moment.

'Where are we going?' he asked.

'Back home.'

Cormac grimaced to himself. 'Back home' usually meant a return to his schooling, and suddenly the idea of sitting around watching his mother dig up fossil bones became attractive.

'Do we have to?'

'I'm very much afraid that we do,' she replied. 'I think we are going to need to be somewhere familiar.'

As Cormac lay on his bunk with his hands behind his head, fingers interlaced, he felt the ship surface into the real – a horrible twisting sensation throughout his body and a momentary but utterly bewildering distortion of his perception – but like the three recruits he was bunking with, he just pretended it was no bother. They were ECS regulars who had gone through a year of tough intensive training, and a little perceptual displacement shouldn't be a problem.

Carl Thrace, a lean man with cropped blond hair, elf-sculpt ears and slanting dark blue eyes, put aside his pulse-rifle, which he had been tinkering with yet again, then picked up the room remote and used it to turn on their screen. Revealed against the black of space was a planet utterly swathed in pearly cloud, a debris ring encircling it. Distantly, in that ring, ships could be seen, about which occurred the occasional flashes of either detonations or particle cannons firing.

'I thought Hagren was Earthlike?' said Yellow N'gar – a woman with a boosted musculature, semi-chameleodapt skin and hair in the usual military crop. The skin of her face partially mirroring the colour of her uniform collar and her own hair, she turned to the Golem Olkennon, who wore the not very convincing emulation of a grey-haired matron.

Olkennon focused on Cormac. 'You tell them, since it seems you are the only one who has bothered to do any research on our destination.'

Damn, teacher's pet, thought Cormac. But it was true that the others hadn't seemed inclined to find anything out about this world. Carl's obsession had, in the two years Cormac had known him, always been weapons technology, and he looked set to become a specialist in that area. Yellow seemed intent on becoming the best groundside fighting grunt possible, hence her skin adaptation. Neither of them seemed to show an interest in anything outside of their narrow focus.

'It *was* Earthlike,' said Cormac, 'though point seven gravity, and with three quarters of its surface being landmass. There's a native ecology under a hundred-year preservation and study order—'

Carl let out a snort of mirth at that, because ever since the first runcible had gone online, the preservation of ecologies had become something of a joke. Instantaneous travel between worlds also meant the instantaneous transference of all sorts of life forms. Many people fought to preserve and record, down to the molecular/genetic level, alien forms on alien worlds. In some cases they were fighting a losing battle when stronger alien or Terran forms were introduced, in other cases those forms they were studying became the invaders elsewhere. It was evolution in action, stellar scale.

Cormac shrugged an acknowledgement and continued, 'An Earthform GM ecology was constructed for formerly bare areas everywhere inland, but only a small amount of that survives – most of those areas are now forested with skarch trees.' He sat up. 'I do know that Hagren didn't have a debris ring when we colonized it.' He pointed at the picture. 'That ring consists of the remnants of about five space stations, a couple of thousand satellites and a selection of Polity and Prador warships.'

'Ah,' said Yellow. 'And the people, on the surface?'

'Coil-gunned from orbit – I don't know all the details, but only about half the original population of eighty million survived.'

'Fuck,' said Carl, picking up his pulse-rifle again and perhaps wishing for an enemy to shoot, but though the Polity was still clearing up the mess, the war had been over for ten years.

'Okay,' said Olkennon. 'Now you're acquainted with some of the facts, it's time for us to get moving. Get your gear together: Earth-range envirosuits, impact armour, small arms and usual supplies. The heavy stuff is already down there.'

'Shit,' said Carl, 'are there Prador down there too after so long?'

'Apparently there are a few,' Olkennon replied as she headed for the storage area to the cabin's rear, 'but they are not the real problem.'

Beyond the door to the cabin Cormac shared with the other three, the tubeway network of the ship was zero gravity. Gravplates had been provided only in cabins and training areas – all set to the pull of Hagren so the troops aboard could become accustomed to it. Cormac's pack was heavy over those plates, and now out in the tubeways it possessed a ridiculous amount of inertia and a seeming mind of its own, but he managed to keep with the others despite the tubeways filling with troops heading for the lander bays.

Finally, in their assigned bay, Cormac studied his surroundings. All seemed chaos, with troops and equipment shifting through webworks of guide ropes to a row of heavy lifter wings parked one behind the other like iron chevrons. The three followed Olkennon along one guide rope to their assigned craft, and joined a queue of waiting troops winding between floating masses of equipment. When his turn came, Cormac gratefully scrambled aboard, pushed his pack into the space provided behind the seat in front of his, strapped it in place, then pulled himself into a position over his seat to get out of people's way. There were hundreds aboard this craft, mostly four-person units of regulars like his own, but also plenty of 'specialists' and units of Sparkind – the latter distinctive by their faded envirosuits and rank patches, but mostly by the smooth unhurried way they moved in zero-gee.

'Get yourselves strapped in,' Olkennon instructed – the same instruction other unit leaders were also giving.

Before he pulled himself down in his seat, Cormac noticed a man and a woman taking the seats nearest the end of the spine aisle where it led into the cockpit. They did not wear uniform, just comfortable clothing that included a mismatched combination of fatigues, denim, enviroboots and chameleoncloth capes. Peering at the equipment strapped before their seats he saw two stretched multipurpose sniper rifles. Maybe these two were just specialists, but the way they had been talking to the lifter's pilot and the deference with which he seemed to respond to them made Cormac suspect they were ECS agents.

Killers, he thought.

'Is there something about the instruction "Get strapped in" that confuses you, Cormac?' Olkennon enquired.

He hurriedly pulled himself down and drew the straps across

his body. Once secure, he glanced at Carl, who was sitting right next to him. 'Be nice to know what we're dropping into.'

Carl grimaced. 'Cormac, we're little more than trainees. It'll be guard duty and urban policing. Anything heavy goes down and the Sparkind will be on it like a Zunniboot on a bug. We get to experience a new environment, do some scutwork and earn a few points towards our final assessment.'

Carl evidently wanted a fight, and knew it would be some years before those in charge would let him anywhere near one. Cormac wondered what it was that he himself wanted. He'd joined ECS because he felt a responsibility towards the society that had raised him, but also because it seemed like a good way to travel to places usually off the map. So many other careers would have resulted in him being planet-bound and travelling only when he could afford to, and then to the usual tourist traps. What was the old joke? Join the army, see interesting new places, meet interesting new people, and kill them. He hoped that wouldn't be necessary, but he was prepared to do his duty.

Am I naive? he wondered, then shrugged. Of course he was, compared with some of the people here who, despite their appearance, were in some cases five times his age.

The lifter shunted forward in the queue, and viewing screens along the bulkheads before them powered up. Cormac considered the wing shape of the lifter. The vessel was capable of AG descent but had been built in such a shape to enable glide re-entry and landing should anything go wrong with the gravmotors. Only ECS still built these things, the landing craft constructed by other Polity organizations coming in all shapes and sizes. He supposed those other craft were less likely to go wrong, since there was less chance that anyone would be shooting at them.

Finally he felt the lifter stabilize on maglev fields, then abruptly surge forwards. The screens ahead of him showed the bay walls receding, and then the lifter fell into flecked blackness. Internal lights dimmed automatically as the craft tugged sideways and brought the planet into view. This seemed to be the signal for everyone to settle and prepare for the hour-long flight to the landing field. Seat lights came on here and there; palmtops, laptops and even the occasional paper book were opened; some passengers sat back with their eyes closed, seeking entertainment or instruction from the augmentations affixed like iron kidney beans behind their ears and surgically linked to their brains.

Cormac opened the top of his pack and took out his own palmtop, quickly calling up the sites that had provided him with information about the planet below. Glancing aside, he noticed that Carl had what might be described as the breech section of a pulse-rifle on his lap, plugged via an optic cable into a palmtop. Yallow, sitting next to him, was leaning back, eyes closed and fingers tapping against her chair arm. Perhaps she was listening to music through her aug, or watching a musical, or even taking part in one. Olkennon was reading a paper book – *The Art of War* by Sun Tzu. She could have uploaded a recording of the book straight to her crystal mind, so Cormac guessed this was all for show.

Hagren had been an idyllic place to live. Its cities had been very open-plan, but most of the planetary wealth was generated by concerns growing GM crops used in the manufacture of esoteric drugs and biotech construction units, or raising vat-grown meat and other comestibles. These concerns were scattered like farms and ranches over the four main interlinked continents. The spirit here had been a pioneering independent one, and this resulted in a lot of problems when ECS ordered the evacuation. It had gone slowly – only two million shifted offworld by the time the Prador arrived. At first Cormac couldn't understand what had gone wrong, then studying news items of the time he realized someone had been sowing some quite strange memes. The Polity, apparently, was not to be trusted and the Prador were not as bad as portrayed – they were in fact being used as an excuse for the evacuation so ECS could get a firmer grip on this world. Cormac sat back. It all started to make sense to him now – the requirement for so many troops here.

'Separatists,' he said.

'Outstanding,' said Olkennon, without looking up from her book.

From orbit the impact site was teardrop-shaped with a wrinkled area just beyond the blunt end, and beyond that a curiously even and radial pattern spreading to the coastal cities. It seemed a geographic oddity, a curious formation, until you were there, and saw what it meant.

The heavy lifter deposited them on a flat expanse of plasticrete that extended into misty distance out of which autogun towers loomed. Other lifters were coming down, smaller transports like flying train carriages were picking up troops and supplies, gravcars and floating platforms zipped here and there. A massive snake of troops clad in body armour was winding its way into the mists, but they were not to join it.

Holding her fingers to her ear as if listening to something, when in reality the radio signal was directly entering her artificial brain, Olkennon said, 'There'll be a transport along for us shortly. Fifty of us are on special assignment out in the sticks.'

The air was breathable but left an acidic taste and smelt of burning hair. Cormac breathed through his mouth and took fre-quent sips from the water spigot of his envirosuit to wash the taste from his palate. Peering intently through the mist, he tried to discern his surroundings. Over in one direction he was sure he could see trees, and in another direction he was sure lay the sea – either that or the expanse of plasticrete extended to the horizon.

Some of the troops who had come down with them peeled off

in disciplined groups to join the departing column. Some Sparkind moved off with them, whilst others were picked up by a small open-topped transport. The two figures Cormac guessed were ECS agents opened a crate that had been deposited, amongst many, from the lifter's belly hold. Eventually they dragged out a grav-scooter, unfolded it and prepared it for use, then mounted one behind the other and shot off into the sky. Cormac wondered who they were off to assassinate.

Finally two train carriage transports landed for them and they boarded. Their journey took an hour, and gazing down through one window Cormac saw that they were approaching the impact site they had spied earlier. After the transport departed, leaving fifty of them on the peak of a spoil hill, Cormac gazed around. Through slowly clearing mist he could see the edge of that radial pattern, and now knew it consisted of skarch trees, millions of acres of them, all flattened and pointing in the direction of the blast wave. The spoil hill they stood upon had been thrown up by the impact, and was one of a whole range of them. Below this range, the scalloped inner slope of the crater delved down to something massive, brassy-coloured, and still smoking.

'I have given your unit leaders the positions for each unit and the area to be covered by each,' said someone.

Cormac turned to see some grizzled veteran standing balanced on a couple of packs. He glanced at Carl, who rolled his eyes – it had been a dictum in the regulars that so long as your commander never felt the urge to make speeches, your chances of survival were higher. However, after more closely studying the one addressing them, it dawned on him that the veteran was a Golem. In reality, he realized, all the new human recruits here were being nurse-maided.

'I cannot overstress the importance of what we are doing here. There are those who would like to gain access to what lies below us, and having gained access might obtain weapons whose destructive power we have seen the effect of in orbit, and on the surface of this world. Now I'm not going to ramble on – I'm not one for speeches. Your unit leaders will take you to your areas of responsibility.' The Golem grinned and stepped down.

'What did I tell you?' said Carl. 'Guard duty.'

'Yeah, but we're guarding something pretty important,' said Yallow.

They'd been given a screen display aboard the troop transport – almost a documentary. It had taken a swarm of Polity attack ships and drones to drive the Prador dreadnought down into the atmosphere. The linear accelerator that had finally done for its engines had been sited down the length of a deep mineshaft in the ground. That mineshaft had become a crater itself shortly afterwards. The dreadnought, suddenly gaining the aerodynamics of a million-ton brick, had dropped, attempted AG planing, then ploughed into the ground below where Cormac stood.

'Comunits on,' said Olkennon. 'Let's go.'

'This is to give us an authentic taste of soldiering,' commented Carl, as he gazed out through his monocular into the darkness.

Cormac squelched his feet in the mud in the bottom of their foxhole and surmised, from his reading, that an authentic experience should include leaky boots. Carl's cynicism could be wearing at times. He raised his own monocular and peered from his side of the foxhole. The infrared image he saw showed him leggy things with bodies about the size of a human head crawling about on the slopes below. They'd been given no warnings about anything dangerous . . . then again, maybe that was part of the learning process. Maybe they had been supposed to find this out for themselves.

'Are you seeing these beasties?' he asked.

'Scavengers,' Carl replied. 'Called cludder beetles. They'll eat anything organic.'

'I thought the inland ecology was Terran.'

'Imports – the eggs probably came in on the bottom of some-one's boot.'

That accounted for Carl knowing about these things, for to Cormac's knowledge he certainly hadn't done any research on this place.

They kept watching into the long hours of the night. The stars here had a reddish tint and there were no recognizable constel-lations. About three hours into their watch a group of four aster-oids tumbled up over the horizon, flashing reflected sunlight, then falling into shadow as their course took them overhead. When he began to feel weary, Cormac took out a packet of stimulant patches and pressed one against his wrist. In moments his bleari-ness cleared and he abruptly realized one of the cludders was now only a few yards downslope from him. He pointed his monocular at it and brought it into focus.

'Fancy a swap round?' he suggested to Carl.

'I'm fine where I am,' his companion replied.

The cludder looked horribly like a human skull without eye-sockets and with eight arthropod legs sprouting from where its jawbone should have been. He could hear it making sucking slobbering sounds as it drew a skarch twig into some unseen mouth.

'About these cludders—' Cormac began.

A flashing, like someone striking an arc with a welding rod, lit up their surroundings. This was followed at once by the stutter-ing of pulse-rifles, then the clatter of some automatic projectile weapon. Cormac turned and located the source as lying behind a mound to his right, possibly down in the crater itself. His comunit earplug chirped, and obviously addressing both himself and Carl, Olkennon said, 'Have you had a nice sleep there, boys?'

Since Carl outranked Cormac by a couple of points, it was his prerogative to reply. 'We have not been asleep, Commander.'

'Then perhaps your monoculars have malfunctioned, or maybe even your eyes?'

When Olkennon got sarcastic, this usually meant someone had seriously fucked up.

'If you could explain, Commander,' said Carl primly.

'Well, it seems a commando unit of six rebels just tried to get into the Prador dreadnought. Luckily they were running a small grav-sled – probably to take away a small warhead on – and one of our satellites picked that up on a gravity map. I'm looking at that map now and previous recordings. They came in right past you.'

'Were they caught?' asked Carl.

After a long delay, Olkennon replied, 'Hold your positions and stay alert. Four of them were taken down but the other two are heading back your way. If they arrive before I get there, try for leg shots or try to pin them down, but don't hesitate to kill if necessary. Out.'

'How the hell did we miss them?' wondered Carl, bringing his monocular back up to his eyes.

'Some sort of chameleonware?' said Cormac, doing the same.

He scanned the nearby slopes then concentrated in the direction of the crater. As far as he understood it, the only portable camouflage available for a soldier was chameleoncloth fatigues – the same cloth the outer layer of his envirosuit was made from and which turned it to the colour of the mud he was lying in. And such cloth did not conceal one from someone looking through a monocular set to infrared, which was why they had dug in – that, and the possibility of gunfire.

'Maybe they slipped past while you were studying cludder beetles,' Carl suggested.

Cormac immediately felt a flush of guilt. He'd only been distracted by the creatures for a moment – nowhere near enough time for someone to get past him. Then he felt anger. Carl's accusation seemed not only unjust but spiteful. Had Carl himself fallen asleep or not been following the required scanning patterns? Was he now trying to find a way to shift the blame onto Cormac? The anger existed in him for a short time, accelerating his heartbeat as he searched for a sufficiently cutting reply. Then it seemed to hit a cut-off, and he abruptly reassessed his situation.

'Maybe they did,' he said without heat.

Aren't we on the same side? he thought. Carl might want to step on people's hands in a scramble up the promotional ladder, but no matter. Cormac had joined to do a job, and do it well. He abruptly felt an utter coldness towards his companion, a detachment. It was as if the man had suddenly become a malfunctioning item of machinery he must account for in his calculations. He would watch Carl.

Following his search-grid training, Cormac continued to scan the slopes on his side of the foxhole. Carl was doing the same. A belligerent silence fell between them.

'I'm half a mile from you and will be there soon,' Olkennon informed them through their comunits.

Carl, as if in response to this, abruptly stood, bringing his rifle to his shoulder while flicking up its infrared sight screen. Cormac spun, monocular still to his eyes. The rifle thrummed, spitting an actinic broken beam into the darkness. It fired again, then again.

'Got 'em,' said Carl.

Olkennon had specified leg shots, or keeping the two escapees pinned down, probably because someone in ECS wanted to interrogate these people. What had Cormac seen? Two people struggling towards them, one supporting the other, obviously wounded. The light from the pulse-rifle tended to blank infrared viewing for brief periods, but still, Carl's shots had all torn into upper bodies and heads.

★

'I fucked up, okay? I fucked up.' Carl turned and gazed out the wide window of the troop transport. Other soldiers aboard gazed across enquiringly, and Cormac felt this a conversation to best have at some other time.

'But that's not like you,' Yallow insisted.

'End of conversation,' said Carl, without looking round.

At that point Olkennon rejoined them, after speaking with a grizzled sergeant seated towards the front of the transport. She gazed at them for a moment then sat, and it was difficult to tell whether she could read the unpleasant atmosphere. Cormac wondered if Golem could sense such things . . . probably, though by picking up pheromones and reading the tensions in facial expressions. Likely they used some sort of formula.

'The barracks adjoin a temporary township down by the coast adjacent to the old city,' she said without any ado. 'You are located in Theta bubble. Cormac, your room is 21c, Yallow, 21b and Carl 21a. Get yourselves settled in, then use the local facilities – I doubt we'll have any reassignment until after the inquiry.'

Carl grimaced and turned to gaze out of the window again.

'We get our own rooms?' asked Yallow.

'Certainly,' said Olkennon. 'There's no shortage of living space and no limitations were put on the size of the township.'

Without any hint of a change in her expression of mild interest, Yallow looked across at Cormac. It had been over a month now since they'd had their own rooms and certain activities had been neglected. He felt a pleasurable anticipation seat itself in his groin.

Within a few minutes the troop transport descended and landed on an area of grated plasticrete over mud. A short walk away bonded-earth domes stood clustered as if the earth had bubbled. The domes were a uniform grey-brown, scattered with green and the occasional flashes of red, which Cormac identified as some adapted form of geranium gaining a root-hold in the bonded earth. There were numerous windows set into the lower floors of the domes, but fewer in the upper levels since they were mainly used for storage. Some of the domes had large hatches open in those upper areas, and extending below them were landing platforms for military AG cargo drays.

They departed the landing area onto a path of the same grated plasticrete, leading across churned mud sprouting skarch shoots like blue asparagus.

'Not difficult to find our dome,' said Yallow, pointing. The main entrance to each dome had one letter of the Greek alphabet incised above. And even as they approached these buildings, Cormac picked out the letter theta.

'You go on now,' said Olkennon, waving a hand at them and turning onto a path heading off around the collection of buildings. 'I'll contact you when we have our next assignment.'

As Olkennon departed, Yallow returned her attention to the barracks and the surrounding area. 'Doesn't look a whole lot of fun.'

'I'm sure you'll think of something,' Carl sneered.

Cormac gazed at him steadily, but Carl did not meet his eyes, merely striding ahead of the other two. That just wasn't like Carl – it seemed utterly out of character, worryingly so.

Carl entered the building foyer well ahead of them, and by the time they arrived at their rooms he had dumped his stuff and was on his way out again.

'There's bars in the township,' he told them as he hurried past. 'I'm going for a drink.' Then he paused and looked back. 'I'm sorry to be such a pain, but it seems I might be looking at the end of my military career.' He moved on, and Cormac could not help but think that his explanation seemed stilted, wrong.

'Let's get ourselves settled then,' said Yallow, watching Carl depart, then turned to the door to her room and opened it using the simple mechanical handle.

Cormac opened his own door and entered to look around: simple bunk; combined shower, sink and toilet cubicle – the sink folding up into the wall and the toilet seat telescoping from the floor; net access on a narrow desk, more of a shelf really, and a window giving a view of the bonded-earth curve of the neighbouring dome, on which, fortunately, some of those red geraniums had taken root. Entering, he dumped his pack and his pulse-rifle on the bed, then proceeded to strip off his envirosuit. Beside the shower he noted a small sonic cleaner box and, after stripping the suit of its detachable hardware, shoved the suit inside and set the device running. He then stepped into the shower and luxuriated in needles of hot water, washing himself thoroughly with a combined abrasive sponge and soap stick. It had been many days since he had been able to do anything more than wash himself from a small bowl. After he shut off the water a warm air blast ensued, complemented by a towel from a dispenser actually within the booth. Once dry, he inserted the towel back into its dispenser for cleaning, then stepped out.

His skin feeling almost like it was glowing, he walked over to his bed and opened his pack, taking out fresh underwear and uniform shirt and trousers. These he laid out neatly on the bed, and before dressing proceeded to pack away everything else in the cupboards. Shortly after having completed this chore, while he was checking round to see if there was anything he'd missed, there came a sharp rap at his door. He stepped over, opened it a crack, and saw Yallow standing there all but naked, holding one of the small towels about her hips where it didn't stretch far enough.

'Well let me in,' she demanded.

He opened the door and she stepped in, still holding the towel in place. Even as he closed the door his cock felt like it was a steel rod. He gazed at her. Her chameleon-effect skin now looked little different from the skin of any normal woman, apart from a slight scaled effect which he knew, though visible, could not be felt. The skin wasn't adapting to her surroundings right now, for she possessed conscious control over it. He focused on her breasts for a moment, which weren't large, since that would have interfered with her chosen profession. She was athletic, as muscular as a man but very definitely not a man. Abruptly tossing away the towel she then reached down and closed her hand about his penis. Looking down, he could see that her mons was bald, since pubic hair could be a problem when trying to stay clean out in the field. He realized, only after the fact, that he'd made a grunting sound as her hand closed.

'Oh dear,' she said. 'I don't think you're going to last very long, and I'm going to need your undivided attention for a good hour.'

Sometimes Yellow could be hard work. He knew that she possessed enough control to hold off on her orgasm, and that she liked to do so because the longer she held off, the bigger the multiple explosion at the end.

After releasing his penis she strode over to the bed, swept his clothing aside – an act that offended his sense of neatness – then climbed on her hands and knees. Looking back over her shoulder at him, she said, 'Time to get you into a state when that will last,' then parted her knees and stuck her arse out at him.

She was right, he didn't last long the first time. Over the ensuing twenty minutes she dictated to him his every lick, bite and caress as his youthful and hyperfit body returned him to the state she required. Next came a marathon that had sweat running into his eyes, and when she came, her hands clenching in the bedding to stop herself tearing the skin off his back, she lost control of her chameleon skin, and blushed with bursts of red, blue and yellow like a slow firework display.

★

'There'll be no inquiry,' said Cormac, as he and Yallow strolled from the barracks along the short curved track to the adjoining military township. Somehow he felt the need to return focus to things military, even though his legs felt wobbly and he really wanted a beer.

'Carl is in the top percentile for marksmanship,' Yallow observed, gazing at him with an amused quirk to her mouth.

Cormac took a slow breath of the cool evening air, which for a change right then tasted clean. The urge for a beer being understood, he also felt utterly relaxed, and understood the reason for that too. He felt the need to pause for a moment – not to hurry on to the next thing. Halting, he gazed at the nearby skarch trees. These were young examples of the plant that had managed to get a root-hold on many worlds. He walked over, rested a hand against a fibrous surface and peered at little green beetles gathered like metal beads in a crotch where one of the thick leaves sprouted from the trunk.

The young trees stood a mere ten feet high with trunks as thick as a man's leg. They were a tough terraforming hybrid of the kind sowed on worlds to rapidly create biomass for the production of topsoil, and therefore grew fast in even the most extreme conditions, rapidly gaining height and bulk. As he recollected, the plants were a splicing of maize, bamboo and aloe vera. It occurred to him then that this was the first time he had seen them up close, though he had seen distant examples on the spoil hills about the Prador ship and pieces of them rotting underfoot in those same hills. This was what it was all about: actually being here, seeing and experiencing – not gazing at a picture on a screen.

He turned back to Yallow, who had halted too and was watching him.

'It is understood,' he said, 'that in his first fire-fight a soldier may not perform to standard. They thought he got a bit overexcited and just blasted away.'

'Young soldiers do tend to get overexcited and blast away,' she said, grinning.

He half-frowned half-grinned, and waved a dismissive hand at her.

She shrugged and continued, 'Well, he won't be blasting away at anyone back there now.'

Too true: the cases had arrived on the morning after the shooting, and they had spent most of the day unpacking and assembling their contents. Carl, whose speciality seemed likely to be weapons tech, had been in charge whenever Olkennon was not around. Assembled, the mosquito autoguns walked on four gleaming spidery legs, fat bodies loaded with ammunition and a minitok power supply, tubular snout for firing rail-gun projectiles at a rate capable of turning a man into slurry in a second. With them now guarding the perimeter around the Prador ship there would be no more mistakes. The guns had been programmed to go for leg shots, though whether there would be anything left of the legs after the shooting was debatable.

Yellow gave the Skarch grove a long suspicious look, then began striding along the track again. Cormac followed, guessing she was thinking about how many enemies such growth could conceal

'Where's he gone, anyway?' Yellow asked, jerking her chin towards the military township.

'As you may have noted he's not very talkative lately, so he didn't tell me,' Cormac replied. 'Who wants to talk about their screw-ups? Maybe we should give him some space.'

Yellow glanced at him. 'He has spoken some to me, though it always strikes me as a bit false. He probably doesn't talk so much to you because you're a hard act to follow sometimes. When was the last time you screwed up?'

Cormac was surprised. He had always admired both Carl and Yellow, and thought them likely to be better soldiers than him. He shrugged. Of course he screwed up, didn't he?

'Let's go get that drink,' Yellow added, after an embarrassed pause.

The township was again comprised of bonded-soil domes, with plasticrete gratings over the mud lying between them. The place swarmed with soldiers, and with those locals who had come from the partially ruined city nearby to sell their wares. A number of eateries had been established, along with a selection of bars that were already gaining a reputation as not the best place to visit and be sure of retaining your teeth. ECS command could have clamped down on that, but felt that allowing the troops to blow off steam here was one of the better alternatives to prescribed drugs and cerebral treatments. It was also true that there were many veterans here who preferred this old-fashioned approach. They took the view that busted heads and broken bones could be repaired, but naivety could kill.

The first dome with a lit façade that they came to was called Krong's. Cormac gazed at the sign and smiled to himself, remembering his childhood fascination with that character. Apparently Jebel U-cap Krong had survived the war and now ran a salmon farm on some backwoods world, though Cormac was not entirely sure he believed the story.

He and Yellow entered the smoky atmosphere and looked around. The place was starting to fill up but there were still some tables available, so Yellow snagged one and sat down, gesturing Cormac to the bar. He walked over and pushed through the crush there, ordered two beers, then scanned around while the barman, a brushed-aluminium spider with limbs terminating in three-fingered hands, poured his drinks.

Carl?

Carl was ensconced with a few of the locals around a small table in one of the dimmer parts of the bar. They were drinking and talking, but did not show the animation evident at the tables surrounding them. Their discussion appeared serious, whispered and vehement. With his drinks finally before him, Cormac took them up, returned to Yallow and told her what he had seen.

'Works fast,' she commented. 'I don't think I've even spoken to a native yet.'

'They don't look happy. Should we go over there?'

'Nah, if they start slapping him about it'll be character-building for him.'

Yallow's attitude to violence had ever been thus, but then few people would ever be tough enough to slap her about. In training he'd seen her flip a Golem instructor – something only one in a hundred recruits were capable of doing. Then, thinking of her earlier comment, Cormac remembered the first time he'd managed to get the upper hand against the same instructor. Maybe he took his own achievements too lightly. He frowned, took a drink of his beer, and decided then to keep a wary eye on any inclination to arrogance growing in him. Then he drank more, keeping pace with Yallow.

They took it in turns to go to the bar for each round, and he was feeling a pleasant buzz when he saw one of the locals standing and pointing a threatening finger at Carl. Carl stood too, glanced about warily, then leaned forward to say something. The man backhanded him and Carl took it, blank-faced, then turned and headed away. Cormac tracked him across to the door, watched him depart, then observed some altercation back at the table. The man who had slapped Carl abruptly turned and hurried for the door, and it didn't escape Cormac's notice that he was checking the positioning of something underneath his coat as he went.

'I think we'd better finish up and take a walk,' said Yallow, obviously having watched events too.

They downed their beers and stood, quickly heading for the door. Once outside, they scanned the floodlit brightness and the deep shadows between buildings. No sign of the local, but Carl was a

26

little way up the street, strolling as if he hadn't a care in the world, which struck Cormac as quite odd.

'You follow him,' said Yallow. 'I'll go the back way.'

She would be better there – sneaking about in darkness was her preferred pastime.

Cormac kept Carl in sight along the curving street, then saw him abruptly take a left heading for the barracks. The route there was dark, so Cormac picked up his pace, but reaching the turn could see no sign of Carl.

Abruptly someone seemed to appear out of nowhere to ballet-ically kick Cormac's feet out from under him, step beyond him and drop into a crouch.

'Carl—'

Carl was aiming a nasty squat little pulse-gun at Cormac's head.

'Ah fuck,' said Carl, then abruptly came upright and scanned about himself. Out of the darkness came the flash-crack of a projectile weapon, the sound of a fleshy impact, and Carl was flung back.

'Thanks for that, boy,' said a figure stepping out of a nearby alley.

Cormac froze for a moment, then began to move towards the interloper.

'You want some, soldier?' the man enquired, swinging the stubby barrel of some weapon towards him. Carl was coughing blood – not dead yet. Maybe all it would take was another shot—

Something slammed against the man's back, and he oofed and staggered. Glimpsing a rock thudding to the ground, Cormac moved in close and crescent-kicked the gun from the man's hand. As the weapon clattered to the gridwork then down into the mud, he moved in close for a heel-of-the-hand strike, and just managed to duck the swipe of a blade. The guy was fast – used to this sort of encounter – and Cormac realized, by the way his opponent was poised, that a crescent kick would not work again.

'Come on, Yellow!' shouted Cormac.

'Oh I'm here,' said Yellow, from just behind the man.

There came a thump then, and the man lifted up off his feet and sprawled. Cormac thought Yellow had hit him, but looking round saw Carl lowering his gun – certainly not military issue, and certainly not something he should have been carrying here. Carl dropped the gun to the grating, then passed out.

'We need to get him to the infirmary,' said Cormac.

'I've already called a medivac team.' Yellow tapped her aug.

Cormac stooped beside the attacker, checked for a pulse and found none. He then found the charred hole right over the man's heart, next turning him over to gaze at the fist-sized cavity in his back and realizing a low-energy pulse shot had been used. A higher-energy pulse would have cut a perfect hole right the way through; this kind, however, was more damaging at close quarters and more likely to ensure a kill. He stood and moved over to Carl.

Yellow had wadded up her jacket and pressed it against Carl's sucking chest wound. Cormac stooped to take up the gun Carl had dropped, then studied it. The weapon had to be adjusted internally for low-power shots – something Carl was quite capable of doing – but his doing so demonstrated that he had felt the need for the weapon to perform in that way. Carl was into something, that was sure.

Soon, flashing lights lit the night above them and an AG ambulance settled. Three medics piled out followed by two self-governing floating stretchers. The medics dismissed Cormac and Yellow and set to work, and soon Carl and his opponent were on the stretchers and on their way towards the ambulance. Inevitably, before Cormac and Yellow could depart, another grav vehicle descended, the logo of the ECS military police gleaming on its doors. Cormac was tempted to slip Carl's weapon inside his jacket, but decided at the last moment not to. Maybe unit loyalty should be encouraged, but only so far. Two military policemen stepped out of the vehicle, then one of them paused, holding up his hand to the other while listening in to his comunit. After a moment they both returned to their vehicle and it took off again.

'Odd,' commented Yallow.

As the ambulance finally ascended, another vehicle descended from the sky. This was a rough-looking gravcar without anything to distinguish it from a civilian vehicle. A lean woman stepped out and Cormac recognized her instantly. She had long blond hair tied back with a leather thong, and was clad in a worn grey envirosuit and long leather coat. She was one of the couple he had tentatively identified aboard the heavy lifter wing as ECS agents.

'Well, you have been busy,' she said, gazing up at the departing ambulance, then down at the dark stains on the gratings. She now looked steadily at Yallow. 'I've viewed your recording.' She tapped the discreet aug behind her ear. 'But now I want detail from both of you.' Looking at Cormac her eyes focused on the weapon he was holding.

'Carl's,' he said, and tossed it to her.

With supreme ease she snatched it out of the air, inspected it briefly, then removed its gas canister before inserting the gun inside her leather coat.

'Let's go somewhere more convivial for a chat.'

2

Sitting before his screen, Cormac called up his word lists for the third-stage Basic Language module, and wished for that brief time when there had been no strictures on education conducted by direct download. Picking up his pack of mem-b drug patches he took one out, peeled off its backing and pressed it against his neck. There was no rush, no buzz, but he knew that after he had read through this list and tracked through its numerous hyperlinks the imprinting proteins and enzymes in the mem-b would have etched the knowledge into his mind after one reading.

At random, he chose a word from the list – cestode – followed the hyperlinks and learned more than he cared to know about parasitic flatworms. Language links gave him the equivalents in his chosen languages of New Mandarin, Hindi, Jovian Argot, Italian and Sinhalese. Here he learnt the associated nuances, and rather more about the parasitic worms that had once plagued the relevant cultures. A side study enabled him to delve into helminthology, which he bookmarked to look at later during biology. His time-warning icon began flashing, so with some reluctance he navigated back to the main page and selected another word. Some twenty words later, the icon greyed out, marking the end of the module. Next would be Physics, then Biology, then Mathematics, followed by Synergistics, which was a combination of all the previous modules. But right now it was time for Association.

Now Cormac wished for the time some centuries ago when, after the collapse of the old schooling systems and the introduction of the first AIs, pupils had received all their education at home via their home's netlink. But after they took over, the AIs decided that such methods did not provide sufficient 'interaction', so centralized schools were once again created. He didn't really mind Association, he just resented the interruption when he'd found some interesting stuff to look at. In his report, which he'd peeked a look at over his mother's shoulder, this was called 'Autistic Spectrum Focus subcritical, adjustment to parental choice'. He hadn't quite figured out what all that meant, since any searches he made turned up esoteric brain function and psychological studies which in turn usually led him elsewhere.

He stood up from his seat, peeling off and discarding the drug patch from his neck. Other children of about the same age as him were also rising from their seats and heading for the door.

'Ian, where've you been?' asked Culu – a small blond-haired girl with a junior aug behind her ear. Like Cormac she was too young to take direct downloads to her brain, but she was getting the nearest to it possible that the laws allowed. Cormac had seen her parents once: twinned augs, visible cybernetic additions like multispec eyes and arm-sockets to take nerve-controlled tools. Culu would not remain long in this class, since she would soon outstrip those receiving a more conventional education like him. When he'd said something about Culu to his mother, her reply had been, 'I want you to remain human until such a time as you can make an informed choice to be otherwise.' Culu seemed human enough to him, and she seemed to like him.

'Digging up dinosaur bones,' he told her, which wasn't strictly true, but sounded great. 'And I am to be called Cormac from now on,' he added. Seeing her fascination with both the bone digging and the name change, he began telling her all about his trip to Montana as they walked outside into the playground. However, he found it difficult to talk about the name change, and how it had stuck when, just before their return here, his mother had started treating it with an almost frightening seriousness.

'Hey, Cormac!'

A ball was heading directly towards his head. Almost without thinking about it, he snapped up a hand and caught it. He glanced up, seeing that a security drone had spun on its post above. Had it decided the ball was going to hit him in the face, it would have knocked the object out of the air with a well-aimed projectile of its own, or safely incinerated it. The drone, which was a submind of the school AI, would have had plenty of time to do this, since in the time it took Cormac to raise his hand to catch the ball it could probably have completed a couple of crosswords and read a book.

Cormac gazed across at Meecher, the boy who had thrown the ball. Meecher was one of the oldest boys in this school. Cormac wondered if, in another time, he would have been a school bully. Such a creature could not exist here, since the AI just watched too closely.

'There, I told you,' said Meecher to a couple of his oppos.

Cormac moved out, throwing the ball back, hard. The drone swivelled again. Meecher reached for the ball, but didn't get his hands together quick enough and it thumped into his solar plexus. He oomphed, then after a moment shrugged that off and went running after the ball. For reasons beyond the comprehension of an eight-year-old, the AI did not intervene all the time.

Rugged carpet grass coated the playground, and upon this rested play equipment in abundance including climbing frames and slides. There was also access to bats and balls, grav-skates and much else besides – though no information access, since this was all about exercise and 'interaction'. Already someone was crying because he'd miscalculated a jump on one of the frames, and a human attendant was hurrying out. The AI did not intervene in such circumstances: injury by malice was mostly not allowed, injury by stupidity was a learning process.

Running around the edge of the ground was a high fence, mainly to prevent balls from bouncing out onto the nearby road still traversed by some hydrocar ground traffic, even though most people were now buying gravcars. Cormac joined in with a game of catch, in which the initial aim was to try and get the drone to intervene, but it turned its sensors resolutely away. This continued until Meecher tried a throw at the back of Culu's head, whereupon the ball disappeared in a puff of smoke, and Meecher shrieked as briefly he became the target of an electron-beam stinger. This hadn't happened for a while, since Meecher had been learning to control those impulses stemming from his stirring hormones.

Now the ball game was over, Cormac climbed a nearby frame and gazed about himself. Across the road stood a row of balconied three-storey apartment buildings, roofed in photo-electric tiles and the gaps between the blocks filled by self-contained waste-composting, incineration and water-recycling plants. Wide tree-lined pavements stretched in a curve round to a large water-park, and beyond that rose the mile-high edifices of city central. Gazing in the other direction, Cormac observed suburban sprawl which he knew ran all the way to the coast and beyond, where an underwater city lay. He continued gazing in that direction until something began to nag at him, and he finally returned his gaze to the curving pavement.

At first glance it had looked like a car, but now it rose up onto its many legs, and waving its antennae, swung its head from side to side as if trying to pick up some scent. Two green eyes, peridots, seemed blind. It possessed what looked like short mandibles, but they probably weren't used for eating – more likely they were used to clean and maintain the particle cannon and two missile launch-ers residing where its mouth should have been.

War drone!

Surely this could not be the one they had seen in Montana? Ian Cormac felt certain it was, and he felt certain that it was looking for him.

★

The ship loomed like some tarnished bronze mountain, slowly being exposed as autodozers cleared the charred earth and stone around it. Some of the cleared areas were fenced off, but such was the work still to do that numerous points of access had to be left open for the equipment being used – hence the mosquito autoguns now replacing the guard units that had been ensconced in the surrounding spill piles.

Before a deep hole excavated in the ground – apparently where a main hold entrance had been opened – was a small town of bubble units. ECS personnel, not all of them in uniform, swarmed like ants before this behemoth.

'There's still Prador in there?' Yallow asked.

'Certainly,' Olkennon replied. 'Too many hiding places, and the exotic metals used in the ship's construction make it difficult to scan effectively.'

'How have they survived for so long?'

Olkennon glanced at her. 'Old food caches, cannibalism, and one or two other methods. They're primitive – were hardly out of their eggs when this ship went down.'

'There've been problems?' Cormac suggested.

'Two of our people from Reverse Engineering disappeared about a month ago. We found their bones dumped below a hatch on the other side. Prador second- and third-children have been seen – usually running away.'

'Hence our presence,' said Cormac.

'Hence your presence,' Olkennon agreed noncommittally.

Cormac was not so sure he believed her. Since the installation of the autoguns in the area they had been guarding, it was inevitable they would be reassigned, but he felt a suspicion that their reassignment had something to do with Carl and the subtle interrogation they had undergone from Agent Spencer. She had wanted to know every detail of recent events, and much detail of their past association with Carl. Then, with a smile and a wave, she departed – giving them no explanation for her questions. He guessed that being grunts, it was not necessary for them to know.

Departing the gravcar that had brought them down by the ship, Yallow and Cormac followed Olkennon towards the bubble-unit encampment. The soil here was orange and dotted with flintlike rocks and pieces of what looked like petrified wood. Such details Cormac took in, but his eyes kept straying back to the Prador vessel. Some structures on the exterior had survived the impact. He recognized the stubs of once-jutting frameworks that surrounded the throats of rail-guns, the remains of reflector shields around lasers – some for communication and some for combat. Inset ports gleamed like spider eyes around a jutting section like a balding head – the upper part of the squashed pear-shape of the vessel.

Soon they arrived at the encampment, where a man wandered out to meet them. He looked old, which was an uncommon occurrence with the treatments available nowadays. Cormac had seen people like him before – usually their lives were so busy that they didn't get round to taking the treatments until something actually pushed them into it. His head hair was as grey and wiry as his beard, and his civilian clothing showed signs of wear and the occasional chemical stain – sure sign that he was the type who didn't give a fig for physical appearance.

The man held out a grubby calloused hand, which Olkennon shook, then he turned to study Cormac and Yallow. 'So these are the two who will be going in with me.'

'They will, Professor Dent.'

'Very well,' he sighed, 'let's get moving.'

Olkennon turned to the two of them. 'You understand your duties?'

Both Cormac and Yallow nodded.

'Keep him alive,' she said, then turned on her heel and marched off.

Professor Dent led the way into the encampment of bubble units, onto the main gratings, then to a narrow packed-soil alley, finally stopping at a door and opening it. They all trooped inside and, scanning the cluttered interior, Cormac felt his assessment of the man confirmed. However, no matter how apparently slovenly his appearance or how messy his dwelling, Cormac knew the professor would not have been here had not some high-level AIs considered his presence important. Dent picked up a large case with a shoulder strap, then pointed to two large backpacks resting beside a desk occupied entirely by a tangled mess of Prador technology.

'I'll be needing some help with those,' he said. As he moved his pulse-rifle to hang before his stomach, Cormac caught Yallow's frown. Burdened like this they would not be so effective.

'Quick-release button on the front,' said the professor – obviously not an absent-minded scientist, but someone aware that soldiers needed to be able to respond both quickly and unburdened.

The two hoisted on their packs and the professor led the way out.

'We'll be going to the Captain's Sanctum, and since that is where the Prador adult was located, it is deep within the ship,' he said.

'As much armour as possible between itself and anyone attacking,' said Yallow.

'Certainly.'

They trudged out of the encampment and onto a wide road of crumbled stone and sticky mud, which ran level for a little while then cut down into a wide excavation. Soon they saw a metal ramp ahead of them, a heavy autodozer parked on it, perhaps to hold it down. The entrance itself was a sideways oval – designed to accommodate the shape of Prador, but much larger than the largest of their kind.

As they drew closer, the first thing Cormac noticed was the smell, which rolled out like a palpable fog, laden with the putrid decay of things washed up on a seashore, damp and miasmic. He saw Yallow hesitate when this hit them, her expression annoyed perhaps at the way she had reacted.

'You get used to it,' said Dent.

'So some of the Prador in there are dead?' Yallow noted.

'Certainly – we haven't found them all.' He glanced round at them. 'But what you're smelling at the moment is a food store we only discovered recently, and then only because someone accidentally cut its power supply a week ago and its contents began decaying.' He pointed back to a group of people clad in full envirosuits gathered around a couple of grav-pallets. 'They'll be moving the rotten meat today.'

Cormac wondered if any of that meat included something once described as 'long pig', for Prador were not averse to eating human flesh. He considered closing up the visor on his envirosuit, but Yallow hadn't, and the professor wasn't even wearing a suit. Perhaps better to go without his visor closed – even with all its systems operating, a closed suit tended to blunt the senses. With Prador in here, on their home territory, he needed to stay sharp.

The floor of the hold felt utterly solid underfoot, and distant walls appeared to be constructed of layers of ragged slabs on which grew pale green weed like dead man's fingers. There were stacks of Polity-manufacture bubble-metal crates here near the entrance, but further back were objects that had occupied the hold before this ship came down. To his left a small scout vessel or shuttle rested like a squat submarine – a miniature copy of the vessel they had just entered, since it seemed all Prador ships were modelled on the creatures' own form no matter how impractical that modelling might be. The craft was secured to deck rings by cables extending from holes in its sides. Behind the vessel were racks of thin pale blue cylinders – perhaps ordnance of some kind for that same vessel.

At the back of the hold they came upon one of those diagonally divided doors needed to accommodate the Prador form. It was only partially open, a heavy lock bolt welded to it to slot down into a hole drilled into the floor, so it lay open only wide enough to allow humans through, and not wide enough to allow Prador second-children out. Doubtless the doors had not been permanently welded in place in case they needed to be opened further to take heavy equipment in. Beyond this door lay a smaller hold, on the right of which stacks of hexagonal crates rose to the ceiling like pillars, and just beyond them—

Cormac and Yallow simultaneously raised their pulse-rifles and took aim, but neither of them fired.

'If they'd been occupied your weapons would have had little effect,' said Dent. 'But it's good to see you're alert.'

Arrayed in a long framework were what looked like five large Prador second-children. But this was armour for the crablike monsters – open at the back and with carapace lids hinged out in two halves, all ready to be quickly occupied. Nearby stood a rack of weapons: vicious looking rail-guns, power-packs and magazines from which hung belts of projectiles, a row of gas lasers and one large particle cannon either for tripod mounting or to be carried by a first-child.

'If there's Prador here,' said Yallow, 'isn't it dangerous to leave stuff like this lying around?'

Dent just pointed towards the ceiling where material had been cut away and something inset. Though very little showed there, Cormac guessed a security drone had been installed. The AI controlling this excavation and reclamation wanted the Prador aboard to take the bait here, but Cormac suspected that any left alive would avoid so obvious a trap.

At the back of this hold another set of those doors, this time fully open, led into a dim corridor. Cormac and Yallow moved ahead to check it, and immediately brought their weapons to bear on movement along one wall. Ship lice: boot-sized multi-legged arthropods that scavenged after Prador leavings. In essence they served the same purpose as beetlebots aboard Polity ships, though they were also pests that needed to be controlled – the Prador version of rats in the walls. One bent its ribbed carapace into an arc and dropped to the floor. Cormac tracked it across with his pulse-rifle as it headed towards him, tri-mandibles clicking. Professor Dent stepped forward to trap the creature under his foot, then brought his full weight down and twisted. His boot sank with a liquid crunch, gelatinous ichor squirting out from under his sole.

'Damned things,' he said. 'They're getting bolder as they get hungrier. If they get locked on to you, you have to cut behind the pincers to get the things out.'

'Charming,' said Cormac.

As they wound their way through numerous corridors, then up one level via a ladder welded to the side of a very wide dropshaft, Cormac realized Dent was following directions given on small flimsy screens stuck at intervals to the walls. Cormac and Yallow kept to the training manual by checking all areas at junctions before allowing their charge to come on, and Cormac felt that the professor was assessing their every move.

'Warheads in here,' he said at one point, gesturing to an open door to one side. 'Big rail-gun launchers to the port of the main turret.'

Why did they need to know that? It seemed an odd piece of information to provide.

'We go down here,' Dent added, pointing ahead to a corridor slanting steeply down into the depths of the ship.

This finally debarked into an even wider corridor. Cormac guessed they must now be close to the Captain's Sanctum, for this new corridor was wide enough to allow a Prador adult through. A bad smell wafted along it towards them, and as they rounded a corner Yallow shed her pack and went down on one knee, taking aim. Cormac just continued walking.

'You don't quite have the reactions of your partner, it would seem,' commented Dent.

'I'm guessing they don't smell like that when they're alive,' said Cormac, now thoroughly aware that Dent was not all he seemed.

Chagrined, Yallow stood, hoisting up her pack again and cinching it into place.

The Prador first-child lay tilted against one wall. Most of its legs had fallen away, as had one of its claws, exposing carapace sockets in which ship lice were as busy as maggots. As Cormac watched, one of the horrible scavengers came out of the Prador's mouth between the rigid mandibles.

'How did it die?' Yallow asked.

'Most of them survived the crash,' Dent supplied. 'But they didn't survive the irradiation, the gassing and the subsequent assault.'

Cormac glanced at him. 'Irradiation?'

'Neutron tacticals were dropped here,' Dent replied. 'Then when the Sparkind assault teams arrived they drilled a hole through the ship's turret, which remained exposed above ground, and pumped Hazon nerve gas inside. Then they followed the gas inside and finished off what survivors they could find.'

'But some survived even that,' Cormac suggested.

'Yes, they were third-children in a sealed hatchery-cum-nursery. They grew into second-children by feeding on the remains of their relatives while we dug the ship out.' He gestured about himself. 'We reckon five or six survived out of about thirty of them . . . Anyway, we go here.' He pointed at a set of wide closed doors just beyond the first-child corpse.

'Why not gas the place again?' asked Yallow.

'A waste of resources for a few second-children,' Dent replied. 'Though we don't always know where they are, we're always certain where they're not.'

It seemed a strange statement to make, especially when Dent needed guards to escort him down here, and especially when people had been killed.

Dent went over to a Polity console that had been mounted beside the door, its optic feed plugged into the control pit where a Prador manipulatory hand would have usually entered a code and been sampled for genetic tissue. Deliberately positioning himself so that neither Yallow nor Cormac could see over his shoulder, Dent worked the touchpads then stepped back. Something moved in the wall with a grinding crash, then with a whine of hydraulics the doors began to part along their diagonal split and revolve back into the walls.

Dent turned towards them. 'Don't be surprised by the—'

Something shrieked then crackled, and it seemed some invisible rope snatched Dent sideways through the air, his body folding at the middle. Loose-limbed he bounced along the floor to lie in a broken heap directly before the door. Packs discarded, Cormac and Yallow crouched, covering each direction along the corridor. Something smashed into the wall above them, showering them with hot fragments. Cormac rolled for cover beside the first-child corpse, whilst Yallow backed up to the opening doors.

'In here!' she yelled, and reaching down dragged the professor through the widening gap into the Sanctum.

Where the hell had that come from?

Then Cormac saw them: Prador second-children coming down through a hatch in the ceiling. For a second he just froze, unable to process the nightmarish sight, then his training kicked in and he fired a concentrated burst at exposed carapace and glittering spider eyes. One of them lost its grip and crashed to the floor. The fallen second-child lay on its back with its legs kicking the air for a moment, then it abruptly flipped upright – one claw and the side of its carapace smoking. It raised some sort of jury-rigged weapon in one of its underhands. He nailed it again, across its visual turret, saw its two palp-eyes fly away in burning fragments, then recognized that the weapon it held consisted mainly of a compressed gas cylinder. Briefly, an almost cryonic calm settled on Cormac as he assessed the situation and considered the best response. Aiming carefully at the cylinder, he squeezed off a concentrated burst of fire. The cylinder exploded, flinging the creature hard against one wall, but Cormac did not have time to relish the moment. More fire from above showered him with stinking flesh, shattered carapace and squirming ship lice.

'Get in here!' Yellow opened fire through the still-opening door. Cormac stood and ran towards her, felt something tug at his leg, and fell through into the sanctum past her. As he tried to stand again, his leg gave way, and glancing down he saw blood, ripped-up Kevlar, exposed flesh.

Fuckit.

He felt his suit leg automatically begin to tighten to prevent blood loss.

'They're coming through the ceiling,' he said matter-of-factly. Cold numbness now suffused his leg as the suit injected analgesics and antishock drugs. He turned his head sideways and vomited once, hard, wiped his mouth and turned back. He felt wired, like he'd drunk too much coffee, but the drugs were quickly numbing him.

'I spotted that,' said Yellow, then fired out into the corridor again.

Ignoring the sarcasm, Cormac went on, 'Looks like most of them out there, if Dent was right about only five or six surviving.'

'Oh, I was right,' said Dent.

Cormac glanced across. The man was standing, his clothing ripped about the waist but no sign of blood there, only syntheflesh and something hard and white that probably wasn't bone. Dent was an android of some kind, but he didn't possess the ceramal skeleton of a Golem, probably because that could be too easily detected. Some other sort of facsimile, perhaps remotely controlled?

Dent continued, 'Just like I was right about them watching the Sanctum. In here they would have had a chance, though remote, of gaining access to the ship's systems, and maybe getting away from here.'

'What?' said Yellow, ducking back for a moment.

'Move away from the door,' said Dent.

'We can't let them get in here!'

'Move away from the door – that's an order!'

Yellow reluctantly backed up whilst Cormac looked on with distanced bemusement. He knew his disconnection was due to the drugs and considered administering a stimulant, then reconsidered, reckoning this would all soon be over and that he and Yellow had already done their part. Now gazing about himself he spied a huge carapace, nearly fifteen feet across, that was all that remained of the Prador adult aboard – the captain. He noted there were neither legs attached to the carapace nor any lying nearby. Adult Prador tended to lose their limbs, and doubtless there were grav units shell-welded to its underside. He could not see them, though he could see, fixed in a row below the creature's mandibles, the hexagonal control units it had used to control everything aboard this ship. It was those the second-children had been after.

This time there came no sounds of hydraulics or rough mechanical movement as the doors slid rapidly closed. Cormac glimpsed yellow and purple carapace and the glint of an eye through the remaining gap. One of those gas-propellant weapons hissed and stuttered, projectiles slamming against the heavy metal, then becoming muffled as the doors finally closed. A hissing bubbling ensued, and white foam issued around the door and along its diagonal slit, rapidly solidifying. Cormac recognized the astringency of breach sealant.

'The engineering of these ships was high-tolerance when they were built,' said Dent in a calm tone. 'But that was some time ago and much in here is very worn, though rugged enough to continue functioning.'

Ah, thought Cormac.

'What are you saying?' said Yallow.

Dent continued, 'Prador are not too concerned about secure atmosphere seals in their doors. Like their engineering they are rugged and can survive large pressure changes. They can even survive in vacuum for an appreciable length of time.'

'What?' said Yallow, in what was rapidly becoming an annoying habit.

'I think,' Cormac said muzzily, 'that the Prador have been lured into a trap, and we were here to bait the hook: one apparently old man and two raw recruits to open up this Sanctum.'

'We're being used as decoys?' said Yallow disbelievingly.

'Outstanding,' said Dent.

Cormac gazed with suspicion at the facsimile human – that was one of Olkennon's favourite comments, so perhaps their Golem unit leader was controlling Dent?

Yallow now turned and gazed at the hardened breach sealant.

'A trap,' she repeated.

'Hazon nerve gas, I would guess,' said Cormac.

Yallow's expression became grim. 'We could have died out there,' she said flatly.

'Sort of comes with the territory,' Cormac replied.

From out in the corridor, despite the thickness of the door, could be heard the sound of heavy objects crashing about violently. Prador were certainly rugged – it took a long time for even that highly toxic gas to kill them.

★

The pedestal-mounted autodoc crouched over his injured leg like a chromed horseshoe crab feeding on the wound. With a nerve-blocker engaged at the base of his spine, Cormac could feel nothing, but his hearing was fine, unfortunately. He kept his eyes averted from the mechanical surgeon's messy work, but couldn't block out the liquid crunching or the two-tone notes of bone and cell welders.

Olkennon, gazing at a screen mounted on the rear of the 'doc, also insisted upon giving him a description of what was going on – neglecting not one single gory detail.

'It's finished removing the fragments of metal and is now welding up the shattered knee-cap. Dissolving clamps will go in next, since welded bone is always a bit weak. We wouldn't want all this coming apart on you again.'

Cormac guessed Olkennon so relished describing this stuff because she didn't want her recruits becoming too blasé about such injuries. Yes, the medical technology was available to over-haul a human with the ease of repairing a broken toy, but some breakages could not be fixed and autodocs weren't always available.

'There, the clamps are in – calcium fibre staples. Cell welding now, and neutral cellular material and collagen to replace all that dead icky stuff it's sucking out.'

Yeah, Cormac could now hear a sound like that made by someone sucking up the dregs of a drink through a straw.

As he understood it, ECS had once experienced problems with recruits becoming careless of injury. At that time, the idea had been mooted that such repairs as this should be made with-out killing the pain – just to drive the point home. Too crude, however. The AIs had thereafter used subtle psychological manipu-lation, part of which involved making the autodocs look just plain scary, another part being the design of training regimens that included real pain. Cormac winced at the memory of hand-to-hand combat resulting in broken bones, ruptures, torn ligaments and gouged eyes. Pain was certainly a good learning tool, but too much pain could make a soldier averse to doing a job which was, after all, one requiring those who were less than realistic about mortality.

'Weaving muscle fibres now and joining up the broken blood vessels. All the small capillary clamps coming off now. Oops, some clotting there – it'll have to cut that bit out.'

Thanks, Olkennon, thought Cormac. *I really needed to know that.*

He said, 'So you used us as decoys?'

'They would have seen through any emulation I could have made,' she replied. 'They're good at detecting metals.'

'Who was running the facsimile?'

She focused on his face for a moment. 'The AI in charge of the excavation.' Returning her attention to the autodoc screen, she went on, 'It's closing up the skin now – layer by layer. It'll feel weird while the nerves heal, but there should be no pain.' She looked up and gave him a smile. Certainly the Prador would have recognized her as Golem and known to keep away. Her emulation wasn't very good at all.

With a hissing sound and a smell of burnt hair, the autodoc raised itself from his knee and began folding its sharp legs and other surgical cutlery into its body for sterilization. It looked rather like an insect grooming itself after eating something rather messy.

Cormac gazed down at his knee and saw it was bright red as if sunburned, and hairless. No sign now of torn flesh or broken bones. Of course, ECS medical technology had to be good. It was all about efficiency, for the time a soldier spent in hospital was wasted time.

Abruptly feeling returned, and it felt odd. In his mind lay knowledge of a serious injury juxtaposed with evidence of none.

The leg itself felt hot and cold – a local flu-like phenomenon – and it also felt full of unfamiliar lumps, as if a bag of marbles had been sewn in underneath his skin.

From beneath his lower back the autodoc retracted one more limb: a long flat hinged affair terminating in a platen for extruding nanofibres, which until then had been engaged with his spinal nerves to cut all feeling below his waist. The autodoc pedestal now moved back from the surgical table, turned and folded down into itself, finally presenting nothing but smooth mirrored surfaces. Stepping round it, Olkennon dropped a sealed packet of paperwear clothing on Cormac's stomach. 'Get dressed.'

Warily, even though he knew there should be no problem, Cormac sat upright. The area of the wound pulled slightly like a strained muscle, and the lumpiness there felt something like cramp. Muscle tension there had yet to readjust and toxins saturating the area needed to be cleared. He swung his legs off the side of the surgical table and peered over at his envirosuit, bagged and lying in a corner, ready to be either repaired or scavenged for usable components. Standing, he tore open the package of paperwear and dressed, trying to ignore Olkennon's unwavering stare since, after all, she was a machine and not a woman.

Finally dressed, he met her gaze. 'We were put in danger – used as decoys – but there's something more to all this.'

'The AI observed you both through the facsimile.'

Being closely watched by AI often resulted in substantial changes. He knew of troops who had come under such scrutiny and been summarily dismissed from ECS, and of others who ended up in the Sparkind, whilst still others, it was rumoured, simply disappeared.

'I can't say I'm happy to hear about that,' he replied.

Olkennon studied him for a moment longer, then continued, 'You understand there are Separatists on this world who would very much like to get their hands on a Prador warhead?'

'You're stating the obvious.'

'Yes . . . presume yourself bored, presume you feel under-utilized by ECS, under-appreciated.'

'Okay, I'm presuming.'

'Perhaps you want greater material wealth.'

Silly, really, when in the Polity every need could be catered for and the greatest ill of society was boredom.

'No,' he said. 'I'm hooked on my own adrenalin, looking for further excitement, and I feel no inclination to get intervention to wean me off my addiction.'

Olkennon bowed her head for a moment. She was smiling. Cormac did not allow himself to react to that – it was only emulation after all. Olkennon raised her head. 'Eminently plausible, considering your psyche reports.'

'I don't get to read them.'

'Of course not . . . now let us go and see Carl.'

They left the room to traverse the aseptic corridors of the medical centre. Cormac knew when they had come to Carl's room because few other rooms here possessed coded locks. Olkennon moved in close to the lock to deliberately block his view of it, rapidly punched in a code, and then opened the door to step inside. Following her, Cormac gazed across at the bed on which Carl lay motionless, a life-support shellwear enclosing his chest with various tubes and fibre optics trailing from it to an autodoc pedestal.

'Unconscious?' Cormac enquired.

'Definitely.' Olkennon gazed at the bed. 'The weapon fired at him was a dirty one: plutonium fragmentation bullet. However, it didn't detonate but passed straight through. He's as healthy as you now, but with what we now suspect about him, better he remains unconscious.'

'I see,' said Cormac. 'So what is it you now suspect about him?'

Still gazing at the bed, Olkennon continued, 'According to his record he's about a year older than you, Cormac. Medscan has revealed some anomalies – he may be older, he may not be who his record claims him to be.' She turned to Cormac. 'Tell me what you think is going on.'

The stuff about Carl's possible age and identity only complemented the suppositions Cormac had already made. 'I don't know how it happened, but I think Carl is working for the Separatists here.' He glanced at the Golem for confirmation.

'Go on.'

'I think that learning he would be guarding part of the Prador ship's perimeter, he allowed Separatists through so they could obtain some weapon . . . a warhead. When that mission failed, he killed those who were on their way out of the ship before they could be captured and then, inevitably, reveal his involvement. Subsequently, the Separatists took vengeance upon him for that killing.' Cormac gestured towards the bed.

'Very close, though not exact in every detail.'

'Perhaps, if it is not too much to ask, you could fill in that detail.'

'Ah, you have an overdeveloped tendency towards sarcasm in one so young.'

'It's a result of my cynicism – something I believe to be a useful survival trait for one working for ECS. Now, must I keep guessing?'

'Vernol's brother was one of those who died at the ship, but Vernol attempted to kill Carl because he believed Carl to be an ECS plant. As we understand it the man always put "the Cause" before family and didn't really like his brother very much.'

Cormac felt uncomfortable with all this. Without his intervention Carl would probably have taken Vernol down, but did this matter? Carl was obviously guilty of something . . .

'Vernol is no longer with us,' Cormac observed, 'and Carl, I suspect, will not be leaving ECS *care* this side of eternity.'

Olkennon shrugged – not her decision.

'The situation now?' Cormac asked.

'Removing Separatists from play is the main purpose of ECS here. Through Carl we might have been able to take down a number of cells.'

Cormac said nothing, for he was tired of having to squeeze information out of her. He knew Olkennon would eventually tell him all he needed to know, but no more.

'As we understand it,' she continued, 'there is divided opinion amidst the Separatists we know of in this area. Some believe Carl an ECS plant and that Vernol was right to try killing him. Others believe Vernol's motive was vengeance only and that he tried to kill a valuable asset.'

Annoyed at himself for prompting again, Cormac asked, 'And my role?'

'According to his record, which we are not entirely sure of right now, Carl came from Callisto. His family were members of the Jovian Separatists, though they never went so far as violent protest or terrorism. We can alter your records to show you came from there too. Any enquiries sent directly there can be fielded by our agents, since the Separatist organization on Callisto was penetrated long ago – it is only allowed to continue functioning because of the leads it gives us to other Separatist enclaves.'

'I see; I am to be the partner Carl never mentioned.'

'Outstanding.' Olkennon grimaced. 'I do hope you understand how dangerous this might be, especially considering the doubts about Carl's antecedents?'

Cormac snorted in annoyance, waving a hand as if to brush that aside. Yeah, maybe there were anomalies about Carl's past, but didn't that rather tie in with his nefarious dealings here and now?

'They'll take some convincing,' he said. 'They'll know just about all information is falsifiable, and there might be those who will want to take me down.'

'Certainly – can you be convincing?'

Cormac considered the situation. He was being roped into an undercover operation because he was conveniently placed. Such operations were usually the province of those with decades of training and experience in the field. He was only twenty-two.

'Yeah, I think I can be convincing.'

3

'Cormac, Dax is back,' said his mother. Again she was wearing old-style sunglasses – a habit that seemed to make her unapproachable, just like her perpetually distant tone, just like her perpetual affirmation of his name change. Cormac abandoned his p-top and school bag and broke into a run for the stairs. 'Don't bother him for too long – I've packed your suitcase with clothes and you need to sort out what else you'll be taking with you.'

Cormac skidded to a halt at the bottom of the stairs and turned. 'We're going away again?'

'Yes, we'll be spending a week with Dax in Tritonia.'

Cormac felt a flood of joy. *Tritonia.* He loved the city which stretched – with intermittent breaks – along the seabed from the south coast of Britain to France. His mother might allow him to take a haemolung out, especially if Dax went out with him to keep watch. He charged up the stairs yelling, 'Dax!' but halted before his elder brother's door. Dax, who had lived at home until finally shipping out with the medical arm of ECS, liked his privacy, especially so since the time Cormac had charged in while he had been having sex with Marella. She had been sitting astride him naked, bouncing up and down – the image was forever etched in the young boy's mind. Cormac knocked on the door.

There was no answer for long seconds, and Cormac was about to open the door to peek inside when he heard the sound of movement from within. He waited a little longer and, disappointed, was about to head to his own room when there came a gruff, 'Come in, Ian.'

'Dax! We're going to—'

The sight that greeted him brought him to a confused halt. This was Dax? His elder brother had always been a big heavily muscled young man with jet-black hair and an easy smile. This thin, haunted individual with flecks of grey in his hair did not seem like the same person.

'Dax,' he said, but could think of nothing else to add.

Dax was still wearing the camouflage fatigues of an ECS medic – the blue uniform had been abandoned during this war, since to the Prador a medic was just as much a target as any human being. He stood with his back to the window, and was smoking a cigarette – something he had once frowned upon, even though body nanites could negate the adverse health effects. 'You're thin,' Cormac finally managed.

Dax nodded contemplatively and stared with what Cormac could only feel as a complete lack of engagement. After a moment he shrugged, shook his head, then tried a weak smile.

'It's hard out there, little brother,' he said.

Hoping for some return to normality, Cormac asked enthusiastically, 'Tell me about it!'

'No.' No excuses, no explanation or justification, just *No*.

'What's it like?' Cormac wheedled.

Dax just shook his head, then after a moment turned to the window. After a drawn-out silence he said, 'We'll talk once we've reached Tritonia – maybe I'll feel better then . . . maybe.'

After another long delay, Cormac finally retreated, closing the door softly behind him.

They were going to take the hypertube in the morning, and when he was sent to bed Cormac observed his mother opening a bottle of whisky while Dax sat in strained silence smoking cigarette after cigarette. Already deft in the art of learning things he shouldn't, Cormac left his p-top open on the side table, its camera screen directed towards the two of them, the microphone functioning, all its other functions in silent mode. Retiring to his bedroom he turned on his room console, linked in, and watched his mother and brother.

'—when I'm ready,' his mother was saying, 'and if it doesn't get to him first.'

Dax gulped his whisky as if to sate a terrible thirst, then replied, 'Do you want me . . . ?'

'No, that won't be necessary,' she replied. 'So, are you going to tell me, Dax?'

More whisky. 'What's to tell? It's a fucking nightmare out there.'

'But you knew it would be.'

Staring at something distant, Dax said, 'Our first assignment . . . we set up a treatment unit for flash-burn victims. They came in with their skins coming off. We handled it to begin with, but then one of their scout ships started taking out our supply ships. We handled that – using nerve-blockers and anything else we could scrape together.' He shrugged. 'They weren't in any pain, but they just kept on dying on us. Then Prador ground troops attacked and we had to withdraw. About eight hundred of our patients we just couldn't move – it would have killed them. Our commander was green and he decided that we should leave them with nerve-blockers in place. Maybe the Prador would ignore them. That commander ended up being shipped back with the other wounded when one of the ECS regulars found out what he had done. Smashed him up real bad.' Dax looked up at his mother. 'You know what Prador do with the wounded?'

'I think I can probably guess.'

'Maybe you can, but it's in the detail. They eat them alive.'

'So they died, which would have happened if you had moved them. At least they weren't in any . . .'

Dax shook his head. 'No, mother – they took the nerve-blockers off first, then they ate the worst cases and spent a number of days with the remainder. They're as technically advanced as us, so they know how to keep someone alive.'

'That's . . . horrible.'

Again the shrug. He held out his glass for more whisky. 'After that, things were moving too fast for us to set up the big portable hospitals. Mostly field work. I've seen just about every injury you can possibly imagine.' He drank, shook his head. 'Tough bastards, some of those regulars. When you see a guy walk up to you carrying his own severed arm, the stump cauterized by laser, and when he tells you he wants it reattached quickly so he can get back to his unit.' He paused. 'Are you sure you want to hear this?'

'I want to hear. I want to know that he faced nothing trivial.'

Dax drew on another self-igniting cigarette. 'It's day after day after day of it. You think you're getting used to it, then find you aren't. Me and three of the other guys were sent to one location where we found two soldiers hanging from a snake tree. They'd been skinned alive, fitted with drips feeding them anti-shock drugs and fluids, and were still alive. Two friends climbed that tree to cut them down. Booby trap. A thermal grenade went off and fried all four up there. I wake up hearing them screaming and I can't go anywhere now where pork or bacon is being cooked.'

Mother looked sick. She took off her sunglasses to expose raw eyes. This was affecting her badly, Cormac guessed, his spine crawling. He wished he'd left his room light on.

'Then there's the Olston Peninsula,' Dax continued relentlessly. 'About a hundred troops waiting for transport from the front. No one really noticed anything odd about them. They were brought into the camp where I was waiting to tend their injuries. They just stepped out of the ambulances and opened up with their weapons. Killed four hundred before they were all themselves killed. I watched an autopsy on one of them. Cored and thralled.'

'What?' his mother asked.

'Humans taken captive . . . I don't know the full story, there's something about an alien virus in them that makes them more durable. Part of the spinal cord and the brain removed – a metal Prador thrall unit sitting in their place.'

'I don't know what to say to you, Dax.'

'There's nothing to say. I'll get all I need in Tritonia.'

'Editing?'

'Damned right. There's people I work with who know how to deal with all sorts of stuff they can never remember having dealt with before. I'll get the bad memories cut away, cauterized out.'

Dax stood, a little unsteadily, and stretched. He turned and walked directly towards Cormac's point of view and gazed straight into the p-top screen. 'And I think you've heard enough now,' he said, and closed the screen down.

The moment he entered the old city, Cormac knew he was being watched by someone other than the one tailing him, for this place was known to be scattered with pin-cams. With the street map at the forefront of his mind, he scanned the row of ramshackle shops to his right, and chose a clothing shop in about the correct position. He walked over to the plastic-draped racks of streetwear, raised some of the clear film as if to inspect a suit, then abruptly turned to look behind, but his tail was good, already turning away to select some food from a vendor's display. Cormac grimaced, then entered the shop where the young girl in charge immediately approached him.

'Hi,' he said cheerfully. 'I need a fog robe and mask.'

'We have a wonderful selection of . . .' She began guiding him to the racks on the left, but he stepped to the right where packs of the cheapest exchange garments lay, and selected a robe and mask. They were necessities here if you didn't possess an enviro-suit, since acidic fogs frequently descended in the evening. The girl reluctantly followed him over when he held up an octagonal ten-shilling piece and then placed it down on a counter beside him. Tearing open the pack, he quickly donned the baggy protective robe and the mask.

'I want to get out through the back of this place,' he said.

She eyed the coin, which was about five times the value of his purchase. 'I don't want to be involved in anything illegal.' It was a rote protest and a test to see if she could push up the price. He didn't have time for this – the one following him would shortly be in here.

'You won't be involved in anything illegal if you let me through, though if Shelah's husband comes in here after me, things could turn nasty.'

'Shelah's husband?'

'I haven't the time.'

Coming swiftly to a decision she snatched up the coin. 'This way.'

She led him to a back room stacked with plasmel or cardboard boxes – the former bearing some burns which attested to their provenance before the end of the war. The rear door was a heavy pseudo-wood affair with numerous bolts, which she slid back. Cormac had no doubt that 'Shelah's husband' would also be conducted through this same door, just as quickly, and for the same price. Afterwards the girl would slide the bolts back into place, dust off her hands, and be quite happy with her profits for the day.

An alley led along the back of the row of shops, with ruins along the other side, some of which were gradually being rebuilt into homes whilst others were being used as dumping grounds. Cormac dodged behind a crumbled wall, the foamstone of its upper surface fused glassy by the intense heat of some weapon, probably a Prador particle cannon. He slipped a small hand-held scanner from his pocket and ran it over himself from head to foot.

One of the bugs – a device the size of a pinhead – lay in the collar of his envirosuit. He discarded it in the rubble heap behind him. The other bug was microscopic and bonded to the skin of his forearm so, employing another function of the scanner, he used a burst of EMR to disable it. Then he clicked over a switch on the scanner and tossed it away, for a simple ECS grunt out for a stroll should have no need of such a thing. The device smoked then burst into flame, incinerating fingerprints and trace DNA along with itself. Now, from his sabretache, he removed a small pepper-pot stun gun, and waited with his back against the war-scarred wall.

The bolts clonking in the door gave him plenty of warning. He placed the fog mask against his face and felt the skin-stick bond, then pulled up the hood of his robe and listened. The one who'd been dogging his footsteps moved with hardly a sound, just the occasional unavoidable crunch of grit. It occurred to Cormac then how simplistic his trap was here, how obvious to anyone sufficiently trained. What would he do? What would he do if he had been trained properly?

Cormac quickly stepped out into the alley, but whoever had come through the back of the shop after him was not visible. Moving as fast and as silently as he could, he returned to that back door, scanned around, and noted a way through the ruins to his left. Yes, had it been him he would have taken a circuitous route to where he had detected the bug. Cormac moved down that way, checking all possible ambush points as he went. There: the shadow of one wall on the ground before him with something moving along it. He dropped into a crouch, aimed upwards and fired at a half-seen shape.

Just clipped by the blast of neurotoxin pellets, the figure fell, swearing, and landed in an unsteady squat whilst groping for something under his coat. Cormac fired at the wall beside the figure, not wanting to take the neurotoxin dose up to lethal levels.

As the pellets fragmented, their contents turning into a choking gas, he charged forward to slam a thrust kick into the man's chest. The man hit the wall behind and bounced back, whereupon Cormac side-fisted his temple and he went down like a sack of sand.

The one they had sent to follow Cormac was young, looked no older than Cormac himself, his face unlined and scattered with freckles, his hair ginger. He had been good, fast and dangerous, but not lethal. Apparently this youth was a recruit like himself, but one undergoing espionage training. The possibility of Cormac being involved in Carl's treachery had been downgraded in importance, it being decided that he should merely be watched. He was not considered sufficiently important or dangerous for a *real* agent to expend valuable time upon.

Cormac quickly sprayed an impermeable covering over his hands, stooped by the man, and began searching him. This had to look like a robbery, and he needed plausible deniability. All the money went into his own pockets, along with other items of value like identification and a small palmtop. A gold finger ring and gold earring he left, since no local would steal such items here where they had been digging that metal out of the ground in industrial quantities since the colony was established. He paused over the thin-gun the youth had been trying to draw. He liked the heft of the narrow, easily concealed weapon. It was an agent's weapon or equally the kind used by others about nefarious deeds. It went into his pocket along with some spare clips. Later, when the mission was over, he would return these items, but for now veracity was all. He considered shifting the man into a recovery position – people had been known to choke on their own vomit after stun – but that would show any watchers that he was concerned, so leaving the man where he lay, he moved off.

Now he needed to get to The Engine Room, since that was the brief instruction given him when he used the com-code obtained from a secret file concealed in Carl's palmtop amidst his weapons-adjustment programs. Whoever Cormac met there would reveal himself – or herself, since the voice he had spoken to had been electronically disguised – as Samara.

At the end of the alley he ducked into yet another alley which in turn led to a square, where mounds of rubble had been bull-dozed to one side and adapted blue grass was sprouting once again, though patchily, since the acid fogs stunted its growth. A statue had been hauled upright again, a scaffold built round it and repairs commenced, though no one was working on it now – perhaps the exigencies of building new homes and infrastructure were more important than the image of some long-dead dignitary.

Locating himself by the position of the still-standing clock tower, Cormac headed for a wide boulevard lined with red-leaf lime trees bearing more dead limbs than live. He turned left at a scummed-over pond and caught sight of the polluted harbour down at the bottom of the hill; the smell rising from there reminded him of the interior of the Prador ship. Fortunately the oceans weren't dead here, but a substantial proportion of the sea life had been killed, so sometimes the shores stood feet-deep in rotting detritus.

He walked down to the harbour, which unlike the city above had not taken any direct hits, but which had taken the brunt of tsunamis generated elsewhere on this world. To his left a thousand-foot-long cargo ship lay on its side, houses and warehouses crushed underneath it. Holes had been cut into its hull to provide accom-modation inside, and spelt out on the blades of the two sets of twinned screws were the words *The Engine Room*. He headed for the low door sliced through the rear of the hull, mounted steps leading up inside over a huge drive shaft, and arrived in the Escher-esque engine room where new floors and stairways had been built in level without removing the old. Removing his fog mask he

headed straight for the bar, which was set over a very retro generator of the kind not normally seen outside a museum. Glancing
round, he understood how wealthy the society here had once been,
for this ship had been someone's privately owned and lovingly
restored and maintained antique.

Behind the bar a man clad in greasy overalls, and with a large
improbable beard bound with copper wire, said, 'What can I get
you, matey?' Maybe he was the owner of this ship.

'I'll have a large espresso and a brandy.' One to counter the
other was his theory, since he needed to stay alert here.

The espresso came from a machine that actually used real
ground beans, and the making of it was a lengthy process. The
brandy came from an old pottery bottle. The price reflected both
these sources.

'Thank you,' Cormac paid without quibbling, since Olkennon
had given him a generous budget. 'I'm looking for someone called
Samara – can you help?'

The bearded barman laughed, then repeated the words,
'Looking for Samara.'

'If you could explain?' Cormac enquired politely.

'Someone's played a joke on you. If you're "looking for Samara",
you're searching in vain. It comes from just after the bombing. A
guy had lost his mind and was looking for Samara. He had no other
details – couldn't remember – and there were thousands called
Samara here in the city.' He looked contemplative for a moment.
'Lot of them changed their names since.'

Cormac nodded his thanks and turned away to head for a
nearby bench table. It did not surprise him that his contact had
not given a real name or method of identification. Doubtless he
was being watched in here, as he had been watched since the
moment he entered the old city. He placed his drinks down on
the compacted-fibre surface of the table, shed his fog robe and

stretched his back before sitting so that any watchers would be able to see he was wearing ECS fatigues. The barman saw, for he frowned and looked quickly away.

The espresso was good, the brandy better, but Cormac sat with deliberate fidgety impatience and scanned his surroundings. He spotted a man clad in similar robes to his own sitting at the far side of the room. He hadn't been there a few minutes ago and he had no drink before him – sloppy, and easily spotted.

Then, as Cormac finished his coffee, three individuals entered the place and headed directly to where he sat. The two men were heavily built – the archetypal thugs employed by many criminal organizations. They either possessed boosted musculature and reinforced bones, or had serious steroid habits and spent most of their lives pumping iron. They wore a mixture of local clothing and the kind of fatigues on sale anywhere, in this case consisting of long heavy coats and the kind of hats worn by gangsters portrayed on ancient celluloid film. The other figure was a woman in a leather tabard-like garment split up the sides of her legs to reveal black trousers and heavy trekking boots. Her face was made up: heavy on the blue lip gloss and face powder to cover a rash of pocked scars. Her hair was black and coiled on top of her head.

With practised ease the two thugs slid onto the bench on either side of Cormac, one pressing a hand down hard on his shoulder as he made the obligatory attempt to rise. He felt something pressed against his right side and peered down at the lethal stiletto prodding him. It protruded from the left arm stump of the thug sitting there. The thug to his left drew a heavy iron flack gun and rested it on one ridiculously meaty thigh, pointing it down towards Cormac's legs – a rather foolish move, since if he pulled the trigger the woman now taking the seat opposite would be hit too. Stiletto still in place, the right-hand thug held a scanner up over Cormac's head then ran it down his front, holding it level with his stomach for a moment before placing it on the table. The device would have detected any active bugs and would now pick up the signal from any that were activated – by spoken word, perhaps, or some other signal. The scanner also possessed a laser interface head, so no one would be able to use laser bounce or any other distance-reading technique. It would also blur the movement of their mouths to outside view, so even a lip-reader would be unsuccessful.

'I hear you're looking for Samara,' said the woman.

'Apparently I was misled,' Cormac replied. 'Very few people here with that name now.'

'Well, you've found one of them.'

He could play this game too. 'But have I found the right one?' He did not need to study her too closely to know she was not one of those who had been sitting at the table with Carl, but in his briefing from Olkennon this Samara matched the description of one of those Carl had been in contact with. 'Carl's descriptions of those he spoke to were somewhat vague, just as were his accounts of what was said.'

'And you claim to be his partner?'

'I thought myself his partner, but whether he intended me to retain that position is open to doubt.'

'Convenient, if you feared not getting your story straight.'

'Well, I know enough to know that there's some payment due.'

'To Carl.'

'To Carl, who courtesy of one of your people is now breathing through a tube.'

'We feel Carl did not fulfil his side of the deal.'

Cormac stared at her for a long moment, then casually said, 'Is this goon going to remove his penis substitute from my side or am I going to have to break what's left of his arm?'

'You talk tough for a new recruit to ECS. Do you think you could break his arm before he skewered your liver?'

'It's not something I'd like to try,' Cormac replied – deliberate retraction of bravado. 'But I would like our discussion to be on a more civilized footing.'

The woman waved her hand and the blade was retracted. She no doubt thought Cormac incapable of dealing with these two, even without that blade at his gut. He felt she had just removed the one thing he could have done nothing about, though he didn't want things to go that far.

'Thank you,' he said. 'Now, you were saying that you feel Carl did not fulfil his side of your deal. As I recollect, he gave you access to the Prador ship. He showed you where to go in under our watch.' Necessary to use the 'our'. They would have known, or at least knew now, who had been in that foxhole with Carl.

'He gave us access – agreed,' she said grudgingly.

'Therefore the deal had been fulfilled.'

'The idea was for our people to go in, grab a Prador warhead, and get out again. They didn't get out again.'

'Which is hardly our fault, now is it?'

'Then there's other issues.' Cormac waited for her to continue. 'Carl's motivation to help us wasn't all about money. He is a Jovian Separatist and believes in the Cause, in bringing about the fall of the AI autocrat and all its minions. Are you here to tell me you are the mercenary side of the partnership?'

Cormac deliberately looked uncomfortable. 'No, I'm not saying that – I'm from Callisto too. But both of us follow the Cause only so far. Yes, we will help it along its way if we can, but the pay had better be worth the risk.'

Her expression remained dead as she said, 'I see.'

Cormac could feel the thugs either side of him sit up a little straighter and prepare themselves. Now was the time for the lure.

'But seeing how things went wrong for you, I am prepared to compromise.'

'Compromise.' Tone flat. She thought he was just a mercenary on the make who now, seeing his danger, was trying to worm his way out of it. She would not believe what he had to say next unless that threat was removed.

He let something relax inside him and adrenalin surged, screwing his stomach into a ball and seeming to pour heat down his spine. He turned slightly, to give himself more leverage. Silly thugs to sit so close. He brought his elbow back into the throat of Mr Stiletto, caught the knife hand as it came across from his choking victim, twisted and pushed down. The blade went straight through the wrist of the other thug as he brought his flack gun across. The man struggled, leaning forward, blood spurting from the wound, but his grip was wet and slippery. Cormac took away the gun and smacked it hard against Mr Stiletto's temple, then almost as an afterthought crashed the head of the one he had just disarmed hard down on the table. Both of them were now unconscious, or as near enough to that state as to make no difference.

'Yes, compromise.' He rested the weapon on the table, its barrel pointing towards Samara. He paused for a moment, taking steady breaths, and noted his hand wasn't shaking at all. He did, however, feel sick, but refused to throw up here, now.

He continued, 'After we let your people through they screwed up and got themselves killed. We can't be held responsible for that, or at least I can't.' He added, 'The opportunity to get your people in that way ended when they put autoguns on the perimeter and moved us on. But together we could have made new opportunities if one of your ill-disciplined idiots hadn't taken it upon himself to blow out Carl's lungs.'

'I did not agree with that,' she said. 'Nor did the Central Committee.'

Central Committee – interesting.

'Whatever.' Cormac abruptly picked up the weapon and rested it across the crook of his arm pointing at Stiletto, who seemed to be recovering. The other one was making odd snoring sounds, and Cormac hoped he hadn't hit him too hard. 'The net result of that action is that Carl will face some hard questions when they put his larynx back in. I am also under suspicion. I was bugged earlier and I was being followed.'

'Yes, I do know.'

Of course, someone knowledgeable in the ways of subterfuge would not have let Cormac know that. This Samara wanted to appear tough and clever.

'You know?'

'I had you watched from the moment you left ECS Base Camp. Why did you use the stunner, why not kill him?'

Cormac shrugged. 'I wanted it to look like a robbery and killing him would only have increased suspicion. As it is, suspicion will have increased, especially when they find out I dumped the bugs.'

'So why are you here?'

Stiletto revived with a grunt, so Cormac abruptly pressed the barrel of the weapon against the side of his head. 'Move away slowly and go and sit over there.' He nodded towards a nearby bench table. Once Stiletto had obeyed, Cormac returned his attention to Samara. 'They can't run autoguns all around the perimeter. There's not enough of them here yet, and with earth-moving equipment travelling in and out the logistics get a bit untenable.'

'So.'

'So, after they replaced my unit with autoguns and after Carl ended up coughing up bits of his lungs, they put what remained of us – without our Golem sergeant – on a guard detail inside the ship. They actually used us as bait to draw out those Prador remaining hidden inside. We nearly died.'

'So, you're pissed off about that.'

'A little, not a lot – comes with the territory.'

The gun wielder snorted a mixture of blood and snot onto the table surface. Cormac edged away from him a little.

'What you should be interested in is what I managed to pick up while I was in there. You see, I know precisely where there is a rack of four one-megaton warheads – all small enough to be carried by a man apiece, and I know how to get you inside to them.'

4

The numerous views through sheets of chainglass directly into the English Channel were often turbid, but when they cleared they were astounding. Magnifying sections picked out local sea life, bringing up clear pictures of rays, cod shoals and glittering storms of a GM version of whitebait that had escaped the farms and burgeoned in the oceans over two hundred years before. As Cormac understood it, the idea of wiping them out with a tailored virus had been proposed a century ago, but put on hold. These rugged little fish filled certain niches that had been emptied and were a ready source of food for other creatures. In fact, other emptied niches were steadily being filled in the same way, with life recreated from dry museum specimens. The oceans now teemed.

Neither Dax nor his mother had mentioned last night. Both of them were drinking from litre bottles of Coke and had earlier popped a few Aldetox. In fact they weren't saying much at all, and both of them were wearing sunglasses.

Departing the maglev station they headed straight out into the tubular streets of the undersea city, one Loyalty Luggage chest groaning along behind them on roller leg spokes like a particularly fat and short-legged dog. Ian had his own case hanging from his shoulder with his own necessities inside, which obviously didn't include such ephemera as clean underpants and socks – they were in the luggage.

'The Watts?' suggested Dax.

'Of course,' said their mother. The Watts – named after some long-dead science fiction writer – possessed the best undersea windows, airlocks and diving facilities. They'd stayed there before on numerous occasions, and one of Ian's most enduring memories was of their father taking all three boys out into the sea for the first time. Back then they didn't have the full-skin pressure suits, so the hotel's rooms had been pressurized, and actually venturing beyond it had not been an easy option.

As they headed for their destination, Cormac scanned his surroundings for places he recognized, but except for the exterior shapes of the streets themselves, everything had changed. A lot of the shops seemed to be closed down and the usual cornucopias of goods were not on display.

'It's hitting here,' Dax observed.

'Everywhere,' their mother replied. 'I don't think it's because of lack of supply, but more to do with guilt about supply.'

'There's a war on,' Cormac piped up.

His mother raised her sunglasses to expose reddened eyes, and gave Dax one of those knowing looks that irritated the boy immensely.

'That's the opinion,' she said. 'It seems to have brought out the Puritan in many.'

Dax shook his head. 'Stupid,' he said. 'Most of what's sold here won't even impinge.' He paused for a moment, thoughtful. 'Unless things get a lot worse.'

They moved on down the concourse and eventually arrived at the portico of The Watts. Arrayed across the front of this building were five heavy oval chainglass doors, which were the original pressure locks for this building. Hannah placed her cash card into the slot of a console beside one door and made her room selection on the touch screen. Peering up at the screen Cormac was gratified to see she had requested three interconnected rooms, all en suite, so he would have his own room, his own space. The last time they'd come here he had shared with her, whilst Dax and Alex had their own rooms. He felt this meant he was not so much of a child any more.

The nearest pressure door opened upon insertion of one of the three key cards the console had provided, and he and his mother stepped through into the lock whilst Dax waited his turn with the Loyalty Luggage. They entered a vestibule containing a central auto-kiosk packed with those items the hotel's guests might need while venturing out into the city. Around the walls numerous doors opened into the accommodation areas, whilst between them were mounted screens showing undersea scenes.

'They were going to get rid of them,' said Dax as he came through, gesturing back to the pressure doors.

'A lot of people objected and there were moves to put a preservation order on them,' Hannah replied. 'The hotel owners finally realized they were an attraction rather than a hindrance to their usual guests – keeps the non-diving riff-raff out.'

She walked over to one of the doors at the end of the vestibule, inserted the key card again, and they moved on down a long corridor giving access to rooms on either side. When she halted by one of the doors on the left Cormac was made even happier, for he remembered enough to know that the rooms on this side were those nearest to the sea, so were provided with real undersea windows.

'You're there,' she said to Dax, pointing to the room they had just passed and tossing him one of the cards. 'And you're there.' She handed Cormac another card and gestured to the next room along. 'I'll send the luggage to you, Dax, once I've unpacked, and you can send it to Ian.' She paused for a moment. 'I mean Cormac.'

Cormac inserted his key card into his door, entered, closed the door behind him and gazed about himself with relish. A large bed lay to his left, interactive netscreen up in one corner opposite the bed, large blacked-out window taking up the entire wall to the right of that, plenty of cupboards, some low comfortable chairs arranged around a coffee table and a door to an en suite in the right-hand wall. He stepped over beside the bed, dropped his shoulder bag on it, then picked up the room remote from the bedside table. It took him just a moment of checking through the touchplates to find the window control. He walked over, turned one of the comfortable chairs round to face it, plumped himself down in the chair, then hit the control to make the window once again transparent.

Starting in a swirl pattern right in the centre, the photoactive liquid, sandwiched between two layers of chainglass, began changing from black to transparent. Cormac remembered spending hours gazing through a window like this. He remembered the crustaceans bumbling along the bottom out there: the masses of winkles gathered like multicoloured pearls, the whelks oozing across the glass and the occasional scallop jetting past; the hermit crabs, lobsters and edible crabs; the shrimps, prawns and crayfish; and the endless varieties of fish. But what sat out there was not quite what he expected, and he shrieked with fright.

Giant iron scorpions were not in the guide book.

The autodozer garage was surrounded by a security fence with cameras mounted on the posts. Floodlights were on, their glow extending out into the darkness, and also reflecting off the polished bodies of two mosquito autoguns patrolling inside like skeletal metallic guard dogs.

As he strode towards the big gates, torch beam stabbing down at the churned earth ahead of him, Cormac glanced back at his three companions. Stiletto – who Cormac now knew to be called Pramer – wore a false hand in place of his blade and appeared quite fitting for this role, since many of those who did this sort of job boosted their musculature and took pride in being able to carry out heavy work normally the territory of some drone or Golem. The other two didn't really fit. Layden was a scrawny pale and sickly individual who looked plain uncomfortable in his baggy overalls, and Sheen was a teenage girl with a perpetual expression of sulky rebellion. No problem, their physical details had been logged into the personnel databank.

Cormac halted and peered up at the security drone extending out from the gatepost on a stalk like some iron and plastic seed pod. It tilted towards them and after a moment said, 'Admittance approved.' He stepped aside and now Layden received the same approval, as did Pramer, then Sheen moved into place. With her the drone paused for a moment, and tilted as if curious about what it was seeing. Cormac suspected the AI was deliberately racking up the tension – it didn't want this to appear too easy for them.

'Identicard,' the drone demanded.

Cormac was amazed at the teenager's sudden calm as she reached into her engineer's belt bag, took her card from amidst the numerous small packs that would open out into monofilm rucksacks, and held it up. He saw the flash of laser scanning pass over the card and hand, then after a moment Sheen received a grudging 'admittance approved', whereupon a personnel door popped open in the main gates and they entered.

'It must be your acne,' said Pramer.

'Fuck off,' Sheen replied.

Cormac had already instructed them to confine their talk to the kind of exchanges expected from such workers, but hadn't expected these two to show such talent for it. Not a word could be uttered about their real reason for being here, since watch programs would be running here listening for key words and phrases and assessing for out-of-character behaviour. Grinning, he glanced at Pramer, but was surprised to see he seemed chastened by the teenager's reply. Odd, decidedly so.

Beyond the fence lay a plasticrete yard, much of it chewed up by the action of dozer treads, along the back of which stood a row of huge garages each containing the heavy equipment being used about the Prador dreadnought. Cormac waved for the others to follow and headed for the third door along. Here he took out his identicard and pressed it into the reader beside another personnel door, which opened for him. The others followed suit and trailed him inside to where a row of dozers loomed like steel dinosaurs.

'Number one,' he instructed, pointing to the first in the line.

The dozer was a five-hundred-ton monster with caterpillar treads, a dozer blade to the fore and two rear excavator arms which could choose from a selection of buckets within the machine's body. It possessed no cab for a driver since the machine could be slaved to AI, loaded with a submind or telefactored to some other operator. There was no necessity for the thing to be permanently full-AI, since such intelligence would be wasted on a piece of earth-moving equipment.

'Sheen, Layden.' Cormac directed their attention towards the tool racks along one wall.

Layden walked over and collected a console and length of optic cable. His technical expertise was why he had been 'invited' – that invitation spiced with a promise of a large supply of whatever drugs were slowly killing him. Sheen collected a screwdriver kit – she was just along to carry one of the CTDs and possessed no expertise that Cormac could see. He himself strolled round the dozer inspecting its treads whilst Pramer went over to peer inside the compartment containing its digger buckets.

This dozer had recently developed a fault in the mechanisms used to shift the elected digger buckets into position for its digger arms at the back. It had been difficult to convince Samara that Carl had managed to introduce the fault preparatory to using this as a back-up way of getting into the ship. But the Separatists here really wanted those CTDs and were quite prepared to lose personnel just to find out if the opportunity of obtaining them existed. It was noticeable, however, that Samara had not seen fit to include herself in this, and that as far as Cormac knew her only close associate here was Pramer; a thug who for reasons Cormac had yet to fathom, had fallen out of favour with her.

'Let's see what we've got,' said Cormac.

Sheen had taken out a multidriver and was removing a small panel from the side of the dozer. Once this was off, Layden plugged the optic from his console into one of the revealed sockets, and input instructions. With a low whine the first enormous dozer arm immediately elbowed upwards, extracting a two-yards-wide earth scoop from the bucket compartment, which it swung to one side – sending Pramer dodging from its path – and crunched down on the plasticrete. With a clonk, pins disengaged, then the arm rose again leaving the earth scoop on the floor, whilst within the dozer's body mechanisms moved the next bucket forward in the compartment. The second arm engaged with this, lifted it out, and deposited it on the floor too whilst the first arm swung back for the next implement.

'Seems okay,' said Cormac, 'but best to be sure.' Removing a small memstore from his pocket, he now headed over to the com console set in the wall beside the tool racks. Upon reaching the console he noticed Sheen watchfully coming up beside him, and guessed her purpose here might be more than it appeared. Perfectly to script Cormac called up the dozer specs and then the relevant maintenance log, which showed them presently working on said machine. He inserted the memstore into the relevant slot in the console and set its contents to load. Deliberately looking pleased with himself, he nodded to Sheen then turned to head back.

The digger arms were now laying out the last of a selection of ceramo-carbide rock drills in neat rows on the floor either side of the dozer's rear end. These were the last items from the digger compartment. As Cormac walked over, one arm detached from a drill then swung over to engage again with the large earth scoop, and there paused.

'Ready?' he asked Layden.

Nodding, the man unplugged the optic, and Sheen, now back at her post, quickly replaced the cover she had removed. By now Pramer had climbed inside the compartment, quickly followed by Layden – who retained the essential console – then Sheen. Cormac stepped into the cramped compartment just as the digger arm started moving again. After a moment the earth scoop swung across then in, blocking out the light as it crashed into the slot at the mouth of the compartment. After a moment a greenish hue filled the space as Pramer stuck a chemical light ball to one ceramal wall.

'Can we talk now?' asked Layden.

'Certainly,' said Cormac, 'but I'd advise against doing it too loudly – there's still ears out there.'

'Tell me about the program you used?' Layden was very doubtful any human could create a program capable of penetrating the security around the dreadnought, for he possessed sufficient expertise to know what it would be up against.

'It was a mutagenic worm,' said Cormac. 'Carl knew more about it than me. It apparently causes a viral fault to develop in the garage memory, and erasing the fault wipes that part of the memory too. The AI will know maintenance was scheduled but the details will be gone.'

'The drone?'

'Shares memory with the garage com system – quite primitive. Most of the security in the area is outside these garages.'

Layden frowned. 'Very useful guy, this Carl.'

Cormac pretended anger. 'Which is why you people were stupid to try killing him.'

'Not my people.' Layden held out his hand to Sheen, who passed over the screwdriver kit, from which he selected a multidriver and started removing the screws securing a panel within the compartment.

'How long?' asked Pramer, whilst fiddling with his artificial hand.

'Twenty minutes,' Cormac replied. 'Then this dozer sets out to shove a spill away from the north side of the ship. Despite its supposed fault it'll be used because only the dozer blade will be needed, not the digger arms.'

Cormac sat down with his back against one wall. All the others made themselves comfortable too, then fell into desultory silence. Cormac closed his eyes and tried to force himself to relax, or to at least display a veneer of that state. But inside he was tightly wound, both scared and elated, all too aware that at any moment this could all go badly wrong and he could end up dead. He had never felt so alive.

'What are you going to do with them?' asked Layden.

It took Cormac a moment to realize the question had been directed at him. He opened his eyes and saw that all three of them were gazing at him as they awaited his reply. He could have shrugged this off mercenary-style and said that was none of his concern, but he too was supposed to be a Separatist, a fighter for the Cause.

'That will be decided by the Central Committee.' Agent Spencer had queried him upon his return from the meeting with Samara, and had been most interested in that. The Separatists here had not, since the Prador bombardment, been able to organize themselves into the usual cell structure. There were still those in charge, and it was still possible to find an easy way back to the leadership. He went on, 'But if it was up to me I'd get them offworld – hit a runcible AI on one of the high-population worlds like Coloron where it would do most good.'

'Really,' said Layden, blank-faced.

Cormac realized he was making an error here – Layden was a reluctant recruit, and knowing the possible consequences of his actions might result in him being more reluctant still.

'But whether they will ever be used like that is a moot point,' he added.

'Why not?' Layden asked.

'Trading,' said Sheen.

Cormac flicked a glance at her, certain now that there was more to her than met the eye.

'Precisely,' he said. 'They'll be traded to richer groups for things of more value to the long-term struggle: personal armament, money, secure computer time, propaganda.'

That was accepted writ, but the truth was somewhat more sordid. Those who ran planetary Separatist organizations usually ate high off the hog. Their ultimate aim might be the downfall of the ruling AIs, but the real short-term goals were racketeering wealth, drugs to sell for more wealth and power within the organization. That all fell apart when someone delivered a major blow, which wiping out a runcible AI with a CTD would have been, for it usually resulted in Earth Central Security coming down hard on those who previously had been an irritation not worth expending resources to be rid of.

The dozer vibrated slightly, which was the only warning that its heavy internal fly wheels were winding up to speed. It then jerked forwards to rumble across the plasticrete, flinging Layden sprawling. Cormac noted how fast Sheen moved to catch his console before it swung on its optic to smash against the compartment wall, and slotted the memory away for future reference. Light from external floodlights abruptly lit a halo around the earth scoop behind them as the dozer departed the garage. Layden picked himself up and accepted his console back from Sheen, giving her a sour look as he took it.

'Watch yourselves,' said Cormac. 'This isn't set up for passengers.'

That was a lie, because alterations had been made to this dozer's structure and operating procedures. A machine like this was quite capable of hammering, without damage, straight over the massive potholes and rocks about the ship. However, that might have resulted in broken bones for any inside, so it would be taking an easy route. Also, no other dozer had an access hatch inside the bucket compartment to its controls – that security weakness had been taken out long ago.

'I've accessed its cams,' said Layden.

Cormac stood and carefully made his way over to the man, and the others gathered round too. The console screen now showed the view ahead, which at that moment was of a track winding between piles of stone, mud and charred and shattered skarch trunks and their decaying leaves, with the occasional glimpse of mosquito autoguns patrolling the area. Then, after a few minutes, the rear upper surface of the ship became visible off to the right, behind a high security fence. Following the track towards this behemoth, the dozer halted at high gates between two framework watchtowers, waited while they opened, then continued down into a shadowy quarter-mile-wide box trench cutting round the rear of the dreadnought. Soon six autodozers and two KiloTees came into view ahead, working to clear a fall of the trench wall. Four of the dozers were pushing heaps of mud and stone before them to the two others, which were using earth scoops to load KiloTees – autotrucks capable of shifting and tipping loads of a thousand tons.

Cormac studied the wall of metal to their right, curving up towards the sky. A scaffold had been erected against it, epoxied to the exotic metal armour and stretching up for eight hundred feet.

'This is where we get off,' he said.

Layden immediately banished the picture, called up some queued programs and set one running. He then pulled off a lower piece of the console – a remote control for it.

'Shouldn't we wait until we're closer?' asked Pramer.

Cormac shook his head. 'Get too close to the other dozers and they'll pick us up with their cams, then we'll have autoguns down here faster than you can write your will.'

'Right.'

With a clonking and scraping, the earth scoop retreated from view on its arm and they moved to the back of the dozer. It was moving fast, but not as fast as such a machine usually travelled along ground like this. Cormac jumped first, managing to keep to his feet because he had no wish to break his fall by rolling in the mud. Layden landed badly, sprawling in the porridge of mud and stone. Pramer rolled neatly and came swiftly upright. Sheen landed with graceful ease and walked over. Cormac wondered if she was a teenager at all. Maybe her look was just cosmetic camouflage, spots too.

Cormac studied them all for a moment, nodded, then set out at a steady trot towards the scaffolding. Glancing back he saw them following, heads bowed, trying to move as fast as they could over the uneven ground. Doubtless their lack of weapons made them very nervous.

Mounted upon a foamstone block right next to the ship, the scaffolding was completely in shadow. As he stepped up onto the block Cormac paused to watch a number of those scavenger creatures he and Carl had seen, scuttling away from him to drop down the gap between the back edge of the block and the hull of the ship. Then he stepped up, moved over to an elevator platform and studied its controls.

'We're in luck,' he said as the others mounted the block behind him. He turned to them, noticing how Layden was gasping and looked almost on the point of collapse.

'How so?' asked Pramer.

Cormac gestured to the platform. 'Simple clamp wheels and electric motor – no monitoring system, so we can use it without being detected.' He studied Layden. 'Which seems a good thing, because I'm not sure all of us would have been able to climb up there, let alone climb back down carrying a CTD.'

'Yeah,' said Layden, gazing determinedly at Pramer. 'I need something.'

Pramer nodded as if he had expected this, reached in his pocket and took out an inhaler which he tossed across to the man. Layden took three pulls on the thing in quick succession, then abruptly stood more upright with colour returning to his complexion.

He grinned. 'Better . . . much better.'

Some sort of stimulant, Cormac realized, though there were so many different kinds it wasn't worth trying to guess which one. He stepped onto the platform, waited until the others were in place, then hit the up arrow on the simple touchpad. Clamp wheels closed on the four poles positioned at each corner of the platform and began turning, rapidly taking them up. More scavengers scuttled out from underneath the platform itself, and Cormac wondered why they were here. Was the port above them the one out of which those Prador second-children had dumped human remains?

Soon the autodozers and KiloTees were toys below them and they could see all the way in both directions along the massive trench. The air was fresh and clean for a little while, then started to take on a putrid smell as they neared the entrance into the ship. Eventually the platform jerked to a halt beside a metre-wide circular port in the hull. Stretching inwards, evenly spaced around this port, were eight crescent-section rails, their inner faces microridged all the way down with doped superconductors. Coolant pipes, s-con cables and various control systems ran through the jacket enclosing all this. It would have been impossible to enter had not a hole been cut through at the base of the port. Cormac eyed the ladder, epoxied in place there and stretching down into darkness, took out his torch and turned it on, then climbed down.

The ladder got them into a chamber over five hundred feet long, with the rail-gun sitting above them like a fallen redwood. To one side lay the magazine and related mechanisms: a belt feed still loaded with one-ton iron-and-ceramic projectiles, whose impact energy when fired by this thing delivered the destructive potential that in the past had been reserved for atomic weapons. Two more torches came on, their beams stabbing here and there about the interior.

'Stinks,' said Pramer.

Cormac nodded and checked his palm screen. He displayed the map he had made and studied it for a moment, quickly realizing he had forgotten nothing about the route.

'You say there'll be no one here this late?' asked Layden. The man looked wired – pupils dilated and motions all jerky and overextended.

'It's unlikely there'll be anyone this deep in the ship, though there might be some nearer the main entrance.' He waved a hand about him. 'Dealing with this is not so crucial any more, so the work is confined to the daylight hours. They also don't like coming in here at night, since it was during the night they lost personnel.'

'The Prador,' said Layden, eyes wide.

'They think they got the last of them.'

'They think?'

Cormac eyed Layden with pretend contempt, shook his head and moved on.

The corridor beyond smelt even worse, but then it did not have the ventilation. Ship lice dropped from the uneven walls and scuttled across the floor towards the torch beams. Kicking them away hardly discouraged them, so every few paces at least one of the four needed to crush one of the creatures under a boot heel. They climbed down a ladder bonded to the side of a Prador drop-shaft, where the lice were even more of a danger as they tried to nip fingers or drop on heads. More corridors, one now filled with the stench like that of rotting seafood from Prador second-children heaped on a grav-sled outside the Captain's Sanctum. Here the ship lice did not bother them, so busily were they feeding on the corpses. Cormac led the three past these and eventually brought them to their goal.

The room was narrow. To the right was a plain if slightly uneven wall, but to the left was no wall, just the exposed section of a carousel. Many of the compartments in the face of this huge wheel were empty, but four contained smoothly polished cylinders each about two feet long and ten inches in diameter. As Cormac understood it, this was not an actual loading carousel, but just one component in the mechanisms the Prador Captain used to select the explosive load for the missiles he was firing.

'Don't look like much,' said Pramer.

'Perhaps not,' said Cormac. 'But detonate one of these in your home city and that city would be gone, along with a fair portion of the coastline too.'

Pramer nodded, then reached out to grip the top of one and pull it – it seemed immovable. 'How do we get these out?'

'You pull very hard,' said Cormac. 'The clamps are sprung, but to a tension for Prador.'

Pramer started heaving at the CTD, putting all his consider-able muscle bulk into the effort. Cormac reached in from the side and tried to help, but though the device moved out of its clamp slightly, the moment they took the pressure off, it snapped back into place.

'We need a lever.' Cormac stepped out into the corridor and headed back towards the Captain's Sanctum. It did not surprise him to find Sheen walking beside him, still watching him warily.

'There,' he pointed. The remains of the gas-propellant guns the Prador second-children had used lay jumbled in a pile to the rear of the grav-sled loaded with their corpses. Cormac and Sheen sorted through the mess, selecting lengths of hard Prador metal that might be suitable. Cormac was just hefting up a flat length of square bar, its end flattened like that of a crowbar, when a high, girlish and terrified scream echoed along the corridor.

'Layden,' said Sheen.

This was no part of Cormac's plans. A man would not scream like that because ECS had come to arrest him, but because he was terrified and in pain. Only two causes seemed probable: either Pramer had done something to him, or something else had just arrived.

Armed with their makeshift weapons, Sheen and Cormac charged back towards the other two, and upon rounding a corner saw Pramer hurtling towards them. He skidded to a halt, and Sheen tossed him one of the handles from those gas guns: a heavy metal ring attached to a short thick chunk of metal, sharp all around its edges from where it had broken away. He gripped it in his natural hand and hefted it like a massive knuckleduster, then turned. Cormac noted his artificial hand was missing to expose the short stabbing blade now dripping something like green oil. Then the Prador second-child came.

Cormac felt that familiar surge of adrenalin, but it didn't seem so intense this time. Maybe this was because this Prador wasn't the size of the ones that had been gassed back in the sanctum corridor, or maybe it was because he was becoming accustomed to the feeling. Certainly, with a shell over a metre across and claws big enough to snip off someone's head, this Prador was not something you wanted to encounter without a large gun in your hand. Cormac eyed the length of metal he held, then the Prador as it ceased its pursuit and began scuttling from side to side in the corridor, obviously wary of attacking the three humans now facing it. Seemingly without effort, Cormac remembered everything he had been taught about Prador physiology. The manipulatory arms folded underneath the creature's body weren't anywhere near as dangerous as the claws unless they were holding some weapon, and they weren't. The top of the shell, behind the visual turret and palp eyes, would be as hard as stone, as were the claws themselves. There were only a few vulnerable points.

'Hit the visual turret, leg joints and claw joint nearest the body,' he said. 'Don't let that fucker close a claw on you, or you're dead.'

'No shit,' said Sheen, stepping to one side and hefting a chunk of metal like a long-handled cleaver.

The Prador second-child came to a decision and surged forward, its claws spread wide, ready to snap closed on any available flesh. Cormac hesitated for a moment, seeing how he and his companions were going to get in each other's way, then abruptly ran towards the creature. The Prador emitted a hissing squeal, now snapping its claws open and closed perhaps in an attempt to intimidate. Before they came within reach of him, Cormac threw himself over the creature, somersaulting in mid-air with a claw just brushing his head, and came down feet first on its carapace. He had time for one swipe with the metal bar, bringing it down hard on one palp eye and crushing it into the creature's visual turret, before his momentum spilled him behind.

Shouldering into the floor, he rolled and came upright, the creature stopping and half turning towards him. But Pramer and Sheen now attacked, and undecided which way to turn, it presented only one claw to them, whilst unable to deploy its other against any of them. Sheen fenced with the snapping claw, whilst Pramer tried to get in close to use his shorter-range weapons. Seeing an opportunity, he ducked in close and managed to drive his makeshift knuckleduster straight into the monster's mouth, breaking one mandible.

Rushing in on the rear quarter of the creature, Cormac leapt and came down with both feet on the knee of one leg. The leg broke and the creature squealed, partially collapsing. Cormac brought his bar down on another leg, breaking a joint. Foaming from its broken mouth it turned fully towards him. He hit the base joint of the claw swinging towards him, then backed off. Sheen hit another leg, severing its sharp tip, and the Prador swung back towards her, but it was Pramer who did the most damage. He leapt onto its back, drove his knife down hard, punching through carapace to anchor him, then began pounding on its visual turret with the gun handle until the carapace there began to crack and green gore began to spatter.

Cormac now concentrated on the claw shoulder joint on his side and copying him, Sheen attacked the other claw joint. They both realized Pramer was in a position to finish the job, only needing those claws kept away from him. Five heavy blows and the claw on Cormac's side was dragging on the ground. Sheen, though she did not disable the claw immediately, obviously opened a gap in the carapace, for she drove her lump of metal deep in beside the claw joint.

The creature jetted foamed bile from its broken mouth. Its visual turret was all but gone, and now the blows Pramer was delivering were punching down into its main body. Abruptly it collapsed completely, its legs shivering and breath rasping wetly. Pramer sat back, and began picking unpleasant gobbets from his arm. Stepping up beside him, Cormac gazed at the hole the man had punched through, estimated the positions of the internal organs, then drove his bar in at a sharp angle. The Prador convulsed, its breathing ceasing all at once, though its legs continued to shiver. Cormac turned the metal, then sawed it back and forth, finally pulling it out.

'Is it dead?' asked Sheen.

Cormac stepped away for a moment, turning his back on

them. The surge of nausea had come quickly, but taking steady breaths for a moment he forced it into retreat before turning back to face them.

'If not,' he said, 'then it soon will be. I was able to sever its main ganglion.' He rested a hand momentarily on Pramer's shoulder. 'Thanks to our champion here.'

It was an odd feeling. He admired both Pramer and Sheen for their bravery, liked them a little better than before, yet he was going to betray them and, one way or another, that betrayal would lead to them dying.

'What happened to Layden?' he asked the big man beside him.

'Pulled his guts out,' said Pramer.

Sheen tugged her chunk of metal from the Prador's shoulder joint, but it responded not at all now. Cormac pulled out his gore-soaked implement, stepped down to the floor and headed back towards the cache of CTDs, the other two falling in behind him. Within a few minutes he saw that Pramer had not exaggerated: Layden was sitting up against the wall of the corridor opposite the door into the cache, a pool of blood spreading all around him and his intestines trailing in a long line right back to the door. On the wall above the man Cormac noted the spatter marks and surmised that the Prador had driven its claw into his guts and flung him, those intestines unravelling like the string of a yo-yo. He walked over to the man, squatted down beside him and checked his pulse. Nothing. An artery had been cut inside him and he'd quickly died of shock and blood loss. It was a good thing that the artery had been cut, else he would have suffered a long and lingering death here – Samara's instructions were that the CTDs took precedence over injured comrades.

'Dead?' Sheen enquired.

'Thoroughly,' Cormac replied. 'Let's get this done and get out of here.' He reached down and opened Layden's belt bag, removing the remote control, took up his metal bar and followed the other two into the cache. Cormac and Pramer levered out the four CTDs and placed them down on the floor whilst Sheen removed the monofilm rucksacks from her belt cache, unfolded them, and placed the CTDs inside. The weapons were very heavy and Cormac considered suggesting they leave one behind, but knew that after what they had just been through, it would be the wrong thing to say.

'We'll carry it between us,' he said to Pramer.

Donning their rucksacks they stepped out of the cache, Pramer and Cormac holding a strap each of the fourth rucksack hanging heavily between them.

'What about him?' asked Pramer.

'They'll know someone got in here when they come to move the CTDs,' said Cormac. 'But maybe we can cover things a bit.'

They put the spare rucksack down and, taking a leg each, they dragged Layden to the Prador, over it, then to the grav-sled stacked with the gassed second-children. With some heaving and shifting, and much swatting away of ship lice, they managed to shove him out of sight underneath one of the dead creatures. Next they returned for the freshly killed Prador, managed to pick it up between them and carry it back to heave up onto the same stack. Returning for the extra CTD, Cormac observed smaller ship lice, perhaps those unable to compete in the scrum about the dead Prador, scuttling out from hollows in the walls. He saw two conducting a tug of war with a length of Layden's intestine, others were snatching up bits of carapace and Prador flesh, whilst still more had come to revel in the sticky pools of human and alien blood.

'Should clear up more evidence of our visit,' he said as they retrieved the fourth CTD and made their way out. Pramer gave him a sour look and Sheen a blank one.

5

It moved fast despite looking heavier than a truck and despite being underwater. His room door opened and in a moment both his mother and Dax were there beside him.

'What is it?' Hannah asked. 'What's wrong?'

No sign of it out there but for a cloud of disturbed silt, which could have been caused by anything. Even before he spoke he guessed how this was going to run.

'That war drone was out there,' he said.

'War drone?' Dax asked.

Cormac turned to look at them, realizing the remote was displaying the red fail light because he was clutching it too tightly and pressing down on too many controls at once.

'It was the one we saw in Montana, and the one I saw outside School,' he said, carefully unclenching his fingers.

'Are you sure?' Of course she had to ask that.

'I'm sure,' said Cormac.

'Outside your school,' Hannah repeated, her voice flat.

She and Dax exchanged an unreadable look, then returned their attention to him.

'Ian,' she said, 'it was probably one of the maintenance bots.'

Dax took up her line. 'They're always working out there, scraping off the barnacles or keeping the windows clean or unblocking vents – this place requires a lot of maintenance.'

Cormac recollected a word he'd recently looked up on his p-top, because he'd just caught the tail end of a conversation between his mother and Dax which he felt sure was about him. The word was *patronizing*. He was being patronized; he was being treated with *condescension*. Determined to protest about this he gazed at his mother and brother, but then he noticed something. His mother was not looking at him but at Dax, who was pallid and appeared frightened. With a shaking hand, his brother opened a packet of self-igniting cigarettes, only just managing to get one to his lips and puff it into life. Cormac understood then that his own fright, which was fading fast, was of the least concern. There was something badly wrong with Dax.

'When's your slot?' Hannah asked Dax.

'Any time today, though there's no guarantee I'll get in quickly.'

'We'll head over to the clinic now,' she said, to which Dax replied with a mute nod. Hannah turned to Cormac. 'Unpacking can wait – we're going out now.'

Dax turned and left the room, trailing a cloud of smoke behind him, and their mother followed. Cormac turned to the room window, picked up the remote control and blanked it. So he had seen the war drone out there. Maybe it was coincidence. Maybe, for reasons he just could not fathom, it was following him. What did that matter? War drones were only harmful if you were a Prador.

Cormac opened his bag and took out his p-top, quickly calling up a site he had found earlier which covered in lengthy detail the effects of Post Traumatic Stress Disorder. Throughout this war the effects had been aggravated by alien environment shock, something given the antiquated term 'shell shock' but which referred to some of the effects upon soldiers of certain esoteric weapons deployed across the front. On top of that, there were the other stresses resulting from the numerous protective inoculations and nanotechnologies running in a soldier's bloodstream. He understood that Dax was suffering from something that came under the general term 'battle stress'. He hadn't read through much of the site, but he knew now that these aftereffects could kill, in many different ways.

His mother poked her head into his room. 'Are you ready?'

Cormac closed his p-top and hooked it on his belt. He moved to follow her out, but had to pause for a moment whilst the Loyalty Luggage entered and settled on the floor.

'I'm ready.' He followed her out into the corridor.

Dax was smoking again, and he chain-smoked all the way out of the hotel and along the streets of Tritonia until they arrived at the clinic. The building frontages here were little different from those of other streets, with bubble windows, stone façades and pressure doors. However, down the side of one entire street the bubble windows were blanked out so that they looked like blind white eyes, the actual pressure doors had been removed and cams were mounted above each entrance, and there were electronic notice-boards scattered at intervals all the way along. Cormac realized at once that 'the clinic' occupied the whole side of this street, which was also crowded with a high proportion of people wearing ECS uniforms, many of whom were either leaving or entering the clinic.

Before they themselves entered the third door along, they had to wait for someone else to come out from inside. The man was a soldier clad in desert fatigues, but Cormac recognized the discreet military decorations of a Sparkind. There was something vague and dreamy about his expression, which seemed in contrast to the burn scarring on the side of his face and his ceramal artificial hand. He nodded to them pleasantly, then moved off into the crowded street.

'Why the hand and no cosmetic surgery?' their mother wondered.

Dax glanced at her. 'Resources get stretched a bit thin out there, sometimes a hand like that is more useful than one of flesh.'

'But his face?'

Dax shook his head as he stepped through the doorway. 'Some

retain their scars in memory of lost comrades.' He bowed his head, leaning against what had been the interior of a pressure lock, suddenly panting for a moment. 'Sometimes, out there, a scar like that means more than medals or military rank.' He shook his head, trying to dispel something, then continued inside.

They walked into a huge and crowded waiting room; the people here occupying row upon row of comfortable chairs, all with personal entertainment or net access systems, or the private booths along the side walls. Along the far wall was inset a row of bland-looking numbered doors, doubtless leading to where the work of the clinic was done. On either side of the aisle leading across this room stood pedestal-mounted palm readers. Dax pressed his hand down against one of these. After a moment it beeped then issued him an electronic plaque from a slot below.

'Does it tell you how long you have to wait?' Hannah asked.

He peered at the plaque. 'No, but I don't expect I'll have to wait as long as some here.'

'Why not?'

He gazed at her with something like pity in his expression. 'Because one soldier at the line is just one soldier, whereas one medic in the same place can put soldiers back together and keep them fighting.'

'About saving lives?' she said, the irony evident in her voice even to Cormac.

'Yeah, sure.'

They found three seats at the end of a row, next to a woman who had a VR band across her eyes and a virtual glove pulled on. She was utterly motionless and there were tears running down from under the eye-band. Gazing around, Cormac saw that many were using the entertainment or information access systems. Very few people were talking. The far doors opened intermittently either to admit people or let them out. It was noticeable how those coming out did so faster and with much more ebullience than those who went it. Those leaving quickly departed the clinic, without looking back.

'Here we go.' Dax, who had just lit up another cigarette, showed them his plaque, which now displayed the number eight. They stood to head for the relevant door.

'You only just came in,' came a flat voice from behind.

They looked round at a beefy, boosted man in worn green fatigues and a wide-brimmed camouflage-patterned hat. Dax pointed to the ECS Medical logo printed on the flap of his shirt pocket. The man rubbed at the side of his nose and nodded tiredly.

'Of course,' he said.

As they continued towards the doors, Hannah noted, 'You don't argue with someone who might be plugging holes in your body next week.'

'Precisely,' said Dax.

Waiting beyond Door Eight was a very attractive but strangely doll-like woman dressed in a nurse's uniform. The room she occupied was a vestibule containing a few chairs and a vending machine for food and drink. It took Cormac a moment to realize she was a Golem – one of the early series with the less realistic syntheflesh.

'If you would like to come through,' she said, gesturing to another door behind her. 'Would you like your family to be present?'

Dax, who had already started for the next door, paused and glanced round at Cormac and their mother. 'Yeah, why not?' He continued through.

Hannah reached down and took hold of Cormac's hand, towing him in after her. Gazing at the aseptic surroundings Cormac recognized a nanoscope, an independent autodoc, a nano-assembler, netlink and an old-style bench-mounted diagnosticer on the work-tops mounted around the walls. In the centre of the room rested a surgical chair with the required hydraulics to turn it into a surgical table, beside which stood the ubiquitous pedestal auto-doc.

'Please,' the nurse gestured to the chair.

Dax looked around for somewhere to put out his latest cigar-ette. The nurse held out a hand and he passed it to her. She closed her hand on it, snuffing it out, then tossed it down in the corner of the room. Immediately a beetlebot cleaner came out of its little home set in the skirting board and gobbled up the cigarette butt, before scuttling out of sight again.

Dax turned and lowered himself into the chair, his movements slow and palsied like those of an old man in another age. Resting his head back against the support he sighed and closed his eyes.

'So how does it go now?' he asked.

The nurse moved the pedestal autodoc across beside him. After a pause, its top half, which looked like a chromed horseshoe crab, rose on a hinged arm.

'When the connections are made, you must remember what you want to forget,' said a voice from a source somewhere above.

The autodoc delicately reached out with one jointed limb to a point underneath Dax at the nape of his neck, and as his body abruptly became still, it was only then that Cormac realized how much Dax had been fidgeting. The doc then lifted and swivelled round until it was squatting directly over his head. Now many of its limbs folded down, some of them bloodlessly penetrating his temples and scalp. Cormac felt his mother's hand tighten on his own, but was too fascinated by the spectacle to concern himself about it.

'It will of course be impossible to completely remove all memories related to the relevant incidents. Rather, I will trim synaptic connections to reduce their importance to you, so that when the events themselves are deleted their absence will not concern you so much.'

The voice was obviously that of a high-status AI, Cormac realized. All the equipment in here likely telefactored from it, perhaps even the Golem nurse too, since she now stood with unnatural stillness behind the chair. Quite likely that same AI was conducting numerous similar editing sessions simultaneously. The autodoc seemed motionless too, since its main work was concealed inside Dax's skull as it inserted nanofibres to cauterize neural pathways and injected neurochemicals to rebalance things inside his head. There was more involved than this, Cormac knew, for he had only read up on the basics of how a mind could be edited. Dax's expression was at first pained, tight and locked up, then his mouth fell open and he seemed to be struggling to keep his eyes from closing. Abruptly the nurse shifted into motion and walked around the chair towards them.

'The process will take approximately half an hour,' she told them. 'Perhaps you would prefer to wait in comfort outside.'

'Is there a problem?' Hannah asked.

'Every case is different,' the nurse replied. 'With someone of Dax's training and experience, more care must be taken not to lose much of value.'

'So if he'd just been a normal soldier,' Hannah said, 'it would have been quicker. I'm not sure I find that comforting.'

The nurse's expression lost its sugary smile, which was replaced with something more complex, more human. The AI must now be paying full attention through this telefactored Golem. 'The simple reality is that experience of complex surgical techniques for dealing with injuries caused by some of the new weapons being deployed out there is more important than knowing how best to gut a Prador.'

'I see,' said Hannah, and with her hand still tightly gripping Cormac's, she headed for the door. Soon they were ensconced in the vestibule waiting room, Hannah getting drinks for them from the vending machine.

'Will he be all right?' Cormac asked, as he took out his p-top and opened it.

She paused for a moment, just staring at the front of the machine as it produced coffee for her and chilled pineapple juice for him. When the drinks were ready, she took them up and turned to him.

'Yes,' she replied, 'he'll be all right.' She stared at him for a long moment before placing the drinks on the low table then taking the seat beside him. 'But I wonder about the morality of editing out bad memories of war.'

'But we were attacked,' said Cormac, 'so surely survival questions come before moral questions?'

She stared at him with a raised eyebrow and a slightly unsure expression – the one she always wore when he said something too 'adult'.

'Exactly,' she said.

He was not quite sure what she meant by that, nor entirely sure he'd understood what he himself had just said. He shrugged and quoted something else he'd recently read too, 'War is Hell,' and returned his attention to his p-top.

But Hannah would not let this go. 'Is it worth winning a war if you become worse than the thing you are fighting?'

Cormac thought long and hard about that one, then replied, 'But you can become good again, which is not an option if you're dead.'

'You're too young to follow this,' she said dismissively.

Cormac picked up his juice to take a drink, rather than disagree with her.

Half an hour later the door opened and Dax strode out, straighter and somehow more substantial now. He was smiling, and though he looked tired he did not look so strained.

'That's it,' he said. 'The cancer is cut out.'

Cormac piped up, 'Hasn't the cancer got a right to live too?'

His mother gave him a poisonous look.

City patrol – it was just the kind of job the AIs would give to those whose loyalty was questionable. They were here to help the local police, whose force was nowhere near up to strength and struggling to control the persistent organized crime in the city which, according to Agent Spencer, kept money flowing into Separatist coffers. However, their help only consisted of showing a presence on the streets, and trained military back-up on the few occasions required, and nothing else.

'You'd think we'd be in the clear by now,' said Yallow, not in the least impressed with this duty. 'If I didn't know he was up for a mind ream I'd do it to him myself with a rusty knife.' She was even less impressed with Carl.

'It's statistics,' said Cormac. 'The AI probably knows we weren't involved in whatever he was up to, but a small element of doubt is enough for it to assign us duties away from the ship.' He added, 'I don't see that guard duty there, even if available, would be any better.'

'Yeah, I guess.'

'In fact we've more chance of some action here.'

Yallow grunted non-committally. They had been patrolling for six hours and were now heading to the rendezvous with their replacements. The only excitement in that time was seeing a drunk vomiting down a drain before passing out.

Because of their neophyte status, their chances were remote of getting any 'action' that wasn't strictly controlled. The incident with the Prador inside the ship had been an aberration, apparently not to be repeated until they had gained sufficient experience. This bugged Yallow even more because of rumours of insurgency two hundred miles north, of fire-fights in the skarch forest up that way, of reconnaissance, of search-and-destroy missions and rumours that illegal arms traders were operating in the area. She wanted to be there, since that was the environment she had trained for, and she wasn't even getting a sniff of it. Here they were patrolling along nearly empty streets, powerless to search any suspicious characters, ordered not to go near known Separatist bars or other gathering places, only to respond when asked for help either by a member of the public or by the local police.

Cormac desperately wanted to tell her about his secret mission – it burned inside him, but he knew that if he opened his mouth his discharge papers would quickly follow, probably shortly after Agent Spencer had tap-danced on his face. Maybe he could get Yallow included in any future action if, in fact, he was going to be involved in anything more. The chances seemed slim – Spencer had remained out of contact for some time and Olkennon had answered his queries with, 'Just do the job you trained for, and don't even hope to know what happens with those CTDs.'

At the end of the street awaited two grunts little different from themselves. Nothing to report, of course, and as they departed, Yallow's 'Be careful in there' was greeted with snorts of derision. In a relaxed mood they began the twenty-minute trek back to the military township.

The gravcar dropping out of the sky like a brick ahead of them came as something of a surprise.

Recognizing the vehicle, Cormac said, 'Agent Spencer.'

Olkennon poked her head out of the passenger window. 'Get in. Now.'

Yallow glanced queryingly across at Cormac. He shrugged. What did he know, after all? He was just as much a grunt as her. Unshouldering their weapons, they climbed into the back of the vehicle. Spencer, who was driving, immediately launched the vehicle into the sky whilst Olkennon peered back at them.

'We're going off-planet very shortly,' she said. 'It's become too much of a risk for you to remain here.'

Cormac guessed she wasn't referring to Yallow.

'What's happened?' he asked.

Olkennon gazed at Yallow for a moment, then shrugged and returned her attention to Cormac. 'Carl escaped.'

'Fuck,' said Yallow, 'and that's enough reason to move us out?'

The car now abruptly descended and, whilst she brought it in to land in the middle of the township, Agent Spencer glanced back and spoke to Yallow. 'You'll be apprised of the reasons for your departure after you're aboard the transport.'

'Go and pack up your own and Cormac's kit and head over to the depot – a car will be waiting for you,' Olkennon ordered. 'You have permission to remain armed until you're aboard the transport out of here.'

Yallow gazed at her unit commander, then switched her attention to Cormac. Her look said it all: he would have to update her soon or she would be seriously annoyed. Cormac remembered the bruises from last time she'd been annoyed with him, though he had given as good as he got. She climbed out of the vehicle and headed off to their quarters amidst the composite domes.

'He escaped?' he asked. 'How the hell could he escape?'

Spencer took the car up again, then in a moment brought it down beside the hospital. Olkennon climbed out, but Spencer remained at the controls.

'Out,' she said to Cormac.

He just cleared the car as it launched into the sky again.

'Come on,' said Olkennon.

Finally reaching Carl's room, Olkennon punched in the code as before and led the way through the door. The bed was empty –

shellwear discarded on tangled sheets. Cormac did not under-stand why he had been brought here. Olkennon walked around to the other side of the bed, gesturing Cormac over. As soon as he stepped round beside her she pointed down at an object on the floor.

'Medscan didn't pick this up,' she said. 'It's very sophisticated for a twenty-three-year-old recruit and certainly confirms Carl was more than that.'

Cormac prodded at the flap of rubbery material with the toe of his boot. It looked like a thick piece of skin.

'The body has been removed,' Olkennon added.

'Body?'

'What you are seeing there is what covers my kind, though the newer of my kind. It's Golem syntheflesh, but unlike mine this has embedded chameleonware.' She stooped, picked up the piece of synthetic flesh and dropped it on the bed. 'A medic came in here to check on him, to make sure the shellwear was still keeping him unconscious. Apparently it was not. We don't know for sure what he had concealed underneath this,' she said, gesturing at the flesh, 'but something transmitted a localized virus that froze all systems connected to his room.'

'You were using a nerve-blocker to keep him unconscious,' suggested Cormac.

'Yes – it knocked that out too.'

'He killed the medic.'

'Broke her neck then took her clothing,' said Olkennon bit-terly. 'Then he just disappeared.'

'Why did you bring me here?'

'Because you have earned the right to know.' Olkennon seemed chagrined for a moment. 'It also seems likely, judging by your recent performance, that you'll be offered the chance to train as an agent, and seeing this sort of thing forms part of your education.'

Cormac nodded, and shrugged his pulse-rifle's strap more firmly on his shoulder. He wasn't sure what to make of that, and really, he didn't think he was ready for that kind of advancement.

'Head back and link up with Yallow,' Olkennon instructed. 'Whether you tell her about all this is entirely up to you.'

Cormac turned and headed out, his head buzzing. Carl would probably rejoin the Separatists here, and once that happened they would know Cormac was not his partner. From then on he would become a target and a danger to those around him. This was why they were being moved out, and he didn't suppose Yallow would be too pleased about it.

Within five minutes he reached their quarters, in time to see Yallow dragging out two heavy packs. He walked over, put down his rifle while hauling on his pack, then once again hung the rifle from his shoulder.

'Are you going to tell me what's going on?' she asked, as she hoisted up her own pack.

Cormac paused for a moment. How to explain all this?

'Olkennon showed me how Carl escaped,' he said. 'He killed a medic. I think she showed me this to drive home that Carl certainly isn't my friend. I think the AI was watching – checking my reactions. They still don't trust me because I was in that trench with Carl.'

The lies spilt so easily from his mouth, and they were simpler than the truth. Perhaps he *was* cut out for agent training.

'But the AI didn't need to *observe* me?'

'I don't know, Yallow, I'm not an AI,' he said. 'Let's go.'

As they marched off towards the main transport depot in the camp, Yallow was silent and contemplative, and kept glancing at him as if hoping to catch something in his expression. He maintained a slightly bewildered and angry expression, and after a little while she seemed to accept what he had told her.

'I still don't understand why we have to go,' she said.

'Trust, I think,' Cormac replied. 'I guess they just can't afford to trust us on a world with this much Separatist activity.' He glanced at her. 'Or rather they can't afford to trust me – you just get to come along for the ride. I'm sorry.'

Yellow grimaced

The hydrovan that slowly cruised past them was not a particularly uncommon sight, it being one of the bland green and beige vehicles used for carting about ECS equipment. It slowed ahead of them, pulled over and stopped, whereupon the back door popped open a crack.

The vehicle emitted a stuttering crackle, which for a second Cormac thought was produced by its exhaust, but Yellow just disappeared from his peripheral vision. He turned, seeing her sprawl loose-limbed. Her uniform looked untidy – torn and frayed – then she made an odd grunting sound and the blood began to soak through. In seeming slow motion Cormac hit the quick release on his pack then threw himself to one side, unlimbering his pulse-rifle. He shouldered the ground, rolled with the weapon clutched against his chest, came upright with it up against his shoulder and fired into the back of the van. The pulses of ionized aluminium cut a punctuated line across the back doors. Something thumped at the ground by his feet and flew apart with a loud crack, the blast sending him staggering. Around him things detonated in the air, punching what felt like needles through his exposed skin. With one hand going down on the ground he shook himself, tried to push himself into action, but couldn't get his breath and seemed to be gazing down a pipe at his hand.

Neurotoxin stun grenade, he realized, as the ground came up into his face and his consciousness fled.

'They would have been removed,' said Samara. 'After our first attempt they would have been removed.'

Cormac blinked. She seemed to be drifting about before him.

Though she had said something a moment before, he could not remember it. He felt terrible: where his body wasn't numb it was afflicted with horrible bone-deep ache. He tried to move, but the only result of that was a sudden hot sweat.

'Wha?' he managed.

Something pressed against his neck, and hurt. From that point a wave of chill spread both up into his head and swiftly down his right arm to his fingertips, which abruptly felt as if each nail had been rapped with a hammer. In his chest the sensation was not unpleasant, until it encountered his stomach and seemed to close a hand around it. Abrupt nausea ensued and he vomited, just managing to turn his head so it didn't go into his lap. Seeing a couple of boots retreating, he blearily peered up at Pramer, who was capping a syringe. Now, becoming a bit more aware of his surroundings, he realized he was tied naked to a chair in some cramped building with charred walls.

'Where were the tracers?' Samara asked.

'In the casings,' someone replied – the voice somehow familiar. 'We left the casings in the hole and took the antimatter flasks only.'

'Are they okay?'

'Couldn't find anything, but we photo-etched the outside of them anyway.'

'What about him?'

Cormac abruptly realized that Samara was standing right in front of him and the one she had been talking to was somewhere behind. To his left Samara's other heavy stood cradling his flack gun. A wound dressing covered his hand and his face bore that shiny look often left by inferior doc-work. It was he who answered, not the other voice.

'His uniform was full of them, and there were microscopic ones embedded in his skin,' said the heavy. What was his name? Skyril, that was it. 'While we were in the sewer we removed them, along with his uniform, then gave him the full-saturation EM to kill any others we might have missed. The search parties were above ground and couldn't get to an entrance into the sewers quick enough. In fact, when they did try to move fast they ran straight into a couple of sticky mines. Seemed to make 'em less enthusiastic.'

Full-saturation EM to kill any bugs planted on him, Cormac realized. Then his mind drifted for a moment, before a hand connected hard with his face, snapping his head round.

'Are you listening, soldier?' Samara asked.

He focused on her, almost grateful for the slap because it seemed to have shaken something into place in his mind.

'I'm listening,' he replied, and further studied his surroundings.

The charred walls and the roof of plasmel sheets told him very little about his location. However, the big ceramic manhole cover behind where Samara was now standing indicated major drains below, so he was probably in the city. Hadn't someone said something about sewers? Behind the manhole cover was a heavy wooden door with a screen mounted upon it showing the feed from a pin-cam obviously positioned outside. All he could see there though was a brick wall with what looked like blackened roof beams resting up against it. To the right of the door a narrow worktop extended along the wall, two swivel chairs before it and further screens upon it. He recognized some city scenes, which seemed to confirm his location.

'So you know,' she said, 'that no one is going to be coming to rescue you, and that no one is going to be tracing those flasks. It didn't work, soldier. ECS fucked up and now we've got the tools to really hurt them.'

Cormac tried to think fast, but it wasn't easy. 'So they played me,' he said.

Samara just stared at him.

'But you've got what you wanted, which means you still owe me,' he tried.

She continued staring at him, a nasty smile starting to twist her features. A hand rested on his shoulder and a mouth came down close to his ear.

'Cormac,' said a now utterly recognizable voice. 'I think she knows you're not my partner.'

Carl.

Then the memory of Yallow sprawled bleeding on the ground hit Cormac in the guts.

Carl continued. 'But knowing that, I really really want to know whether ECS chose you because you were conveniently positioned, or whether you, like me, are not quite what you seem.' Carl reached up and grabbed Cormac's chin, dragging his head round so they were face-to-face. 'You see, if it's convenient positioning, I'll know ECS had no suspicions about me until the fuck-up at the ship, and will consequently know that our method of penetrating ECS military remains sound. However, if you're an agent, that means they've been on to me for some time . . . and we really need to know about that.'

The hand released and Carl retreated. His neck vertebrae clicking, Cormac turned his head to peer behind. Workbenches back there. Carl, dressed in an army maintenance technician's overalls, began loading instantly recognizable antimatter flasks into a large brushed-aluminium case.

'We left the casings in the hole and took the antimatter flasks only.'

Cormac brought his focus back to Samara.

'How did you get to them without being detected – they were being watched?' he asked. It seemed important to keep talking, keep delaying.

'Sewers,' she said, proud of herself now. 'You buried them

twenty yards from one. It took a bit of tunnelling to get to them, but was worth it.'

She looked past him to Carl. 'Are you done now?'

'Ready to roll,' Carl replied.

To Pramer and Skyril she said, 'Cut him loose and give him some clothes. If he tries anything, break his arms, but don't kill him. We want to have a talk with him back at base.' She glanced at Carl. 'A long long talk.'

Back at base . . .

When they cut the ropes tying him to the chair he could not have attacked anyway, since he had enough of a problem just standing up. Skyril stood back while Pramer brought over a bundle of clothing and dumped it on the chair. Cormac struggled into a pair of jeans and a black T-shirt with a holographic logo over the right breast. The only other item there was a worn hat with a wide floppy brim, which he left. Though his feet were hard from combat training he would have liked boots – it was easier to run if your feet were well protected. Pramer picked up the hat and jammed it on Cormac's head.

'Move,' Skyril prodded him in the back with the flack gun, then stepped out of reach. As Samara opened the door, Carl came round and up behind her, clutching that brushed-aluminium case.

'If you look up,' said Skyril, 'I'll cut out your right eye.'

Cormac now understood the reason for the hat. They were worried about satellite surveillance and recognition systems that would certainly be on the lookout for him. If he looked up there was a small chance he would be spotted and that a Sparkind unit or some such would be sent to rescue him, but was that chance worth an eye?

'He won't be looking up,' said Carl. 'Cloudy day today.'

Skyril caught Cormac's shoulder and shoved him towards the door, whilst Pramer watched, his expression neutral. He and

Cormac had been in combat together, so maybe that made a difference. Keeping his head down, Cormac stepped out after Samara and Carl. A glimpse from under the hat brim confirmed the cloudy sky, so there was little chance of him being spotted from up there. They turned left to where a large old hydrocar limousine was parked across the end of the alley. Beyond that he recognized the top part of a statue surrounded by scaffolding and realized he wasn't far from where he had first met Samara. Glancing to the right he saw that the alley stretched for thirty feet, beyond which lay weed-choked ruination. He could run, but doubted he would get ten feet before someone brought him down.

Carl placed the case in the limousine's boot and walked round to climb inside. Only as he drew closer did Cormac realize that the driver was Sheen. Pramer climbed in beside her, whilst Samara climbed into the back next to Carl where sets of seats faced each other. Skyril waved Cormac in next and followed him in.

'Move up against the door,' he instructed, flack gun pointing down at Cormac's legs.

The man wasn't going to make the mistake of sitting close again.

With the whining note of a turbine imbalance, the limousine pulled away. Cormac decided to relax as best he could since he was in no condition to attempt escape at that moment. He'd taken the full brunt of a neurotoxin stun grenade and now felt extreme sympathy for the ECS agent he'd hit earlier with a pepperpot stun gun, which fired the same toxin. Without intervention, it apparently took the toxin sixteen hours to clear from the bloodstream. Medium functionality, as the combat lecturer had informed the class Cormac once attended, returned within two hours. If no other option was available, take vitamin supplements and drink plenty of water.

'Do you have something to drink in here?' he asked.

Carl grinned at him. 'Like some vitamin supplements too?'

Cormac turned to gaze through the window. After a moment he asked, 'Was it you who killed Yallow?'

'Certainly,' said Carl. 'That woman had been the bane of my life since I entered basic training three years ago.'

The frustrated rage growing in Cormac seemed too much to bear, and he knew it was that, and not the aftereffects of stun, which now made him feel sick. He wanted to throw himself at Carl but, suspecting this was what the man would have liked, he controlled his rage and tried to turn it to ice.

'Understandable.' He nodded. 'She pissed on you in hand-to-hand combat and, despite all your claims, was the better marksman.'

Carl's grin remained in place, but it lost its sincerity. After a moment, he folded his arms and turned to gaze out of the window. Reaching under her seat Samara pulled out a squeeze bottle of mulljuice and tossed it across to Cormac. Carl glanced back and frowned at this, his gaze focusing on Samara, then after a moment shrugged and returned his attention to the passing scenery. Clamping down on nausea, Cormac drained the entire bottle then placed it down on the seat beside him, where Skyril retrieved it and jammed it behind him. But it wouldn't have been any use as a weapon, it being flimsy plastic.

'Thank you,' said Cormac to Samara.

'You're going to need all your strength,' she said unpleasantly.

Cormac folded his arms, made himself as comfortable as he could, and stared at Carl, just trying to figure him out.

'How old are you?' he asked.

'I was killing ECS soldier boys before you appeared in your daddy's testicles.' Carl glanced round. 'That's if you are what you appear to be.'

It sounded so utterly wrong coming from the recruit Cormac had known for over two years, so wrong from someone he thought his own age. He tried to think of something else to ask, but it was almost as if the juice he had just drunk was alcoholic, for abruptly he could no longer see straight. Perhaps he had been drugged, but it was just as likely the aftereffects of the toxin. He closed his eyes and drifted . . .

'Out!'

He fell backwards, just managing to catch hold of the door frame to stop himself tumbling out of the car, swung his feet round and staggered out. It was dark, but not so dark he could not see Skyril's grin. Though he might hesitate to kill Pramer, Cormac felt he would not hesitate for a second if the target was Pramer's partner. Utterly weary, Cormac stood, shoulders hunched, and seemingly without the strength to even lift his arms. They were in the midst of a skarch forest, with only the odd glimpse up through the foliage of cloudy sky backlit by the glow of the orbital debris ring.

'Get in.'

Skyril was holding open the hatch to the luggage compartment of a corroded ATV with worn bubble-plas tyres. Cormac walked over slowly, gazed into the oily space and hesitated.

'Wasn't the instruction clear enough for you?'

Something prodded him in the back and he glanced back to see Samara brandishing a pulse-rifle, probably his own. A few paces back from her Carl stood holding a thin-gun – probably the one Cormac had stolen earlier – his expression glacial. Beyond him Pramer was driving the limousine away, Sheen sitting beside him. Cormac was glad to see the both of them go. Should the opportunity arise, Sheen was another he might hesitate to kill. He climbed into the luggage compartment, whereupon Skyril slammed the hatch shut on him. Closing his eyes, he tried to make himself as comfortable as possible in the cramped space. In a surprisingly short interval he drifted into sleep, but was then snapped out of it by the first bump – a sequence of events that was to repeat for a nightmarish time.

6

The diving suit felt clammy and sticky, but that was due to the internal gel layer. The top half of the suit was ribbed and padded since it incorporated a haemolung and a breathing-assist formed of artificial muscle. Fortunately all this equipment had been positioned to flatter the wearer, so when Cormac donned it and clicked his room's viewing window to its 'mirror' setting, he gazed upon an eight-year-old who was either heavily into weight-training and steroids or had been boosted. There were gill slits positioned at intervals down either side of his chest, signs of the additional ribcage within the suit for deep-water work, but the joint motors for that same work were artfully concealed.

Next Cormac pulled on the gloves, engaged them at the wrist and flexed his fingers. He ran a finger down the palm of one glove and it felt to him almost as if there was no intervening material as the glove transferred the pressure of his touch inside. After a moment he toggled a touch control at the base of his forefinger with his thumb and webbing extended between his fingers; another touch and it receded. Now he pulled the hood up over his head, felt the pressure phones ooze into his ears, then pressed the face mask into place. Air was fed to him from the haemolung through holes where the mask engaged with his collar ring, so there were no inconvenient dangling tubes. The mask itself was a simple hemisphere, the top half transparent and separated from the opaque bottom breather half. A membrane pressed against his face running in a line which centred on the tip of his nose.

'Diagnostic test,' he said.

'I am fully functional,' the suit replied in his ear, a little snootily he thought.

'Run a test anyway.'

'I just did,' it replied. 'And again.'

Entertaining a suspicion he asked, 'Are you AI?'

'Yup,' the suit replied. 'Lot of processing power in these suits nowadays and sometimes subbies like me hitch a ride.'

'And if I don't want a submind in my suit with me?' Cormac asked.

'Aw, don't be a spoilsport.'

Cormac considered dismissing the interloper, but curiosity, and perhaps a little in the way of a loneliness he wouldn't admit, got the better of him.

'What's your name?' he asked.

'Well,' replied the mind, 'I can give you the name of the AI that made me about twenty years ago, but I prefer to be called Mackerel.'

'Then Mackerel it is.'

'Are you ready yet?' Dax leaned in through the door, also suited up. He was grinning and had a harpoon gun resting across one shoulder.

Cormac understood this utter change in his brother's character, but still felt uncomfortable with it. He pulled the mask from his face and the hood back off his head, stooped and took up his flippers, then headed for the door.

'Are you allowed to use a harpoon?' he enquired.

'Special dispensation,' Dax spoke over his shoulder as he headed for the water locks of this section of the hotel. 'There's a lot of very large g-mod turbot out there. If I get one, the hotel will cook some of it for us and pay us for the rest – or rather take the cost off our bill.'

As he followed his brother he looked round for his mother, expecting her to be here to see them off. No sign of her, but then lately when she wasn't talking to Dax she was often ensconced alone in her room.

The corridor dog-legged at the end and along one wall were three pressure doors with windows spaced between them. Halting by the first door Dax turned to Cormac.

'Let's take a look at your suit,' he said.

Cormac grimaced in annoyance, since he felt himself more than capable of checking out his own suit. Really, having an adult check your suit was the kind of thing that needed to be done for infants. He held up his arm, showing the small screen attached to his wrist. Dax waved it away.

'Put your mask on and your hood up, and put on your flippers,' he said.

Cormac obliged, while Dax did the same.

'Your suit is fine,' said his brother, turning towards the pressure door. Of course, Cormac's was a child's suit and would have a computing channel open directly to his brother's. If there was any problem with Cormac's suit, Dax would receive an alert at the same time as Cormac did.

The inner door opened with a slight hiss of equalizing pressure and Cormac noted a change since the last time he had been here: the door that opened into the sea which had once been made of ceramal had now been replaced with chainglass, which made the whole experience of going through the lock a lot less claustrophobic. They both stepped inside and the door drew shut behind them. Immediately, seawater began pouring in through nozzles set in the walls. Cormac remembered with some embarrassment how frightened and helpless he had felt when first experiencing this.

In moments the water was up to his knees, then to his waist.

'We'll head straight out to flat sands above the reefs,' said Dax, his voice clear through the phones in the plugs filling Cormac's ears. 'The turbot are out that way hunting mackerel.'

'Nasty turbots,' said the submind Mackerel.

Cormac glanced at his brother, but Dax showed no sign of having heard the submind speak. 'Don't worry,' said Mackerel, obviously guessing what Cormac was thinking. 'I'm not letting him hear me and I won't let him hear any replies you make to me . . . unless of course you want me to?'

'No, keep our conversations private.'

'Thought that's what you'd want.'

The water reached his neck then was soon over his head. It occurred to him then to wonder about what the submind had just said.

'How . . . will you know?'

'How will I know when you're speaking to me and not to your brother?' it said to him. 'Remember, I'm your suit and I'm monitoring you on many different levels.'

Cormac wasn't sure if he liked the idea.

A clear bell tone rang in the airlock and the water swirled around them as Dax pushed open the chainglass door.

'Let's go,' he called, something odd in his voice.

Dax pushed off and drifted out into the sea, his suit immediately adjusting to give him negative buoyancy. Cormac peered down at the bottom twenty feet below him, rocky and forested with weed, mussel beds lying between like spills of coal. As he pushed off, he dislodged something from a ledge below the door and turned over on his back for a moment to observe a scallop jetting unevenly away from him. Now, in this position, he gazed back at what he could see of Tritonia. On either side the convex wall curved away, filled with viewing windows, many of them lit from inside and crowded about outside with undersea life attracted to the light. To his right he saw a robot crawling along the exterior of the structure, a clean trail behind it as it stripped away barnacles, a shoal of fish dogging its course as they tucked in to the bounty of shredded shellfish it provided. The machine looked like a large aluminium lizard with a wide flat head and a mouth like a manta ray's. It wasn't something that could be mistaken for a large iron scorpion. Cormac now focused on the undersea city's roof. Up there, a secondary seabed had been provided and upon this had burgeoned a forest of kelp. Around the numerous artificial islands and moorings, sea otters had become established, feasting on a cornucopia of abalone.

'Come on sea slug!' shouted Dax. 'Shift yourself!'

Cormac rolled over again and kicked hard after his brother, who was lower down now, sculling over a bed of oysters and menacing a large edible crab with the barbed point of his harpoon. Once he saw Cormac coming after him, he kicked away over above the crab, which held its claw high and scuttled backwards, falling over the edge of the oyster bed. Crab had been a menu favourite for over thirty years and despite the availability of the big GM sea farm versions, demand still outstripped supply. Cormac peered down at the crustacean as it righted itself and now raised its claws threateningly. It did look very much like one of the Prador, the difference being size, intelligence, and who was likely to eat who – though there had been news stories buzzing around the nets of some human soldiers trying a new addition to their diets. It was only fair, Cormac thought, as the Prador showed no reluctance in adding humans to their menus.

The start of the reefs was marked by the *Tesco III*, which had been sunk by an eco-terrorist cruise missile over two hundred and fifty years ago. This had been during the time when Middle Eastern oil was both running out and being supplanted by fusion power. Cormac had studied some of the history of the time, but found it boring in its repetition of idiocies stemming from the political corruption of science. The two-mile-long oil tanker was only vaguely recognizable as a ship under the masses of marine growth. Down by one side of its hull lay an entrance for divers who found such a claustrophobic environment enticing, and who might enjoy hunting the massive conger eels that haunted the huge dark spaces inside. Dax increased his buoyancy and abruptly rose beside the wall of this tanker.

'Take me up,' said Cormac, then abruptly felt himself rising too. As he went up he felt the breathing assist of the suit beginning to slacken off as pressure decreased. He also felt other subtle adjustments as it sought to protect him from the pressure change.

He swam in closer to the cliff and studied the corals and multi-coloured blooms of weed that owed their existence to a craze, over a century ago, for seawater fish tanks containing colourful GM seaweeds. Amidst these he observed numerous hermit crabs. Many of these had made their homes in varieties of natural whelk shells, but others had found some quite odd-looking residences.

'What is all this stuff?' Cormac asked.

Dax replied, 'Indestructiphones,' but said nothing more.

'Mackerel?'

'Here you see the result of early twenty-second-century industries producing cheap and incredibly hard-wearing ceramics and glass,' the submind replied. 'Those are the ceramic cases of Indestructiphones, just like your brother said, also webcams, glass pipe fittings for plumbing and bottles and jars.'

Cormac could see that some of the latter still bore inset labels of their erstwhile contents – coriander, mustard, tabasco, pickled ginger. He then paused to gaze at the ghoulish sight of a hermit crab that had taken up residence in the remains of a ceramic artificial hand.

Soon he passed the crumbling rails of the tanker and swam after his brother across the wide deck, now occupied by a garden of brain corals which, like all the corals in the vicinity, were no product of evolution, instead having been adapted to grow fast and survive in the cold waters here. Beyond the ship the reefs proper began: corals stretching as far as they could see. Only by pausing and gazing for a long while could Cormac discern the regularity of this waterscape.

'Mackerel,' he said, 'what was it they dumped here?'

'Hundred-year tyres,' the submind replied. 'They were carbon-filament tyres that gave even the most advanced recycling equipment of the time indigestion. They epoxied them together in tubes and dropped them to make a conservation area impossible to trawl.'

'Was that before the *Tesco* got hit with a missile?'

'Yeah.'

'So they were still trawling then?'

'Oh yeah – Oceana Foods was still struggling to get started and there were pollution problems with the sea farms. You couldn't fart back then without some environmentalist following you about with a gas monitor.'

'Should be there in a few minutes,' called Dax, now a good hundred yards ahead.

Cormac swam harder to catch up, but Dax was not slowing down. In fact, as the sand beds beyond the reefs came into view, he began swimming harder.

'There is something wrong with your brother,' said Mackerel abruptly.

'Dax!' Cormac called. 'Slow down!'

Soon Dax was low over the sand beds swimming hard just above a shoal of fish. Something was stirring up the bottom there, and in a moment Cormac spotted the harpoon spear shoot down, its trailing string the bright orange of instantly clad monofilament. Dax was jerked down as something two yards wide and as long as Dax was tall took off along the bottom. Some kind of huge flatfish.

'What's he got?' Cormac asked, panting as he continued to swim hard.

'Turbot,' Mackerel supplied. 'They're big buggers out here – crossbred with escaped sea-farm stock from Oceana Foods.'

'Right.'

Dax was clinging to his harpoon gun as the massive fish just kept on going. Now a trail of blood was streaming from the fish.

'Dax!' Cormac called again.

'No it's not,' Dax replied. 'They weren't . . . they weren't . . .'

'I have summoned help,' said the submind.

Suddenly the great fish jerked and shuddered, coming up from the seabed. Cormac realized the harpoon gun must be the kind that could deliver a massive electric shock. The turbot was almost certainly dead now. It slowly turned over, exposing its milk-white underside, blood clouding around it.

'No . . . no it . . . no please. I didn't mean . . .' Dax's voice slowly lapsed into an indistinct muttering. He just hung in the sea, still clinging to his harpoon, still linked to the dead fish.

'You must return to your hotel now,' said the submind.

'I will not,' said Cormac.

'Sorry about this,' said the submind.

Suddenly Cormac turned and began swimming back, only it wasn't him swimming, it was the suit.

'You can't do this!' he protested.

'Assistance is coming for Dax,' said the submind.

Then far ahead, Cormac saw a shape hurtling towards him, a white water trail behind it. As he watched, it swung wide, so it remained distant enough for him to be unsure, but certainly it was insectile, with many legs folded underneath.

'I hate you,' said the boy, not sure whether his hate was directed at the submind controlling his suit or at that distant unknowable drone.

Cormac could not tell how many periods of sleep and rude awakening passed as the ATV travelled over rough terrain, but eventually they arrived somewhere, and the compartment was opened. Samara peered in at him for a moment, backlit by dawn sky, then reached in and slipped something over his head.

'That's braided monofilament around your neck,' she said, 'so climb out very carefully and be careful not to snag on anything, or your head might end up on the ground.'

Cormac climbed out, unable to take his time as she kept up the tension on the glittering strand extending from her hand to his neck.

'The neurotoxin is leaving your system now, agent,' she said. 'Don't make any errors of judgement at this point.'

'I'm not an agent,' he said, though he wasn't sure why he bothered.

The ATV had been parked beside a copse of stunted and charred skarch struggling to put out leaf. Ahead, a track disappeared between a sprawl of low buildings interspersed with the occasional silo.

'Head for the door.' Samara pointed to the nearest building.

He was about to nod, but thought better of that and just walked. Halting at the door he glanced back past her at Carl, but Carl was gazing thoughtfully off into the distance, his whole physical pose seeming completely wrong to Cormac.

'The door,' Samara instructed.

Cormac pushed the handle down and stepped in.

It seemed some sort of control centre had been sited in this warehouse. Numerous foamstone pillars supported a smoked glass roof. There was a lot of wiring, fibre optics and items of hardware up there. Similar wiring and optics snaked across the floor from sets of consoles gathered about two newer-looking ATVs, whose bodies were all sharp angles and plain faces – a sure sign that they deployed chameleonware. He then realized what all that stuff up in the roof must be: a similar camouflage shield.

There were people busy at the consoles whilst others, mostly armed and clad in chameleoncloth, conducted typical army tasks with a worrying professionalism. Samara towed him over to one of the pillars, wrapped the monofilament about the foamstone and locked it off. Cormac had no doubt that the loop of filament wrapped around his neck was locked off too. Then, seeming to lose interest, she went over to stand with Carl, who was now talking to one of those working a console. After a moment she said something, then pointed across the warehouse to where Skyril had handed over the case of antimatter flasks to two individuals at a set of workbenches. Carl nodded and headed over as Samara returned to Cormac.

'Sit down,' she said.

Cormac was grateful to do so, but it hadn't occurred to him, which told him he still wasn't thinking straight. He sat with his back against the pillar and Samara squatted before him.

'You do understand that we knew right away that it was a trap – that the AIs wanted us to take those CTDs so they could trace them back here, Agent Cormac.'

'I've already told you, I'm no agent.'

He glanced across, saw that Carl and Skyril were now heading over, and guessed it wouldn't be long now before the *real* questioning started.

'I do hope you are,' she replied. 'Because if you're not, I don't see any reason to keep you alive. Just like Carl says: you're either a raw recruit who was conveniently placed in the same unit as Carl when suspicion fell on him. A raw recruit, I might add, who was capable of taking down Pramer and Skyril. Or, more likely, you are a Polity agent.'

'He's almost certainly an agent,' said Carl, stepping up beside Samara. 'He was always a bit too good, a bit too efficient and a bit too fucking moral. Much as I hate to admit it, I think they knew about me right from the start. I don't see ECS using a plain grunt for an operation like this – too much chance of it going wrong, and they wouldn't want that with CTDs involved.'

Samara glanced up at him. 'So he's probably like you, Carl – a damned sight older than he looks.'

'Well let's find out,' said Carl nastily.

Cormac reached up to the monofilament around his neck and toyed with the join. It was a friction grip which, if he pulled hard enough, would slide down the line. Unfortunately, pulling hard on a piece of monofilament wrapped around your bare neck could lead to some nasty side-effects.

'Supposing I am an agent,' he said. 'Do you honestly think you could get anything useful out of me?'

Carl gazed steadily at him. 'Possibly not, but we'll certainly have fun trying.' He focused on Cormac's fingers at the mono-filament join. 'Best we get that off his neck, Samara.' Perhaps in any other circumstances him saying that might have been reassur-ing, but Cormac knew precisely why Carl now wanted the filament removed – it was far too much of an easy way out. Samara stood up and moved round to the foamstone pillar. He considered going for her, but even as he considered it, Carl was abruptly standing over him pointing a thin-gun down at his legs. Samara unhitched the monofilament from the post, inserting its end into a neat little winding device that quickly took up the slack. A tap against another control on the device released the friction slide at his neck and the filament came loose there.

'Remove it,' she instructed him.

Maybe a tough ECS agent would have used the filament on his own throat to prevent any vital knowledge he possessed falling into enemy hands. Maybe such an agent would now use the filament as a weapon to bring down at least a few of his captors before he was killed. He was no agent, and not anxious to die or be tortured, and so tried to delay the inevitable.

'I don't know if it's occurred to you yet,' he said, leaving the filament precisely where it was, 'but maybe Carl is your ECS agent. He's here now in your base . . .'

'Remove the monofilament,' Samara insisted.

'How did he get in contact with you, by the way?'

'Remove the monofilament or Carl will burn off your knee-caps.'

Since he rather expected something like this was the intention, he considered delaying further. Carl fired his gun, the ionized pulse punching into the plasticrete by Cormac's feet and spraying him with hot fragments. Cormac reconsidered. Maybe they would soften him up first with a beating, which he could survive, or with drugs . . . He removed the filament from about his neck.

'Stand up.'

Every move in slow motion, he obeyed. Samara wound in the monofilament then tossed the winder to Skyril, who caught it and moved in behind Cormac.

'Hands behind your back.'

Ah, he was beginning to see now. They didn't want him truncating the questioning by cutting his own throat, but it didn't matter if he sliced up his wrists or even cut off his hands, because they could still keep him alive. Maybe now was the time—

Carl's foot went like a swinging beam into his stomach, driving him back against the pillar. It seemed the man could read his intentions before they turned to actions. Skyril then grabbed his T-shirt and shoved him forward, catching hold of his arms and pulling them back. Cormac went down on his knees, unable to do otherwise. Skyril looped monofilament about his wrists. He started to slump forwards, but the filament began to tighten as Skyril once again attached the other end to the post, so with a huge effort of will he forced himself upright again. Skyril now pulled his ankles together, looping a plastic tie about them – Cormac recognized the clicking sound as it closed. Then the man stood and stepped past him, bringing his flack gun sharply back and smashing it into Cormac's mouth. He nearly went over again, but fought to maintain position, then shuffled back up to give himself at least a little slack. He spat out fragments of tooth, felt his lip swelling and blood running down his chin.

'That one I owed you,' said Skyril. He then glanced at Carl. 'Want some?'

Carl shook his head. 'In good time.'

Skyril shrugged, holstered his flack gun, then turned back to Cormac and delivered a hard kick to his guts. Then he reached inside a poacher's pocket in his coat, took out a length of reinforcing rod, worn shiny by handling, and stepped in close. Three hits in rapid succession – one felt as if it had snapped Cormac's collar bone, the next slammed hard across his stomach and the next across an elbow as the previous one bowed him over. Cormac went down on his side, fighting for breath. Skyril delivered a few more kicks for good measure, then stepped back.

After a moment Cormac managed, 'Aren't . . . you supposed . . . to question?'

Carl now stepped up close and squatted down. 'As you well know, Cormac, this is the softening-up process. You must be brought to the point where the pain and the damage to your body is too much. We'll use psychotropics on you then, and extract every last shred of information from your head.'

At that moment one of the troops came over to speak to Samara. 'We've got one ready now.' Cormac recognized him as one of those who had been at the workbenches where the CTDs had been delivered.

'But we should wait two hours longer before detonation,' the man continued. 'We've intelligence that another whole battalion is moving into Dramewood within that time.'

'Carl,' said Samara.

Carl grimaced in annoyance and stood. 'I take it you want me to do this?'

'It's more important than him.' She gestured at Cormac then turned back to the trooper. 'Carl will go with you to position it,' she continued. 'Rindle and his squad can take the old ATV, and tell the others to get ready to move out.'

'You won't be able to pull all your people out of Dramewood,' said Carl.

'No, but that's a small price to pay to take out two ECS battalions,' she replied.

They were going to use one of the CTDs here, on this world.

'It'll tidy up things here, too,' Samara added, glancing at Cormac.

Carl shook his head. 'No, I have to veto that.' He gazed steadily at her. 'He stays alive until we find out one way or another if he's an agent – that's essential, that's important to more operations than your one here on this world.'

Samara was annoyed about that, but nodded acceptance. Cormac wondered about the hierarchy here. Samara seemed to be in charge, and yet Carl seemed to have some power but was being careful not to step on too many toes, like some envoy from another Separatist group.

To salve her injured pride he added, 'By all means keep working on him, but don't kill him. If he is an agent he's probably high-ranking, and using the right techniques we could be extracting information from him for months.'

Carl grinned at Cormac, 'Have a nice day,' then moved off with the trooper. Cormac watched him join a group of five other troopers, one of them hoisting a heavy rucksack onto his back – a rucksack certainly containing an active CTD. They began climbing into one of the ATVs whilst the trooper who had originally come over now spoke to some others, who quickly began packing away equipment and heading towards the door.

'Should we burn off his face or his testicles?' Skyril wondered.

'Carl says we've got to keep him alive,' said Samara.

'Carl's an offworlder,' said Skyril.

Grimacing she replied, 'Best we do what he says, but there's a big difference between alive and undamaged.' She waved a hand at Skyril, and smirking he moved off.

'Now,' she said to Cormac, 'let me bring to the forefront of your mind the kind of stuff I'm going to want to know, so you'll have it ready when this all becomes too much.'

Skyril was collecting an ancient oxythane bottle with a tube wound around the top to a cutting torch. Behind him, the ATV with Carl and the CTD aboard set off towards a roller door at the end of the warehouse, which opened ahead of it. The last of those carrying loads to the older ATV outside departed, and Cormac heard it start up and pull away. That left one ATV and, including Skyril and Samara, seven Separatists in here.

'First I'll want every AI-net access code in your possession, which I'll check at random while we speak. I'll next want everything you can tell me about the disposition of ECS forces here, inside information on contacts and the status of ECS commanders. Like, for example, who is running you, who your contacts are, and what they look like.' She pulled a palmtop out of her pocket. 'I've got numerous pictures in here I'll want you to look at and identify. I know who many of them are, so if you lie, I'll find out.' She gave a metallic smile. 'Next I'll want you to tell me how you found out about Carl, right from the start, listing who ECS has identified in the Jovian Separatists and the double agents there.'

Something quite cold and hard solidified inside Cormac at that moment. In two hours these people intended to detonate a CTD to wipe out two battalions of ECS soldiers. During the time leading up to that, Samara intended to put him through quite easily imaginable agony. But she wouldn't kill him unless it was proved he wasn't an ECS agent. They intended to take him away and continue . . . interrogating him for *months*. He must do something, and soon.

Braided monofilament . . .

Single-strand monofilament was usually used as a cutting weapon, but never for long, since though it was incredibly tough, it could develop faults and would often break. For many applications ECS used braided monofilament because it was tough and still narrow enough for a lot of it to be packed into a small space, but that wasn't usually used for cutting. Braided monofilament would slice through flesh and, with a bit of sawing, would go through bone. Samara had been exaggerating about the loop round his neck taking his head off if he snagged it, though it would certainly have cut in enough to kill him.

He considered how he was bound: Skyril must have put a double loop through the friction device to go about each wrist, before running the filament back to the pillar. Certainly, the filament cutting in above and below a wrist would cause debilitating injury, severing nerves, blood vessels and ligaments – but cutting in against the hard nub of the radius bone, just up the wrist on the thumb side, would still leave him with a usable hand. Of course the other hand would be useless.

Skyril dumped the gas bottle down before him, whilst Samara stood up and stepped back. Cormac squirmed right up against the pillar as if to get as far as he could from the torch Skyril was now lighting. The flame ignited – a blue spear searing out from a constellation of bright white dots. He played with the controls, shifting that constellation about and adjusting the shape and length of the flame, slipping it from its hole-cutting to sheet-slicing setting and back again. Then holding the torch in his right hand, he stooped over Cormac. Cormac cringed back, turning his right hand behind him to a particular angle, then stretching out the fingers of his left hand and abruptly pulling it against the loop of filament, hard.

It was the worst pain he had ever felt – but it coincided with Skyril closing a hand on Cormac's neck, crushing a knee into his stomach and bringing the torch down on his thigh. Cormac screamed, bringing his left arm out from behind him and round in an arc, not wanting to see the bloody thing that had been his left hand as the edge of it slammed back up into the man's throat. Skyril lurched back towards Cormac's head, taking pressure off the knee. Cormac struck again, keeping the pressure on, pulling Skyril closer, then brought out his right hand, sufficient slack in the filament now available, and reached under the man's jacket. He found the flack gun, pulled it out only halfway and pulled the trigger. Skyril disappeared to one side, most of his guts preceding him in that direction. Samara was moving fast, pulling something tucked into her belt behind her. Not fast enough. The second shot folded her in half, one of her legs flipped up like that of some grotesque ballerina.

Up into a squat now, Cormac fired back into the pillar, severing the monofilament. He stood, brought a foot down on where the hose trailed from the gas bottle, snapping it, then kicked the bottle over. Gas mix coming directly from the bottle ignited from the guttering torch, spewing out a five-foot flame. One good shove with his foot sent it rolling across the floor towards the five others present, who were only now reaching for their weapons. Cormac stooped and stepped back, going for cover behind the pillar as pulse-gun fire cut overhead and rained hot foamstone down on him.

Another shot with the flack gun and the bottle exploded. Someone shrieked over that way, which seemed a good thing to Cormac. He stepped round and out the other side of the pillar, towards where Skyril lay. A flack gun like this held only fifteen shots. He would need more. He fired repeatedly, was satisfied to see someone's arm and head fragment, and continued firing as he stooped down by Skyril. Inside the tattered jacket, slick with blood but still intact: two more clips of explosive bullets. A shot seared across Cormac's shoulder. He considered the bastard task of re-loading with only one usable hand, and gazed fully for the first time at his left hand. The monofilament had taken off his little finger, paring it away from the wrist. It had skinned one side of his thumb and taken off the end of it, flensed his palm and taken the skin off the back of his three remaining fingers. It was complete agony but he could still move those fingers and that stub of a thumb. He used this bloody implement to take up the two clips, then dived for cover behind the pillar again.

A press of his thumb dropped the now empty clip to the floor. Cormac fumbled bloodily to put the next one in, got it into place then banged the gun butt against the floor to engage it all the way. What sounded like three pulse-rifles and some sort of projectile weapon were hammering at the pillar. He sat with his back against the foamstone, waiting for a pause, but it seemed there would not be one. Then a great chunk of stone peeled away and began to fall. A pause. He stretched himself on the floor then rolled out. Targeted and fired. Somebody shrieked and dropped, legs gone, stumps coming down on the plasticrete. Another dived for cover. He realized they cared more about their lives than he did for his, for they had not inhabited the place he had recently occupied. The one diving arrived in cover in pieces. Cormac rolled into a crouch, stood upright. The one with the projectile weapon was fumbling to reload. Cormac walked towards him as he opened fire, and just raised his gun to take careful aim. Material slugs whined past him, flicked his trousers, picked a chunk out of his biceps, pinged the side of the flack gun and hissed past his elbow. He breathed out, squeezed the trigger. His opponent's head disappeared and he slumped out of sight.

Something groaned and crunched. Cormac turned, and watched as the pillar he had sheltered behind twisted, tearing away roof trusses, and collapsed. Wiring and optics fell like lianas dragged down by a falling tree, and were followed by sheets of smoked chainglass which rang against the floor but did not break. He swivelled back, searching for further targets as a wave of dust rolled past him.

There was no one left.

7

Since Dax had seen through his little ruse with his p-top, Cormac had ventured into a local hardware store and bought an underwater pencil cam with a 280-degree viewing head and integral microphone. It now rested in a pot filled with pens and memory sticks sitting on a shelf in his mother's room – where she and Dax usually had their little discussions.

'The editing didn't take,' said Dax. 'I thought it might happen – wanted to retain too much.'

Hannah just gazed at him expressionlessly. After a moment she said, 'It was a bit foolish to take Ian out diving when you knew that.'

Dax waved a hand, smiled. 'He was in no danger. I made sure he had a fully cybernetic suit and for good measure requested a city submind to load to it.'

Cormac swore quietly – a word that was a particular favourite of his brother's during these talks he had with their mother. So Mackerel had loaded to his suit at Dax's instruction. That figured.

'Did they get my turbot?' Dax asked. 'I believe I speared a right monster out there.'

'You don't remember?' she asked.

He shook his head. 'They had to remove a lot more this time. Apparently the adrenalin and the sight of blood and death, even if it was that of a fish, caused a synaptic link to partially excised memories.' He grimaced. 'There was more to it than that, but it caused something akin to amplifier feedback and the whole circuit was reinforced. They had to remove the lot.'

'Your turbot will feed the customers of this hotel for the next week, and we've had a substantial amount deducted from our bill.'

'Excellent! I look forward to trying some myself.'

Cormac had already eaten some of the turbot while Dax had been away for editing again – it had tasted fine but the circumstances that brought it to his plate left him lacking in appetite. He continued to listen, hoping to hear something about the drone that had brought Dax in, but the conversation just didn't go that way. Dax sat back, a glass of beer in his hand rather than whisky this time.

'Do you remember that time Dad went harpoon fishing around the wreck – that shark?' he said.

'I remember,' said Hannah.

'Damn but we were shitting ourselves when he tried to get it through the lock back into the hotel. Even though he got it straight through the head, it kept on moving. It was like being in a confined space with a sanding machine.'

'Sanding machine?' Hannah looked distracted, almost uninterested.

Dax tapped his forearm. 'If it wasn't for my suit I'd have needed a skin graft here. Its skin took off the outer layer right down to the protective mesh.'

'Yes,' said Hannah, 'your father had just finished basic training then . . . That was when Ian was only two. David went to war just six months afterwards.'

'Have you heard anything from him recently?' Dax paused, looking puzzled. 'I'm sure I asked something about that, but can't seem to recollect – something to do with the editing I think.'

'Just the usual,' Hannah replied. 'He keeps me updated with where he is, but mostly he's after news from here rather than telling me what he's doing. He knows I don't want to hear the detail, to know what attack he's been involved in or how it went. He knows I'll only worry about his safety . . .'

What was it about their mother, Cormac wondered. She looked quite ill and there was something odd in her tone.

'You're not interested?' Dax asked.

'I just want to know he is alive.' Hannah put her whisky glass to one side. 'I'm very tired now, Dax. Can we call it a day?'

'Certainly.' Dax drained his beer glass, then stood up to wander over to the drinks cabinet and place it there. 'See you in the morning.' Hannah stood up as he headed for the door, then caught hold of his arm and embraced him. Cormac felt slightly embarrassed – she wasn't usually so touchy-feely.

'Good night Mother,' said Dax, his expression puzzled.

Cormac thought now might be a good time for him to sign off. More diving tomorrow, and perhaps this time without any traumatic aftermath. He was about to switch off his p-top when he observed his mother sitting down in her chair again and taking up her glass. She wasn't heading as expected to her bed. She held up her whisky before her.

'Here's to editing,' she said. 'Please forgive me, David.'

What on earth did that mean?

Cormac walked over and gazed about at the wreckage. Someone was making little grunting sounds and, stepping round a collapsed table and a jumble of burning consoles, Cormac gazed down at a slug trail of blood, plasma and charred fragments of either clothing or skin. The person – it was not possible to tell if it was a man or a woman – had been hideously burnt from the waist upwards. Cormac considered it neutralized, and was about to turn away, then some sympathy kicked in, and he fired once, the shot completely exploding the upper body and sending head and arms bouncing away at three compass points.

What now?

He searched the wreckage, the pain from his injuries steadily increasing as adrenalin washed away. Eventually he found the first-aid kit he sought inside the ATV's luggage compartment. It was difficult to open, for his left hand was now completely useless, and as soon as he tucked the flack gun in the top of his trousers his right hand began to stiffen too. First he found some anti-shock capsules and swallowed two of them dry. Next he found some local analgesic patches, stuck one above his left wrist and one directly over the burn on his thigh. Blessed numbness spread in those areas, also taking the edge off the agony of his hand and the elbow above it, which felt broken. Using a can of analgesic spray skin he completely covered the ruin of his left hand. A tube of wound glue, held in his mouth, he squirted into the deep cut on his right wrist, closing the cut by tilting his wrist and waiting a moment for the glue to bond. Another patch went on his collar bone, then he paused. He didn't want to deaden himself completely – there was still work to be done. Now he found a micropore bandage and wrapped it about his left hand to give it more protection than provided by the spray skin, which was already leaking in places. Sticky dressings on his other wounds, for more padding. Enough. Now weapons.

Weapons weren't difficult to find, since there were pulse-rifles scattered all about the area. He picked up five of these and tossed them in the passenger seat of the ATV. Then, after further searching, he included a satchel of gecko mines and a pack of old-style bullet magazines for a machine gun and, as an afterthought, threw in the first-aid kit too – the effect of the analgesics he'd used was limited. He climbed into the driver's seat and checked the controls: simple start button and single joystick, which was useful when having only one hand. He set the electric motor running, pulled back on the stick and the ATV shot backwards, crashing over burning wreckage and wheel-spinning on a wet corpse as he turned the vehicle. Forwards now and it shot towards the door. No remote door control visible, no matter. The ATV slammed into the door, tearing it out of its runners, the roller mechanism crashing down on the roof. For a moment it hung draped over the vehicle, but when he turned the ATV and brought it to a halt, the door slid off.

Now Cormac took his time checking out the onboard computer and communication system. As expected the radio and line-of-sight laser communications were encoded – it wasn't possible for him to send a message to ECS via that route. All that was available was a netlink, and that had numerous restrictions upon it. He was, however, able to tap in a text message and route it to his own infrequently used net-space, hoping that an AI, somewhere, was keeping watch: *Ian Cormac, location Dramewood, 'ware concealed ATV carrying CTD to be deployed against ECS battalions, am in pursuit in similar vehicle.* He was about to add something about checking targets, but then realized a satellite strike against the other ATV could not be used – it might breach the antimatter flask with the same result Samara and Carl had intended, though of course Carl had not intended to be in the vicinity.

Cormac dedicated a subscreen down in the bottom right-hand corner of the main console screen for any reply he might receive, then called up a local map on the main screen. It flicked up, showing the location of his own ATV within it. He spent a moment sending another message giving the coordinates of the Separatist base behind him, then stared at the map. He had hoped it would show him where the other ATV was, but it didn't. He frantically searched through menus, eventually pulling up a list. Highlighted was Veh3, amidst numerous other designations, presumably including Separatist positions in the woodlands and maybe even known ECS ones. He highlighted all the 'Vehs' on the list and went back to the map. Four were visible. The one on a road behind him he assumed was the old ATV heading away, and there were two others out in the woods. He checked through menus again, selected the coordinates of the nearest vehicle, then chose autopilot. The ATV immediately lurched into motion – chances were that the closest one had the CTD aboard. Now he turned his attention to the weapons on the seat beside him.

Checking the displays on each rifle he chose the two with the highest charge, then laboriously set about stripping both of them of their butt stocks and one of them of everything he could to reduce weight without impairing function. He also removed its electronic trigger mechanism, which would have screwed it up as a single weapon, but he did not have that in mind for it. The ATV was now jouncing over rough ground, so this made his task doubly difficult. Glancing up he saw hundred-foot-tall diseased-looking skarches from which the bark was peeling. Obviously the Prador had hit this area with something, but he had no idea what.

Detaching the end of a wire from the remaining trigger mechanism he cross-linked it to the relevant plug in the wholly stripped rifle. Now, when he pulled the trigger, both rifles would fire at once. He taped the weapons together with surgical tape, tested their weight with the barrels resting across his left forearm, then grimaced to himself. Carl had shown him how to do this.

Next Cormac removed the power supplies from the other three rifles, which were essentially contained in their moulded forestocks. To two of these he moulded two pliable gecko mines, and then he set the mine timers to four seconds once he hit the priming button. To the third he stuck the remaining four mines, and rather than use the timer he set just one of the detonators to a violent movement setting with a delay of two seconds. He put this device back in the satchel, then proceeded to empty the machine-gun magazines of bullets and pack them around it, along with anything hard and small within reach, including the plastic magazines themselves. Last, he lifted his feet up off the floor, braced his back against the seat, and kicked out one section of the front screen. He was ready.

The other ATV was some miles away, and Cormac realized that at the steady pace of the autopilot he would be unlikely to catch up with it any time soon. He clicked the autopilot off, took up the joystick and thrust it forwards. The vehicle accelerated abruptly, kicking up decaying matter dropped from the skarches around him. Now he began hearing the occasional susurration of a distant beam weapon firing, the crackle of pulse-gun fire, the thwocks of detonations and a vicious ripping sound it took him a moment to identify as a proton carbine. That last weapon probably meant there were Sparkind out here. He hoped to fuck that if he ran into any of them they'd not mistake him for a Separatist.

Abruptly he realized he was now rapidly closing in on the other vehicle. It had stopped. This must be where they were going to position the CTD.

'Samara,' said Carl's voice from his console. 'I am quite capable of doing this unsupervised, thank you very much.'

Damn.

He kept driving.

'Samara, reply.'

Carl was going to know something was wrong. After a moment Cormac noted the other ATV turning to head straight towards him. Abruptly the icon representing that vehicle just disappeared from the screen. Cormac quickly reassessed his plans. He switched the autopilot back on, still heading for the original coordinates, then turned his attention to the weaponry. Estimating distances and times he reached inside the satchel and reset the detonator from 'violent movement' to a timing of eight minutes, and hit the priming button. It was the best he could do in the circumstances. Finding a catch on the passenger-seat cushion he hoisted it up. There was a tool bag in a compartment underneath. He pulled this out, dropped the satchel inside then tipped the tools back in on top of it. More shrapnel. He placed the two other mines with attached power supplies into the tool bag, along with his twinned pulse-rifle, and taking this with him he opened the door and jumped.

Cormac hit the ground and rolled, then came up onto his knees swearing and really wishing he'd brought the first-aid kit too. No time for pain. He carefully hung the tool bag, with the two bombs inside, from his left shoulder and rested the rifle across his left forearm, tucked close to his body. Then he set off along the root-laden ground between the dying skarches, giving himself plenty of cover but staying parallel with his ATV. Taking into account the amount of time it took him to get from the vehicle, he began silently counting down from four-hundred-and-fifty. In a moment he was gasping, and the vehicle was pulling ahead of him. A sight to one side gave him pause: a wrecked mosquito autogun, a scattering of bloody field dressings and a single corpse in ripped-up chameleoncloth fatigues. This proved, along with earlier mention of another battalion coming in, that there was more going on out here than evidenced by the rumours Yallow had heard.

The ATV was still in sight . . . *three hundred, two hundred and ninety-nine . . .*

Then he heard the whine of a distant motor, the crashing and bumping of something heavy moving fast through the rough woodland. At two hundred, it came into sight ahead. Cormac crouched behind a deadfall of skarches that had obviously fallen long before the Prador arrived to trash this world, and watched. Something shrieked and he dropped lower.

Rail-gun? A fucking rail-gun?

Chunks of metal flew from the vehicle he had occupied. It shuddered, but just kept on rolling. Pure luck that nothing had struck under the passenger seat, for the vehicle cabin now looked like a pepperpot. The other ATV slowed. A second fusillade smashed into his own, but still no detonation and still it kept on rolling. The other turned abruptly and stopped. His own vehicle rolled on and crashed into its side, its wheels still turning, then abruptly something inside it died and it shuddered to stillness.

Armed with pulse-rifles, three troops piled out. Cormac noted only the driver remaining in the other vehicle, so assumed Carl and one other were back where they came from. They showed no wariness of anyone occupying Cormac's ATV – why should they? Anyone inside would have been paste. One of them climbed up and, after a bit of a struggle, pulled open the door, which fell off its hinges to the ground.

. . . seventy, sixty-nine . . .

Damn, he was a minute out.

The man dropped back down to the ground and turned to his fellows. He said something, then waved a hand towards the surrounding woodland.

Shit.

Light glared inside the wrecked cab and then it just disappeared with a gravelly crump. Things hissed through the surrounding skarches, dropping thick dry leaves and tearing off fibrous chunks in dusty explosions. A cloud of oily smoke occluded view, a red fire burning at its heart, and someone was screaming. Cormac guessed his countdown had been too slow. He stepped out from cover, gazed for a moment at a spanner embedded in the deadfall he had been hiding behind, then jogged towards the mess. The increasing heat of the fire started shoving the smoke higher, but there was no sign of the three troops. He slowed to a walk, carefully surveilling his surroundings. Then he saw the inward face of a skarch coated with bits of flesh and tatters of clothing, and nearby a boot lying smoking like some cartoon depiction of the results of an explosion, only this one still had a foot inside. He trod on offal, warm under his bare foot, and guessed only a meticulous search would find all the remains.

The screaming dropped to an agonized gasping. It was coming from the cab of the other ATV, which was now burning too. Cormac pointed his twinned weapon at where the driver should be and fired. A double line of pulse-fire punctuated the air to that cab, punched holes through metal and sprayed burning debris all about. The groaning ceased. Cormac moved on, breaking into a trot.

Four bad guys down, but Carl and the other one, about a quarter of a mile ahead of him, had now been thoroughly forewarned. He kept moving at a steady jog, now following tracks made by their ATV. He hit an upslope through dead bushes of black convoluted twigs, brittle and crushed flat. Amidst these, knowing he was now close, he slowed, then got down on his belly and crawled. Finally reaching the head of the slope, he could now see down through the skarches to the ruin of a small composite dome house, but there was no sign of anyone nearby. Now he should slowly and carefully work his way down there, continuing to crawl, but he didn't feel physically capable of doing that. He took one of the two explosives out of the tool bag, reset its timer to ten minutes, hit the button and shoved it into the bushes ahead of him, then crawled backwards until the ruin was once again out of sight. Standing up, he ran to his left, where the rise he was upon sloped down again to the level of the ruin. It was counterintuitive, since the best tactical position would be to come down from higher ground to the right.

Running, he damned the dry skarch debris on the ground, since it was near impossible to run on them without making a noise. Shortly he reached the level of the ruin, but it was not yet visible through the trees. He squatted down beside a multiple skarch stump coated in fungus resembling spilt custard, and waited

The bomb went off with a satisfying flash and glaring explosion, and the added benefit that shortly afterwards a number of skarches started to fall. Cormac ran towards the ruin, using what cover he could and frequently altering his course. No sign of anyone. Shortly he arrived at the curved wall of the ruin and squatted down. His best course in any other circumstances would have been to toss his remaining explosive into the building, but if the CTD was in there such an action stood a chance of breaking the antimatter flask. What now? It belatedly occurred to him that Carl and his companion might have moved away from this building and now have it in their sights, knowing it would be the focus of anyone coming here – that's what he would have done in their position. He wasn't thinking straight. He should have waited out there, perhaps for hours, until one of them put in an appearance. Then again, he was in no condition to wait any length of time.

Carefully he surveyed his surroundings, trying to work out where they might have gone to ground. Two locations seemed probable: the bushes on the slope to the right where he had detonated the bomb, or an area to his left where a skarch had fallen and caught in the fork of another, suspending it just off the ground – plenty of cover there. He chose the fallen skarch, since if they had been in the bushes they would probably have retreated from the smoke spreading from where a fire still burned. He selected a skarch with a trunk a yard thick in a straight line to the fallen tree, took a couple of paces to his left and ran for it.

Immediately pulse-gun fire stabbed across the intervening space, past him to the right and impacted the ruin wall. He had moved just in time – whoever was shooting at him must have had him targeted. He fired back as he ran, multiple shots exploding along the length of that fallen trunk, shearing off leaves and blowing up dusty clouds of burning fibrous pulp. The hostile fire ceased momentarily, giving him just enough time to get to cover behind his selected skarch, then pulse-gun hits thrummed against the other side of the tree, flinging everywhere debris that looked like chunks of frayed rope and generating a cloud of dust and smoke, before ceasing again.

'It seems you are what we thought you were,' Carl called.

Cormac did not want to bother replying, but he needed to

know where both Carl and that CTD were. Carl's voice had not issued from by that fallen skarch.

'Wrong, Carl,' he replied. 'I'm just a grunt, which probably tells you something about the abilities of Samara and her crew.' He paused deliberately for a moment. 'Or rather, it tells you something about the abilities they used to have.'

Carl didn't react for a moment, which Cormac hoped meant his jibe had struck home. Carl eventually replied with, 'It doesn't matter. In a little while a great many trained ECS soldiers will be turned to ash, which will more than make up for Separatist losses here.'

Where the hell was he? Cormac could not locate the source of his voice – doubtless some effect of the surrounding vegetation.

'Seems to me your ash will be mixed in too – you don't have any transport out of here now,' he said.

'Ah but I do,' Carl replied. 'I've got an ATV on the way in to pick us up. Tick tick tick, Cormac. It's a shame you won't feel the fire with the rest, since I'll shortly be in a position to get a clear shot at you.'

The comment was obviously designed to drive him from cover, but nevertheless it might be true. He surveilled everything within view, but could not yet see any sign of Carl. Where was the CTD?

'I won't let you detonate that CTD, Carl,' he tried.

'Tick tick tick – there's nothing you can do to stop it now,' he said.

Cormac unshouldered the tool bag, reached inside and set the bomb timer to three seconds.

'Where is it?' he asked, expecting no answer.

'Why it's in the ruin of course,' Carl told him. 'Do you think you can get to it in time? I suggest you start running now before I finish adjusting the sight on this knackered old pulse-rifle.'

Another attempt to drive him from cover, but he had to do

something. He didn't know Carl's position, but he did know the position of the trooper who had opened fire on him earlier, and could maybe do something about him. He dropped his twinned pulse-rifle and stood, sliding his back up the tree and hanging the handles of the tool bag from his right hand. Reaching across he took a slow breath, reached in the bag and hit the priming button, then stepped out to the left, spun and hurled the bag like a hammer straight toward where the trooper was hiding. Pulse-gun fire cut past the other side of the skarch, then jerked across, slamming into fibrous wood just as he ducked for cover again. Following the manual, the man had targeted the side of the skarch to his own left, expecting that would be the side a right-handed gunman would break cover from. Had he been any less proficient, Cormac might have been dead by now.

Cormac grabbed up his twinned pulse-rifle. The detonation followed at once, blasting fire and debris past him. He waited a moment more, to be sure he wouldn't be hit by flying objects, then ducked from cover again, this time from the other side of the skarch.

The bomb had obviously landed by the base of the half-fallen skarch. Long woolly splinters of smoking wood were pointing at the sky. The blast had excavated a crater and fire was spreading through the papyrus-like leaf-litter surrounding it. The skarch, obviously released from its final attachment to the ground, had crashed down flat. Cormac circled it quickly, coming in behind. He saw a backpack by the fallen trunk and three other objects. One of these was a smaller pack of pulse-rifle forestocks – those containing the power supply and aluminium dust charge. The other two objects were feet, protruding from underneath the heavy trunk. Ducked low, because Carl was still out there somewhere, Cormac ran over, then quickly stretched upright to look over. The man was scrabbling at the ground, but he wasn't going anywhere.

Cormac considered putting a shot through his head when something smashed into the back of his own legs.

It felt as if the world had been pulled from underneath him and he crashed down beside the trunk. All the wind seemed to have been knocked out of him. Where was his gun? He looked around for it and realized he'd dropped it over the other side of the trunk. Then his attention focused on his legs. They were smoking. His left leg was bloody and charred, but his right leg was worse – all the flesh flensed away from knee to ankle, just the bones there, and them blackened.

'I told our friend there I was going to get round behind you,' said Carl. 'But I thought it better to step back and use him as bait.'

Cormac looked up, just in time to get a rifle butt straight in his face. Next he felt hands checking over his clothing, flipping him over and checking again. All he could do was struggle ineffectually until Carl kicked him over onto his back again.

'So you escaped,' said Carl.

Cormac dragged himself backwards. He needed to get up, needed to stop this . . . Carl was squatting in front of him, gazing at him curiously.

'But I don't think you are an agent, not now,' Carl continued. 'Running straight down to the ruin was a dumb mistake of the kind they don't make.'

Cormac tried to shrug casually, but it didn't come off that well. The agony was rolling up from his legs in waves and he was starting to shake violently. Carl stood, walked over to the backpack and picked it up by its straps. He walked round Cormac, climbed up onto the trunk and walked along it to where it rested between two upright skarches then, shouldering the pack, he found handholds on its scaly exterior and climbed. Twenty feet up he hung the pack straps from a large dry leaf bud, then climbed back down again. Pausing halfway back along the trunk, he drew his thin-gun again then jumped down on the other side. After a moment came a shot. A sound from the other side of the trunk that Cormac had only half been aware of, ceased at once. Carl had just killed the trapped man. There came further sounds, then Carl dropped down beside Cormac.

'It's a shame,' he said, 'but I haven't the time to get him out from under there, and he would be a bit of a burden if I did.' Carl checked the time display embedded under the fingernail of his right forefinger. 'My ride should be here shortly. In an hour we'll be beyond the blast perimeter.' He gazed up at where he had hung the CTD from the skarch, took a remote control device from his pocket, pointed it up there and pressed a button. It beeped, then he hurled the remote away.

'I'm not going to kill you, Cormac,' he continued. 'In fact, if you can climb that skarch, you might even be able to save yourself and over a thousand ECS troops.' He smiled, 'Ciao,' then he stood and walked away.

Cormac felt his consciousness fading. He tried to fight it, drifted, and jerked back into a world of pain at the sound of an ATV pulling away. No chance of climbing that fucking oversized weed – he doubted he would be able to even get himself up onto the fallen trunk. But there was another option: his rifle. Laboriously, using one workable and one maimed arm, he began dragging himself along the ground to get round to the other side of the fallen trunk.

Blackout.

Cormac recovered consciousness in a panic, having no idea how long had passed, for he possessed no handy timepiece under his fingernail. Dragging himself on, he finally reached the crater. The ground all around was smouldering, and he would have to drag himself through embers to reach his goal. He did so, and it added little to the agony he was already suffering.

The dead man came into sight and Cormac looked around frantically for his weapon, any weapon . . . They were gone. Carl must have picked them up and hurled them away. Cormac lay there with his face in the fibrous leaf-litter, swearing, but without much energy and with his voice slurred. It would be so nice just to stay in that position and wait until everything went away.

Cormac forced his head up, turned and began crawling away from the fallen trunk. Somewhere out here lay his weapon and maybe others. He couldn't see them, but surely there was a chance . . .

The thing crashed through the skarch canopy like a giant ingot of lead. Cormac gazed in bewildered recognition upon a nightmare iron scorpion scrambling through the leaf litter towards him. It poised above him, silhouetted against the sky, huge long claws each over a foot long opening and closing, then those claws came down and closed upon his body. Something groaned and he felt the hard metal digging into his torso as those claws tucked him underneath a head sporting lethal weaponry and green peridot eyes. Acceleration. The thing now crashed up through a canopy, and Cormac glimpsed acres of dead forest below like a maize field long overdue for harvest. The last thing he saw was a searingly bright light igniting and the disc of a shockwave spreading out from it, shredding the skarches in its path.

8

The concourse, one of four leading in towards the lounges and runcibles of the Paris Runcible Port, had been stripped of its gardens and kiosks, and a divider fence erected to separate the bidirectional flow of human traffic. Over the other side of the fence Cormac observed those newly arrived from offworld, and was reminded of scenes he had seen in historical films or interactives, for there was no doubt he was seeing soldiers and support staff returning from the front line. Most of the returnees were in uniform, some of them had limbs missing and limb-caps in place; some were in hover chairs, their leg stumps also end-capped. Others had areas of their bodies clad in shellwear, a kind of exoskeletal prosthetic that enabled wounded soldiers to keep functioning, whilst the damage underneath was healed by advanced medical technology. Often there were Golem, rendered either partly or wholly into macabre metal skeletons because some damage had removed their human outer covering. And scattered throughout this crowd were numerous full-life-support containers drifting along on AG, some of which were burnished cylinders large enough to hold a whole body, whilst others were the size of hat boxes.

'You'd think they'd use two concourses for departures and the other two for arrivals,' said Hannah.

Gazing across at the returnees, Dax shook his head. 'The idea was suggested, but the AIs scotched it. The reason given was that though we face a vicious enemy in a costly war, there will be no secrets and no massaging of casualty figures.' Dax paused contemplatively. 'Personally I think this is maintained so those departing to war will be reminded of what it's like out there, and be more cautious – the enthusiasm of many new recruits, or those returning after medical treatment or rest, tends to kill.'

They continued to make their way slowly towards Dax's departure runcible, troops of soldiers all about them, others like Dax clad in the blue dress uniforms of ECS Medical, Golem, occasional war drones and occasional units of Sparkind. Cormac, who until now had never thought more deeply about the war than wondering how many more Prador Jebel U-cap Krong had splattered, suddenly had a moment of realization. What was happening here was happening at main runcible complexes all around Earth, up on the moon and out where similar complexes had been established on the worlds of the Solar System. It was happening beyond on populated worlds throughout the Polity. Trillions of people were on the move, marching to the beat of the same drum. And it had been happening for over forty years.

Soon the concourse debouched into a wide runcible lounge in which the seating areas were wholly occupied and groups of people had made little camps on the carpeted floors as they awaited their runcible slot. They joined a queue to an information terminal mounted in one of the ersatz cast-iron pillars supporting the lounge's decorous cathedral-like roof. They waited there only a moment before Dax turned to Cormac.

'Your p-top,' he said.

Cormac handed the device over as the three of them stepped out of the queue. Dax flipped it open, tapped away for a short time, then abruptly snapped it closed and handed it back.

'My slot is right now – Runcible Six,' he said. 'They're set for group departures and mine's got only eight minutes to run.'

'So quickly?' said Hannah.

Dax grabbed her and hugged her. 'I'll be in contact as soon as possible.' He released her and stooped down to Cormac. 'I could say look after our mother, but I won't be so patronizing. Look after yourself . . . Cormac.'

'I will . . .'

'Where are you going?' Hannah asked, as Dax began heading away.

'A place called Cheyne III – never heard of it.'

And that was it: he was gone.

Cormac abruptly found his mother seizing hold of his hand and holding it tightly. 'Let's go,' she said, her expression grim.

Following arrows painted upon the floor they joined the crowd of arrivals and trudged out with them. Now amidst that crowd rather than gazing at it from a distance, Cormac gained a better view of the grotesqueries it contained. Certainly there were those here with missing limbs, but many other injuries were on display too. He observed a woman, her skin reddened and cracked like the river mud in a drought, but protected by a translucent layer. Had these injuries been burns the injury could have been dealt with by tank growth, grafting or repair under shellwear. With what little he knew of such things Cormac supposed the injury the result of some biological or chemical agent, hence the protective layer.

'Don't stare,' said his mother.

The woman, noticing his inspection, smiled, the skin of her cheeks cracking open. She didn't seem to notice.

Also travelling parallel to them was a man in a lev-chair. He was just a torso and head, all his limbs missing and the point of severance visible under the same sort of translucent layer the woman wore. Only later, checking his p-top, did Cormac discover that the translucent layer slowed the action of diatomic acid – a substance that was very difficult to neutralize. These people were heading for one of the few clinics where a successful neutralization process had been found. Some of the others he had seen here in shellwear, he understood later, were those with old acid burns, who had lost large areas of skin and necessarily wore shellwear permanently until a cure could be found.

Finally they reached the lev-train station and boarded a carriage to take them back to Tritonia. The numbers of the walking wounded were lower on the train, though there were still plenty of those wearing military uniforms. Doubtless their injuries were not physical and were due for mental cautery.

His head felt stuffed with cotton wool and recent events seemed to sit divorced in his mind, for he could not quite believe what had happened to him nor all the things he had done. Yet, when he looked down at himself, he found confirmation.

The shellwear enclosing Carl's chest while he had been in hospital had been an example of this technology not being used for the intended purpose. Shellwear had been developed during the Prador war to enable severely wounded soldiers to continue functioning. Cormac flexed his damaged hand and carefully studied its new covering. Really, it looked just like the glove from a medieval suit of armour, but for the optical data ports along the section covering his wrist and the odd LEDs scattered here and there to give an immediate warning in the location of any problem. The underlying thumb, new little finger and various other skin, tendon and flesh grafts were functional and hurt not at all, but they needed protection and time to knit together. Now he gazed down at his legs. Much the same there, though as far as he could recollect, medieval armour did not actually have toes, nor those nutrient feed pipes, blood scrubbers and various black boxes containing selections of nano-factories. The medics here hadn't given him new legs, merely further grafts. Apparently they didn't like to replace entire limbs when there was no immediate need.

His spare set of legs was being kept on ice.

Cormac gazed at the cylindrical tank resting in the corner of the room. It was bar-coded, and affixed to it was a mini-console that could display a manifest of its contents.

'So, just like every mosquito autogun or grav-tank, each soldier comes with a package of spare parts,' he said.

'It's only practical,' Olkennon replied.

He glanced at her. 'I never knew.'

'Well, we wouldn't want you getting careless with the originals.' She grimaced. 'Didn't seem to work in your case.'

Cormac picked up the pack of clothing she had slapped down on his chest, then swung his metal legs over the side of the surgical table and sat upright. He felt a slight dizziness, just as the medic, who had recently departed, had told him to expect. Sitting there he hoped for further clarity – some emotional connection with recent events – for he had seen a friend murdered, he had been tortured and he had killed so many, yet still it all seemed like VR fantasy. And what seemed to aggravate this unreality was the scorpion drone that had rescued him, for it seemed to have flown right out of childhood memory.

After a moment he stood up, and found that his legs supported him without problem. He was slightly out of balance as he pulled on the undergarments and fatigues, but a steadying hand from Olkennon was enough. Once finished dressing, he gazed around at the other familiar furnishings of this room and wondered, with his chosen profession, about the regularity of his visits to places like this.

'How many died?' he finally asked – one of the many questions nagging at him since the moment he woke up.

'Your questions will be answered during the debriefing,' Olkennon replied. 'Follow me.' She headed towards the door.

Cormac peered down at his feet, twisted one of them against the floor to test its grip and, finding it sufficient, followed Olkennon out of the medical centre and along one of the township streets. As they walked he found himself scanning about him, half expecting to see a big steel scorpion crouching in the shadows nearby. Maybe he had imagined it; war drones tended to be quite similar in their choice of nightmarish body-shapes, so perhaps it had just been a similar drone. After all, he had lost consciousness shortly after the CTD blast, and hadn't been exactly lucid and clear-headed just prior to it.

Now they reached another composite dome which, as far as Cormac knew, was used for storage. Olkennon led him inside, lights automatically switching on for them. Cormac gazed round at the stacked crates, racks filled with ordnance and crash-foam-wrapped items. To one side stood a column of disc-shaped anti-gravity tanks, stacked one upon the other like inverted plates. Assembled mosquito autoguns squatted in lines in one rack, occasionally shifting and twitching as if trying to get more comfortable in slumber. She took him into the shadows between racks loaded with engine components and what looked like bundles of pulse-gun barrels, then finally through an internal security door into an area packed with specialized equipment, where Agent Spencer sat behind a table spread with the component parts of various hand weapons.

'Pull up a chair,' said Spencer, gesturing to where some folded camp chairs were resting against the wheel of a low-slung ATV. Olkennon grabbed two chairs, handing one to Cormac, and they sat themselves before Spencer's table. Cormac was glad Olkennon had positioned herself next to him, for this indicated she was taking the position of advocate rather than interrogator.

'Are you paying attention?' asked Spencer.

Cormac only realized the question wasn't directed at him when a crab drone resting folded on some packing cases behind her unfolded gleaming legs and said, 'I am always paying attention.'

'So, Cormac,' said Spencer, without looking up from the pulse-gun power supply she was inspecting, 'in your own words, and in as much detail as you can supply, tell us what happened from the moment trooper Yellow was murdered.'

149

That hit him in the stomach and immediately seemed to high-light his memories, or maybe the potent cocktail of analgesics and anti-shock drugs washing about inside him was beginning to wear off.

'She's dead,' he said.

Spencer looked up and nodded once.

'What about the CTD blast?' Cormac asked. 'How many were killed?'

'None at all.'

'What?'

'We'd already spread the rumour that another battalion was moving into the woods because we suspected that would be where a CTD would be deployed and knew the Separatists would want to wait on a larger target. At that point, we were preparing the battalion there to pull out. And they pulled out fast once we got the warning you posted on your personal net-space.'

Cormac sat back, feeling some of the tightness in his chest slacken.

'Now, from the moment Yellow was murdered . . .'

Cormac told them the story, in detail. There were no interruptions until he reached the point where he escaped.

'So let me get this right,' said Spencer. 'You deliberately sacrificed one hand to enable yourself to get free, and thereupon managed to wipe out seven Separatists?'

'Of course, the forensic examination of his wounds seems to confirm his story,' Olkennon observed. 'As does the examination of the bodies recovered at the Separatist base.' She turned and gazed at Cormac for a moment. 'It would appear that this soldier is a walking abattoir.'

Cormac absorbed that, understanding in an instant that they must have pieced together the sequence of events in Dramewood before this debriefing. However, he felt they really didn't under-stand what he had faced and why he acted as he did. 'My choices were to either do nothing and be tortured, eventually to death, or to try and fight back. I was lucky, I was prepared to die and my opponents were not.'

Spencer, who had long ago abandoned her inspection of the components before her, placed her elbows on the table, interlaced her fingers and rested her chin on them. 'Then having been pre-pared to die and managing to survive, you went after Carl. If you could continue your story?'

Cormac did so, including in detail the mistakes he felt he made at the end.

'You made no mistakes,' said Spencer. 'Your time was limited both by your injuries and by the detonation time of the CTD, so you needed to expose yourself to draw them out. Carl was wrong about that. If you had held back and spent your time trying to stalk them, you could have lost them, faced reinforcements or been forced into an encounter when your injuries further impaired your efficiency.'

It was a distinctly cold analysis.

'What about Carl?' he asked.

'What about him?' Spencer leant back, holding her hands out in appeal. 'The Carl whose records we have grew up on Callisto and there joined ECS, but it now seems the Carl here was not the Carl there.' She turned towards the crab drone. 'Anything?'

The drone replied, 'I have made inquiries: childhood genetic and medical records match with recent scans and samplings taken whilst he was in the medical unit here. The Callisto AI has now dispatched agents to bring in his parents for questioning, for genetically it seems they are not his parents.'

'The records have been altered?' Spencer suggested.

'They have,' the drone confirmed. Cormac realized it must be telefactored from the local AI to have made such fast inquiries.

'So he has escaped,' said Cormac, which was the real question he had been asking.

'Unless he was caught in the blast,' said Spencer, 'it would seem so.'

Cormac paused for a moment, wondering how he was going to broach the next subject. 'A drone rescued me.'

'Your actions in the Separatist base resulted in their chameleonware crashing, but it seemed quite possible to us that they did that themselves to lure more ECS personnel within the blast radius of the CTD, so we left it. The explosion from your ATV was picked up by satellite shortly after our friend here,' she stabbed a thumb back at the crab drone, 'picked up your warning on your site. We then moved anything that could fly fast enough into the area. Lucky the drone found you and grabbed you when it did.'

This was frustrating. How could he say to them that the drone looked just like one that had haunted his childhood? They'd probably send him back to the medical unit for brain scans.

'I can't say that I'd seen many war drones here,' he said.

Spencer studied him for a short while, then shrugged. 'There aren't many.'

'Where's it from . . . has it been here for a while?' Cormac grimaced. 'Drone or otherwise I'd like to thank it for getting me out of there.'

'Hagren?' Spencer enquired, her use of the planet's name indicating that the AI using the crab drone behind her was the main planetary runcible AI.

'Amistad is a free drone and merely answered the call I put out for assistance. He is now no longer connected to the planetary net and is not responding to calls. I have no idea where he is.'

'Amistad,' Cormac repeated. 'Do you have any other information about him?' As he finished speaking he wished he'd kept quiet, for now both Spencer and Olkennon were studying him carefully.

'There's something more to this,' Spencer observed.

'I'm sure I've seen this drone before,' Cormac admitted.

'Where?'

'On Earth – over ten years ago.'

'I see,' said Spencer, abruptly looking irritated. 'Might I suggest you utilize your free time to research the matter?' Cormac nodded. 'Now, let's get back to where we were.' Spencer glanced across at Olkennon. 'Obviously you no longer have a unit.'

The Golem dipped her head.

'And, I understand,' Spencer continued, 'you'll be heading for . . . Cheyne III to train further recruits?'

'Such seems to be my burden,' Olkennon replied.

Spencer turned back to Cormac. 'You, Cormac, lack training and experience, but it seems that our masters,' she glanced back at the crab drone, 'feel, after your recent heroic efforts, prepared to take a risk with you.' She picked something up from the table before her and gazed at it for a moment. 'Though your warning enabled us to get the main battalion out of Dramewood, there were still plenty of casualties there beforehand. A unit working there, directly for me, lost one of its members. The remaining three members of that unit have been observing this briefing, and it has only been down to their approval whether or not you replace their missing comrade. Apparently they approve.'

She tossed something to him, fast, then smiled approvingly when he snatched this object from the air with his right hand. He opened his hand and gazed at a badge fashioned out of gold and platinum. It depicted a round shield with spears crossed behind it, topped with an ancient Greek hoplite war helm, all on a disc of milky crystal.

'Welcome to the Sparkind, Cormac.'

'This is standard issue,' said the medic. 'I'd advise you to stick with it.'

Cormac gazed at the augmentation lying on the plastic tray

affixed to the side of the pedestal-mounted autodoc. It looked like a two-inch-long broad bean rendered in chrome. The aug was optional for most of those in the military and he'd seen many soldiers wearing them, but he had not been inclined to try such an invasive technology himself. Perhaps it was silly, but he felt a deep aversion to anyone tampering with what lay between his ears. He didn't know where it came from, and had not noticed the same in others. However, to become one of the Sparkind, wearing one of these things was now compulsory.

'But I have sufficient funds now to pay for something more sophisticated,' said Cormac. He still didn't like the idea of this, not one bit, but if he was going to have an aug, then he intended to have the best available.

'I give that advice every time,' said the medic, 'and mostly it is ignored.'

'Then explain to me why you advise so.'

'You understand that the aug makes nanofibre synaptic connections inside your skull?'

'Who doesn't understand that?'

The man grimaced. 'You'd be surprised how many but, be that as it may, up until recent years it hasn't been possible to disconnect those fibres or remove them from the skull. It is of course possible to remove the aug itself, but the fibres remain in place. They don't cause any harm – well, not much. This also means the only kind of upgrade possible has been to the aug itself, not the fibres.'

'Then surely that's a good reason to get the best one you can?' suggested Cormac.

'You'd think so, but no.' The medic sighed, obviously groping for the best way to explain something complicated to this stupid soldier. 'Methods of extracting the fibres are now just becoming viable, and meanwhile the sophistication of aug technology is advancing very fast. Within a year it will be possible to completely remove an aug like this one – however, it won't be possible to remove one of the more advanced ones presently available.'

'Yes,' said Cormac, not entirely sure what the man was driving at.

'What I'm saying is that for military purposes, the standard aug is more than adequate. You don't need to do any sophisticated modelling or need to put together an assault plan for an entire army, and I'm presuming you're not conducting any genetic research or studies of U-space mechanics?'

'No,' said Cormac, still at a loss.

'Well,' said the medic, 'what I'm driving at here is that if you have one of the more sophisticated augs now, it will be outmoded within a few months and you won't be able to replace it. If you have this aug, it will be possible to remove it completely when you have decided, having used an aug for some time, what your requirements are, what aug you want. Do you understand?'

'Yes, I understand,' Cormac replied, but what really decided him was that 'possible to remove completely', since he still did not like the idea of these things. 'Go ahead and fit me with that one.'

'If you would.' The medic gestured to the surgical table.

He sat on the table, lifted his legs up and lay back, his neck coming down into a V-shaped rest with his head overhanging the end of the table where various clamps were ready to be engaged. The medic quickly tightened these clamps then stepped back and swung the autodoc over Cormac's face.

'I've got your medical record on file,' he said, 'but I want to confirm that stuff about the editing.'

Editing?

The underside of the doc was a nightmare thing – like looking at the underside of a woodlouse fashioned from chrome and glass.

'Close your eyes.' He did so, and felt an intense glare and warmth traversing his face from forehead to chin. 'Okay, that's done.'

Cormac opened his eyes. 'Editing?'

'Yes,' said the medic thoughtfully, probably whilst studying the scan result. 'Obviously it was done while you were a child, which seems rather drastic, but then it wasn't an uncommon occurrence during the war.'

Now the doc, down beside his head, stabbed out one of its many appendages. Something stung at the base of Cormac's skull and suddenly his head turned into a dead rock. His vision now seemed to be down a dark tunnel, his hearing distant, both divorced from reality. He could no longer speak, no longer ask questions, but what more information could this man provide? He would know only that Cormac had received cerebral editing during his childhood.

When something crunched on the side of his head, Cormac expected some sort of explanation of the sensation, but none was forthcoming. Of course, this man was a military medic, so did not possess the bedside manner of those who fitted augs to civilians. Next the inside of his skull felt as if it was filling with ice-water, and something began hurting behind his ear. Then, nowhere he could precisely locate, a lid opened on the imaginary third eye he now possessed.

'Raise your hand when the status text appears,' the medic instructed.

The pain started to fade, and as it faded blue text appeared in the vision of that third eye and blinked intermittently: STATUS >

Cormac raised his hand.

'Okay, now visualize the words "search mode" and let me know when the words appear.'

How was he supposed to let the man know? He visualized the words, felt an odd sensation as of a plug going into a socket somewhere inside his skull, then raised his hand when SEARCH MODE > appeared.

'Now search for something.'

SEARCH MODE > EDITING

After a pause these words blinked out to be replaced with: CANNOT EDIT SEARCH MODE.

'Something else,' the medic suggested.

SEARCH MODE > PRADOR

NO NET CONNECTION. NO MEMSTORE.

'Now you should have "no net connection" and "no memstore".' The man sounded bored, and Cormac wondered how many times he had said those words before.

He raised his hand.

'Now, let's get to the other functions.'

The process took a further hour, was sometimes confusing and sometimes exhilarating, especially when he connected to the AI grid and found out how much information lay but a thought away. He was run quickly through the tutorial contained within the aug and shown how to access its user manual. When the autodoc removed its nerve-block and feeling returned to his head, Cormac waited impatiently for the clamps to be undone, then quickly sat upright.

'What can you tell me about this editing?' he asked.

The medic shrugged. 'No more than that you were edited as a child. That's something you'll have to take up with your parents or guardians.'

As he left that place Cormac was determined to discover more about whatever had been done to his mind, but knew he would not be finding out for a while. Now he had another VR training session, followed by weapons practice, then tactical assessment training and analysis, and knew that after them he would be falling exhausted into his bunk.

9

Cormac gazed at the crowds standing in the large waiting area of the editing clinic and briefly wondered where Dax had got to. Perhaps he had gone to the toilet, or to buy more cigarettes. Soon, he knew, they would enter Door Eight where a smaller waiting room was situated, then they would go into the editing suite itself, where a Golem nurse, telefactored from a local AI, would conduct the editing process on Dax. It would take some time, of course, because Dax was a medic, and much of what lay between his ears was too useful to lose. Ah, perhaps Dax was already in there being worked on . . . no, that couldn't be right, for they had remained in the smaller waiting room until the work was done . . . but that was in the past . . . it had already been done.

Cormac looked around, realized he was sitting, then glanced across at his mother, who was sitting beside him doing something with her laptop. She had a look of extreme concentration until, abruptly, she realized Cormac was gazing at her.

'I was just making sure I kept copies,' she explained. 'They're notoriously unstable in the carbon memstores they're using here.' Then she paused, as if reviewing what she had just said, and cursed quietly to herself. After a moment she went on, 'Are you alright now?'

Cormac had absolutely no idea what she was talking about. He just gazed at her, unable to articulate the weird déjà vu he was experiencing – the sensation of reliving memory, and being offended because memory wasn't matching up to reality. Hannah popped a memtab from the side of her laptop and dropped it into the top pocket of her shirt, slid the device back into its carrycase and hung the strap from her shoulder. He continued staring at her while something tried to realign inside his head, then he abruptly grasped that memory came after reality, not before it. They were not here with Dax – that was all in the past and Dax was, right now, many light years away on a world called Cheyne III.

'What?' he said, then after a long pause, 'What happened?'

Hannah stood, her hand closing on his and pulling him to his feet. He felt a bit wobbly and realized be must have been asleep or something.

'You felt faint,' she explained, 'and this was the nearest place where you could sit down.' They moved back into the aisle and started heading towards the exit. 'Best I have you checked out,' she added, 'though it's probably due to the excitement of the last few days.'

Cormac still couldn't quite get things clear in his mind. They'd seen off Dax at the runcible port in Paris, then returned by lev-train to Tritonia, but he couldn't remember if they'd returned to the Watts Hotel or were still on their way back there.

They stepped out into the street, where his mother scanned about herself carefully before towing him off in the direction of the Watts. Yes, he remembered now. They had returned to the hotel to clean up and change, before heading out to try a local restaurant. He couldn't remember if they had eaten. It certainly felt to him like they hadn't.

'Weren't we going to get something to eat?' he asked.

Hannah came to an abrupt halt and gazed down at him. 'Do you feel up to it? I thought it better to get back to the hotel for a rest . . .'

'I'm hungry,' he complained.

She smiled a secretive smile then turned them right round again. Within a few minutes they came opposite a restaurant where the tables and chairs spilled out onto the street through the arched frontage. Inevitably, considering its location, this place served seafood. The moving holographic sign above the arches depicted a crab holding a large gun in one claw with which it was blasting all about itself. The gun then evidently ran out, at which point the crab began backing away from the human who now stepped into view – Jebel U-cap Krong – who advanced with a pulse-gun in one hand and a mine in the other. The crab ended up backing along a plank over a large cooking pot of boiling water, into which it fell when Krong jumped onto the back of the plank.

Cormac was mesmerized; he loved this place at once.

They seated themselves at one of the outside tables, where-upon they were approached by a metalskin android with a head like a platinum ant's. Cormac immediately made his selection from the menu and the android said, 'Good choice,' then turning to Hannah, 'Crab salad for you too, madam?'

Cormac adjusted his night goggles and gazed about himself for a moment, impressed at how well they worked – he could hardly distinguish his surroundings from how they had appeared during the day. Could this be a hindrance? Might he neglect to take advantage of concealing darkness because he was less aware of it? Then again, it might also not be a great idea to get compla-cent and assume all his enemies blind, for any of them could be sporting similar goggles. Nevertheless, he adjusted them slightly so his surroundings took on an unnatural tint, just to remind him that it wasn't day, then returned his attention to his companions. Not much of them was visible at the moment, for like Cormac they all wore chameleoncloth fatigues, and until they moved it seemed three disembodied heads, six hands and various pieces of unconcealed hardware occupied this clearing in the woods.

Gorman, when wholly visible, looked like a thickset and brutal thug. He carried a lot of body weight, easily, his head was stubbled with grey hair, his neck bulging, his eyes grey and his teeth slightly crooked and yellowish. He smoked cigars, liked eating mouth-strippingly hot curries and drinking vast quantities of beer, but only when off-duty and relaxing. The rest of the time his appearance and general demeanour belied the speed of his mind, his reactions and the way he assessed the data coming in through the small flesh-coloured aug affixed behind his ear like some sort of growth. Travis was neat and lean and ridiculously good-looking, with jet-black hair tied in a pony tail and startlingly green eyes. He grinned a lot and his sense of humour was distinctly odd. Crean's appearance was Asiatic, big-breasted and lush, dark-haired, dark-skinned and dark-eyed. It had taken a little while for Cormac to realize that, like Travis, she was a Golem. Gorman was so obviously human, and delighted in being so.

'These gods like to have their ugly pets along as a contrast,' said Gorman, stabbing a lit cigar to where the two Golem were assembling a mosquito autogun.

Mills was the missing member. A Separatist sniper had hit him right in the head with an explosive bullet. It was Crean who got to the sniper first. Tore him in half and hung the bits from a tree. Cormac hadn't understood how Gorman seemed to be so accepting of Mills' death, until he learned from Travis that Gorman had been edited. This reminded Cormac of when his brother Dax went for editing during the Prador/Human war, and of the other events of that period, and of the drone he now knew to be called Amistad. He reached up and touched the bean-shaped lump of computer hardware behind his own ear. In his new aug he had files about Amistad he wanted to review at leisure, but with the VR training and now this fast deployment, he hadn't had a chance. Also, sitting in the aug was a message he had been drafting to send to his mother, asking why he himself had been edited as a child, and what memories were missing.

'So here's the plan,' said Gorman.

Cormac made that odd unnatural effort to call up his inbox in a frame that appeared to the right of his visual field, and saw he had received one message. He opened it and studied a visual file showing a mugshot of someone immediately recognizable: Sheen, one of the Separatists who had accompanied him during the raid on the Prador ship.

'Any problems?' Gorman asked.

'I'll let you know when you tell me the plan,' Cormac replied.

Gorman grinned. 'Okay,' he said. 'Agent Spencer wants her alive. Sheen is Samara's sister and is likely privy to much that went on at the top.'

'Sister?'

'You didn't know that?'

'No, I didn't know that.'

'Everyone else in the caves is dispensable.' Gorman shrugged. 'In fact, that's *all* they are. They've got no information we want nor do we want to bring them for trial, since sentence has already been passed on them all.' He studied Cormac carefully. 'Can you handle this?'

Cormac nodded, but swallowed drily. This was so different from killing those who had already attacked you and intended to torture you. It seemed too cold, too harsh. Would he hesitate? Might he find it difficult to pull the trigger on someone unarmed, even if that person was a Separatist? He picked up his stubby machine pistol from where it rested on the ground beside him, then stood up. The weapon was perfect for this kind of work, being easily manoeuvrable in confined spaces and, unlike most pulse-weapons, its discharge was invisible. It also bore a fat silencer that not only absorbed the crack of the shot, but also broadcast an inverted phonic waveform that covered most impact sounds. The result was, in most cases, utterly silent and eerie killing. Its magazine contained two hundred bullets, each projectile a high-pressure explosive p-shell just a millimetre across and three long. All four of them carried weapons like this, and also wore pepperpot stun guns holstered at their belts for when they came upon Sheen.

'Okay,' said Gorman, standing up. 'Time to get bloody.' He pulled up the hood of his fatigues, pulled across his face mask and slipped on his gloves. Via his aug Cormac instructed his goggles to respond to the recognition signal each of his fellows was broadcasting. Gorman at once became visible again, as if clad in some orange suit – it wouldn't do for Cormac to end up shooting his own side because he couldn't see them.

The two Golem, also now apparently clad from head to foot in orange, had finished setting up the mosquito and now stepped back from it. The weapon abruptly stood up on its six silvery legs, disappeared for a moment, then reappeared as a red outline as it engaged its chameleonware and Cormac's goggles picked up its signal. It then abruptly targeted them each in turn, recognized them then moved on, finally falling into a routine of surveying the tree-covered slope leading down into the valley before them.

'I'm glad you're so confident of your programming,' said Gorman sarcastically.

Cormac realized they'd onlined the gun without doing a test, an option considered risky until they were sure its recognition software was working properly. Travis glanced round at them, and Cormac imagined his usual maniacal grin under his face mask.

'I delayed the loading of its dust magazine,' the Golem said. 'If my programming had been wrong it would only have given you a bit of an electric shock.'

'Nice,' Gorman replied. 'And it'll recognize Sheen when we bring her out?'

'Of course it will!'

Crean now spoke directly to Cormac. 'Don't let him get to you. The chances of him programming a mosquito wrong are about the same as any of us getting hit on the head by a meteorite.'

Gorman flinched, put a hand on his head, and peered up at the sky.

Nice little humorous exchange, just before the four of them went down into that valley to slaughter people.

'Let's go,' said Gorman, and led the way down the slope. The two Golem strode along beside him for a moment, then abruptly headed off at speed. Cormac glanced back at the autogun, which was now loping along behind himself and Gorman like a loyal hound. Checking the assault plan in his aug, he saw that the two Golem were heading out wide on either side to come in above the cave mouth from either end of the valley. His own and Gorman's routes diverged ahead, so they would also come upon the opening of the cave from two different directions.

'Go forty per cent infrared,' Gorman advised. 'They're sure to have guards out here.' He reached out and slapped a hand on Cormac's shoulder. 'You come on any, you take them down nice and quiet before they can send a warning.'

Now they parted company, the mosquito following Gorman. Cormac located himself on a map of the locality called up in his aug, then transmitted the data from that to a small screen display mounted in the upper surface of his gun, which shortly displayed a low-lumen arrow pointing to his destination. The reason for them splitting up and approaching from four different points was precisely so at least one of them would hit the expected guard outpost. They didn't want anyone positioned behind them when they finally went into the caves. Continuously checking ahead and moving swiftly and silently from tree to tree, he advanced. It was a small glow-worm luminescence that gave them away.

I've found some watchers, Cormac sent, using the text function in his aug.

Can you take them? Gorman enquired.

Cormac eased up the infrared in his goggles. The small glow

of heat came from an ancient style of lamp. Obviously it had recently been used and its filament had yet to cool down. Now, with infrared at a hundred per cent, Cormac could see the spotlight itself, the hide below it, and the glow of two bodies inside.

I believe so, he replied.

Belief is not sufficient, came Travis's interjection.

Quite, said Gorman. *And make sure you check identification first.*

Of course: one of those two there could be Sheen.

Cormac raised the magnification of his goggles as he got down on the ground and began to crawl towards the hideout. He shut off the cooling function of his clothing so nothing would be visible from its vents should those ahead possess night goggles. Now they would not be able to pick him up in infrared, since his chameleon-cloth fatigues also possessed a near-perfect insulating layer, hence the need for cooling and vents. Immediately his temperature began to rise and he started sweating.

He worked his way carefully forwards, using as much cover as possible, avoiding twigs and patches of dry leaves, moving in a slow muscular motion that produced very little noise. He hadn't believed it possible to be so silent until training in VR, but this was his first time doing it for real, so he was as careful as he could be. In ten minutes he reached within five yards of the hideout. One of the figures was peering out through the front of the hide and by its bulk it was evident to Cormac this wasn't Sheen.

'At least it ain't raining,' said a male voice from the hide.

Cormac reached forward, pressed a hand against the tree directly in front of him, then using that to take his weight, slowly eased himself upright.

'Always fucking positive,' replied a second male voice. 'We get to spend the night out here with beezle grubs crawling up our arses and you're seeing the bright side?'

'It could be worse.'

'Yeah, the coffee could be cold and there could be grit in my pie.' The man paused for a moment. 'Oh right. The coffee *is* cold and there *is* grit in my pie.'

'Yeah, okay—'

Two men, that meant Sheen wasn't here, so Cormac must kill both of them. For a moment he considered other aspects of his training – the stuff about an enemy being humanized, about maintaining an emotional distance – but he found, even having listened to these two talking, that he was utterly cold. Yes, these were two people with lives of their own, with kin, families, maybe wives and children. However, he also knew it was quite likely that had he been tied up before them, one of them would have been bitching about 'grit in his pie' whilst going to fetch the blow-torch. He soft-linked via his aug to his weapon, throwing up a targeting frame in his goggles, stepped out from behind the tree and walked forward, bringing that frame over the head visible before him.

'Hey, I think I see—'

Cormac pulled the trigger and his machine pistol shuddered and whispered. Pieces still glowing in infrared splashed out behind the man as most of his head disappeared. The other was now visible through the hole in the front of the hide, crawling fast on hands and knees to reach for a pulse-rifle nearby. Cormac hit him once, slinging him against the back earthen wall, then centred the frame over his head as he tried to haul himself upright. The face, almost skull-like in infrared, cratered, and the top of his head lifted like a lid.

Cormac paused for a moment, took a slow easy breath, then reactivated the cooling function of his clothes. With a red mist rising from the vents about his waist, he moved to the side of the hide, found a door and kicked it open, then altered his goggles to optimum night function: everything clear as day. The man he'd hit second was still breathing, but in short little gasps, his right leg shivering and blood spreading on the ground underneath him. The other one was down on his knees, what remained of his head resting against the front wall of the hide, blood painting a stripe down the wall. There was brain tissue spattered everywhere, the odd piece of hairy skull and, grotesquely, one ear was stuck to the back wall. After a moment, the gasping noises of the one still breathing ceased.

'The problem has been dealt with?' Gorman enquired, now through the verbal com function of Cormac's aug.

Cormac realized Gorman had probably been monitoring Cormac's weapon and so knew when it fired, how many shots were fired, and when it ceased firing.

'The problem has been dealt with,' he replied, quietly, calmly.

'Continue to the cave mouth,' Gorman ordered, 'but stay alert – just because you've killed some guards doesn't mean there aren't any more out here.'

Cormac stepped back out of the hide, then continued along his course, following the direction arrow atop his gun. Oddly, he had felt no surge of adrenalin before the assault, and now wasn't shaking and didn't feel sick. Previously this had been his reaction in violent situations, with the exception of that time when he had faced torture. 'Stone Killer' was a description that occurred to him, but it seemed far too dramatic. Maybe he was just becoming accustomed to the life . . .

There were no further guards either at the bottom of the valley where a stream wended its way between the trees, nor on the slope leading up to a rift of stone in which the dark mouths of caves were clearly visible. Cormac paused twenty yards below the caves and scanned his surroundings. He soon saw Crean and Travis coming down the cliffs like orange spiders and Gorman, mosquito still walking at his heel, coming up through the trees to his right. Gorman came over to him whilst the two Golem waited up by the caves.

'Were there any other guards?' Cormac asked.

Gorman pointed upslope. 'Travis found a watchtower, but it was automated for air defence – no problem for us.' He glanced back behind him. 'I found another hide just like yours. Not a problem either.' Gorman pointed a finger up the slope and set out. Cormac fell in behind him, and soon they were up with their backs against the rock wall between two caves.

Travis gestured with a thumb to one cave. 'This one only – the other two only go back about ten metres. There's an autogun about five metres inside.'

Gorman tugged at his fatigues. 'Will this get us through?'

Travis shrugged. 'One way to find out.' He stepped in front of the cave mouth, then ran inside. There came a cracking sound then a fizzing as from a severed cable. After a moment he strolled out lugging a primitive auto pulse-gun trailing various cables.

'Apparently not sensitive enough to pick up chameleoncloth,' said Travis, driving the gun barrel-down into the earth.

Gorman now turned to the mosquito. 'Stay,' he said. The mobile weapon took a few paces back, tilting its body up towards him like an obedient hound watching its master. Quite odd the way weapons like this sometimes behaved, which was apparently due to their original design being a Tenkian one. The four entered the cave.

Gorman and Cormac took point, Gorman holding his machine pistol casually at his hip, slowly swinging it back and forth. Cormac copied him, the targeting frame in his goggles veering from wall to wall of the cave. Gorman doubtless saw a targeting frame too, though did not wear goggles since the mods were actually in his eyes. They stepped past the autogun tripod and followed the tunnel round to the right. After a moment Cormac had to knock down the light amplification of his goggles, for there were lights ahead. Twenty yards further in they reached a fork in the tunnel. A woman stepped out of the right-hand one. Cormac brought his frame over her as she turned: black hair, wiry frame and apparently quite young. He triggered once and she slammed back against the wall, spun and went down.

'*Fuck*,' said Gorman via aug.

'*It wasn't her*,' Cormac replied.

'Michele?' someone called, stepping out of the same tunnel shortly after her. This man must have seen her abruptly fall, but had heard no shots nor the impacts of any bullets. He gazed down at her for half a second before shots from Gorman abruptly flung him on top of her.

'*Crean, Travis*,' Gorman sent, '*take the left fork.*'

The two Golem headed left whilst Gorman led the way down the right fork, gesturing for Cormac to follow. Stepping round the corpses, Cormac took another look at the girl's face. No, definitely not Sheen. It occurred to him that he should feel something about killing a young woman. He felt nothing at all.

They moved deeper and deeper, Cormac needing to keep on reducing the light amplification of his goggles, until, feeling stupid, he called up the menu related to the goggles and set them on automatic. Shortly after that he heard the murmur of voices from around a corner ahead. Gorman held up his hand, halting them.

'*Remember – check your targets.*'

At that moment, the familiar sound of pulse-gun fire echoed from behind them – obviously one or both of the Golem had been spotted.

'Fast now,' said Gorman out loud.

They broke into a jog and rounded the corner, where the tunnel expanded. Against one wall stood a stack of crates beside which a group of three people stood smoking cigarettes. Beyond them the tunnel sloped down, lined along one side with regularly spaced doorways from which the light shone. Cormac tracked the arc of a cigarette as it curved towards the stone floor. Reaching for the pulse-gun at his hip the smoker squinted back up the tunnel towards Cormac and Gorman. The man could not actually see them, but he could see something and those shots had made him suspicious. His two companions were reaching for pulse-rifles resting against the crates. Two machine pistols purred and the three went down as if someone had instantly removed alternate bones throughout their bodies. Now shadows loomed and flitted as people began exiting what appeared to be rooms carved into the rock.

Gorman slowed to a walk. 'Let's not get overexcited,' he said. 'You check the first one.'

Someone came out of a room and sprayed pulse-fire up the cave. Gorman nailed him immediately and Cormac wondered about checking identities now, but then realized the collapsing figure was too big to be Sheen. More pulse-gun fire from around a door jamb five doors down. They both slammed back against the wall, then Gorman tossed a small spherical grenade down that way. It went off with a smoky crump, hurling sooty fragments all about the corridor as well as through the open door. Somebody groaned and a rifle clattered to the floor. Pulling a similar grenade from his belt, Cormac moved to the first door and tossed it in ahead of him, waiting until it went off, then immediately ducking in. A big man, wearing only a pair of shorts, was staggering from a bunk. At once Cormac realized the man could hardly see to aim the thin-gun he was holding, even if Cormac had been clearly visible, for that neurotoxin worked fast. Cormac knew. Now, for the first time, he hesitated. There was no need to kill this man, for in a moment he would be unconscious.

'Pramer,' he said in surprise, now acknowledging the real reason for his hesitation.

'You,' said Pramer, abruptly swinging his gun towards the doorway where Cormac stood.

A slight pressure on the trigger, the machine pistol hummed contentedly to itself and Pramer staggered back, shots stitching up his front. A cloud of vaporous blood and bits of flesh and bone exited his back as he crashed against the bunk beds, then he abruptly sat down as if suddenly very weary. Blood gouted from his mouth. Cormac brought the targeting frame onto his head, triggered again and watched the top of Pramer's skull disappear, then turned to exit the room. Now he was suddenly angry, and not entirely sure why.

Gorman stood poised by the next door.

'*We've got her,*' Travis informed them all.

Gorman leant around the door jamb and fired twice. 'Okay,' he said, 'we're out of here – fast.'

Gorman was past him and heading back along the cave at a run before Cormac realized it was over – they'd got what they'd come here for. For no reason he could quite fathom he ducked into Pramer's room, studied the man for a short moment then picked up his thin-gun. A trophy? He felt that to be so, but no trophy of any victory. He turned and followed Gorman, for a moment feeling utterly bewildered. Pulse-gun fire issued from behind. He turned, fired, saw someone fold up. No need to check targets now.

In moments they reached the junction where Crean stood firing intermittently back down the way she had come. Travis stood there with a body slung easily over one shoulder, nodded to Gorman and Cormac, then broke into a fast run for the exit. As they followed him out, Cormac noticed Gorman removing a short black cylinder from a pouch on his belt. He primed this with his thumb then sent it skittering back into the cave. Cormac recognized the item: gas grenade, probably Hazon. In a moment they were outside and moving back into the trees, the mosquito still poised at the cave entrance behind them to finish any who made it that far.

'Good work, people,' said Gorman.

Cormac wondered who would come here to clear up the mess. Certainly someone would come, for there might be information in there useful to ECS. He wondered momentarily if the cave would then be sealed. Probably not; they'd just take what might be of use and burn the bodies.

As they headed down into the trees Cormac heard yelling, and the mosquito opening fire. He didn't look back.

It being imperative the prisoner stayed alive, no lethal weapons were to be put within her reach, so Cormac and Gorman armed themselves with stun batons only. Cormac thought it all a bit over the top – but then he had been a captive too, and look what he had managed to do. Gorman was smoking one of his big cigars, a contented look upon his face as he digested the huge chicken madras he had eaten, tempered only by the fact that he had been unable to wash it down with numerous beers. But later, he had said, they'd drink some beer later.

'We normally don't get to see this side of things,' he announced.

'Then why are we seeing it now?'

'This is for you,' Gorman replied. 'I've seen it before and know what's involved, but you haven't. ECS likes its Sparkind to be thoroughly aware of the consequences of what they do. None of this "I didn't know" or "I was only following orders". You can choose to leave the military at any time, you know?'

The cell-block corridor appeared little different to how such corridors had looked for hundreds of years, though someone from a past age might have mistaken the pendent ceiling drones for light fittings. Cormac and Gorman halted at an armoured door with a screen display fixed centrally. Gorman tapped the screen and it came on, showing the interior of the cell and reassuring them that the prisoner wasn't crouched beside the door ready to jump them. It seemed unlikely she would be in any condition to do so, though, since she would still be suffering the aftereffects of stun toxin and a robust scanning routine. Gorman pressed his hand against the side palm lock, the door swished open silently and they stepped inside.

A bed, washbasin and toilet were provided. The bed was fixed to the floor and the washbasin was a flimsy thing that folded down from the wall. Neither of these items offered an opportunity for the prisoner to hang herself, just as the bed possessed no sheets that could be turned into ropes and the paperwear she wore consisted of a tissue that turned powdery when torn. Also, there were no sharp edges to be found in here, nor anything that could be turned into a sharp edge. Via pin cameras positioned up in every corner of the room the prison submind kept perpetual watch, and other hardware in the walls monitored the prisoner's vital signs. ECS did not want its captives to die here, though it had been known to happen. Gorman had already related to Cormac a tale of the man who managed to drown himself with his own urine, though he was revived shortly afterwards, and a story about a woman managing to tear out her own jugular artery.

'Hello soldier Cormac,' said Sheen, easing herself upright and swinging her legs off the bed. He noted that she looked bruised, and there were a couple of raw spots on the skin of her bare arms. However, no one had beaten her – the marks were a result of the full-spectrum scan she had undergone, just to be sure she had no pieces of syntheskin attached about her body. They had learned their lesson with Carl.

'Stand up,' said Gorman, then removed his cigar butt from his mouth, dropped it to the floor and crushed it out.

'No civilities then?' Sheen enquired.

173

She still looked like a teenager, but the information they had available put her age at fifty-two. Her present appearance was the result of cosmetic work, perpetually maintained by whatever suite of nanomachines she was running.

'You heard the man,' Cormac said. 'You can walk out of here or we can carry you out of here – makes no difference to me.'

'Ooh, tough talk.'

'Zap her on the tit – that usually gets their attention,' said Gorman.

Cormac began to step forward, but Sheen abruptly lurched to her feet. He and Gorman moved in on either side of her, Gorman closing a hand just above her elbow, his stun baton held in his other hand casually down at his side.

'Let's go.' He marched her towards the door, Cormac, as instructed earlier, falling in two paces behind Sheen.

'You have to keep them off balance,' Gorman had also told him earlier. 'If they're untrained, you usually have no problem because they continue to maintain the hope that somehow they're going to survive, to get away with what they've done, or that ECS might be forgiving if they cooperate.' He had paused for a moment to spread a piece of poppadom with lime chutney and then chomp it, washing it down with a swallow of fresh mango juice. 'This one isn't going to be like that. She's trained and she's wily, and she knows no one gets given amnesty by ECS. Ever. She'll go for one of us once we leave the cell corridor and step outside the range of the security drones there, and she'll fight for her life knowing that if she loses, that life is certainly forfeit.'

At the end of the cell corridor the door stood open. Gorman turned her into the corridor beyond. Sheen lurched sideways as if losing balance, then turned, her foot coming up in an arc towards Cormac's head. It was smoothly done. Perhaps she hoped Gorman would lose his grip and that she would have time to relieve Cormac, obviously the less experienced of the two, of his baton.

Gorman's grip was iron. He turned slightly, dragging her truly off balance whilst planting a foot against the back of the foot she kept on the ground. As she started to go over backwards, her kicking foot coming well short of its target, Gorman casually touched the baton to her chest.

Sheen gasped, then hit the floor on her back convulsing, her spine arched. Gorman and Cormac stepped forward to grab a wrist each, and they dragged her the rest of the way, leaving shreds of her paperwear clothing in the corridor behind.

Sheen never truly lost consciousness, though she did lose some awareness of what was happening to her and where she was. That awareness only returned once she was strapped on the surgical table. She focused first on Agent Spencer, who stood at her head fiddling with a pedestal-mounted autodoc, then on Gorman and Cormac who stood beside the door.

'I'll tell you nothing,' she said.

Gorman grinned, then groped about in his top pocket for a cigar, which he lit with an old petrol lighter.

'As you have recently experienced, Cormac, when an aug is installed,' Agent Spencer continued the explanation she had been making before Sheen's interruption, 'the patient cooperates in the interfacing process, enabling the aug software to recognize its targets and thus guide the nanofibres to synaptic connection.'

'Which takes me back to my previous point,' said Cormac. 'It's a difficult process to first install an aug, even with the recipient's cooperation, then a lengthy learning process afterwards to get it to work properly – the recipient's mind learns how to use the aug and the aug itself learns how to interpret the recipient's mind.'

'So I'm just meat now,' said Sheen. 'You're just going to ignore me?'

Agent Spencer picked up an item from a glass tray mounted

on the side of the autodoc. It was a large translucent plastic plug with a hole bored through the centre, attached to a skin-stick strap. Spencer kept it from Sheen's sight, which was easy enough with the Separatist's head being secured in a clamp.

'On the contrary, Sheen,' she said. 'You are a very valuable piece of meat and you are going to receive my utter attention over the next few hours.'

'You can't—' was all Sheen managed before Spencer leant across, clamped a hand on her chin, pushing her jaw down, and shoved the plug deep into her mouth, pressing the skin-stick strap down on her cheeks. Now all Sheen could do was make sounds from deep in her throat.

'It's to stop her swallowing her tongue,' Spencer explained. 'Or biting it off.' She now moved the autodoc into place beside Sheen's skull.

'You were saying?' Cormac enquired.

He'd been told the process was easier to conduct if the subject remained conscious. He understood that some would find all this rather distasteful, cruel even, and feel it something those of a civilized society should not do. Trying to feel some sympathy for Sheen, since they had fought together, he only felt cold. Criminals like Sheen tortured and killed with utter abandon, they ruined people's lives and, when they wanted information, they got out the blowtorch and disc grinder.

'Yes,' Spencer continued, 'interfacing with an aug is an act of cooperation. Limited synaptic contacts are made and both mind and aug learn to use the communication channels they provide. Increasing the amount of contacts can lead to problems: destructive feedback, destructive synergy of the kind that killed Iversus Skaidon when he invented runcible technology and, of course, organic damage. In this case we are worried about none of these.'

Cormac noted the sudden look of panic on Sheen's face. She'd just understood what Spencer intended doing to her. Perhaps she'd expected interrogation under drugs and torture, or maybe just a plain old execution, but ECS was more *civilized* than that.

'We'll be making multiple nanofibre connections, recording synaptic and neurochemical data all the while. The process records the structure, both architectural and neurochemical, of her brain, meanwhile building up a virtual model of it. It takes an AI then to deconstruct that model and interpret the data from that deconstruction as thoughts, images and memories.'

'And Sheen's brain?' asked Gorman, watching Cormac as he asked.

Spencer glanced up. 'It's mush afterwards. We maintain the connections to keep the autonomous nervous system going and the body is handed over to ECS Medical. I think they're trying now for direct download of recorded minds.'

Sheen's eyes were wide as she stared sideways at the autodoc. Terror? Maybe, though Cormac doubted she would be so scared of death. More likely she was frightened about all she was due to betray.

'Download?' queried Gorman. 'I'd heard it's theoretically possible . . .'

'I'm told the physical and neurochemical structure of the brain has to be changed to accept the mind in waiting,' said Spencer. 'It is actually restructured by nanomachine throughout the download process and takes some months.'

'Interesting,' said Gorman. 'I've been thinking about getting myself a memplant.' He tapped the side of his skull.

'Even more interesting if you ended up occupying the body of your killer,' Spencer quipped. She now tapped a control on top of the autodoc and it immediately extruded a probe like a chrome and glass tubeworm against the side of Sheen's head. She started yelling from the back of her throat, the sound made into an odd whine by the aperture of her mouth plug.

'Goodbye Sheen,' said Spencer. 'The next person you encounter will be the AI that takes apart your mind and turns it into a report for ECS.'

After a little while the sounds Sheen was making tapered off to a sighing. Cormac crossed his arms and watched for a short time.

'Is it necessary for us to be here any longer?' he finally enquired.

'Why?' asked Spencer. 'Are you uncomfortable with all this?'

'No, bored, and Gorman here was going to buy me a beer or two.'

Spencer waved her hand in dismissal.

Some hours later, Cormac returned, and watched the blank-faced drooling thing that had been Sheen being wheeled out on a gurney to be taken to the spaceport. He thought it good that in her new incarnation she would serve some useful purpose. Beyond that, his concern was nil.

'Waky waky,' said Gorman, slamming into the room and whipping the heat-sheet from Cormac's body – his presence turning on the light.

Cormac's instincts told him he had been asleep for about thirty seconds, but his aug told him precisely fifty-five minutes had passed since his consciousness fled into the pillow.

His instincts also told him his immediate course of action should be to punch Gorman on the nose, turn off the light and return to bed. However, he swung his legs over the side and sat on its edge for a moment, deliberately not swearing at his unit leader, since that was precisely what Gorman expected.

'Some problem?' Cormac asked.

'Get your stuff together,' said Gorman, scanning the room's sparse collection of belongings and frowning. 'We're shipping out.'

'Why?'

'Apparently Agent Spencer will be giving us chapter and verse aboard the attack ship,' Gorman explained.

Now Cormac did swear, and his unit leader grinned. He had obviously known that if the fact that they were still under orders from Spencer wasn't enough to get a reaction, then knowing they would shortly be aboard an attack ship would. His work done, Gorman now departed, whistling tunelessly and leaving the door open behind him.

Cormac stood up, walked over to close the door, then returned to his bedside locker from which he removed a self-heating coffee and a stim-patch. He pulled the tab on the coffee and set it down, and after stripping off its backing pressed the stim-patch down on his forearm. He pulled on disposable undergarments, his enviro-suit and then dragged his pack out of a cupboard, into which it took him only a moment to shove a few more belongings, by which time the stimulant was kicking in and the coffee steaming. Next he released his pulse-rifle from its coded rack by pressing his hand against the palm lock beside it. The clamps dropped open and he took the weapon out and hung it by its strap from his shoulder. From under his pillow he took Pramer's thin-gun, which he shoved into his belt, then he was ready – just in time to receive a demand through his aug for his presence outside the barracks. Sipping hot coffee, he headed out.

Gorman, Travis and Crean awaited him in the darkness outside, standing beside a low-slung ATV with big smooth tyres, its chameleon-paint body only revealed in this darkness by its scratches and unpainted replacement components. He noted that only Gorman possessed a pack, which lay on the plasticrete grating beside his leg. The two Golem carried nothing, not even weapons, and they wore chameleoncloth fatigues oversuited with white paper-wear for courtesy's sake. Upon seeing Cormac, Gorman hoisted up his pack, turned to the ATV and pulled open its side door to reveal the lit interior. It seemed almost as if he was opening a door in the very darkness. He climbed inside, Crean and Travis following. Cormac took the opportunity to employ a visual enhancement program in his aug, which made everything surrounding him more visible but turned the body of the ATV into something that kept flickering in and out of visibility. When he ducked into the vehicle he saw that Gorman and Crean had taken the two front seats, Gorman in the driving seat, whilst the two behind were for himself and Travis. Cormac shoved his pack in the space behind the remaining seat and climbed in, closing the door behind him.

'Where to?' he asked.

'Where you came in,' Gorman replied, immediately setting the ATV into motion.

The landing field was fifty miles from here, so Cormac could not understand why they were using a ground vehicle to head for an apparently urgent rendezvous there. He didn't have time to ask just then, as he quickly strapped himself in before Gorman threw the ATV round the corner at the end of the street. The vehicle, with its computer controlling suspension, tyre pressure, individual wheel torque and the actual grip of the tyres, shot around the corner as if on rails and continued accelerating.

'Okay,' he said, 'why on the ground?'

'Travis,' said Gorman, concentrating on his driving.

The Apollonian Golem turned to Cormac. 'Though you are the prime target, having offed a considerable number of Separatists here, those surviving won't balk at killing us too, since we are also responsible for many deaths.'

'It's still not clear to me why we're not flying.'

'Agent Spencer's departing gift to the forces here was to request our presence over an uncoded channel,' Travis explained.

'Sheen's deconstruction has revealed that the remaining Separatists here have missile launchers concealed within the vicinity. The AI has calculated a high probability that a launcher will be deployed to shoot at the automated gravcar that will depart in about four minutes.'

'I see,' said Cormac, awaiting further explanation but receiving none.

Gorman had now taken them into a track winding between the carnage of felled skarches left by the crash-landing of the Prador vessel. All around lay a jumble of thick trunks draped in dry leaves, jags of cellulose spearing into the air and trailing fibres like frayed rope, the whole scene scattered with the bright yellow-green of new sprouts stretching up towards the sky. Even with augmentation all this was only just visible through the screen – Gorman had not put on the lights so had to be also using his own visual augmentation. Soon the track began winding to the left around a hill, past a couple of parked autodozers which had been used to clear the track, then turning uphill. Here, where the hill had sheltered the area from the direct shockwave from the crash landing, the skarches were still standing, and beginning to sprout grassy yellow flowers. Upon reaching the top of the hill, however, they found it utterly clear of vegetation. Gorman skidded the vehicle to a stop and disengaged the drive.

'How long?' he asked.

'About a minute,' Crean replied.

'Let's take a look then,' he said, turning to Cormac, who opened the door.

They climbed out into a sultry evening, some local animal making a gobbling sound from downslope in a deadfall. Gorman nodded to a nearby stone promontory and led the way up on to it. From here they could see the pattern of felled skarches spearing inland to where the Prador ship had come down. The vessel was invisible behind the distant hills of detritus it had thrown up, but the work lights created a sunrise glow over there. Directly below them lay the military township, partially conjoined to the shore city, and beyond lay the sea, a couple of ships and some smaller boats visible upon it.

'It could be right here, you know,' commented Travis.

'I doubt it,' said Gorman, 'but let's hope not.' He added, 'Here it comes.'

Even as he spoke a gravcar rose from the township, its navigation lights switching on as it accelerated up and out to the left of them. Almost immediately there came a flash down in the skarch wreckage, perhaps two or three miles to their right, and a dim spot of light ascended, curved over, and began heading towards the car.

'Close,' said Gorman, 'but I win, I think.'

Something flickered and the missile briefly trailed a luminescent green cloud before, with a thunderclap, turning into a long cloud of fire.

'Laser,' commented Travis.

'Now the bet is on as to whether—'

There now came another thunderous crash to their right from the missile's launch site. Peering over there Cormac saw the ground seem to bubble up for a moment then erupt in a localized explosion.

'Rail-gun strike,' he said, just to try and feel part of all this.

'Exactly,' said Travis, turning to Gorman, 'which negates the bet.' He grinned crazily. 'You thought it would use a particle beam.'

Gorman shrugged. 'Fifty-fifty really, once it was located outside of any populated areas.'

'And if it had been fired from the city?' Cormac enquired.

Gorman turned to him. 'We had squads decked out in night gear ready to move in once the power supply in the grid area concerned was cut.'

Cormac nodded. They had known all this was going to happen and had been making bets on how it would happen. It all brought home to him that though he was officially the fourth man in this Sparkind unit, he was not really part of it yet.

'Let's go,' said Gorman.

They returned to the ATV to continue their journey to the makeshift spaceport. As Cormac stepped inside the vehicle after the others, he pulled the stim-patch from his arm and discarded it, reclined his seat and was soon dozing fitfully, only coming fully awake an hour later as they arrived at their destination. Through the screen he saw a ship down on the acres of plasticrete: a lumpen vessel like a giant beetle, battle-scarred and old, with ramps down from which currently gravtrucks were disembarking. The four departed the ATV and began heading towards this vessel.

'I would have liked to have bet on both the firing position of that launcher and the weapon deployed against it from orbit,' he commented to Gorman.

'Would you have won?' Gorman asked.

'Yes,' said Cormac. 'They would have wanted to be close to the city to fire the missile but not actually in the city where they could be located and apprehended. If they'd known we had anything up there capable of taking them out, they wouldn't have fired at all. And a rail-gun strike was used because though it would kill whoever was near the launcher, it would leave evidence for investigation, whereas a particle-beam strike would have incinerated everything.' Cormac paused for a moment, before continuing coldly, 'Also the beam strike might well have started a fire in all that dead skarch wood that would have required further resources to extinguish.'

'Good job we didn't include you,' said Gorman.

'Why didn't you include me?'

'There was no certainty you would be coming offworld with

us until just ten minutes before we left – it seemed the AIs were having some debate about that.'

'Why am I coming with you?'

'Two reasons,' Gorman replied. 'The first concerns our mission to capture Sheen. I've seen the analysis of everything that happened in there. You killed Pramer – without much hesitation it would seem.'

'And the second reason.'

'I'll leave Agent Spencer to tell you about that.'

Soon they were aboard the large shuttle and ensconced in one of its cabins with the Polity agent. The explanation was quite simple:

'Carl Thrace,' Spencer supplied.

The cabin was cramped and seemed as packed with equipment as Spencer's office down in the military encampment. The two Golem stood back against one wall whilst Gorman snagged the only free chair and Cormac sat on a plasmel crate which, by its label, contained fragmentation grenades. Cormac wondered if Spencer dragged around a collection of stuff like this wherever she went, or if she had merely taken a cabin previously vacated by another of her kind.

When no one else seemed inclined to ask, Cormac enquired, 'What about him?'

Spencer was sitting at a cluttered desk gazing at a screen, occasionally pressing buttons and manipulating a ball-control she held in her right hand. 'After searching through millions of hours of scan data, the Hagren AI eventually managed to track his course from when he abandoned you in the Dramewood,' she said, still paying attention to the screen. 'The ATV delivered him to a rendezvous with an old hydrocar limousine' – now she did look up – 'driven by Sheen, who took him to a guest house in the old city. The data showed no sign of him leaving the guest house, but Sheen was kind enough to inform us that as well as having syntheflesh patches for concealing weaponry, Carl has a whole kit for drastically altering his appearance. The AI checked its recordings and tracked everyone who left the hotel – all but one have been tracked down and eliminated from the search.' She now turned her screen towards them all to show a portly individual with yellowish and slightly scaly skin, and mouth tendrils that wound into a large spadelike beard. He was clad in brown leather and wore a leather trilby. 'He's calling himself Marcus Spengler now.'

'I'm still not quite sure why I'm here,' said Cormac.

Spencer eyed him for a moment. 'There was some discussion about whether to allow you to continue in the Sparkind. Though you have shown an aptitude for the job, your training is lacking. The powers that be were considering sending you for further training whilst the rest of your unit' – she flicked a glance at the other three – 'took a vacation.'

'Damn,' said Gorman. 'What made 'em change their minds?'

The room lurched at that moment and a deep vibration shook the vessel they were aboard. There was no doubt it was now launching.

'My request changed their minds,' Spencer replied. 'My aim is to bring Carl Thrace down and I prefer to work with those whose methods I'm familiar with.' She glanced at Cormac. 'I wanted Cormac included for two reasons: having known Carl for two years he might well be able to identify him despite any disguise but, most importantly, Carl Thrace will recognize Cormac.'

Bait, thought Cormac.

'I take it Thrace has left Hagren?' suggested Travis.

'After leaving the guest house,' Spencer replied, 'he headed for the inland commercial spaceport and boarded a small but very fast light-cargo hauler.'

'Smugglers,' said Gorman.

Spencer nodded. 'Almost certainly, since that ship's destination seems to be the Graveyard.'

Gorman cursed, and Cormac understood his reasons.

'Get some rest now,' said Spencer. 'We dock with the *Sadist* in three hours.'

'The *Sadist*?' Travis enquired.

'AI humour,' said Spencer, 'go figure.' She waved them away.

After Spencer had dismissed them, Cormac received a message in his aug from the ship's AI giving a schematic of the ship itself and in that the location of a cabin he could use for the brief time he was aboard. Crean and Travis headed off somewhere else in the ship, perhaps to occupy themselves with Golemish things while the soft humans of their unit sought home comforts and sleep. Gorman accompanied Cormac, since his own cabin was nearby. As they walked, Cormac considered everything he knew about the Graveyard. Originally this borderland and buffer zone between Prador and Human space had been called the Badlands, but the name was soon dropped in favour of the more accurate description. Polity AIs did not intervene there or, rather, they did not intervene overtly, beyond sending in the odd warship to drive off Prador vessels that were getting too close to the Polity for comfort. The place had become home for some nasty types, but the worlds and stations they occupied were few in number compared to the other once-habitable worlds that could now be described as war graves.

'It should be an interesting experience trying to find him there,' Cormac opined.

Gorman snorted derisively. 'You can bet it'll get dirty and bloody within an hour of us making landfall.'

Cormac paused by the door to his cabin and Gorman slapped him on the shoulder before continuing on to his. 'Get your head down, boy – you're going to need your rest.'

Cormac pressed his hand against the palm-lock and the door slid open. He stepped inside and looked around, feeling a grab almost of nostalgia on seeing that he had been given a four-berth cabin just like the one he, Carl, Yallow and Olkennon had arrived at Hagren in. Obviously this ship, having dropped off its passengers, had room to spare. He dumped his pack and his pulse-rifle on an empty bunk, then stepped over to the wall to pull the screen remote from its slot and turn on the room screen.

Immediately the screen showed an image of the ground far below and quickly receding. The old city and the military township were no longer visible, though the crash site of the Prador vessel showed as a shape like a small eye just inland. Trying a few other views, he got the curve of the horizon and the glint of one or two objects in orbit. Magnification brought into focus a coin-shaped satellite and a ship shaped like a canal barge with three U-space nacelles jutting equidistantly on vanes at its rear. It was an old-style attack ship and he wondered if it was the *Sadist*. Logging on to his present ship's server he requested details on all ships in the vicinity and discovered that it was. He peered down at the remote, found a touch control marked 'voice' and pressed it.

'Ship,' he said, 'can you hear me?'

'Of course I can hear you,' replied the voice of a grumpy old woman, 'and my name is Pearl.'

'Nice to . . . be aboard you, Pearl,' Cormac replied. 'Can you tell me why it is going to take us three hours to dock with the *Sadist* when it's clearly visible out there?'

'The attack ship is waiting on further targets below and, for our own safety, it's best not to dock when it might open fire at any moment.'

'Fair enough.'

'Is that all?'

Cormac considered something else he'd been delaying for some time. 'I would like to send a message to Earth . . .'

'And you're telling me this why?'

'I . . . I've never done this before.' He felt a bit stupid, for he knew how to go about sending a simple message, even if it was over a vast distance. The truth was that he wanted to talk to someone about it. However, this AI's attitude did not encourage conversation.

'Simple enough,' said the *Pearl* AI, 'you just address it correctly and send it to my server where it'll sit in the queue until I make my next U-space transmission, which should be in about three minutes. Now is *that* all?'

'That's it, thank you.' Cormac hurriedly thumbed the 'voice' control again.

Now he sat on one of the bunks and called up the message in his third eye to review it. First he described his journey from the training camp on Mars to Hagren, then he went on to describe some of what had happened on that world, though his internal censor had been working overtime. As he reviewed it, he wondered if this was the same sort of message his father had send to Hannah whilst he had been away fighting the Prador. At the end of the message came the part of most importance to him:

Having been promoted to the Sparkind it has been necessary for me to have an augmentation fitted, and only during this process did I discover that my mind has been edited. The medical data indicates this was done to me when I was between the ages of eight and twelve, but since there was so much editing going on during the Prador war, the AIs did not feel it necessary to keep detailed records. I know no more than that memories have been extracted from my mind and remaining memories of the time have been 'cut and pasted'. What can you tell me about this, Mother? Which of my memories did you feel it necessary for you to destroy?

For some time he had been toying with the wording of this last bit, unsure if he was being too harsh, or not harsh enough. In the end he placed it in a packet file, attached his mother's net address, and sent it. There: it was done now. Cormac rested back on the bunk and tried to catch up on his sleep.

It evaded him.

10

Cormac gazed at the image on his new p-top. Its screensaver showed scenes from an encounter between one of the big Prador dreadnoughts and the *My Mary Rose* out in deep space, where usually the crabs won. It was a slugging match: massively powerful weapons being deployed by both ships, shield generators burning out on both of them and poxing them with fires, bigger and bigger weapons getting through defences so the two ships strewed armour and molten metal across a couple of million miles of void. Then came the big CTD hit straight in a particle-beam hole bored through the Prador vessel's hull. The explosion gutted it, leaving only the heavy-armour hull to tumble glowing through space like a mollusc from which the soft body had been scraped out.

But it was old news.

New weapons being deployed at the wavering line of defence had been having a positive effect for over a year. The latest ships from the factory stations, their armour as effective as that of the Prador dreadnoughts, were fighting direct one-to-one engagements and winning, and this recording was of the first of those. Now there were many new recordings of similar events and more coming in every day. Cormac consigned the recording to memory and pulled up another one of a ground conflict in which mosquito autoguns were hammering into a line of Prador second-children. It was a messy but satisfying scene.

Even to Cormac it was noticeable that the holographic three-dee maps of the Polity had begun to display appreciable areas of regained territory. And now stories were appearing about worlds that had been occupied by the Prador and incommunicado since before he was born, and he viewed them with the utterly morbid curiosity of a ten-year-old.

When it was possible for any ECS trooper wearing an aug to easily record thousands upon thousands of hours of sensory data – and transmit that data directly onto the nets once within range of a suitable server – it wasn't so much impossible for the AIs to keep a lid on the news, but a pointless exercise. Better, they thought, for people to know what was really happening than to let the rumour mills fill the void. Censorship, which had been forever placed in the hands of the end-user, was mostly applied by parents to what their children were viewing. However, since access to information was universally easy, it was almost a rite of passage for most children to find their way around parental blocks. Cormac had long ago looped his mother Hannah's censorship programs and now watched whatever he desired.

It seemed that on these worlds Prador adults had ensconced themselves like feudal lords amidst their own kind, but the position of humanity had been little better than that of cattle in some previous human age. Cormac observed the drone recordings of huge camps like those seen in human genocides – but noted a lack of bodies not because few people died there but because those guarding the camps simply ate the corpses. However, he did glimpse one recording broadcast by some ECS ground troops of a massive abattoir containing row upon row of gutted human corpses hanging on hooks. He also saw the initial pictures of the release of some captives – these ones were bulky with fat and could hardly carry their own weight, for the Prador had been keeping them like veal calves. It was also the case that many of these captives knew of the Polity only as a word-of-mouth story passed down to them by their parents, for many of them had known nothing but the camps and Prador rule.

'Anything new?' asked Osiah.

Cormac glanced up from his p-top at his friend. Osiah was

working on a missive back home to his extended family – a combination of audio, video and holographic recording with explanatory texts that could be accessed throughout it all. He wanted to be a documentary maker, and in the year Cormac had known him it seemed not a moment passed when he wasn't either recording, or editing those recordings.

'You can check for yourself,' Cormac replied.

'But I want you to tell me – don't give me news, give me reactions to news.'

Cormac shook his head and closed up his p-top. He was bored now and bubbling with energy, which was good, since soon he would be having an hour of zero-gee training, usually followed by a handball match in the same gym.

Zero-gee training, familiarization with station and ship safety protocols, were the main reasons for them coming to the orbital school, but their days were also filled with numerous other lessons covering all aspects of extraplanetary existence. Cormac found that his underwater swimming at Tritonia had stood him in good stead for most disciplines. He was good in zero-gee, with spacesuits and with most of the safety stuff regarding vacuum and pressure changes, since a lot of it applied to diving. He was less able when the lessons concerned solar radiation, field technology and the mechanics of space travel.

'Y'know we're well advanced compared to kids our age a few centuries back,' Osiah once told him. 'Back then we would still be playing with plastic toys.'

Cormac had investigated this and been astounded at how dim the children of past ages had been, soon discovering that his own advantages were due to the AI redesign of education methods. It seemed his mental development was at about that of the late teens of the heavily politicized education systems of the twenty-first century. Damn, kids of ten back then didn't even know about simple stuff like vector analysis. Some of them couldn't even read and write their own language, let alone the three or four that most of Cormac's contemporaries managed. And none of them were much good at the sciences and, strangely, didn't really like learning them.

There was no sudden announcement that it was all over. During his first two months at orbital school Cormac was too involved in his lessons and zero-gee handball to take much notice of the news. When he again started checking, he found that for the past two months the news services had been full of reports of some kind of internecine conflict within the Prador Second Kingdom, and of their dreadnoughts pulling off from attacks and heading back there. Then, just a month before his eleventh birthday, Cormac realized that though plenty of Polity victories were detailed, they were usually over Prador first- and second-child ground armies abandoned by their support ships. Then, after his birthday, it seemed that past stories of battles and atrocities were being recycled. Nothing much was going on out there. Upon his return to Earth he discovered that there had been a revolution within the Prador Second Kingdom, that the king had been usurped and many other ruling Prador slaughtered, and that it was now called the Prador Third Kingdom.

'I think the war is over,' said his mother one day.

Cormac nodded, for so it seemed. The Prador had withdrawn behind their original border and were building defensive stations, whilst on the Polity side similar construction was taking place. There had also been as yet unconfirmed rumours of tense meetings between Polity and Prador ambassadors.

'You understand that your father won't be coming home,' Hannah continued.

Cormac nodded again. He was not sure when this had become evident to him, maybe a year or so back about the time Dax had last visited, but he couldn't remember being told.

'He's dead,' he said.

'Yes,' Hannah confirmed, though there was something in her expression Cormac found difficult to fathom. He did not pursue it – there seemed no need.

The interior of the *Sadist* rather belied its ominous name, and whereas Pearl had been a crotchety AI, Sadist was chatty and cheerful.

'Welcome aboard!' it boomed from the intercom system the moment they stepped into its thickly carpeted interior.

Cormac immediately received a schematic of the ship's interior and directions to his cabin. 'Cheerful AI,' he observed.

'Probably enjoys its work,' said Gorman, 'if its choice of name is any indication.'

'I've some stuff arriving in the hold here that I need to check over,' said Spencer. She stabbed a finger at Cormac. 'We're five days away from the Graveyard, and in that time I want him to lose that rod up his arse.' She turned and headed off.

'The rod up my arse?' Cormac enquired.

'Your military bearing, my son,' said Gorman. 'It was fine enough on Hagren where your cover included you being a soldier, but if we go undercover in the Graveyard, you'd be spotted in an instant.'

'It's all those marching drills,' said Crean dryly.

'Yeah, right,' said Cormac, never having marched in his life.

Travis patted him on the shoulder. 'You need to slouch a bit more, maybe acquire one or two bad habits – seemed to work for Gorman.'

The four of them headed off down a corridor thick with carpet grass. At intervals framed pictures hung on the walls, each displaying what looked like Egyptian papyrus scrolls that were certainly copies. Soon they arrived at a row of doorways – Cormac halted before his.

'We'll meet up in the midship training area in half an hour,' said Gorman. 'Meanwhile, take a look at this.' A message arrived in Cormac's aug.

The luxurious accommodation contained a wide bed, plenty of cupboard space, an en suite bathroom and even his own dispensary port from the ship's synthesizer. He dumped his pack and rifle on the bed and immediately turned back to the dispensary, since he had not eaten in some hours. First he got himself a coffee, which arrived behind the chainglass hatch in a porcelain cup and saucer, then, checking through the menu, he found that just about anything was available from the ship's synthesizers. He ordered a bacon sandwich in rye bread, which arrived whilst he sipped his coffee. The sandwich tasted wonderful, though what it contained had never come from a pig.

Whilst on his second sandwich and second coffee, he opened the message Gorman had sent, which was empty, then the attached file. Therein lay the main factors that could identify someone as a soldier. Some things he could do nothing about – he could not unlearn his familiarity with weapons. The rest was about speech patterns, combat techniques, choice of nutrition, neatness and the importance of slouching and bad habits. After skimming through the extensive lists, he headed over to his pack then opened it and upended it on his bed. From the contents he pulled out his casual clothing of jeans and a sleeveless light-blue shirt and, after stripping off his uniform, donned these, retaining only his enviroboots – nothing in the list about wearing crappy foot-wear. He then headed for the door, deliberately leaving the mess on his bed and deliberately not putting his cup and plate into the waste port next to the dispenser. Then he slouched down the corridor.

Gorman and Crean were awaiting him, both of them dressed casually. Gorman wore baggy black trousers and a brightly col-oured Indian shirt, whilst Crean wore karate slippers, white com-bat trousers and a tight little green top that exposed both an expanse of cleavage and her flat stomach. Certainly she possessed assets that might distract anyone seeing her from being suspicious of who or what she was, and her chameleonware should be able to fool most scanners. However, her emulation wasn't perfect – Cormac had yet to see a Golem he did not recognize as a Golem, and guessed there were many others like him.

The training area was merely a cylindrical room with a hard floor and numerous lockers about the circumference, doubtless packed with training equipment. Cormac surveyed it all as he walked out and stopped before the other two. Smiling, Crean stepped up close to him and, despite her being a Golem, when she reached up and began running a finger around one nipple jutting against the fabric of her shirt, he could not help but be distracted. The next thing he knew her other hand had closed around his testicles and squeezed, hard, just prior to her forehead slamming into his nose, then she kicked his feet out from underneath him and stepped away.

'Now,' she said, whilst Gorman looked on grinning, his arms crossed, 'you are going to learn how to fight dirty.'

The analgesic patches had taken the sting out of his grazes and bruises, the repair to his front teeth was invisible, and the ache in his foot would fade once the bone and cell welding had settled. He had learned a lot over the last four days. Certainly there were the specifics, like which brands of drink came in breakable bottles and therefore could be broken on the edge of a table and shoved in an opponent's face, but generally it was an attitude. Everything was a weapon from spittle to drinking straws, and it was always better to take the initiative: if it looked like a situation was about to turn violent, better for it to be *you* that turned that situation violent. He had learned something else too: knowing the difference between Golem emulation of humanity and humanity itself was not quite so cut and dried as he had liked to believe. Crean sweated, she smelt of woman, and grappling with her it was sometimes difficult for him to keep his mind on fighting techniques.

Cormac took a long slow breath. He needed a shower, but first he turned on the room screen and gazed at the world the *Sadist* had now fallen into orbit about. Apparently Polity operatives scattered throughout the Graveyard had been told to keep watch for the light-cargo hauler Carl had departed on, and it had been seen landing here. Cormac was about to apply to the ship's server for details about this world when there came a tap at his door.

'Come in,' he said, without looking round.

'How's the foot?'

Cormac looked round to see Crean standing there. She was still dressed in the skin-tight low-cut top and similarly clinging leggings she had been wearing earlier, whilst taking him through the finer points of kick-boxing with your hands tied behind your back. He had broken his foot on her hip.

'All stuck back together again, though still aching a little,' he replied. 'I'd ask you how your hip was, if it weren't for the fact that your bones don't break and you don't bruise.'

'Now,' she held up a finger, 'you're only half right. Look.' She took hold of the top of her leggings and pulled them right down to show her hip, incidentally exposing the side of her pubis and neatly waxed traditional Brazilian-style pubic hair . . . or was it waxed? Cormac didn't know whether synthetic Golem hair grew. It seemed crazy to him that they would want growing hair, but then it seemed odd that they emulated flawed humanity. After a moment he focused on what she was supposed to be showing him: a growing bruise on her hip.

'Does it hurt?' he asked, a catch in his voice. He could not help but notice that her nipples, invisible when she entered his room, were now very definitely visible. Did she consciously control that, or was her emulation program an unconscious thing?

197

How deliberate was any of what she was now doing? It then occurred to him that men often asked themselves that last question about flesh-and-blood women.

She looked up. 'Yes, it hurts.'

'But it doesn't have to.'

'And that is different to you in what way?'

It was true. Cormac did not even have to put up with his foot aching, and many troopers he knew now possessed pain-management systems installed in their bodies. In fact, it was possible for him to manage pain through his aug, but he had yet to study those functions. He nodded acquiescence, and felt a surge of disappointment when she pulled the waist of her leggings back up into position. She walked over and stood with her arms akimbo, gazing up into his face.

'You've got a little bit of a problem with Golem, haven't you?' she suggested.

'No problem, as such . . .'

'But we're machines?'

'Yes . . .'

'And you're not?'

'Well . . .'

'I was programmed by an AI that could run a human mind inside itself as a sub-program,' she said. 'The way my mind operates is not any less human than yours just because its physical substance is a form of memory crystal. Honestly, Cormac, if you had not been told, you would never have known I was Golem.'

He could have argued that point, but right then he didn't want to: his own particular male programming was responding to her even though she wasn't human. He felt some reservations – a seedy part of his mind telling him that sex with her would be more like VR porn than the real thing, but then, VR porn had felt just as good . . .

'Here.' She reached up and pulled down her top to expose

those all too perfect breasts, reached out, took hold of his hands then pulled them up to her breasts. He squeezed gently, rubbed the nipples with his thumbs and she made a perfectly plausible little grunting sound. 'Human enough for you?' she enquired.

They were warm and taut, and certainly there was a part of his anatomy telling him there was no difference at all. She pushed closer to him, her expression coquettish as she undid his jeans and pulled them and his underwear down about his hips, then abruptly she slid down, took hold of his cock, ran her tongue around the end for a moment, then took it into her mouth, which felt sufficiently wet and warm.

'Is this part of my training?' he asked breathlessly.

She pulled away for a moment. 'My programming AI told me not to speak with my mouth full.' Then she abruptly stood, walked past him to the bed, where she stripped off her top and then her leggings, holding herself bent over for a moment before clambering onto the bed and rolling onto her back. She reached down and with slow leisure began playing with herself, watching him enquiringly as he hurriedly stripped off his clothes and rushed over to join her.

Throughout the ensuing hours they both acquired a few more bruises.

The *Sadist* had only left U-space for a moment when the ship's AI informed Cormac, 'I've got a message for you! It's from your mother!'

Cormac, who at that point had been lying back on his bed studying pictures of their new surroundings on his viewing screen and wishing Crean would come and join him, abruptly sat up and paid attention. He had half expected there to be no reply.

'What format is it?'

'I've got a video transmission along with another large file that looks like mem-code,' Sadist informed him.

He sat up even straighter then. Mem-code was how memories were stored, its format dependent on the human brain it had
been extracted from or destined for. Did this ship have the kind
of equipment he would require? It was certainly possible now to
implant such code – to allow people to live the memories – but
it usually had to be done under very controlled circumstances.
There were also augs out there that could do it, the Sensic range,
which were not recommended but which had not been made
illegal, since the AI view was that if you were stupid enough to
use one then that was your look-out. Many people did use them.
Many were addicted to experiencing other people's memories.
There was also an illegal trade in memories extracted from people
as they were tortured and murdered, though how some became
addicted to that, Cormac had no idea.

'Can you transmit both files to my aug?' he asked.

'I can transmit the video message to you, but not the mem-
code,' Sadist replied. 'The code file would be too large for the
storage in your aug.'

'Is there any way I can . . . load this code?'

'It is possible. The initial file would have to be divided into
three at preset chapter marks. I can then load them each to your
aug through an adapter, though after each you will need to take
a rest.'

'Why?'

'If these are, as I suspect, memories that have been edited
from your mind, when you re-experience them the contradictions
will give you an extreme headache,' Sadist explained. 'They will
not mesh with your mind – you'll experience them as actuality,
but afterwards will certainly have trouble integrating them.'

'I see.'

'It will also be necessary for you to seek permission from
Agent Spencer and your unit commander, since the process may
affect your performance.'

'Perhaps the video first?'

'To your augmentation or on your screen?'

'Send a copy to my aug, but also play it on the screen for me.'

The screen blinked on to show a frozen picture of his mother, Hannah. After a moment she jerked into motion, raising a hand to rub her forehead as if she had a headache. Then she looked up.

'Cormac,' she said, then paused for a long moment. 'I'm still not used to calling you that. I wonder if, after being in ECS now for a while, you've retained the habit of insisting people call you by your surname. Doubtless you have, since I rather suspect the habit was more firmly established in your mind by the editing process.'

Again a long pause.

'Yes, I did have your mind edited. It was perhaps a foolish thing to do, but I wasn't thinking straight back then anyhow. And once it was done there was no way of putting those memories back. Even now, it isn't really possible to restore them, especially after this lapse of time. Everything you are now is a structure built upon what went before, and by altering the shape of a building's foundations you risk toppling it.'

She smiled tiredly, and Cormac wished this was a direct link so he could point out how dependent a building was on its foundations, and how if you screwed with them in the first place the same building might not be stable anyway. But he rather suspected she knew that.

'I took you into the editing suite shortly after Dax departed to Cheyne III, when you were eight years old. I had received the news about your father . . . we had both received the news about your father, and at that time, the way I was, it was difficult enough for me to handle my own grief. On his second session in the suite even Dax had those memories deleted because he didn't want to deal with them then. As for you, it just seemed easier to relieve you of that pain. There is nothing advantageous about suffering—'

Cormac, having picked up the remote control, paused the video at that point and thought long and hard about what she had just said. At the end of the war he had understood that his father would not be coming home. This fact had penetrated his growing mind by some form of osmosis during the three years between his eighth and eleventh birthdays. Would it have been better if he had known at the time that his father had been killed? He thought yes. Here he utterly disagreed with his mother's assessment. Life, if you really wanted to *live* it, could be sometimes wonderful and sometimes hard, and he felt you couldn't fully appreciate the good stuff without experiencing the bad. He also felt that to get on in life, you also needed to acquire a few emotional calluses. She had been selfish and overprotective, but then, throughout history that had always seemed a parental prerogative. He started the recording running again.

'—and experiencing pain only hardens you, desensitizes you. That was how I thought about it all back then. I now understand I was just being selfish, like a parent giving an unruly child drugs to calm him down. Pain, whether physical or mental, always serves the purpose of teaching the recipient to avoid it, but more important than that, it can teach said recipient to empathize with the pain of others. We need pain to be human.'

Abruptly his mother shot up in his estimation of her, and though he resented what she had done, he could only forgive her.

'Along with this message I have attached a memcording of the memories excised from your mind. It comprises three incidents. However, it was impossible to include all the small alterations made to your memories or the natural tendency of the mind to fit things into a logical order.' Hannah grimaced, now gazing down at her clenched hands. 'I am told this is rather like what happens the moment you wake up from REM sleep. Your mind has been processing masses of unrelated rubbish, yet when you wake these masses are aligned in a coherent order, which we call dreams.'

Now she looked up. 'Experience these memories if you feel you must, but understand they are not the ending. I am not sure if there is an ending – the only way to find that out is from the horse's mouth . . . or to be more precise: the scorpion's. You need to speak to Amistad.'

What the hell?

'I hope you can forgive me, then perhaps I can forgive myself.'

The video feed froze.

Cormac sat staring at the screen for a moment, then rewound it and replayed the last bit again, then once more to be sure. No, he had no idea what she was talking about. The memories of when he first found out about his father's death had been edited from his mind. How could death be any more of an ending? And what had that drone got to do with it all? Cormac immediately began reviewing the information he had obtained about that drone, information that had been sitting untouched in his aug since the AI back on Hagren had found it for him.

The drone Amistad was apparently constructed in the infamous factory station Room 101. Certainly the AIs had so named that station because its intended use had been to turn out some of the nastiest cybernetic fighters of the war. A lot of experimental work was done there, and it was apparently where the first assassin drones were made. But most of the experimentation involved taking the minds of surviving drones, who in themselves had been quite nasty to have survived, and upgrading them with further traits useful in the fighting, like aggression, amorality and immorality. It might be apocryphal, but there were those who said that before it was destroyed by a Prador kamikaze – essentially a spaceship packed with CTDs and flown into the station by a Prador first-child – Room 101 was turning out the AI equivalent of psychopaths.

After his initiation in Room 101, twenty years before the end of the war, Amistad went off to the front, where he was involved in numerous vicious conflicts. However, the information Cormac had been given to cover that period was mainly sections of net-retrieved text. After studying them for a while longer he realized they were sections of aug text communications expanded to read-ability: *Sparkind unit 243v23 with drone support sent to Horia Caves. Minimal resistance encountered and now area B is secured. Enemy casualties: one first-child and fifteen second-children. Nix relevant intelligence. Nix relevant tech for Reverse Engineering.*

A further check of hyperlinks in the text gave him the names of those in the Sparkind unit, also revealing that 'drone support' had been Amistad alone. There were numerous entries like this, which only confirmed what he already knew: Amistad was a war drone. Then Cormac had a moment of inspiration, and using the integral search engine in the aug, searched for his father's name. Just two entries appeared:

*. . . I sent Sparkind units 243v20 through 243v28 to the Olston Peninsula sect. 104, with atmosphere gunship (*Vlad *and* Rickshaw*) support. They cleared sect. Enemy casualties: 3 first-children, 4000 second-children (est.). Own: 8 Humans, 3 Golem (2 minds retrieved). After Prador counter-attack: Lost: gunship* Vlad *with all personnel. Lost: all Sparkind units. Survivors: gunship* Rickshaw, *drone Amistad, SUC David Cormac. I tell you, it was a fucking nightmare . . .*

. . . Specialists SUC Cormac & drone Amistad report Prador snatch squads working in the area. The attack in the Hessick desert will give time for runcible evacuation of 10% population of Patience. South Hessick impossible. Advise clearance . . .

The Olston Peninsula, Cormac remembered, was one of those places Dax had been stationed. But was his memory of that con-versation overheard between his mother and Dax true? It seemed that after the disaster there, Amistad and his father had been recruited to some specialist unit. He wondered what 'Prador snatch squads' were, and immediately started a search. Nothing came up in his aug, but it offered him the option to link to 'local server'. He approved this and immediately got the bad news:

Prador snatch squads were those especially introduced by the Prador to capture humans alive for transportation back to the Second Kingdom, where they were used for entertainment or food. During the later years of the war, these same squads captured humans who were then transported to the planet Spatterjay, where they were infected with the local viral fibres which impart great physical toughness and durability. The purpose of so infecting these captives was to make them strong enough to physically survive Prador coring: a process whereby the brain and part of the spinal column is removed to be replaced by thrall technology.

Clear enough, he felt, and one of those horrifically grotesque things the Prador did that he still could not quite believe. Now, studying the rest of the entry, he called up data about the Hessick Campaign, which was the last Polity action his father had been involved in – the one he had died in. Though the final battle for planetary dominion had taken place on the ground in a region called Hessick County, which terminated in the Olston Peninsula, the deciding factor had been out in space. The Polity, it seemed, had expected to lose, but were fighting a delaying action so as to evacuate as much of the population as possible. However, after six months which had seen over a million humans dead (mostly civilian casualties) and an estimated two hundred thousand Prador, the tide turned with the assassination of two of the three Prador adults in charge on the ground. The remaining adult quickly retreated and headed for its dreadnought, which was hunting down Polity ships much further out in this Solar System. Whilst that adult was in transit from the planet to its distant ship, a new Polity dreadnought arrived and destroyed its shuttle, killing it. Further new Polity dreadnoughts arrived and began to get the upper hand. On the ground, the now headless armies of Prador gradually fell into disarray, but it still took a further month to defeat them.

That was the summation of it all, but there was a lot more available to Cormac if he wanted it. He chose another search, this time for 'South Hessick Clearance', and received an unexpected response: Access Restricted.

'Sadist,' Cormac enquired, 'why is access restricted to "South Hessick Clearance"?'

There was a long pause before the AI replied, 'It is restricted because it is restricted. If I tell you why, then I will be revealing what is restricted, won't I?'

Cormac contained his annoyance. It seemed he had gone as far as he could for the moment. His next option must be accessing his edited-out memories. He opened a familiar channel direct to Gorman's aug.

'Gorman,' he said, 'I need your permission—'

'You have fifteen hours,' Gorman interrupted. 'If Sadist estimates that you can recover within that time, then you can load one chapter of your excised memories. If there's any doubt of your performance coming up to scratch, then no chance.'

The channel closed.

11

Cormac and his mother, Hannah, were on their way back from the Fossil Gene Project excavation when she abruptly turned their gravcar. It tilted over, swinging round in a wide circle, and she peered past him towards the ground. He looked in the same direction and saw something down there, perambulating across the green. It looked big, its metal back segmented. As they flew above this object, it raised its front end off the ground and waved antennae at them, then raised one armoured claw as if to snip them out of the sky, clearly revealing itself as a giant iron scorpion.

'What's that?' he asked, supposing it some exotically shaped excavating machine controlled by the AI running the Fossil Gene Project.

With a frown his mother replied, 'War drone,' then abruptly used grav-braking to halt the gravcar in mid-air above the drone. Cormac tried to stand and peer down at it, but his mother grabbed his shoulder and pulled him down.

'Behave yourself or I'll put the child safeties back on.'

A war drone!

Ian Cormac tried to behave himself, but could not keep still in his seat as his mother now brought the car down towards the ground. They landed kicking up a cloud of dust and a scattering of dead leaves. Hannah shut down the car and peered through the cloud towards the drone's location. Shortly it became visible, approaching like some nightmare monster emerging from a sinister fog.

'You stay here,' she said, hauling herself up on the passenger cage and, without opening the door, clambering out.

'Aww,' Cormac whined.

She walked round to his side of the car, towards where the drone was approaching, and stabbed a finger at him, 'You stay there – these things might be fighting for us but some of them can be damned dangerous,' she said, then headed towards the drone.

Thirty feet out from the car the drone and his mother drew face to face, and Cormac felt a sudden rush of fear as the mechanical monster rose up above her, exposing its ribbed underside and forward legs. It reached towards the sky with its claws, as if again trying to catch hold of something invisible. She looked small and vulnerable before it, and he thought it was about to fall on her. Then she gestured with her flat hand, waving it towards the ground, and the drone dropped down again. Cormac had a feeling she had just told it off, but could not hear what she was saying.

The two stood talking for a short while, Hannah occasionally gesturing or the drone waving a claw in the air, but they were just far enough away for their conversation to be an indistinct noise with no single word clearly audible. Cormac fidgeted in his seat and wondered if he might be able to get away with climbing out and creeping up behind her.

'No!' his mother yelled, and abruptly collapsed to one knee as if her legs could no longer support her. The drone was still speaking, moving and snipping one claw to emphasize each point.

'Mother!'

Cormac scrambled from the gravcar and began moving hesitantly towards her. The drone dipped its nightmare head, antennae waving above Hannah, and said something further. Hannah immediately heaved herself to her feet and whirled round.

'Get back in the car!'

He had never seen her so angry, and could now see she was crying. He still hesitated.

'I won't tell you again!'

Cormac returned to the car, his stomach tightening and tears behind his eyes. As he climbed in he saw his mother turn once more to the drone, say something brief, then head over. The drone sat utterly motionless for a moment, then abruptly came after her. Upon reaching the car, Hannah turned on it.

'There's nothing else to be said,' she told it, almost choking as she spoke.

Cormac, tears abruptly forgotten, stared in fascination at the machine's peridot eyes, its slowly grating mandibles and what looked like missile and beam ports below its mouth.

'The boy should be told,' it intoned, its voice sonorous but with a hint of steel.

Hannah walked around the car, grabbed a passenger cage bar and heaved herself in. 'That is my decision.' She scrubbed away tears on her sleeve, reached out and engaged power then grasped the joystick, lifting the car from the ground.

The drone surged forward, its claw coming down with a crash right beside Cormac and closing on the top of the door. The car made a whining sound and tilted as it struggled to rise.

'I think I know more about what is best for my son than you,' said Hannah. 'As I understand it, with the one-oh-one classification you have, you shouldn't even have been allowed to come here. Release us. Now.'

The drone abruptly obeyed, and the car soared into the air.

'What should I be told?' asked Cormac.

Hannah slammed the joystick forward, but her shaking hand imparted its motion to the vehicle, which swayed from side to side through the air. Abruptly the safeties cut in, a single tongue of plastic folding out of the seat beside Cormac and closing around his waist, then a voice issued from the console.

'Are you experiencing difficulties, Hannah Lagrange?'

'I am,' she replied. 'Can you take me on automatic back to our house.'

'Done.' The car abruptly stabilized, now controlled by some remote AI, but Hannah kept her hand on the joystick.

'What was the drone talking about?' Cormac persisted.

'Be quiet,' she said mildly, reaching into her top pocket to take out her sunglasses and place them over her reddened eyes.

The campsite beside the lake soon came into view and Hannah said, 'Okay, I can take it from now on.'

This time, rather than land the gravcar beside their bubble house she took it into the carport, and upon landing there sent the instruction for the floor clamp to engage.

'Are we going?' Cormac asked.

'We certainly are,' his mother replied.

As they clambered out of the car he peered at the damage the drone had caused to the door, then hurried after his mother when she shouted for him.

The instant Cormac opened his eyes it felt as if someone was driving a dagger straight through his forehead. For a little while it was difficult to even think about the missing memory he had just experienced. His right eye seemed to be filled with a large black blob and zig-zag patterns were flashing in the left peripheral vision of his other eye. He groped to his right for the medical table, couldn't find it and so turned to look, feeling something dragging across his left shoulder.

There.

He snatched up a strip of three analgesic patches, peeled one from its backing and slapped it straight on one temple, then after a moment peeled another and stuck it on his neck.

'Careful of the optics,' Sadist warned him.

Only then did he remember the optic feed trailing across his shoulder. It had come as a surprise to him that the aug hinged open to reveal numerous optic plugs, that in fact most of its internal space was taken up with them and the device's computing hardware wasn't much bigger than the tip of his thumb.

'Can you initiate detach?' the ship's AI enquired.

'I don't think so,' Cormac managed.

'No problem.'

Words blinked fleetingly across his vision but he could identify none of them except 'CLOSED', which by some mental quirk went to join the zig-zags for a party.

'You may now remove the optics,' Sadist informed him.

He reached up, grabbed the bundle of fibre-optic threads plugging into his aug, and pulled. They detached easily and when he released them the device standing at his side, which bore only a passing resemblance to a pedestal autodoc, quickly wound them in, afterwards retreating across the med-bay to its alcove.

'How are you feeling?'

Cormac looked up and saw Gorman standing just inside the door. He hadn't heard him enter.

'Like someone's been scraping out the inside of my skull with a rusty knife.'

'Yeah, been there myself.'

Cormac gazed at him. 'Really?'

'They weren't my memories, but those of someone like Sheen,' Gorman replied. 'I'm told it made the process easier precisely because they weren't my memories. Didn't feel easy at the time.'

The pain was ebbing now, to be replaced by nausea. There were sick bags on the medical table. Cormac took up one, opened it then eased himself upright, immediately having to make use of the bag. A cool hand rested on the back of his neck as he finished and wiped his mouth with one of the tissues also provided.

'Was it worth it?'

He gazed at Crean in surprise, then looked around for Gorman. Where the hell had he gone? Then he remembered Sadist's

211

explanation of the likely aftereffects, a particular phrase about 'temporal dislocation' coming to the forefront of his mind.

'Ask me later,' he replied.

She took her hand away and, after what seemed only a moment, he looked up to find she had departed. His back aching, for he had obviously been sitting in the same position for some time, he eased himself back and lay down again.

So, the memory of his mother's encounter with the war drone Amistad had been excised from his mind. It now sat in his skull much clearer than the current memories of his childhood but refusing to integrate. After a moment, he realized that no, this was not a memory of his childhood, rather the memory of very recent experience. It did not fit because it was out of sequence and he was no child. Now he kept feeling that he was just too big; his hands and arms were like great lumps of meat and bone, and his testicles felt as if they were made out of lead. Some part of him wanted to cry, but was vetoed by the rest. The only feeling that did not seem contrary was his fascination with that drone, which seemed to have been reinforced.

His mother had removed this memory from his mind for, during that meeting, she had learned from the drone of the death of her husband. Why the machine had travelled many light-years to tell her, he could not fathom, nor could he fathom why she had not learned earlier in the conventional manner. Perhaps the death of Cormac's father had not been recorded by ECS and only the drone had known about it?

Reaching out to take up another sick bag, Cormac eased his legs off the surgical table and sat upright. Nausea surged through him, but he managed to hold on to what little was left in his stomach.

What, he wondered, would the other two chapters of excised memories contain? Since all three were about the death of his father and that news had been delivered in this one, were the other two just tidying-up exercises? It occurred to him that maybe he didn't need to experience those other memories and consequently suffer the horrible aftereffects. However, he knew once he had recovered and this sickness itself had become a memory, he would certainly want to experience those other two chapters.

He stood, a little unsteadily, and headed for the door. His right eye had cleared now and the flashing in the peripheral vision of his left eye broke up into disassociated dots. His headache, which the patches had driven away, was returning but manageable. Opening the door he turned into the corridor beyond and headed for his cabin, now trying to access his aug and use it to obtain information. First he found out the time, and realized that they must now be approaching their destination – a world called Shaparon, which had once supported a small colony of a million. The population was now only ten thousand, most of whom were previous residents but some of whom were those whose dealings were not looked on too kindly in the Polity itself – people who mostly kept to the periphery and often based themselves in places like this or retreated there when things got a bit too hot for them.

'*You've got four hours, Cormac, are you up to it?*' It seemed as if Gorman was speaking directly into his ear, but the question came via the military comlink channel of his aug.

'*I'm up to it.*'

'*Briefing in the gym in half an hour.*'

'*I'll be there.*'

Entering his cabin, Cormac first noted a large glass of some muddy orange drink sitting in the mouth of his synthesizer. He didn't recollect ordering anything, but then, there was no guarantee his memory was working properly.

'The drink will help,' Sadist abruptly informed him. 'If you can keep it down. It contains everything a growing boy should need, along with stimulants, anti-nausea medicine, anti-inflammatories and a tailored Valium.'

213

Cormac picked it up and gulped it, keeping it down by sheer effort of will. Then he lay down on his bunk, thinking nothing and moving not a muscle for twenty-five minutes, whereupon he heaved himself up again and headed for the gym.

'Our informant on the ground,' said Spencer, 'positively identified the ship Thrace took passage on and positively identified Thrace himself departing it.' She grimaced. 'Or rather our informant identified someone with the same appearance as Thrace when he departed that guest house back on Hagren.'

'Was he carrying any luggage?' Gorman asked.

Spencer glanced at him, then said, 'Sadist, give me the screen.'

A virtual screen abruptly dropped down like a curtain across one side of the gym. It was blank grey at first, then flickered on to show a ramshackle spaceport whose support facilities consisted only of a clump of low nissen huts beside a couple of large silo-like tanks. The latter, Cormac guessed, probably contained pure water, hydrogen and maybe even deuterium fuel for the aged ships scattered on the surrounding dusty white plain. Abruptly the camera view swung up and fixed upon a craft descending on antigravity. The thing looked just like a slab of granite with a framework mounted on its upper surface securing a long cylinder terminating in three evenly spaced U-space nacelles. As it approached the ground it jetted a series of thrusters from its underside to slow its descent and bring it down in the right place – obviously its antigravity system lacked finesse, or was not sufficient for the weight of the vessel.

It landed quite heavily, stirring up a cloud of the white dust that took some time to clear. When the ship finally became visible again, a ramp was down and an autohandler – a squat treaded machine with double grabs to its fore – was carrying a large cylinder down it. Walking down directly behind this were two people with a Loyalty Luggage case like an old sea chest trundling along behind them. One of these was a slim woman with cropped blond hair and who wore orange overalls cut off at the knee. The other figure was a portly bearded fellow in leather clothing: Carl Thrace. At the bottom of the ramp he stopped to chat with the woman for a while then moved off, the luggage following him. Now the camera swung away to point up at the sky as another vessel descended.

'Shit,' said Gorman. 'Why didn't it stay on him?'

'The camera,' Spencer replied, 'was positioned on a nearby water tower and just following a program to record new arrivals. It picked up this before our informant knew to look out for this ship and Thrace, or rather "Marcus Spengler".'

'So, do we know where he is now?' asked Travis.

'Inquiries have been made and are still being made,' said Spencer. 'He stayed in a local hostelry where he met with the local leading light of the community, then rented a car and headed out of town.' With her hands on her hips she gazed round at the three of them. 'That same leading light, an unpleasant individual called Tarren, will be our point of entry.'

Cormac felt the *Sadist* shift underneath him and a change in an engine note he had not even been aware of until then. He guessed the ship had now fallen into orbit about Shaparon.

'We can't land this ship,' he observed.

Spencer shook her head. 'We take a shuttle down – the one aboard is old and battered enough to fit in.'

'Well, thank you,' said Sadist.

Spencer continued as if the ship AI had not spoken. 'No one will know where it came from since we're now geostat on the other side of the world and running chameleonware.' She paused, gazing for a moment at Cormac. 'No need for complications on this world, and not much need to use Cormac here as bait. Our informant tells us Tarren is guarded, but not heavily. We go in, we make a few pertinent queries, then we go find where Carl has gone. Any questions?'

'Do we even have to pretend not to be ECS?' asked Gorman.

'As a precautionary measure, yes. Tarren may be some small-time hoodlum, but Carl Thrace is not. He may have methods in place to warn him should we be too overt. We'll just play the part of bounty hunters who are after Marcus Spengler and are prepared to pay for information. It might even be that we won't have to kill anyone.'

'What about scanning for Carl's location?' asked Cormac.

'Double-edged sword,' said Spencer. '*Sadist*'s chameleonware is not the best, hence our present geostat positioning. Plus, using wide-scale active scanning, which will be what's required since he's had over a week now to lose himself down there, further reduces the ware's efficiency, and might also be detected by Carl.'

'If he is even here,' Crean observed.

'Yes, if he is even here,' Spencer agreed. 'All the departures from the spaceport since his arrival have been uploaded to us. If we don't find him down there then it's back to searching. Now get yourselves kitted out appropriately and get down to the shuttle bay.'

As Spencer had opined, the shuttle would certainly not look out of place. It was a battered brick of a vehicle with a bubble cockpit to the fore and two ion-drive nacelles at the rear which, after a bit of a tweak by Sadist, immediately started coughing and spluttering and burning dirty. It was also dented and scratched, with a large repair patch welded just behind the cockpit where, so Sadist informed them, someone had tried to cut the craft in half with a particle cannon.

Cormac sat back in his seat behind the cockpit and tried to feel comfortable in his jeans, enviroboots, sleeveless shirt, weapons harness and an assortment of well-worn armament. He was supposed to look like a bounty hunter but felt more like an extra in some Old West VR fantasy. Crean and Travis wore similar attire and Gorman wore fatigue trousers, a bomber jacket and baseball cap. Spencer, who sat at the shuttle's controls, had not changed her clothing, her cool-killer long leather coat perfect for the role.

The vehicle started rattling the moment it hit atmosphere, and flecks of smoking matter began shooting up over the chainglass cockpit. Cormac wondered if they might be bits of atmosphere seal, or maybe pieces of the hull. Shaparon loomed ahead: a white orb streaked with umber and black scars. There were no oceans down there and only nitrogen and a few trace gases comprised the atmosphere – hence the breather mask hanging from Cormac's belt, attached via a long thin tube to a high-pressure oxygen bottle there, and hence the reason the place had never been heavily colonized. Apparently that had been due to change, for the residents had started building terraforming installations, but then the Prador had arrived to abruptly terminate the colonial dream.

After a little while the rattling ceased and the world dropped from view as the craft bellied in. Now they were deep in the atmosphere, Spencer engaged antigravity and put them in a spiralling glide down towards the spaceport. They descended through darkness, then into day as the glare of the white sun broke over the horizon. The day cycle here was just over fifty-two solstan hours long and they would be landing five hours after dawn. Peering over Spencer's shoulder, Cormac observed, on a subscreen, the view below of folded gutlike mountains rendered in the colours of cream and butterscotch. Then all at once the shuttle was over a plain, and when the human settlement slid into view it was a bewildering splash of colour on a white sheet. Spencer banked their craft and brought it steadily lower, and it was only when they were right over it that Cormac recognized the spaceport.

'No control tower, then,' Gorman observed.

'It's hardly a busy place,' Spencer replied.

Their dust-down was suitably bumpy for such a craft and in a moment they were unbuckling their safety harnesses and moving back through the cramped interior to the single door. Cormac donned his mask, as did the others, though of course the two Golem did not require them, then Travis undogged the door and pushed it open.

'Remember,' said Spencer over com. 'All you've got to do is stand around looking mean unless the shit hits.'

'Thanks for the detailed briefing,' said Gorman.

Spencer shot him a look, but it was difficult to tell what it signified now she wore a breather mask across her mouth. She stepped outside after Travis and the rest followed, Cormac coming last. He stood there for a moment, blinking in the glare and feeling a momentary stab of pain in his forehead, as if his earlier headache was searching for a way back in.

'Here,' said Gorman, handing him something.

Why hadn't he thought of that himself? These completed the image. With some relief he put on the sunglasses as, gesturing for them all to follow, Spencer moved off. However, the sunglasses didn't help too much as another spear of pain penetrated his forehead and lingered, twisting every now and again.

The spaceport was not enclosed and there was no security of any kind, unless you counted two individuals who stepped out of one of the nissen huts to silently watch them traipse by. Beyond the huts and the fuel silos stood the water tower the camera must have been positioned upon, standing on a ridge. Studying his surroundings, Cormac realized that though this was an airless world, there was still life here. The ground of the spaceport was mainly compacted white dust dotted with chemical spills from the spacecraft, and nothing else. Here the ground was strewn with white and grey rocks either formed from that same bland dust or what had been ground up to form it, and lying amidst them were green globules spreading networks of fibrous brown roots or mycelia over the ground about them. There were also arthropods here that looked like large black four-legged termites, and other things with shells like terrapins but far too many legs.

Beyond the ridge the track curved down into a town consisting of unsealed buildings almost lost amidst burgeoning growth, all enclosed in quadrate transparent plastic or chainglass greenhouses. Every solid building was brightly painted too: individual houses coloured in bright pastel shades. Cormac stared at them for a moment, blinking as a dark spot reappeared in his right eye. Should he tell Gorman that he might be having a problem?

'I guess all that whiteness out there gets wearing,' Gorman commented.

'They look like *homes* here,' said Crean.

'Mostly the survivors and their descendants,' said Spencer, 'though Graveyard scum are in charge. You never know, our visit here may benefit the residents.'

They moved down into a wide street, whereupon Spencer gestured to one of the 'greenhouses' inside which, behind squat palms and bluish cycads that looked like nothing less than giant artichokes, lay a large sprawling flat-roofed building that would not have looked out of place on a Mediterranean coast on Earth. As they drew closer to this, Cormac saw that the building extended out from its greenhouse on either side, to connect to other buildings. Only now was he becoming aware that all the buildings here were interconnected in some way, if not by butting up against each other then via various above-ground roofed walkways, which were either enclosed in glass or walled in with plasticrete or the local stone.

An airlock lay before them – not a pressure lock, for the chainglass doors were too thin and the seals and fittings too flimsy.

Twisting a simple manual handle Spencer opened the first door and they all stepped inside. Once Cormac closed the door behind them, Spencer opened the inner door into the interior.

'Slight pressure differential,' she said. 'Lower inside than out so they don't lose air – contamination with nitrogen is no problem. Okay, we can take off our masks now.'

When he removed his mask Cormac immediately felt some relief. Perhaps there had been a bit of a problem with his breather gear? No, he was kidding himself – he was still feeling the after-effects of recently acquired memory. He took a couple of deep breaths, a moist smell of burgeoning greenery in his nostrils. The pain faded further and the black spot in his eye winked out to leave a vague blurriness. He tried to invest more in what was going on, and not to focus too much on the dull ache in his head, since that seemed to emphasize it.

Glancing around, he realized that though from the outside the cycads and palms had looked decorative, that was not their pur-pose. The palms were date palms and the cycads were a splicing that budded pineapple-like fruits along the edges of their thick leaves. Between these were sunflowers and sugar cane, with vari-eties of climbing beans, peas, tomatoes, squashes and other less easily identifiable fruit vines climbing them. The ground was covered with a mix of brassicas, salad vegetables, and a form of GM Jerusalem artichoke that produced huge starchy roots and was a staple for food synthesizers everywhere. And scattered throughout all this were slow-moving agrobots like steel harvestman spiders, with bodies the size of footballs and each limb terminating in some useful tool. A whole food-growing ecology was being maintained in this enclosed environment.

'They must have problems with contamination,' he said, ges-turing back to the airlock, 'with anyone wandering in like we just did.'

'A year ago,' said Spencer, 'you needed permission to land

and went through a decontamination routine in those huts you saw by the spaceport. That all changed when the scum moved in here. They don't care what dies here – either plants or people.' She was fingering the butt of a gas-system pulse-gun holstered at her hip. He realized that Spencer, under that usually cool façade, was an angry person. This did not bode well for the people they had come here to see.

'We go here,' she said, and a schematic of the building ahead arrived in Cormac's aug, with one of its interior rooms highlighted. 'Tarren is usually sitting in court in his favourite bar at this time.'

'The informant, I take it,' said Gorman, 'is one of the original inhabitants?'

'You take it correctly,' Spencer replied.

The path they traversed, which was made of flakes of red stone – probably the local white stuff dyed for this purpose – wound in through the growth to terminate at an arch. As they moved through this Cormac eyed an old-fashioned gimbal-mounted holocam above, turning to track their progress. The short entry tunnel opened into a central courtyard occupied by a series of ponds, with water flowing and splashing between them down waterfalls or sprayed up in jets. Within the crystal depths numerous large fish, either trout or salmon, cruised back and forth restlessly – doubtless another food resource.

Now they began to see a few more people. Some were abruptly wary and found reasons to be on their way elsewhere. Other armed individuals also began to appear and follow them.

'How many . . . associates does Tarren have?' Gorman enquired.

'Oh, about fifty,' said Spencer offhandedly.

'I see.'

Pain again stabbed Cormac's forehead, but he could not pull out now.

They ducked through into another tunnel on the other side of the courtyard, took a couple of turnings and then came to a wide tunnel along one side of which people were queueing. Cormac noted that generally these people wore cotton clothing in the same bright shades as their homes, were unarmed and looked scared. On the other hand, those who *were* armed were heavy on the black leather, canvas webbing, odd items of envirosuit or even spacesuit, and didn't looked scared at all. It should be simple enough to select targets, if that became a requirement.

'*Keep an open link now,*' Spencer advised generally over their military comlink.

Next they turned in through the arch at which the queue of locals terminated, and entered a wide bar area with many supporting internal arches, scattered tables and low divans. There were star lights across the ceiling and Cormac could see the occasional servitor-bot, each one immobile, having obviously been used for target practice. Tarren was immediately identifiable, for he sat like some medieval king in a large armchair raised up on plasmel ammunition boxes. However, Cormac's attention was then drawn to others in the room. Prostrate before the throne was one of the locals, and over to one side lay another whose petition had obviously found disfavour, if the angle of her neck was anything to judge by. But most striking was the individual standing to one side of Tarren, a huge man clad in only a loincloth, his skin oddly coloured as if tattooed all over with blue circles, and a star-shaped steel cap atop his bald skull.

'*Fucking hell,*' sent Gorman.

Cormac, because he was only just becoming accustomed to using his aug, did not feel confident enough at subvocalizing to ask what was bothering his unit leader.

Tarren was a small wiry little man clad in an armoured suit which Cormac assumed he favoured because it made him look a little more impressive. He wore an aug and sat with a hand resting on a hexagonal box affixed to the arm of his chair. He eyed them for a moment, then nodded to one of his men, who kicked the prostrate man to his feet and sent him on his way. This local scuttled past them as they advanced.

'*This could be a problem,*' Spencer sent generally.

'*We will both have to focus on him,*' came Travis's reply.

'*If, or probably when we encounter any problems,*' Spencer sent direct to Cormac's aug, '*these are yours.*' An image of the room and its occupants arrived in his aug with four of Tarren's men highlighted over to Cormac's left. He tried to focus first on the image, then on the four men indicated, but felt distanced by the pain in his forehead. But he would not let this little handicap hinder him – he had managed to function with worse than this. There were about twenty of these thugs in the room and he wondered how the others had been assigned. And why were Crean and Travis focusing on only one person? He decided to try asking a question.

'*Who Travis Crean focus on?*' he managed, feeling clumsy as he tried to prevent his lips moving.

'*I see,*' sent Spencer. '*The big guy is a thralled hooper. Under his hand Tarren has a Prador control unit which is probably linked to his own aug.*'

Cormac absorbed that and shivered in almost superstitious awe. He had heard about such creatures, but stupidly assumed they were all gone now, or were confined to the Prador Kingdom. So, Tarren controlled a human once enslaved by the Prador – a mindless human, and one that, because of infection by the Spatterjay virus, would be very very tough and hard to kill.

'That's far enough,' said Tarren, as they reached a point out in the middle of the floor close to the woman's corpse. The hooper had probably broken her neck with the ease of someone snapping a carrot.

Spencer halted and nodded towards the corpse. 'Little problem with the natives?'

'Not an insoluble one,' Tarren replied, 'and really none of your concern. Who are you and what do you want here?'

'You can call me Spencer, if you wish, and I'm here for information for which I'm prepared to pay quite handsomely.'

'Just received a recent update from our informant – seems this little shit's pet hooper has killed eight people in the last week.'

'And how are you going to pay for this information, supposing I even have it?'

Cormac could see where this was going. He kept his right hand positioned over the gas-system pulse-gun holstered at his hip, whilst the thumb of his left hand, apparently hooked into the waistband of his jeans, was also hooked around a stun grenade.

'Prador diamond slate,' said Spencer, carefully reaching into the pocket of her coat and taking out a packet. She held it up and Tarren glanced to his hooper, who lurched into motion and walked over to stand before Spencer, holding out his spade of a hand. Spencer cautiously placed the package on that hand, which closed, and the hooper swung round and brought it to Tarren.

'Crean and Travis, when we're done here and if you're both still intact, go and drive the rest away,' Spencer sent. *'We won't want to be disturbed for a little while.'*

No direct order given, but Spencer was certainly telling them this was about to get bloody. Or had she earlier issued some order that Cormac had missed?

Tarren accepted the package, a simple leather wallet with a buttoned-down flap, opened it and tipped out the contents. Four flat clear octagonal crystals slid out onto his hand – a fortune in diamond slate.

'So what is this information you want?'

'You recently had a visitor,' said Spencer, 'whose current name is Marcus Spengler, though you may know him by a different name, maybe Carl Thrace. His current appearance is of a fat bearded fellow with a tendency to dress in brown leather.'

Tarren frowned and tipped the crystals of diamond slate back into the wallet, then placed that to one side on the arm of his chair. 'He told me there would be people following him and he paid me to discourage them.' He smiled and waved a finger at Spencer. 'Now, as well as being a man of my word I am also a businessman. Spengler told me to discourage you, but he didn't say I should keep quiet about where he went.'

'And that would be?' Spencer enquired.

'Oh, he went out to what's left of this planet's attempt at terraforming. I'm not entirely sure what interest he has in the place, unless it was to find somewhere to hide that interesting piece of luggage he had with him.' Tarren looked theatrically thoughtful for a moment. 'I really ought to find out soon, since he only rented that gravcar for a day and has now been gone for five.'

'Thank you for the information,' said Spencer.

'*Don't kill him – I'll need to confirm this,*' she sent.

'Think nothing of it,' said Tarren. 'In fact that's *all* you'll be thinking of it.'

'*Hit them,*' came Spencer's cold instruction, as she palmed a thin-gun, raised it and fired a short burst of three shots, whilst swinging the weapon sharply across. Cormac had never seen anything quite like it, for each of the three shots separately struck three individuals, two of them beyond Tarren, and one of them the hooper. That shot punched a hole straight through the big blue man's forehead, but it didn't seem to affect him at all as he began moving towards Spencer.

Something then clipped Cormac's shoulder, and stun grenades began to go off all about the room. He felt a surge of adrenalin whose cause was more embarrassment than fear, for he should not have been standing gaping. He threw himself sideways, simultaneously arming the grenade as he pulled it from his waistband, and sent it skittering across the floor to two of those Spencer had selected for him. As it exploded, he shouldered the floor, rolled and came up with his pulse-gun levelled. He fired once on automatic, sending one envirosuit-clad woman crashing over a table, then something punched him hard in the right biceps, spinning him round, his gun flung from a hand that now felt boneless. As he went down on one knee, he used his left hand to draw Pramer's thin-gun from where he had concealed it in the back of his trousers, but he knew he was moving too slowly. His fourth target, a squat ginger-haired man, had already drawn a bead on him with a cut-down pulse-rifle.

Then something flashed in from the side and the man cart-wheeled in the air and crashed to the floor, the upper half of his back now at a completely unnatural angle to the lower half. Cormac glimpsed Crean pausing to fire at someone on the ground. It had been her, moving almost too fast to see. Now she streaked across the room, slamming into the hooper, just a second after that big man picked up Travis and just threw him across the room. This gave Spencer the opportunity she needed. Throwing herself forward she rolled past below the hooper's grasp, came up and flung herself on Tarren as he groped for a gun at his belt. She drove her fist into his gut and, as he bowed over, she reached down and tore the aug from the side of his head.

Tarren shrieked and fell from his throne, and as if this action had removed some sort of block, the surrounding cacophony suddenly impacted on Cormac: yelling out in the corridor, further shooting, someone shouting instructions in a language he didn't recognize. Then the noise grew dull again as the bar's double doors slammed closed. Now, within this room he heard the odd groan and a crackling sound of something burning, smelt a seared pork stench and saw a spreading strata of smoke. Turning, he focused on the hooper.

The big man, just like Cormac, was down on his knees, his head bowed forwards and a bloodless rip in the flesh of his arm slowly zipping shut.

Someone began groaning in agony.

'Gorman, shut that up will you?'

A single shot rang out; the groaning stopped.

Cormac peered down at his own arm.

'Fuck,' he said – his bicep was cooked meat with a neat black hole punched through it. Seemed like his fight was over for now.

12

'Moving a little slow there, Cormac?' Gorman asked, squatting down beside him.

Perhaps he could just keep quiet about it; he made a bit of a mistake, it was a blip, which with further training would not occur again. However, something relentless inside him wouldn't allow such dishonesty.

'Aftereffects of the mem-load,' he explained.

Gorman peeled a patch combining pain-killer and anti-shock meds from a roll and stuck it on Cormac's shoulder, none too gently. 'You should have said.'

'It didn't seem a problem at first, then we were in here and it was too late.' It sounded a weak excuse.

Expressionless, Gorman turned away and gazed across at Spencer, who was sitting on Tarren's chest with the barrel of her thin-gun pressed up against his nose. She was talking low, too low to hear, and Tarren was replying. After a moment Spencer stood and stepped back, then gestured with her pistol.

'Stand up.'

With blood running down his neck from where Spencer had torn away his aug, Tarren got warily to his feet and gazed around at the carnage. Cormac studied it too, and noted that though not one of Tarren's people was standing, they weren't all dead, most of them having been taken down by stun grenades. But what about the rest of Tarren's men? Only then, looking round, did Cormac absorb that Crean and Travis were not present and that distantly he could hear sporadic gunfire.

Tarren now focused on the hooper, briefly glanced back at the control unit mounted on the arm of his throne, then returned his attention to Spencer.

'ECS doesn't come here,' said Tarren. 'When you've gone, more people like me will come back.'

'But you won't,' said Spencer. Tarren did not even get a chance to be afraid before she shot him through the side of the head. She calmly watched him stagger and collapse, then walked over to the throne and, after taking up and pocketing her wallet of diamond slate, pumped numerous shots into the hexagonal control unit, smashing it open and setting it smoking. Then she tore it from the chair arm, dropped it on the floor and stamped it to fragments.

'Okay,' she continued, breathing heavily as she walked back past Tarren, who was still shuddering into death, a pool of blood spreading about his head, 'Thrace did head out to the old terraforming station and hasn't been back. We'll head out there and see what we can find.'

Cormac carefully regained his feet. Now he not only had a headache, but felt dizzy and nauseous again.

'What about him?' he asked, pointing at the kneeling hooper.

'We'll take a DNA sample for ECS Records,' she said. 'At least one more might then be accounted for out of the millions still listed as missing.'

That wasn't quite what Cormac had meant.

'He's still alive,' he said.

Spencer shook her head. 'He died years ago when they tore out his brain. What's left will need to be destroyed, thoroughly. If what you see there is not fed the right antivirals and foods, it'll mutate into something even nastier.'

Just then the doors to the bar crashed open and in strode Travis and Crean, along with two of the locals, a man and a woman, both armed. The woman peered down at Tarren and grimaced. 'You could have left him alive.'

'I wouldn't want to turn you into a killer, Adsel,' said Spencer flatly.

Adsel, who Cormac suspected must be the ECS informant here, said, 'But that's what I and my friends will have to be here if we're to keep people like this away.'

'Certainly, but you're not in any rush are you?' She gazed at Travis and Crean. 'Arms cache?'

'Yep,' said Travis. 'The last of his lot are running for their ships' – Travis nodded at Tarren – 'with the locals in hot pursuit.'

'But we remain focused on the mission,' said Spencer, now gazing at Cormac, who was tying his wrist to one of his harness straps to support his injured arm. 'We need a vehicle.'

'There's one just outside you can use,' said Adsel, who was now standing before the hooper, peering down at him.

'Good.' Spencer nodded.

'Is he safe?' Adsel asked.

Spencer walked over, abruptly stooping and pulling an evil-looking stiletto from the top of her boot. She leaned over the hooper and, with much apparent effort, cut a slice of flesh from the top of his ear, which she then dropped into her wallet of diamond slate. There was no blood.

'Safe as can be,' she said, 'but you'll have to throw him into one of your incinerators if you don't want something nasty crawling around here when the virus in him decides it's time for him to start feeding.'

'Right,' said Adsel, stepping back. 'Right.'

All business, as if what she had just done was of no further note, Spencer asked, 'Could you also get our wounded comrade back to our shuttle, should he need the help?'

Cormac was sickened by a reality which until now had been of mild academic interest to him. He had seen the ruins, the spaceborne wreckage, the casualty figures, he had heard of Prador snatch squads and actually fought the creatures himself, but this,

this hooper, brought home to him more than anything the horror of the war his father had fought and died in. Dragging his gaze away from the big man he focused on Spencer, trying to bring himself back to the moment. He considering arguing against being sent back to the shuttle, but rejected the idea. He had been a liability and now, with this injury, he would be even more of one. Doubtless, when Spencer and the rest had checked out this old terraforming plant and either captured Carl or ascertained that he wasn't there, he, Cormac, would be in for a tongue-lashing. Quite possibly Spencer would decide she no longer needed his services.

'Can you fly a shuttle injured like that?' she abruptly enquired.

Of course he could; he nodded.

'We'll head straight out to the terraforming plant and start searching. When you get to the shuttle, you bring it straight out there.' As she turned away an area map arrived in his aug, almost like a dismissal. It gave the coordinates of the old terraforming plant some fifty miles away.

'I've told Sadist to come in above us now, since if Thrace is here I rather doubt he's now unaware of our presence. It should arrive in about an hour and begin scanning the plant. But we'll get out there and start searching right now.' She gazed about them. 'Let's move.' She led the way out and Gorman, Travis and Crean followed. Only Crean looked back, her expression unreadable.

'Cold bastards, those Polity agents,' said Adsel.

Cormac glanced across at her, then scanned round for his pulse-gun. He found it lying under a table by the foot of one of Tarren's men, who was unconscious – snoring, in fact.

'What are you going to do with these?' he asked.

'Those identified as murderers become fertilizer, just like him.' Adsel gestured towards the hooper. 'The rest get to leave if there's a ship left, if not they work for their keep.'

Cormac stared for a moment more at the hooper, who now

seemed to be sagging closer to the floor. He felt a stab of sadness. Here was a crime he could do nothing about, a crime that might well have been committed before he was born. Returning his attention to Adsel, he reckoned the people here would probably do all right. Presumably they now possessed weapons, if Spencer's comment about a weapons cache was anything to go by, and the will to use them. It struck him as unlikely there would be any more Tarrens coming here, since people like that, though quite prepared to kill, did not like risking their lives unless there was profit to be made and no other options available. It did occur to him, however, that in this Adsel, they might end up with a completely home-grown despot.

'I'll be able to get to the shuttle myself,' he said, as with difficulty he holstered his pulse-gun.

'I imagine so,' said Adsel, 'but I wouldn't want any of my people mistaking you for one of Tarren's men – it's been getting quite nasty out there.'

The moment he and Adsel reached the courtyard, Cormac saw what she meant. The water in the interlinked ponds was now red, and a shoal of the troutlike fish had gathered underneath a floating corpse clad in a grey envirosuit, but whether to feed or just out of curiosity was difficult to tell. Out in the garden were two more corpses – both also Tarren's men. One of them had obviously been shot numerous times through the back with a pulse-rifle, the other was hanging from a palm-tree, optic cable wound around his neck and secured over one of the sawn-back scales on the trunk. His hands were tied behind his back and his face black, tongue protruding. Trying to be coldly analytical, Cormac realized someone must have held onto his feet while he strangled, to stop him supporting his own weight on the lower tree scales.

'Lot of bitterness here,' he observed.

Adsel just glanced at him blankly, then dismissively away again.

In the airlock she put on a breather mask pulled from within her bright clothing, and now they headed out towards the spaceport. Three ships were rising from the ground and another, still on the ground, was smoking, muted fires visible inside through blast holes in its hull, sustained by internal air supply and doubtless soon to be extinguished by the oxygen-free outer atmosphere. Numerous locals were scattered here and there, and numerous corpses lay sprawled on the ground, many wearing the same kind of bright clothing as Adsel. When they finally reached the shuttle, all under the watchful gaze of a crowd of locals gathered about the nissen huts, Adsel stepped back.

'It's easy to be judgmental when you come from the civilized Polity,' she said, her voice distorted through her mask. 'There's no ECS to protect us here, no wise AIs to govern us.'

Cormac did not know what to say, and so nodded in agreement before climbing inside the shuttle. Only later, as he applied to his biceps a nano-activated wound-dressing from the shuttle's first-aid kit, did he remember that all survivors within the Graveyard had been offered relocation to other worlds within the Polity. Adsel and her fellows had stayed here, which meant they must have refused that offer and were living with the consequences.

The shuttle subscreen briefly showed a view of a grounded gravcar, then swung back to the ruin. The terraforming plant was not much to look at, comprised mainly of big silos like the ones just a few hundred yards from Cormac beside the spaceport. There were also numerous low buildings and networks of big pipes, many of which speared away across the ground beyond view, along with piles of twisted wreckage, and spills of green and rusty brown across the white ground. He assumed this was one of those places that manufactured masses of GM algae tailored to survive in this environment and spread through the ground, slowly multiplying and chewing up oxides to add oxygen to the atmosphere – hence those white and brown spills. Perhaps, if no other plants were built, the stuff already here would spread out and eventually finish the job in a few tens of thousands of years, though more likely the growth spread would not possess enough momentum and would eventually die.

Now the view swung from side to side as Crean glanced first at Travis to her left, then at Gorman and Spencer to her right and just ahead of her.

'Spencer wants you to bring the shuttle here and land it beside the gravcar,' said Crean, her voice issuing from the screen.

Maybe Crean was the only one prepared to talk to him, or maybe he was just being paranoid. Spencer and Gorman would certainly be a bit disappointed with him, but not overly censorious, surely. He had risked their lives by allowing himself to go into combat when not functioning at a hundred per cent, but with him being new to the Sparkind, only recently promoted from the status of grunt, surely some leeway would be allowed? Cormac would have given anything to have heard their conversations since departing for the terraforming plant. Or perhaps he was being both paranoid and egotistical to even think they had been talking about him.

'Okay,' he replied. 'I'm on my way.'

'How are you now?' she asked solicitously.

For a moment he didn't want to answer, since the last thing he wanted was for the others to overhear. Then he damned himself for his stupidity, because Crean was quite capable of talking to him without using her audible-voice generator.

'I am well enough,' he said cautiously.

'Don't sweat it,' she replied. 'Nobody expects perfection from you at once, and certainly not Spencer. She walked us into a situation which, because she had not completely assessed it, could have gone a lot worse than it did.'

'Meaning?'

'Meaning she didn't know about the hooper, and she should have.'

'I see.'

That knowledge did make him feel a little better, but not much. Perhaps he was just being too hard on himself? His arm now properly dressed and the drugs in the dressing numbing both that and his nagging headache, he reached out and quickly initiated the shuttle's start-up routine, then gripped the joystick and pulled it up.

'Sadist, how are you doing?' he asked, as the craft's AG motors lifted it shakily from the ground. He boosted it higher with a couple of spurts from the steering thrusters, and watched the ground rapidly drop away.

'I will be above you in thirty minutes,' the ship AI replied.

Cormac was about to ask if Sadist could send a program to realign the grids in the shuttle's ion drive, as there was no longer any need for the craft to appear to be a Graveyard relic owned by dodgy inhabitants of the area, when he started to pick up military com in his aug.

'*Over there,*' said Gorman.

Crean's view swung across to focus on a gravcar grounded over by one of the low buildings. A chameleoncloth tarpaulin had been slung across it, but obviously the wind had picked up one corner and dislodged it. Crean now began scoping out the surrounding area with magnification, focus, and in spectrums not available to unaugmented humans. There seemed to be no weapons emplacements within view, but in infrared she detected a heat source within the nearest silo close to where the car was parked.

'*Two by two cover,*' said Spencer, breaking into a trot towards the gravcar. '*Pulse-rifles down to electro-stun. We want Thrace alive if he's in there.*'

Crean and Travis reached the grounded gravcar well ahead of Gorman and Spencer. Meanwhile, Cormac urged the shuttle out over the spaceport, checked his position on a terrain screen called up in a frame in one corner of the subscreen, then set the shuttle grav-planing towards the terraforming plant.

Now he asked, 'Sadist, can you do anything about the ion drive in this shuttle from up there?'

'I have sent an alignment program,' the ship AI replied. 'It will take two minutes to take effect.'

He could turn on the drive at once and have the shuttle speeding to his destination, but running such drives dirty never did them much good. They also tended to be noisy, and he guessed Spencer would not want him creating a racket while she and the others were creeping about out there. He decided to wait.

Crean studied the chalky ground about the gravcar, a visual program clearly outlining footprints for her. There were numerous patterns, so obviously Carl had been tramping about this area for some time, but most of them led to a single door in the nearby building. In a second Crean and Travis were over by the door.

'*No booby traps or sensors evident,*' Travis sent, obviously having used his Golem senses to scan through the wall.

The moment she arrived, Spencer twisted the door handle and she and Gorman entered. Crean and Travis followed them in, pulse-rifles up against their shoulders as they scanned the gloomy interior. From Crean's perspective, Cormac observed twisted and collapsed pipework and big ceramic vats, some cracked or shattered. He observed frames picking out various points within that area and understood she was making threat assessments. Meanwhile, Gorman and Spencer reached double swing doors through the further wall, one of the doors hanging by only one hinge.

Now they covered the area behind them as Travis and Crean sped over.

'Your ion drive is now at optimum function,' Sadist abruptly informed him.

Had only two minutes passed? It seemed like hours. Cormac held off engaging the drive as he gazed at the screen. Crean and Travis went through the doors, Gorman and Spencer coming through behind them to cover the area they now sped across. Here lay a long low room walled with chainglass through which ran many transparent pipes – some sort of control area with numerous consoles attached along those same walls. Not too difficult to cover, this. The area terminated against the curve of a silo, where a hole had recently been cut through. Using her infrared vision, Crean detected heat beyond, inside. Travis dived through the hole ahead of her, whilst she turned to cover the other two as they approached. Then she dived through, rolled and came upright in the cathedral space within.

'No one here,' said Travis, out loud, as Gorman and Spencer now entered.

'The heat source?' Spencer snapped.

Travis gestured to a large crate with some fleshy-looking substance seemingly growing over it like a fungus. Crean focused on this, detecting the heat signature inside the crate. They all walked over to inspect it. Cormac felt both disappointed and glad as he engaged the ion drive to accelerate towards their location. He certainly wanted Carl apprehended, but he wanted to be there when it happened.

'Shit!' Spencer exclaimed.

Cormac returned his attention to the screen, and saw that Crean was now gazing down at the face of Marcus Spengler. The stuff strewn over the crate was syntheflesh: Carl's syntheflesh disguise. Then the face spoke.

'Ah, you're here at last,' it said. 'Say bye-bye cruel world.'

The face winked.

'Run,' said Spencer, and chaotic images ensued – too fast for Cormac to follow.

Then a light ignited on the horizon, and he looked up. A fireball expanded there, so bright it seemed to eat into the earth. He just stared, utterly understanding what had happened, yet still unable to accept it. When he looked back at the screen, it was blank.

The crash of the explosion arrived shortly after its glare, and it sounded as if the world was being smashed in half. The shockwave struck just as Cormac was trying to land the shuttle, tilting the vessel nose-down. It automatically fired stabilizing thrusters and Cormac felt a strange wave run through his body as the grav-motors tried to realign too. Immediately the surrounding air filled with white dust, blotting everything from view. He concentrated on bringing the craft level and landing it properly, but it still came down with a crash, and as its systems wound down into silence he listened to the patter of some sort of hail against the hull.

'Gorman? . . . Crean? . . . Travis? . . . Spencer?'

No response over his aug, just static. The electromagnetic pulse from the blast might well have screwed up his aug . . . might have screwed up their augs . . .

Feeling numb, he unstrapped himself and headed for the side door of the shuttle, stood before it for a long moment, then went off to search the craft's lockers for some goggles, which he found – they were Gorman's. Opening the door he stepped out, then stepped quickly back inside when falling cinders burned his bare arms. After a further search he found an envirosuit which, with painful slowness, he began to don. When he finally closed it up he just sat exhausted, not sure how to proceed. Then came a query for linkage through his aug, and he realized, recognizing the source, that the device had lost all its previous settings. He approved the query and a com channel was established.

'Are you alive?' Sadist enquired.

It seemed a stupid question, but for all the ship AI knew it was opening a communications channel with a still functional augmentation attached to a corpse.

'I'm alive,' Cormac replied.

'Are you injured?'

'Got a pulse shot through the arm.'

'I know about that,' said the AI, sounding irritated. 'I wanted to know if you sustained further injuries as a result of the CTD blast.'

On some level he had known that was what the explosion had been, but never really admitted it consciously. Carl had left a nice little booby trap for anyone who came hunting him, with the final touch of that syntheflesh head winking at the victims.

'They're gone,' he said abruptly, but the words did not seem to make any sense.

'At present I can detect no signals either from Travis and Crean or from the augmentations belonging to Gorman and Agent Spencer,' said Sadist didactically. 'However, it is quite possible the EM pulse knocked out all their com hardware – you will have to go and look.'

Cormac jerked himself to his feet and headed outside, where he found that the cinders had stopped falling and the dust had cleared enough for him to see about ten feet ahead.

'I am now within scanning range,' Sadist informed him. 'I cannot as yet penetrate the ionization around the site, but I can see you, Cormac. Might I ask why you are outside the shuttle?'

Cormac stood gaping into the dust, his brain seemingly running on neutral. Why had he stepped outside, what purpose was served by him walking the twenty-odd miles to the terraforming plant?

'Bit of a glitch,' he said, and returned to the shuttle.

'Are you sure you are uninjured?' Sadist enquired.

'I think it's what might be described as shock.'

'Then take an anti-shock med,' said the AI.

Standing inside the shuttle, Cormac gazed across at the first-aid kit, then abruptly turned and smashed his left fist into the wall. 'Fuckit! . . . Fuckit! Fuckit!' Then he forced himself into motion, taking the pilot's chair and re-engaging the shuttle's systems. He glanced at the blank subscreen and abruptly reached out to key the controls that expanded the location map to cover it, then jerked the shuttle into the air. He didn't want to take anti-shock meds; it seemed like a betrayal.

Fifty feet up the dust thinned, and a hundred feet up he was above the worst of it in his present location, but ahead a mushroom cloud stood high in the sky. Turning on the ion drive he thrust the joystick forwards, not bothering to check the location map since his destination was clear. Within a few minutes debris was pattering against the shuttle and occasionally there would be a loud clang as something big impacted. Nearing the stem of the cloud he spun the shuttle around and used the ion drive to decelerate, then descended into boiling whiteness. This was no good – he needed a clearer view. Setting the craft to hover he checked the control panel before him for a moment, then damned himself for not thinking clearly.

He aug-linked to the shuttle's system, mentally sorted through the menus available, noting numerous diagnostic warnings from the EM damage to the craft's systems, and eventually found what he wanted. Shortly a radar map of the terrain below began to build on the screen – slowly because of the ionic interference – but it soon became evident that there was no terraforming plant any more, just a large crater with occasional chunks of silos and pipework scattered about it. Using the radar image for guidance, which was also updating slowly, he eased towards the largest mass of wreckage. Again setting the shuttle to hover, he waited until the picture on the subscreen was again complete, selected a clear area to one side of the wreckage and descended cautiously to the ground, using a high-powered radar pulse to give him the distance to measure his altitude. Still the shuttle settled with a crash.

'Can you hear me?' he asked, via the aug channel to Sadist.

For a moment there was no clear reply, just occasional bursts of static, then abruptly Sadist spoke. 'I can hear you, just.' The AI's voice was clear to Cormac so he guessed it must be using a narrow-beam transmission aimed precisely at his location, whilst using all sorts of clean-up programs to sort out what Cormac was transmitting. He unstrapped himself and headed for the door. There would be a lot of radiation outside, but his envirosuit would protect him from much of it, as would his internal suite of nanites and the anti-mutagenic tweaks to his own immune system. However, he called up the main menu in his aug and sorted through that and numerous sub-menus until he obtained what he required. Once this facility of the aug initiated, a simple dosimeter appeared in his third eye, presently reading in the green. Anyway, even if he received what once would have been considered a lethal dose, the medical facilities aboard Sadist would certainly be able to deal with it – dealing with the effects of radiation was something ECS Medical had become quite expert in during the Prador war.

Stepping outside, he scanned around. Visibility was just over twenty feet and cinders were still dropping from the sky this close to the hypocentre. He wondered what Sadist hoped for him to achieve here, and what he hoped to achieve himself. He knew Golem could move very fast and that maybe, given time, Travis and Crean might have been able to get Gorman and Spencer clear. But they had not been given time. It seemed likely they had all simply been vaporized.

'It is becoming clearer,' said the ship AI. 'I am sending direction-finding to your aug. Key to envirosuit reactive visor.'

241

He hadn't even thought of that. As an information package arrived from Sadist, he searched for the channel to the suit he was wearing, found it and initiated visor projection. Immediately the dosimeter appeared down in the corner of the visor, shortly after that he opened the package from Sadist and ran it too. Now a locator arrow appeared in the lower half of the visor with his present coordinates on some planetary grid, in red numerals, to one side, and coordinates of some other location aligned underneath them in green numerals. The arrow presently pointed to his left; he turned until it was pointing straight ahead, which put the shuttle right in front of him, so he walked round the craft, aligned the arrow again, and headed off. Already the dosimeter had shifted to a pale yellowish-green, and checking one of its attached functions he realized his time here was limited to an hour and ten minutes.

'So what is it you've found?' he asked.

'A regular energy signature, but beyond that I have no idea.'

Cormac again checked the given coordinates against his own and worked out that he had half a mile to travel. Maybe, out there, either Spencer or one of his unit was lying injured. He broke into a jog, then accelerated, going just as fast as he could over the churned ground in this poor visibility. Within a couple of minutes a hundred-yard length of a huge pipe loomed out of the murk to his right, five yards wide and flattened by its impact with the ground, almost like some massive sea creature washed ashore and decaying. Beyond lay chunks of twisted building superstructure, deposited on the ground like sections cut out of a steel forest. He had to slow here because as well as the ground being uneven, the ends of I-beams and jagged edges of metal protruded from it. His own set of coordinates gradually drew closer and closer to the others, then eventually the arrow blinked out.

'Within five yards of your present location,' Sadist informed him.

Cormac halted and scanned around, disappointed, since there was no immediate evidence of any of his companions here. He spotted a short length of aluminium extrusion, tugged it from the earth and stabbed it down upright where he had been standing. Then he walked out in a spiral from this, closely inspecting the ground. Now paying greater attention to what lay about his feet, he noted all sorts of items scattered amidst the earth. There were numerous small fragments of greenish-brown matter. He stooped and picked one of these up and crumbled it between his fingers, guessing it to be a piece of dried-up algae from one of the silos. There were also numerous hard chunks of something, and it was only when he picked one of these up and cleaned the soot from it that he realized these were hardened spatters of molten metal. But still no sign of what he was looking for.

'What was this signal?' he asked again.

After a brief delay, Sadist replied, 'Merely a regular energy signature – possibly from a power supply of some kind.'

Then he saw something he at first took to be a red object on the ground which, only as he drew closer, resolved as a patch of red light cast by an LED. He stepped over and stooped down to inspect it more closely, seeing that the small light was inset in some sort of metal object. He dug underneath it with one hand and levered it up, and as the object came free he recognized the breech section of a pulse-rifle. He grabbed it and pulled it free. The barrel was missing, as was most of the butt stock – the barrel stock, which was in fact the power supply, was still only partially attached. He instantly dropped the weapon and stepped back.

'A pulse-rifle,' he said.

About the rifle the ground was smoking, and he realized he had just had a close call, for the power supply was discharging into the ground.

'Nothing else?' asked Sadist.

'Perhaps I should dig?' Cormac wondered.

'No,' replied the AI. 'There's as much chance of anyone being down below there as anywhere else within a hundred miles. I will however deep-scan that area when the ionization has cleared. Move on to the next coordinates.'

These coordinates appeared on his visor and he saw that the next location was a mile away. His dosimeter had now edged into a yellow-orange on its way across the spectrum to the red. He was about to set out when there came a crack from the ground. The pulse-rifle jerked, sparks momentarily spreading about it, then these drained away and the LED went out. For a moment he considered it an ominous sign, then felt a tight sadness in his chest, because really the time for omens was past. However, he set out, again running as fast as he could. Abruptly, there came a drumming sound and he felt something pattering against his envirosuit. Halting for a moment, he saw it was raining great globular drops of black tar-like rain. This struck him as odd, since there was not a great deal of water on this world. Some sort of atmospheric reaction caused by the heat of the blast? No matter, he set out again.

More wreckage, and acres and acres of churned earth. His dosimeter was into the orange when he reached a great mountain of wreckage, which he realized was an entire building, uprooted to its foundations and dumped on its roof. Was the power source in this? He followed the arrow until it disappeared, and found himself still twenty yards from the nearest wall, though amidst a strewn wreckage of chainglass pipes and large chunks of ceramic he recognized. They were the vats he had seen in the building his unit had entered through.

'Within five yards of your present location,' Sadist again informed him.

He approached this as before, this time picking up a length of chainglass pipe to jab into the ground as the start point of his search, but he did not have far to go. Nearby a sheet of muddy chainglass jutted from the earth, and just visible through it, something was moving against the underside. He stepped over, thinking for a moment he was seeing one of the insects of this world, and then realized it was a black skeletal hand. He paused for a moment, not sure he wanted to see more, then felt a sudden disgust at this reaction and forced himself forwards. As he stepped round the sheet a head turned towards him, severely blackened and burnt, but with shiny metal showing through where some of the crisped synthetic skin had fallen away.

Cormac grabbed the edge of the sheet and with some diffi-culty, possessing only one working arm, tried to pull it away. He could not tell if it was Travis or Crean who lay there. The Golem reached up and pressed its hand against the sheet, which began to shift, and suddenly Cormac was able to pull it clear. The Golem lay with its legs and the lower half of its torso buried in the ground. Cormac grabbed the arm, but the Golem failed to clasp its hand around his forearm, and otherwise seemed to be making no further effort to get free. Perhaps its power supply was down, for surely it could pull itself free.

'I see,' said Sadist abruptly. 'She is refusing to acknowledge my signal – allow me to speak through your envirosuit.'

She?

Cormac wasn't quite sure how to go about that until through his aug he accessed the suit menu and initiated 'external speaker', whereupon the ship AI spoke.

'Crean,' said Sadist, 'Cormac here has now received about half of the allowable dose of radiation searching for you, and now you have been found. However you choose to proceed henceforth, your recent experiences must be recorded – this you cannot avoid.' Then, after a pause, 'Get up.'

Crean lurched to sit upright and it was only then that he realized one of her arms was missing. She turned, her torso revolving further round than a human torso could have, stabbed

245

her only hand deep into the earth and, levering from this point, dragged her legs free. She looked grotesque twisted round like this, but abruptly twisted back and then stood. Cormac studied her, seeing that very little of her syntheflesh remained – she looked like a charred mummy. He wondered if, without Sadist naming her, he would have known this was Crean. Did Golem females possess female ceramal skeletons, would he have known her as female by the shape of her pelvis? Too late now to know for sure, for in his mind he had imposed the shape of Crean over this burned wreck.

'What about the others?' he asked.

Her head swivelled towards him for a moment. 'Dead,' she said, her voice perfect, which more than anything seemed to bring home her unhumanity. Humans needed lips and tongues to form their words; she now possessed neither. He took that in, some weasel part of himself trying to find some way around it. He stamped on that inclination, hard. Whatever he thought of Golem, or artificial intelligences, in this situation Crean would not have said the others were dead without being utterly sure. Cormac felt that had she been human, this would have accounted for her apathy earlier. He felt a moment of confusion: why should she emulate shock and grief?

'Return with Cormac to the shuttle, and then to me,' Sadist instructed.

New coordinates appeared. Cormac turned, until the arrow was pointing directly ahead, and set out. There was no need to run now, and suddenly he felt so exhausted a slow walk seemed almost too much.

13

As Cormac stepped outside the school he scanned around eagerly for a sight of the war drone – the one they had seen in Montana and which now seemed to be here – but there was no sign of it.

'Bye-bye Cormac!'

Glancing round, he saw Culu standing with her father and waved. 'Bye Culu!'

Her father was a bulky bald-headed man in baggy pyjama-like clothing that disguised the physical cybernetic additions to his torso, but which could not disguise his twinned augs, shiny chrome additions on either side of his head. Cormac's mother, on one of the few occasions she met Cormac outside the school, said Culu's father was a 'traditionalist' because he felt the necessity to pick Culu up every day. It had taken Cormac some time to figure out what she meant. Only after stumbling across a historical text about twenty-first-century paedo-hysteria did he understand that Culu's father followed the old tradition of always picking up his daughter at the school gates. It was something to do with that, he thought. His mother also said something about minority-group paranoia also being traditionalist – a comment he still did not quite understand.

The only other individual being picked up at the gates by his parents was Meecher, but Cormac suspected that had something to do with his behaviour today. He watched as Meecher's mother smacked him hard across the back of the head then pointed to their hydrocar. Meecher climbed in and sat down, whilst both father and mother stood discussing him. Cormac watched them until they climbed into the car and headed off. He waited a little longer, dawdling because he didn't enjoy sharing public transport with his fellow pupils – apparently a trait that worried the school authorities.

Eventually he began heading down the pavement in the direction numerous other pupils had gone – all heading for the nearest bus stop. Still scanning his surroundings for some sight of the war drone, he noticed the presence of numerous gravcars parked here and there in the area, most of which seemed to be occupied by one or two individuals. This was odd, since usually such vehicles occupied the roofports of the numerous residences here, or if from outside the area, were parked on public roofports. Then a shadow loomed above and he glanced up, expecting it to be yet another car coming in to land, only to instead see a scorpion, black against the bright sky.

The drone descended fast and landed hard in the road, flinging up flakes of plasticrete and gritty dust. Simultaneously, surrounding gravcars accelerated; blocked the road in either direction and occupants began piling out. With a surge of sheer excitement Cormac realized that many of these people wore ECS uniforms and many of them were brandishing weapons, which they rested across the roofs and bonnets of their vehicles. These weren't any kind of weapon he recognized, having long arm-thick barrels and heavy wide breech sections covered with cooling fins. The drone spun in place, its sharp-pointed limbs scoring the plasticrete, until it came to face Cormac, then it surged forwards to loom over him.

'I do not have much time,' it stated.

Cormac just gaped.

'You need to know.'

'Amistad!' came a bellow from some public address system. Now more shadows drew across, and Cormac looked up to see some huge vehicle hovering above. It looked like a floating barge, but with all sharp corners and flat surfaces, all the dull greyish green of military ceramal armour.

'Amistad! Move away from the boy!' A woman in ECS uniform had walked out, her hands on her hips.

The drone turned slightly to peer at her, then quickly swung back to Cormac. 'Your father—' The drone seemed highly agitated, and Cormac was reminded of those archaeologist friends of his mother who visited; men and women who were not accustomed to talking to children. 'Your father is gone.'

'He's dead?' Cormac asked.

Further agitation from the drone. Its feet were beating a tattoo against the ground, its antennae quivering and it kept extending and snipping its claws at the air as if it could find the words there. It never got the chance.

There came a thrumming from above, a deep sonorous note, and it seemed as if something invisible but incredibly heavy and substantial slammed down from the vessel above. The drone was crushed flat on its belly, its legs spread out about it and its claws immobilized. An invisible wall of air hit Cormac in the face and shoved him straight back against the wall of the building behind. He tried to fight his way free, but the air seemed to have coagulated around him, turning into a cloying sheet.

'Is my dad dead?' he asked, but knew at once that his words reached no further than his lips.

Then there came a blast, excavating a great crater in the road underneath the drone. Somehow, this gave it enough freedom to move and it dropped down into the hollow then bounced out sideways. Beams of a deep red radiation stabbed through the dusty air from those weapons resting across the gravcars, but the drone avoided them all, moving almost too fast to follow. Coiled into a ring it rolled and sprang open, landed on the face of the building opposite and leapt again, crashing against the side of the ship above and bouncing off once more. The bright light of a fusion ignition in atmosphere lit the street, and the drone hurtled away.

The ship above also accelerated away, the invisible force immediately coming off Cormac so that he slumped to the pavement. Down in the street, some of the people leapt into their gravcars and they too sped away. His ears ringing, Cormac gazed down at the pavement, and after a moment noticed a pair of enviroboots nearby. He looked up at the woman who had addressed the drone and she reached down, helping him to his feet.

'You mother will be here shortly,' she said.

'My dad is dead,' he replied.

She gazed up at the sky in the direction of the departing vessel and gravcars. 'So that's what it's about,' she said. 'You can never be sure with them, and it's best not to take any chances.' She peered down at him. 'They can be so dangerous.'

He tried to learn more, but everything he asked was referred to his mother, who soon arrived looking both worried and angry, and quickly led him to her gravcar.

'It said that Dad is dead,' he told her.

'And that's all?' she enquired, handing him a bottle of fruit juice.

'It didn't get time to say much,' he replied, uncapping the bottle. He took a long drink, for he was very thirsty. 'I think they used a hard-field to try and capture it.'

'It shouldn't be here, and it shouldn't interfere in things it's not equipped to understand,' Hannah told him, watching him carefully.

He suddenly felt incredibly tired, and leant back in the seat.

Hannah continued, 'It knows about fighting and killing, but like them all is emotionally stunted.' She seemed to be speaking to him down a long dark tunnel. 'How can something like Amistad explain the truth when even I, your mother, can't think of a way?'

Everything faded to black.

★

Feeling utter betrayal, Cormac opened his eyes.

'She drugged me,' he said, just a second before an invisible dagger stabbed in through his forehead. He glanced across at the side table and reached out to pick up the roll of patches there, his biceps still stiff under the length of shellwear enwrapping it. He took one patch only this time, since he felt that using two last time might have contributed to his nausea, and stuck it on the side of his neck. Now familiar with this process, he then took up a sick bag, and tried to order the detach sequence in his aug for the optic connection. It was a struggle, but this time he managed it. After a moment he reached up and pulled the fibre-optic strands free, then glanced aside as the machine that provided them wound them in.

'I am not aware of what these mem-loads contain,' said Sadist. 'I would require your permission to load them myself.'

Cormac wasn't sure about how to react to the AI's evident curiosity, but he really wanted to talk to someone about all this. Gazing about the room he half expected to find someone standing by his bed, then felt a sick sinking sensation in his stomach. The only one who might possibly have been there was Crean, but she had confined herself to her cabin ever since they boarded. Sadist, having now scanned much of the area around the blast, had reported finding only a heat-distorted ceramal blade belonging to Spencer, the surprisingly intact brass buckle from Gorman's belt, and Travis's legs. All three of Cormac's companions had been vaporized. Crean had survived only because a chainglass wall had peeled up and slammed into her, acting like a sail on the blast front and carrying her two miles from its hypocentre. Total unlikely luck, coincidence.

'I give you my permission to load them.' He paused. 'But for the last one – you can load that only when I do.'

'Thank you,' said the ship AI, then, 'Done.'

Cormac was only momentarily surprised; of course an AI

could encompass those memories in a moment, it was a reminder of the difference between himself and the intelligences that ran the Polity; between himself and the likes of Crean too.

'I note that each chapter also has attachments and you have only been loading the chapters themselves,' Sadist added.

'Attachments?'

'They are incompatible with your mind, apparently.' Sadist paused. 'They are cleaning-up exercises. It seems apparent to me that your mother at first did not think your initial encounter with the drone, out in Montana, of any significance – though she did think your more traumatic encounter with it outside your school should be edited out at once. After seeing Dax's problem with not fully editing his memories, she then decided to remove that earlier encounter from your mind as well.'

'Cleaning-up exercises?' Cormac asked, though he had some intimation of what the ship AI was talking about.

'All those times you thought deeply about that encounter with the drone out in Montana, all those times you talked about it to others. Other less formative occasions were not removed, but the human mind tends to self-edit those memories that do not match up with the life's narrative.'

Now that was a statement that would require some thought, and he wondered how much of what lay between his ears truly reflected reality, even had it not been deliberately tampered with. But his head was aching, he again felt nauseous, and what had once been shock at the loss of his friends was turning to a deep sadness. Was it grief? he wondered. He did not know if it was, for 'grief' was such a vague term. Did it require howling tears from him, irrational behaviour? He didn't know, but certainly he recognized the feeling of betrayal.

'As you saw, she drugged me,' he said.

'It seems extreme to have done so, just as it seems extreme to edit the mind of a child to prevent him knowing about the death of his father, but the action was not so uncommon,' said Sadist. 'During the war, when pain was a frequent companion, many took the easy route of excising it from their minds.'

Cormac sat upright, tightly clutching the sick bag. This time there seemed to be no visual effects, and despite the sudden surge in his nausea he did not vomit, although maybe that was because he had deliberately fasted for a day before doing this.

'But was it right?' he wondered.

'In itself there is nothing uplifting or virtuous about suffering,' Sadist stated. 'Whether it makes its recipient a better person often depends upon whether that person has the ability to change that way. There were those during the war who were turned into monsters by it.'

'Do you think she did the right thing?'

'No, I cannot see how the death of a father you had not seen since you were five years old would be so damaging. Rather, I think she was transferring her own grief onto you. I also think that there is more involved here than mere death.'

'What do you mean?'

'Her last statements to you, before you blacked out, seem to indicate this,' said the AI. 'If forced to guess, without seeing the last chapter of these mem-loads, I would say there is something about the manner of your father's death that is being concealed.'

Cormac swung his legs off the surgical table and stood. He seemed to have gained some control over his insides and so discarded the sick bag before leaving the room. He would have liked to take on the next mem-load, but knew Sadist would not allow it. Walking slowly, he returned to his cabin and lay down on his bunk.

The attack ship had left the orbit of that ruined world over twenty hours ago now. Struggling to mesh with the ship server, he discovered they were now in transit through U-space, though where to, he had no idea. Doubtless, information would become available.

Cormac abruptly glanced to his cabin door, feeling the oddest sensation that Gorman had just stepped inside to chivvy him out of bed. No one there. Phantom presences of the dead – a sign of grief. Cormac could feel something leaden in his chest and tight in his throat. He felt on the edge of tears yet, as had occurred two or three times before, they did not surface, ebbing into a cold and distant sorrow. His headache was definitely fading now and he wondered if his mind was becoming accustomed to the mem-loading process. He sat upright.

'I've been mooning around in this ship so wrapped up in my own concerns,' he said abruptly. 'How is Crean?'

'Crean has ceased to communicate,' Sadist replied. 'As is her right.'

'Where are we going now?'

'I am to deliver you both to the nearest Polity world, where you are to rest and recuperate for a period not less than three months, after which you will be reassigned.'

'What?'

'Was that not sufficiently clear for you?'

'What about Carl Thrace?'

'Did you think ECS would allow you, a new recruit to the Sparkind who has just lost most of his unit, and a Golem that looks likely to self-destruct, to continue the pursuit of this criminal?'

'I . . . don't know.'

Sadist continued, 'For you, the trail after Carl Thrace ended with that explosion. It is possible he is still hiding on that world but, if so, it would take a massive search to find him – one that ECS AIs consider a waste of resources. It is more likely he boarded one of the seven ships departing that world during the time between his and our arrival there.'

'Do we . . . does ECS know the destinations of those ships?'

'It is understood, from information obtained by Adsel, that two of the ships are heading for unknown destinations within the Graveyard and five are heading to a selection of three Polity worlds. Carl could be on any of them, and there is no guarantee that their stated destinations are their actual ones. ECS personnel are watching for those ships, and for Carl. Your involvement in this is now at an end.'

Cormac felt a sudden obstinate anger at this decision, even though, of course, it was perfectly logical.

'I am presuming,' he said, 'that the nearest Polity world might also be one of the three Carl is heading for?'

'The likelihood that Carl has not headed off into the Graveyard is considered low. The likelihood of you encountering him on one of those three worlds, each of which is moderately to heavily populated, is nanoscopic. Also, Cormac, if it came to the attention of ECS that you were making personal inquiries about this, you would be disobeying a direct order to *rest and recuperate*, and so apprehended and sent out of this sector. This is now out of your hands.'

'So what are the names of these three worlds?'

After a long pause his room screen blinked on to show three planets, with their names printed below them. One world he knew: Tanith, a terraformed place of damp moors, dark forests and ersatz gothic castles. It was a tourist place for those with an inclination for such things. The one called Borandel he had never heard of, though wondered if he should have, it being so close to the border with the Prador Kingdom. But it was the last world that riveted his attention: it was called Patience.

He whispered the name to himself, then aug-linked to the room screen to access information about the planet. First to come up was news on current events there, which he quickly scanned through. Areas denuded of life during the war were recovering well, and other areas rendered highly radioactive by bombardment, or unsafe because of the possible existence of human-specific engineered viruses, had been declared safe after many years of decontamination. The building of a massive city, up on mile-high stilts, was nearing completion in the Cavander mountains located in Hessick County, which eventually terminated in the Olston Peninsula. Such a project was apparently an assertive declaration of the new optimism on this world, as was the arrival of the sup-posedly famous 'Thander Weapons Exhibition' – something he had heard of before. But they needed to be forward-looking and optimistic here, they needed to put behind them the memories of bitter battles fought here against the Prador. Battles like the Hessick Campaign, in which Cormac's father had died.

'Crean wants to see you,' Sadist abruptly announced.

Cormac continued staring at the screen, the skin on his back crawling. Of course he had known Patience lay out this way, and he knew odd and mysterious coincidences were an inevitability when billions of humans occupied so many worlds, but actually seeing this happen was creepy.

'What does she want?' he asked, perhaps rather too abruptly.

'She has come to a decision,' Sadist replied, 'and wants to acquaint you with it.'

With a thought, Cormac shut off the screen, then sat staring at the blank surface for a long moment. He recalled now where he had heard of the Thander Weapons Exhibition. It was during his basic training, from Carl Thrace. Cormac stood and headed for the door. He would keep that particular bit of information to himself for now, though it was essential he get Crean to agree that they should head for the world called Patience.

Shortly he had reached the door to Crean's cabin, rapped his knuckles against it and waited. After a moment the lock in the frame clunked, and he pushed the door open.

Crean sat on her bed, utterly motionless. She was clad in a white disposable ship-suit, and now with syntheskin and synthetic hair replaced, her appearance was much improved. Last time he had seen her she had been sitting in precisely the same position, but still skeletal and charred from the CTD blast, still minus one arm. Glancing round he noted burned remnants still strewn on the floor and over the bed sheets. Why she possessed a cabin and a bed was a mystery to Cormac, her requiring no human comforts or even essentials like food or sleep. He guessed it was all about emulation – everything was with Golem. However, he did notice that her ship-suit hung loose and baggy, and that her hands, though clear of burnt matter, were still bare of syntheflesh. The bones of her hands gleamed in her lap like steel spiders.

'How are you?' Cormac asked, then was suddenly irritated by his own politeness. Why should Golem have any problems related to flesh they could replace and minds they could reformat like the drives on primitive computers? Why was he playing the emulation game with her?

She looked up, and once again seeing her face reminded him how he had very much reacted to her on a human level. Remembering their erotic encounters here and in his own cabin irritated him too, for after recent tragic events, that now all seemed a childish game.

'I am what I am,' she said, 'and to be better, to be recovered, it would be necessary for me to cease to be what I am.'

'I don't understand.'

'Of course you don't,' she said. 'You still think that Golem are something less than human. You still view Golem as mere machines. You still retain a primitive archaic belief that the mind produced in flesh is something more. It's almost like a religious belief in souls. You cannot seem to accept that we are as complex as you, if not more so. Nor can you accept that you are merely a machine made out of different materials.'

He wanted to argue, but she had nailed it. He did feel that way, no matter how foolish it might seem. It was all about emulation, he guessed. What use was emotion if it was something you could turn on and off? What was the use of ersatz humanity when it was something you could dispense with? It was a falsity. Yet, in humans, it had become possible to edit the mind and, as a corollary, the emotions. Even now it was becoming possible to turn on and off the emotions in creatures of flesh, and soon memcording of all the data in that lump of flesh enclosed in bone would be refined enough for humans, if they so chose, to become something else.

He shrugged, embarrassed. 'I will learn.'

Crean gazed at him for a long moment and said, 'Perhaps I can help you.' Then she smiled, closed her eyes and bowed forwards, once again freezing into immobility.

'What do you mean?' he asked.

No response.

'Crean?'

'She will not reply,' Sadist informed him.

'What?'

'Crean has chosen to erase herself rather than reformat herself to a condition in which she could bear to be without her companions.'

Cormac found himself backing towards the door. 'What?'

'She has suicided.'

He stumbled out into the corridor, the nausea earlier generated by the mem-load returning in spades. Going down on his knees he vomited, then rested his head against the wall and wished he could cry. But something in him wouldn't permit that, and he wondered if those early edits of his mind had damaged it. He remained in the same position for some time, then slowly eased himself to his feet as a beetlebot peeked out of its home low in the wall.

'Do you want me to move her?' he asked.

'I will send one of my telefactors to deal with her,' Sadist replied.

Cormac gazed down at the beetlebot as it hoovered up the thin bile he had spewed, erasing it to leave clean carpet behind. Wipe these things out, clear the slate, leave it clean and ready to be written on again. He understood his mother now, but refused to choose her course.

It was different this time. He felt no sense of being a child and, though he recognized his surroundings as his mother's home, the place had been redecorated and modernized. He walked into the living room and sprawled in one of the armchairs, just like Dax used to do, and even reached over to take up the conveniently placed bottle of whisky and glass, and pour himself a drink. When his mother walked in, she studied him for a moment before seating herself in the sofa nearby, her legs crossed and her fingers interlaced over one knee.

'I don't know how you commenced loading your edited-out memories back into your mind, Cormac,' she began, 'but it is certain that the mem-file I provided was broken into three chapters, since there is not yet the means to load a file of that size without causing brain damage.'

Cormac sipped the whisky, and found it fiery and good – yet he had only tried whisky once before, and then found he disliked its medicinal taste, and the way it ate into his self-control.

'You are therefore,' Hannah continued, 'on to the third and final chapter after having discovered some things about your past.'

Cormac wanted to reply, but though he placed the glass down on the table beside him and returned his hand to the chair arm, he possessed no control over his movements. His present mind was here, and aware, but he could no more change what played out here than he could have while experiencing his childhood memories.

'You have discovered that I edited your mind twice . . . only twice.' Hannah frowned. 'The first time was when that drone tried to speak to you while you walked home from school. The second time was when I realized how unstable so limited an editing could be, and had our encounter with the drone in Montana edited out in Tritonia.'

So, Sadist had been exactly right about that.

'I have to say that on the second occasion I thought Amistad had told you everything, but the AI who conducted the editing process informed me otherwise.'

Everything? Cormac wondered. What else was there to know?

'The drone of course told you enough for you to infer that David was dead, apparently.' She now paused, a strange unreadable twist to her expression, which she concealed by looking down at her hands. 'Amistad did not really understand much about human affairs and human emotion, but perhaps he did understand that what I was doing was wrong. It remained my choice, however, and Amistad had no right to go against my wishes in this matter.'

Why did you do it, Mother? Was it because you controlled so much in your life and his death lay out of your control? Was it the past you really wanted to edit?

'However, your father's death was by no means the whole story. It was only when Amistad tried again to get to you while we were in Tritonia that I managed to again confront him and persuade him to leave you alone, though only with the direct intervention of the AI running Tritonia and the near shores of Calais.' She looked up. 'There is much more you need to know about what happened to your father, but you were never told, so that story is not contained in these pieces excised from your memory. You deserve to know, I guess, and if you are anything like David I imagine you will not rest until you do know. But I am not going to tell you. I'm sorry, but I feel another has earned that right.'

Again a long pause, whilst she stared directly at him. How, he wondered, had this mem-load been put together? Had she sat someone down before her and told this story, then had it edited out of their mind to be sent to him? Was the person who had sat here Dax?

'You are out in a particular area of space I have not wanted to visit, ever since the end of the war. I don't believe in fate, destiny or any of that rubbish, but the workings of coincidence can sometimes be frightening. Amistad has been lurking out that way for many years, for reasons I . . . know. He learned of your presence out there and, I understand, managed to intervene in some small way during an operation you were involved in? Whatever . . .'

Cormac felt a momentary amusement: it seemed the drone had at last learned to be diplomatic and not gone into detail about that particular *operation*. But why had it contacted his mother?

'You told me you discovered your mind had been edited when you were fitted for an aug, but I have to wonder if the drone's presence out there is really what set you to wondering . . . and perhaps checking.' She shook her head, and he noticed her eyes were glistening with tears.

'Cormac, you are out there near the world called Patience, where the Hessick Campaign was fought and where your father . . . died. Amistad never managed to tell you the truth, so I will let him do so. He wants to tell you the truth there, on that world. I am sure, in the circumstances, you can ask for a leave of absence

. . . Attached to this mem-load is a net address via which the drone can be contacted. Just call for Amistad, and he will find you on Patience . . . And please forgive me.'

The scene blanked out and for a second it seemed as if he was just hovering in blackness, still ensconced in that chair. In that moment he felt a dread of the ill-effects to come. Then all at once he was again flat on his back on the surgical table, an invisible dagger poised over his forehead. Now he felt a surge of anger and instead of just lying there waiting to feel pain and nausea, he thrust himself upright.

Once the optic threads linking him to the machine that had loaded that ersatz memory had detached, he reached up and slapped the aug cover closed, glanced aside at the roll of analgesic patches, then swung his legs off the table and stood. Dizziness and nausea hit, but he just stood there breathing evenly and pushing those ill effects away by force of will. Next he checked his aug's inbox, and there found a small file awaiting his attention – it would be interesting to see what a war drone kept on its netsite.

'Interesting,' said Sadist.

'Oh really?'

'However,' the AI continued, 'the coincidence of the world Patience being one of our possible destinations is not such a great one. Trainees are generally brought into this area because this is where ECS is still most needed, and it is also essential for would-be soldiers to see effects of war which, in the final analysis, is what they are being trained to prevent.'

'You're preaching,' said Cormac.

'Is it so obvious?'

'Yes.'

'And you still intend to resign from ECS?'

'I do, when you can finally bring yourself to tell me what I need to do.'

'I felt it necessary for you to at least have a cooling-off period,' said Sadist. 'I do understand that Crean's suicide hit you rather hard.'

It had seemed the final straw, and Cormac had never known such mental pain, as everything finally impacted on that moment: Carl's betrayal and murder of Yallow, the injuries Cormac himself had suffered and the effect on him of killing his would-be murderers, the deaths of Gorman, Spencer, Travis and Crean, the discovery of his mother's betrayal. Now he felt bruised, things inside him broken, and of course it was plausible that this pain had been enough to drive him to quit his position in ECS. It was perfectly understandable, perfectly, yet a complete lie. He knew that as an ECS soldier, under the 'rest and recuperation' order, there were things he would not be able to do, things he needed to do, on Patience. And how utterly opportune that this last mem-load had given him an unquestionable reason to go there.

'My decision to quit need not be a permanent one,' he said. 'But I do desperately feel the need to be out of it now . . . Sadist, we have had this discussion before and my opinion has not changed. Tell me what I must do.'

'Very well,' said the AI, sighing like any human. 'There are no documents to sign, nothing like that. You merely have to state your intention to me.'

'I resign from ECS,' said Cormac immediately.

'Very well,' it said, the AI's voice now taking on a different tone. 'In four hours I will be landing at the Cavander spaceport on Patience. When you depart this ship you may take with you only those items not directly issued to you by ECS. Here,' it continued, as an information package now arrived in his aug, 'this is the coding sequence you can use to access your back pay. And please, Cormac, remember that at any time you can rejoin ECS in the same manner as you have just departed it.'

'Perhaps I will, but I need time.'

'Very well, Cormac,' said the AI, and it seemed like both a goodbye and a dismissal.

Cormac pushed himself away from the surgical table and headed for the door, and it was only as he stepped out into the corridor that he realized his head did not ache, and he did not feel sick. Perhaps this was because this last mem-load had not been a chunk edited from his own mind, and was in fact no more than a message delivered through the same medium.

He headed for his cabin, and there immediately emptied his pack onto his bed and began sorting through the pile. It did not take long. In the end his own possessions formed a very small pile on the pillow: a few items of clothing, a carbide-bladed knife, a palmtop and finally Pramer's thin-gun. Why was it, he wondered, that he did not feel any great need for possessions? Even when he lived at home, with his mother, and later when he lived away for a while working autohandlers in Stansted Spaceport, the belongings he treasured would only ever fill a small suitcase. All the ECS stuff went back into the pack, which he placed to one side of the room, with his pulse-rifle resting on top of it. He changed out of his fatigues into his jeans, T-shirt, enviroboots and jacket, and everything he truly owned went into the jacket pockets.

The Cavander spaceport rested in the mountains on a platform below and to one side of the city it served, a fantastical place looming above on mile-high legs, each one a vertical city in itself. Cormac walked slowly down *Sadist*'s ramp, carefully taking in his surroundings: the sky of a slightly orange yellow and the shocking pink clouds, the smell like vinegar in his nostrils and the taste of metal in his mouth, the bounce to his walk as he departed *Sadist*'s Earth standard one gravity to this world's point nine. Drifting through the air above him were things like gulls which he knew,

from having studied information about this world when a teenager, to be strikingly similar to miniature pterosaurs.

'Goodbye, Cormac,' Sadist's voice echoed from the interior of
the ship.

'Goodbye,' said Cormac, glancing back as the ramp-hatch
drew closed. Even as he set out across the spaceport he heard the
ramp clonk into place and saw the ship's shadow speed across
the plasticrete as *Sadist* ascended silently. He turned to watch it
float higher and higher, then with a burst of thrusters accelerate
into the sky. It receded rapidly to a black rod against those blowsy
clouds, where its fusion drive ignited and it sped away. Now he
returned his attention to his immediate surroundings.

The spaceport looked almost like a city itself, what with the
enormous ships here like curved edifices. He eyed two great cargo
haulers like blunt bullets stood on their back ends, about them
swarms of autohandlers trundling between blocky mountains of
plasmel cargo crates, and people clad in overalls striding about
importantly clutching manifest screens or handler control modules.
Beside one of these behemoths, a huge loading robot – a tall four-
legged monstrosity with crane arms extending down underneath it
– squatted over some vast cathedral of a container to attach numerous hooks in order to lift and shift the massive weight. Perhaps the
container held something for the Thander Weapons Exhibition,
which had apparently only just opened to the public.

There were also numerous smaller vessels down on this spaceport platform, many of which bore the standard utile shapes seen
anywhere, but others that were utterly exotic. One he recognized
as a replica of a World War II aircraft carrier and another as a war
barge, probably a restoration job, of the Solar System corporate
wars. Still others were ECS fighting ships of one kind or another,
probably decommissioned and voided of their original AIs, or self-
decommissioned, their resident AIs deciding to go independent.

On the whole, it seemed there were few private ships here without some sort of military connection.

They were all here for the exhibition.

Though that same exhibition was not Cormac's only reason for being here on Patience, it was the reason he had resigned from ECS, for he wanted freedom to move, to investigate. He had known Carl for two years, and though so much about the man had been false, one thing certainly wasn't – his fascination with weapons. Perhaps it was foolish of Cormac to feel so certain that Carl had made this world, and the exhibition here, his destination, but it was a certainty he could not shake. Though this whole thing came under the Polity aegis, and remained closely watched, he had divined from the stories about this event that a lot of illegal arms deals went down. Carl, he was sure, would have come here to sell his remaining two CTDs. Of course, certainty about that did not ensure that Cormac would find him – there were hundreds of millions of people on this world, millions here in this city, and millions more who would be visiting the huge displays and demonstrations of armaments.

Now spotting the exit buildings along the far edge of the spaceport nearest the city, Cormac set out towards them. He knew that there would be no need to present identification because Sadist would already have informed the port or city AI of his presence, which would be automatically confirmed as he passed through that building either by scan or a bounce query to his aug. However, he did not want to simply pass straight through that building, for that was where he would begin his search.

Numerous chainglass doors gave access to a lounge two miles long, half a mile wide and scattered with bars and eateries. Net consoles adorned every one of the pillars supporting a chainglass roof that was a confection of moulded-glass pillars, spires and hexagonal sheets. The moment Cormac entered the area an ident-query arrived in his aug and he responded by allowing his aug to send its brief summation of who he was. The lounge area, though huge, was very crowded, and he noticed numerous security drones folded out from their alcoves in the heads of the pillars, while other floating drones of a bewildering variety of shapes zipped back and forth above the crowd. Even as he watched, a number of these drones converged above where four individuals, probably plain-clothes security personnel, politely detained a lone traveller and separated him from his luggage. Cormac wandered over in time to see one of them opening that luggage and taking out a hand-held missile launcher – the kind sporting a ring-shaped magazine. He had trained with similar devices and knew their missiles could cause enormous damage.

'We'll keep this for you until you depart, Mr Kinsey,' said the one holding the launcher. 'I hardly think this falls under the specification of personal defence.'

Though the AIs did not proscribe personal armament, there were limits. Cormac moved on, finally locating a netlink terminal that wasn't occupied. Though he could have done what he was about to do by aug, that would have necessitated him making a request through the local AI or one of its subminds, and he did not want to subject himself to possible scrutiny. Working the touch controls and the simple keyboard he accessed spaceport information, specifically a record of all arrivals and departures. In total, eight ships had come in from the Graveyard within the span required. Making a file containing a copy of all the information obtainable about them, including links to related sites on the net, he then sent that file to his personal net-space, before finally turning away and giving the console up to the first in the queue now gathering behind him. He then headed for the anachronistic-looking lifts on the other side of the lounge to take him up to the city proper.

The moment he stepped out of the lift, it was evident that Cavander City remained a work in progress. Though complete

buildings rose all about him here, the skyline beyond was webbed
with scaffolds, cranes, and the heavy shapes of big grav barges
loaded with construction materials. The street he stepped out upon
was lined with all the usual eateries, bars and shops, interspersed
with numerous entrances to towering apartment complexes above.
Down the centre of the street, set about twenty feet above the
ground, were the two tubes of a fast-transit network, with escalators
leading up to platforms arrayed about them. Cormac swung his
gaze along the street, studying the crowds and noticing a prepon-
derance of military dress, though not necessarily the contemporary
kind. He recognized uniforms from the ages of Earth extending
back centuries, and fashionable variations on such uniforms. He
hadn't realized he'd needed to come in fancy dress.

An enquiry through his aug of the local server gave him lists of
hotels still with accommodation available. Downloading a map
from that same server, he located his current position and then
headed for the nearest hotel. In the automated lobby he paid from
his back pay, pleasantly surprised upon seeing the quantity of
money available to him, and was soon ensconced in a small but
luxurious room. Pulling up a comfortable chair by the window he
gazed out across the busy city and now accessed his own net-
space. Casting a swift eye over the messages therein, he saw one
from his brother Dax and another from an old school friend, Culu,
who was now a haiman working on some project in a distant reach
of the Polity. He left these and instead downloaded to his aug the
information he had sent there himself about the Graveyard ships
here.

Upon checking their departure points, where listed, he was
surprised to find that one of them had recorded its departure
world as Shaparon. It seemed too good to be true, for surely Carl
would not have wanted to leave any trail; but then perhaps he had
no choice in the matter and was relying on ECS being unable to
trace every ship that left that world. Maybe he hoped ECS would

expect him to run for cover in the Graveyard, which would of course have been the most sensible move. Relaxing back, Cormac now found out everything else he could about the vessel, soon learning that it was owned and run by an individual called Omidran Glass, an ophidapt. It was then little problem to trace her net-space and find out how to send her a message. He contemplated this for a long moment; it all seemed too easy. Surely ECS would be onto this already? Deciding to give the matter further thought, he now considered another message he needed to send. He went to his inbox and opened the information package giving him Amistad's net address.

The drone's website was nothing like a human one. It contained no biography, no public images nor any of the usual drivel humans were fond of collecting in their net-spaces. The first page gave communication links, but the pages behind this were loaded with machine code, links to weapons sites with occasional pictures or schematics of some esoteric piece of hardware, and numerous vast and inaccessible files – perhaps stored parts of the drone's mind it no longer felt the need to carry about with it.

Cormac spoke a message, recording it in his aug, then sent it to the first com address given: 'Amistad, I am on Patience, and I think there's something you want to tell me, something you have been wanting to tell me for a long time.'

Then, having done that, he went straight back to Glass's site and recorded and sent another message, deciding to be utterly blunt: 'Hello Omidran Glass. You don't know me and of course I will understand if you tell me to go to hell, but I'm trying to trace someone who was recently on the world Shaparon who I think may have taken passage on your ship. I would like to speak with you.'

With the message on its way he now set about running searches to try and ascertain this ophidapt woman's location, because he half expected her to reject his request. He also tried to find out if she had had any passengers, but no luck there. Then, abruptly and surprisingly, he received a request for linkage from Glass. He accepted it and immediately an image of her appeared to his third eye. This being an aug communication, the image was obviously computer-generated, but her lips moved in perfect synch with her words. She too would be seeing an image of him, recorded aboard the *Sadist*.

'I see by your image that you're wearing an ECS uniform,' she observed.

'It's an old image – I've resigned,' he replied.

Her shoulders were bare and she seemed to be wearing a top of pleated blue fabric cut low, with twin straps across her upper arms. It looked like the top half of a ball gown, which seemed utterly incongruous on someone whose skin bore a greenish tinge and was spangled with small scales. Her jet-black hair flowed long down behind her head, her eyes were those of a snake and as she spoke he could occasionally see her fangs folding down a little as if she was preparing to bite.

'So who is this person you are seeking?' she asked.

'I know him as Carl Thrace, though he may possess a different identity now and even a different appearance, since he's shown an aptitude for that sort of thing. What I do know is that he was likely travelling with a large piece of Loyalty Luggage, probably in the shape of an antique sea chest.'

She seemed to gaze at him for a long moment, but he realized her image had frozen. Obviously she was doing something else behind this. At that moment an icon lit in the top right of this third-eye image: message pending. Then her image abruptly reanimated. 'I am presently aboard my ship and will be departing this world in two hours. There is no way you can get to see me, and this is certainly the last time we will talk like this.'

Her link cut.

Cormac sat in tired frustration. His one possible contact was gone. In annoyance he opened the other message, but his anger evaporated as he listened to a sonorous voice. It made the skin on his back crawl.

'I have been waiting. Meet me at Vogol's Stone.' Appended to this was a time . . . time to talk to a war drone, he guessed.

14

Located on the roof of Cormac's hotel, the gravcar rental office stood by a small fenced-off area of the roofport containing a row of three cars. All were utile vehicles of similar design, with two front seats and two rear ones that could be folded down to make a luggage space. The whole compartment was enclosed in a chainglass bubble, the rest of the upper part of the car being featureless brushed aluminium while the underside looked like a boat hull, with stabilizing fins. Unusually, the rental office actually had a human attendant: a young boy clad in bright yellow overalls. He sat at a workbench scattered with strange archaic-looking engine components. Cormac gazed at these curiously.

'A marine outboard motor,' the boy explained. 'One that actually used to run on fossil fuels.'

Cormac raised an eyebrow, since he thought that unlikely. Even on Earth such things would not be seen outside a museum.

The boy grinned. 'No, not that old – they used them here before the war, and during it. Now that's the alternative.' The boy pointed to the row of gravcars.

'I wondered about the hulls.'

'Some people like the authentic boating experience out around the Peninsula,' the boy explained. 'They also like to put a car down on the surface of the sea and use it as a diving platform – to go after Prador artefacts. Now, how long for?' He held out a palmtop.

'A day should cover it.'

A linkage request arrived in Cormac's aug, identified by the figures on the palmtop screen, and he paid with a thought.

'The one at the end of the row.' The boy pointed, then returned to his tinkering. As Cormac walked over to the car he wondered if the boy was really one of those odd adults who liked to retain the appearance of a child. He felt not, for positioned on the wall of the portable office was a sticky screen displaying images from the war, some of them being of Jebel U-cap Krong – but of course that was not conclusive.

The chainglass bubble automatically rose as he approached, so he stepped inside the vehicle, immediately taking hold of the simple joystick to lift the car from the roof even as the bubble closed back down again. A flock of gull-things scattered above him, spattering the vehicle with white excrement which quickly slid from its frictionless surfaces. City traffic-control took over and the car swept to one side and then up, joining a widely spaced row of similar vehicles punctuating the sky. Tapping the console screen turned it on, and in a moment Cormac called up a map of the area, while a further search scaled the map down to show him Vogol's Stone some two hundred miles away at the tip of the Olston Peninsula. The moment he selected it as his destination, traffic control turned his vehicle out of his present sky lane, then into another, the car accelerating. Within minutes the city was receding behind him and the screen alerted him that he could now take control of the car, if he wished. He so wished.

Below, mountains of grey stone speared above valleys filled with plants like pine trees, though with foliage both dark green and steely blue, and some areas Cormac recognized as being infested with skarch. Gradually, it seemed the grey stone was being sucked down into the trees, which were soon changing to autumn colours of deciduous growth. The mountains became hills, interspersed with the occasional lake along whose shores the local 'gulls' skated their bodies across the mud searching for their favourite delicacy: a thing that looked like a cross between a slug and a cockroach. Next, Cormac began to notice occasional barren areas, some of

273

them fenced off, all of them looking as if they had been ploughed. Spotting a plume of vapour from some machine working one such area, he brought his car down low to take a look. It was a huge cylinder running on numerous sets of treads, conveyors of scoops lifting soil up into its mouth, blackened and smoking soil excreting from its anus. The thing was a massive soil sterilizer, there to kill off potential Prador bugs or nanomachines. Cormac flew on.

Soon the barren areas melded and were only occasionally scattered with copses of trees. He saw great lines of sterilizing machines stretching to the horizon, other devices like mobile oil rigs trundling across the wasteland at a snail's pace, occasional ruined cities or towns, buildings melted and crumbling. Then in the distance he saw the sea, and swung out that way to fly above a long rocky coastline against which waves broke to cast up plumes of water through crevices; spume floated above like confetti in the low gravity here. His console screen pinged, scaled up the map and he saw that Vogol's Stone lay only ten miles away. He was reaching the tip of the Peninsula now, with sea both to his right and left. A series of sharp peaks rose ahead, marching down into the sea. His map now gave him direction arrows, then pinged at him again once he lay above his destination.

The Stone had to be the single canted monolith jutting from a plateau cut into the side of one of the peaks, for there, right beside it, rested a familiar steely shape: a scorpion memory.

The weapons exhibition occupied the centre of the city where permanent buildings had yet to be raised. Here a three-dimensional maze-like structure, nearly two miles wide, had been assembled from portable yet massive tubes of plasmel and strengthened with girders of light bubble metal. Escheresque stairways interlaced all this, also drop-shafts and enclosed walkways. The entrance Cormac approached was a wide arch without human attendants, but the whole exhibition being computer-monitored meant the doors would automatically close once an optimum number of visitors had entered, then open again when the number dropped again. The long tubular foyer lying beyond was crowded but not unpleasantly so. Here numerous exhibits stood in chainglass cases, on pedestals or hung from the plain white walls. Entering brought a query to his aug; he allowed it, and studied the provided menu of options. There were numerous historical tours he could take, general and particular in that he could get an overview of weapons history or track the historical development of specific weapons. He could focus on a chosen era – for example just taking the tour of medieval weaponry, and enjoying ersatz battles between armoured knights. He could select particular battles and inspect every recorded detail, observe how the weapons of the time were deployed, to what effect, hear expert analysis, study tactics and logistics. It seemed there was something here for every variety of war and disaster junkie.

Just inside the entrance Cormac cast an eye over a huge pedestal-mounted rail-gun, obviously of Prador manufacture, then turned and halted to gaze for a long while at a large oil painting. It depicted the battle between the Polity dreadnought *My Mary Rose* and a large Prador dreadnought, with distances shortened to fit both vessels within the frame. This was the first one-on-one encounter between such vessels in which the Polity ship was actually victorious, and as a child Cormac used to run a video recording of this as a screensaver on his p-top. Further along he regarded a case containing a single Prador claw. Keying to the constant signal from the case, he uploaded information and learned that the claw had been recovered in the vicinity of the battle depicted in the painting. Doubtless the rail-gun over on the other side of the foyer had been retrieved from the same location.

Entering a juncture of six of the tubular units beyond the foyer, he now needed to make a decision. Here the exhibitors had obviously chosen World War I as their kicking-off point. Digitally remastered films from the time could be run on various screens or loaded to aug. The centre display was of the first-ever tanks to be used in war; slow-moving iron monsters likely to kill their own occupants merely with the fumes from their engines. In one area, obviously surrounded by a sound-suppression field, visitors were availing themselves of the opportunity to fire replicas of the weapons used at the time – Enfield rifles, heavy revolvers, Maxim machine guns. The targets available ranged from static silhouette boards to moving manikins that actually bled and screamed. Numerous VR booths offered similar experiences and more besides. It all depended on how much you were prepared to pay, for this whole exhibition was privately owned. Heading down from here would take Cormac directly into wars prior to the first to be numbered. Ahead lay the development of the tank, but only the kind that ran on treads; to his right the propeller-driven airplane, and to his left the machine gun, but only so far as that weapon used solid projectiles. Would such things interest Carl Thrace? Certainly, but nowhere near as much as what lay above, far above. Cormac headed for the nearest stair.

Stepping from the gravcar Cormac expected to feel some disappointment upon once again seeing this drone up close, or rather, up close when he was not himself on the point of death. The distant sight of the drone still roused in him all sorts of complicated feelings, along with the excitement he had felt as a child. Amistad also seemed unchanged: still a big iron scorpion with peridot eyes and weapons ports below its mouth. But Cormac had changed, had experienced an array of situations and emotions, was bigger in every way, so perhaps the drone would look small, not quite so substantial as childhood memory told him.

Drawing closer to where Amistad squatted in the shadow of Vogol's Stone, Cormac realized that childhood or otherwise, edited or not, his memories were not lying to him. If anything, from an adult perspective the scorpion drone was even more fearsome, for he now knew there were numerous reasons to fear it. He knew its armour was tough ceramal it would take a particle cannon to penetrate, and it contained enough weapons to tear a city apart. He knew if any individual pissed it off sufficiently, it would probably use its claws to tear that one apart, slowly, for since this machine was a product of the later years of the war, when the aim was to produce fighting grunts as fast as possible, it was not necessarily stable or moral. Its weapons were supplied with power by laminar storage and fusion reactor, both of which the drone could detonate at will. During the war, its kind had often done this if they were somewhere the explosion could do huge damage to the enemy, or if they were in danger of capture. To say that the entity before him was dangerous was understatement, for Amistad was a purpose-built killing machine with 'bastard' being an essential part of its job description.

The drone rose up onto its numerous legs, the fat hooked sting in its tail looping above threateningly, and a single weapons port opening briefly. It raised one long lethal claw and gestured to the stone above.

'He was a Prador first-child, you know.'

That sonorous voice sent a shiver down Cormac's spine. He gazed up at the stone and considered accessing information about it, but such ready knowledge was a conversation-killer. 'So what was this Vogol's story?'

'He was the leader of a Prador battalion: near on a thousand second-children, war drones, armour, portable p-cannons. We smashed them, but he and a few of his kin survived and climbed to the top of the stone with hard-field generators and two p-cannons. He held us off for two whole hours. He's still up there now.' Amistad flicked its antennae to one side. 'Follow me.'

The drone led the way out from the shadow of the stone

around towards its canted back, where a stairway had been cut into the rock. This last was a recent addition, Cormac noted, because it actually cut through the burn marks and heat-glazing caused by the battle here. The drone's sharp feet scraped the rock, sending flakes of stone tumbling down behind. Within a few minutes they reached a slightly tilted plateau, and there stood Vogol. The first-child was much larger than those of its kind Cormac had encountered aboard the Prador ship down on Hagren, its shell lay nearly ten feet across and its coloration was a bright combination of yellow and purple. It stood there perfectly still, a big rail-gun held in one claw, an ammunition belt and cables trailing to a power supply and heavy ammo box affixed to its underside. As he drew closer Cormac saw that a thick glaze covered the creature, and rods supported it, penetrating into the rock below. Vogol had been stuffed and mounted.

'I got to him first,' Amistad informed him. 'Just after your father managed to down their systems with a computer virus and put a shot through one of their power supplies. Vogol never gave up; even spitting stomach acid at me after I tore off all his limbs.' The drone was chinking a claw against the stone below it as it gazed at the Prador. 'Happy times.'

'Tell me about my father,' said Cormac.

After a long pause the drone reared up and spread both claws expansively. 'I met him here on this world. He was a combat veteran and specialist in attack viruses whose usefulness in creating such viruses was coming to an end because of his frustration with being kept out of the fighting. Just like you he was then moved in as a replacement in a Sparkind unit.' Amistad dropped down onto all legs and turned to face Cormac, not that there was anything in that face Cormac could read. 'I first met him in the Cavander mountains where his unit, among others, and among independent drones like myself, was hunting Prador saboteurs. Being allowed to fight once again, he was taking more risks than he should and using Jebel U-cap Krong's methods: wearing chameleoncloth fatigues and sneaking up on Prador with gecko mines to take them out. The AI on the ground did not like this, but knew it had to give him some leeway.'

It was good to hear this and Cormac was glad he had come, but he knew there was much more to be told. 'This was during the Hessick Campaign?'

'No, a solstan month before.'

'When did you meet him next?'

'You understand what the Hessick Campaign was?'

'The Prador occupied this Peninsula, where they had numerous cities under siege. I'm not clear why they wanted to fight a ground war here – why they didn't just bombard from orbit.' Cormac shrugged. 'It was a big and complicated war.'

'Our understanding of the situation then,' said the drone, 'was that we were certain to lose this world, because if we won the ground war the Prador dreadnoughts would then move in to obliterate everything. But we were fighting a delaying action in order to keep the runcibles online, and ships coming in, wherever possible, to evacuate as many of the people here as we could.' The drone brought one claw down to clonk its tip against the stone, as if making a point. 'It was only as we began the campaign to drive the Prador from the Peninsula so we could evacuate the besieged cities, we found out the true aim of the Prador here.'

'Presumably to establish a foothold, but also retain this world as a living environment,' said Cormac.

'So we thought, but we could see no tactical advantage to them.' The drone shook itself. 'You of course know that this was the time when the traitor Jay Hoop was operating out of the world now named after him: Spatterjay. He was processing tens of thousands of human prisoners, ferried there by the Prador. He was infecting them with the Spatterjay virus in order to make them tough enough to withstand the installation of Prador thrall technology. It is estimated that before his operation was shut down he processed over ten million human beings, but the likely figure is much, much higher.'

Cormac nodded, a nasty taste in his mouth. He had already seen a product of that 'processing', the hooper on Shaparon.

'That's why the Prador were here,' Amistad continued. 'Yes they were fighting ECS forces, but they didn't want to bombard this place and kill everyone because they wanted the people here. Their snatch squads were operating all across the planet. Cities we had thought destroyed during the fighting had in fact been emptied then subsequently demolished.' The drone raised that claw and brought it down hard, splintering stone. 'They were not here to gain some tactical advantage in the war, but for slaves.'

The stair wound up past displays of combat knives, uniforms and handguns. Suspended in the central space was a replica Stuka, then an American tank, then a selection of World War II machine guns. Opposite each of these were drop-shaft entrances to take those with more specific interests to the areas dealing with these items. The WWII room contained more weaponry than the one below, as well as more logistical stuff, though it was still possible to have fun blowing away a manikin with a Sten gun. Divergent halls traced the development of jets during the war and for a number of years thereafter. One whole hall was devoted to atomic weapons used on Earth before Solar System colonization, and another traced the development of submarines, though with a brief diversion at the beginning into the submarine used in the American Civil War and WWI submarines. Cormac kept on climbing, heading for the Solar System Corporate Wars and beyond.

After World War II ensued smaller but no less intense conflicts: the Korean War, Vietnam, the Cold War, the numerous squabbles over fast-depleting oil supplies and the subsequent strife over other resources – then, until the human race established itself in the Solar System, everything was labelled a 'police action' rather than a war. It was during this time that the leaden behemoths of government were bankrupting themselves and imploding while the corporations were growing in power. Effectively the governments were bought out by the corporations, asset-stripped and consigned to history. Then, because they were as human-run as the previous governments and just as liable to greed and stupidity, the corporations began to fight between themselves for power and resources.

The whole of history was not covered here, for that would defeat the purpose of this exhibition. There was nothing here about the diaspora of cryo- and generation-ships during the time of corporate power, nor much about the political complications – they only displayed where relevant to some conflict or the development of some new weapon. Cormac paused by an early attack ship, apparently salvaged from the surface of Io, which was used during an assault on Virgin Jupiter by the Jethro Manx Canard Corporation – one of the survivors of those wars, a weapons development and design corporation still in existence now, though controlled by the AIs. Gazing about himself he saw there were few visitors in this part of the exhibition. Perhaps those coming here who, like himself, had probably bought the bargain price week-long pass were leaving these upper levels until later. He decided to take a side route from this point, for he remembered Carl expressing an interest in JMCC, in the weapons it developed, and in one particular designer.

A side passage took him into a hall detailing the weapons developed by JMCC. The corporation was responsible for much that was still extant now: the pulse-guns, proton weapons and particle weapons – it was left to others to find ways to defend against these destructive devices. The JMCC hall rose in steps heading, he realized, for the Prador War levels above, where the corporation expanded massively to develop the aforementioned weapons into something much more effective. Before reaching that area, which he could identify far ahead by the brassy glint of Prador exotic metal armour, he turned into a small and narrow side hall, whose subject was just one man: Algin Tenkian.

As he stepped in, Cormac downloaded a brief history of the man. Tenkian was born two hundred years ago on Mars during something called the Jovian Separatist Crisis, and as yet there was no record of his death. Originally he was trained in the areas of metallurgy and the then quite young science of force-field dynamics. At age nineteen, on his graduation from VIT (Viking Institute of Technology), the Jovian Separatists recruited him and soon moved him to their weapons division. After four years, when the Separatists had resorted to terrorism, he became disillusioned with their methods and surrendered to Earth Security on Phobos, where he served two years of a ten-year sentence. On his release, Tenkian was forced to join ECS, where he worked for six years; and then, aged thirty-two, he joined JMCC, where he worked for five years, after which he was recorded as leaving the JMCC complex. Three years later he turned up on Jocasta as a designer and crafter of esoteric individual weapons. Beyond that, there was no further chronology.

Cormac could delve further into what was known, but felt no real interest, not now. He stepped up to the first display case and peered inside at a huge bulky handgun with a heavy power cable trailing from its butt to a backpack power supply. This, apparently, was the very first ionic-pulse handgun developed by ECS, and Tenkian had been on the design team. In the next case were rows of small mobile weapons: guns mounted on wheels, treads, inside single wheels, and finally on legs – a row of development terminating in the mosquito autogun. Cormac applied for the download from this display but got nothing. The lights flickered briefly, and he was sure he saw one of the autoguns move. Turning, he glanced behind at the mouth of a drop-shaft over which was a sign saying 'Individual Esoteric Weapons'. Down there doubtless were a few examples of those weapons but mostly copies of them, for many were difficult to obtain, being held in private collections. Then, abruptly, a man – for some reason using the side ladder – climbed into view and stepped from the shaft. Cormac felt the shock of recognition, despite the grey hair, the stoop, the crooked nose.

'You know that ECS is using you, don't you?' said the man. He straightened up and pressed a finger against his temple, adjusting his face so it became the one Cormac knew well.

'Using me, Carl?' Cormac enquired.

Of course Cormac could read no expression in the drone's iron face and peridot eyes, but there was no doubt it was angry about what the Prador had been doing here. Why? Why anger at this particular aspect of a race of vicious homicidal aliens when the battle with this Vogol had been 'happy times'?

'Surely the slaves were a resource and thus a tactical advantage?' he suggested.

Amistad remained utterly still for a short moment, then dipped his front end low to the stone and gave a slow writhe. Poised lower down like this the drone looked even more like the arthropod it had been modelled on, and even more menacing.

'The slaves were never a tactical advantage, nor the human prisoners taken for other purposes.' Those big claws clicked together for a moment then the drone rose up again. 'They were spoils of war. The Prador wanted human slaves because slavery is part of their psychology – all the first-, second- and third-children of the Prador are enslaved by the pheromones produced by their fathers, and most of the adults are enslaved in their vicious hierarchy by those above them. Only a few thousands of adult Prador are in any way we would know of as independent, and only then because they possess enough power and resources for other Prador to consider it too high a risk to either enslave or attack them. It is a precarious existence for them, and in the Prador Kingdom murder and betrayal are just politics.'

'Nice,' said Cormac, gazing at Vogol. Cormac knew all about this anyway. He knew that the second-children he had encountered aboard that ship had still been if not pheromonally then psychologically enslaved by their dead father, still fighting humans as originally instructed, incapable of stopping had they even known the war was over. This Vogol was the same. He ranked higher than most, but still would have been utterly under the control of an adult, and following orders unto death. 'And the human prisoners taken for other purposes?'

'Prador eat their own kind. They often eat their own children. They consider the meat a delicacy not because it tastes so good but because it is an ultimate exercise in power.' Amistad shrugged. 'Once it was an act of evolutionary selection: the weak and the stupid children being turned into dinner. Now it works the opposite way around: the adults killing and eating those who might become too clever, too strong, a threat.'

'But humans?'

'Another rare delicacy and ultimate exercise of power. To Prador, human meat is an acquired taste – certain substances must be eaten with it to prevent poisoning, and a perpetual diet of such meat will kill the Prador concerned.'

Cormac remembered the news stories he had seen as a child; about the livestock farms on Prador-occupied worlds – the livestock concerned being humans who had never known any other life but that farm. How were such people now? Had their minds been edited of the horror?

'We seem to be straying from the key subjects,' he said, 'which are my father and the Hessick Campaign.'

'Come with me,' said the drone, now directing its antennae up towards the top of Vogol's Stone and leading the way. They walked up to the very edge, a thousand-foot drop below and much of the Olston Peninsula and Hessick County spread out before them. Amistad pointed a claw out towards the purple misty line of the Cavander mountains. 'Pushing from there we did manage to drive them from the Peninsula, straight into the sea. But that was precisely what they wanted us to do. They wanted us out of the mountains where they could deploy against us more effectively.'

'And the AIs didn't realize this?'

Amistad turned slightly to peer at him. 'Of course they did, but the thinking was that if we could push them back for just a little while, we could rescue the bulk of the population of Hessick County as far as the Peninsula.'

'So how did that go?'

'Me and your father were not involved in the main push. Along with numerous other Sparkind units and war drones, our jobs were sabotage and assassination. We went in ahead of the main Polity forces, under chameleonware, to hunt down the three adult commanders on the ground, and any other first-children commanders we could find along the way.'

'I know about that,' said Cormac. 'It was the assassination of two of the commanders that drove the remaining one to flee.'

Amistad snipped a claw at the air. 'Later, that was later . . . We didn't manage to get close to any of them at first, though we did manage to take out some of the main first-children, like friend Vogol here. The subsequent main assault went very well, we thought. We pushed their forces back into the sea and were set to bring in atmosphere ships to evacuate some cities. It was only then that we began to find many of the cities were empty, and it was then that the Prador detonated the CTDs they'd spread strategically about the Peninsula. While our forces were still in disarray, some thousands of concealed Prador war drones rose out of the sea and attacked. We started losing very heavily and had to retreat.' The drone paused and gazed steadily at Cormac. 'It was the things that happened during that retreat, and what we did, that finally led to the death of your father.'

'And this you will explain to me?'

'First, during the Prador counter-attack, because your father and I were running attack viruses from a grav platform, we were at the edge of the CTD blast that killed your father's Sparkind unit, killed thousands of others and brought down an atmosphere gunship. Prador war drones then came in and slaughtered many more. Apart from the crew of the gunship *Rickshaw*, we were the only survivors of the battle in Sector 104. Your father took that hard, but was professional enough to continue. It was what happened later that made things worse.'

'I picked up something about that Sector 104,' said Cormac. 'What could be worse than that?'

The drone continued in leaden tones, 'You must understand that the Prador wanted to drive us off this world so they could have unrestricted access to the human population. They wanted those people alive for coring. We knew that and we had to do something about it. At the time it seemed impossible for us to evacuate the population of South Hessick.'

'South Hessick clearance,' said Cormac.

'You know about it?' Amistad enquired.

'Only those words – access is restricted.'

'Three cities in South Hessick were certainly doomed, we thought. There seemed no possibility of rescuing even just one person from them. And it took all our guile and the very best chameleonware technology to even get to a position where we could launch missiles at those cities.'

Cormac felt a shiver go down his spine; so that was what was meant by 'clearance'.

'They were occupied by Prador forces?'

'No.'

'Slavery.'

'Precisely.' The drone sighed. 'As we saw it, the choice the people in those cities faced was the most horrific treatment imaginable followed by a living death, or quick utter extinction. We gave them the latter – it was merciful.' Even through its leaden tone the drone sounded dubious. 'Afterwards your father went slightly crazy, as did some other survivors of the counter-attack, including myself. Hate is a great driver. We took appalling risks, we disobeyed orders, we lost many, but we did the job. We got to the first Prador adult in a hardened bunker established under one of the depopulated cities, then, losing almost 90 per cent of our personnel, we managed to kill the other in its undersea base.'

'I've accessed some of this,' said Cormac, 'but the details are never clear. How did my father die?'

Seemingly ignoring the question, Amistad continued relentlessly. 'As you know, the remaining adult commander was frightened by this and fled the planet. Having seen us kill the first adult and knowing we were going after the second, the AIs predicted something like this might happen. They rapidly deployed one of the new dreadnoughts of the same design as the successful *My Mary Rose* and managed to kill that commander on his way back to his ship, subsequently taking out that capital ship as well. From then on, Prador ground forces began to lose direction. The arrival of more Polity dreadnoughts then further turned the tide up in space and they could then give air support down here. Still, it took us a month to finish them.'

'How did my father die?' Cormac asked again.

After a long, long pause the drone turned towards him again. 'This is the thing I have to tell you, Cormac. Your father did not die here.'

★

'They know I'm here but they can't find me,' said Carl Thrace. Cormac began edging a hand down to his side, towards where he had shoved Pramer's thin-gun into his waistband.

'Now now,' Carl raised a finger. 'You are acquired, and if you do anything incautious my friend here will just have to burn out your guts.'

Glancing round at the case, Cormac saw the mosquito auto-gun had risen high on its legs and was turning. He knew the effectiveness of these machines, having set them up himself with Carl. He wasn't so stupid as to think he could beat one to the draw. He tried auging outside, sending a message to the local AI, to ECS, but got only static.

'Using me?' he repeated, realizing Carl must somehow have isolated this area of the exhibition.

'Certainly – they must be desperate,' said Carl. 'They know I'm here to sell the remaining CTDs to one of the big Separatist organizations and they want to stop that. They've got their agents swarming about here but they're easy enough to avoid if you're not stupid. My guess is that they hoped your presence here would draw me out and, obviously, they were not wrong. Imagine my surprise when Omidran Glass sent me the image of someone who was looking for me.' Carl tilted his head, his expression amused, 'She sent it just before they arrested her aboard her ship.'

'So why is it that I drew you out?' Cormac considered his reasons for being here. If the AIs had not wanted him on a world where Carl was likely to be, it would have been easy enough for them to stop him. Serendipity, perhaps, though that was certainly something no AI would believe in.

Carl drew a squat, nasty-looking pulse-gun and pointed it at Cormac's head. 'Take out the thin-gun, drop it on the floor and kick it over here.'

As he reached for Pramer's gun, Cormac briefly considered

trying to use it, but though he might be able to get off a shot at Carl alone, the autogun would have time to individually burn off his fingers before he pulled the trigger. He carefully took out the gun, dropped it, and kicked it over, though not all the way over. Carl smiled and shook his head, stepped forward and squatted to pick the weapon up. He slid it into his pocket, then stepping to one side and circling around Cormac, said, 'You drew me out, Cormac, because you interest me.' He grimaced. 'For the years I was with you I thought you just a recruit, then subsequent events convinced me you must be an ECS agent, *then* further events have apprised me of the truth: you are a recruit, but a surprisingly adept one. Also, Cormac, I have come to dislike you to the extreme. You are adept, intelligent, and irritatingly moral. You see the world in black and white, and so would make perfect ECS agent material. This is why I am making it my personal business to kill you.'

The static in Cormac's aug stuttered, burping up just a time and one word. The time was twenty minutes and the word was 'chainglass'. Obviously, out there, an AI or agents of ECS had some idea of what was going on in here, but what were they trying to tell him? Twenty minutes was perhaps how long it would take them to get to him – too long, he suspected. But 'chainglass'? He glanced across at the autogun. It was one of the very first designs of such a weapon, but the design had not changed very much since. He could see that rather than firing solid projectiles this one emitted pulses of ionized aluminium, which could cut through just about anything, given time. However, he abruptly realized he was wrong about the speed of this gun – it would take at least a few seconds for those same pulses to cause a collapse of the incredibly long molecules of chainglass, and the weapon was sitting in a chainglass case. He felt that the calculations of ECS went deeper than Carl supposed. The AIs knew Cormac's presence here would draw Carl out because Carl was arrogant, and those who were arrogant tended to be overconfident, and to make mistakes like this one.

Cormac threw himself towards the drop-shaft, sudden pulse-fire lighting up the display case. A thunderous crashing rang out behind him, then something slammed into his right shoulderblade as he rolled over the lip and dropped into the deactivated shaft. He smelt burning flesh as he fell. *Not again*, he thought, visions of autodocs hovering over him. But he would be lucky to survive long enough to end up in a medbay, rather than a morgue.

The drop was only ten feet, which was more than enough, especially when Cormac fell back slamming his shoulder against the drop-shaft wall. He swore then thrust himself through into darkness – obviously the power was completely out in the 'esoteric weapons' section.

'*I am through to you now,*' said a familiar voice in his head.

Forcing himself to subvocalize, Cormac replied, '*Sadist, so it was you.*' He moved on through the darkness, bumping against display cases, just trying to get as far from the mouth of the drop-shaft as he could, utterly aware that a mosquito autogun's vision did not depend on light.

'*What was me?*' the attack ship AI enquired.

'*Sent me the clue about chainglass.*'

'*Oh no, that was the Cavander AI. It will be able to get an ECS team to you in eighteen minutes. It doesn't want to send anyone in until all possible exits are assessed and covered. Carl must have a way out that he thinks is secure so it needs time to find that.*'

Great, so Cormac's function was to keep Carl here for those eighteen minutes. That those minutes might cost Cormac his life was probably factored into the calculation, but at an order of magnitude lower than the importance of capturing someone who had CTDs to sell. Cormac resented that, but even so knew it to be absolutely right. The lights came on.

'I reckon I have about fifteen minutes before they're on their way in,' said Carl, as he stepped from the shaft, the autogun squatting at his feet like some faithful chrome dog. Fortunately there were display cases intervening, though the autogun was not firing. Perhaps Carl did not want to damage some of the stuff in here. Cormac's gaze strayed down to a nearby plaque saying 'Sneak Knife'. The device inside, up on a glass pedestal, was just an opalized blade without a handle, though closer inspection through its translucence revealed some intricate technology inside.

'*Can you help me?*' Cormac asked Sadist.

'*I would like to, but I am not authorized to do so.*'

'*What? Why?*'

'*There is one thing I could do, had you been a member of ECS. However, you are a civilian, and in the weighing of values, the loss of a certain item for research purposes outweighs your usefulness.*'

Cormac wondered what that item might be and what calculations were being made. On what basis did the ruling AIs make their calculations? On the loss of human life, potential suffering, danger to themselves, the Polity, or something beyond the exigencies of beings of mere flesh?

'*I hereby rejoin ECS,*' said Cormac.

Carl sent the autogun off like a sheep dog, around the display cases to his right, while he walked round to the left. Complicated code arrived in Cormac's aug, weird code, something he had never seen before. Some elements of it seemed quite archaic, whilst others strayed into the nonsensical. He could load it, but he was damned if he knew what it would do to his aug or even his mind.

'*The author of that is one Algin Tenkian,*' Sadist informed him. '*The device coming under your control will impress on you, hence its loss to the AIs who have often studied it. It will be yours henceforth.*'

Pulse-gun fire slammed into the opposite side of the 'Sneak Knife' display case, and Cormac threw himself backwards, immediately loading the supplied code. The data expanded in his aug like some sort of computer virus, subsuming memory space, deleting information and rewriting the aug's base programming. It felt like the device was burning into the side of his head, and that somehow the synaptic connections already inside his head were worming deeper. He hit the ground, his shoulder agony, scrambled and threw himself behind another display case as something, *something* in this room connected.

Standing, he felt a presence, just like he had felt with Sadist, but it spoke no words and he sensed at once that it was incapable of doing so. It wanted something, at a computer code level and almost at an instinctive level. When he peered through the display case at the autogun beyond it, that other presence seemed to be sitting at his shoulder, and he felt a species of fierce joy thrum through his connection with it.

The thing in this room had found what it wanted: *a target.*

Carl now stepped into view, his gun pointed casually at Cormac's head. The autogun was also moving into position and in a matter of seconds he would be in its range of fire. Carl grinned, enjoying the moment. Doubtless he would have some last words for Cormac, some last sneer. Training with the Sparkind, Cormac had learned one thing that stayed with him always: never grandstand, never hesitate. If you have an opportunity to kill an enemy do it at once, for that opportunity may pass.

A high whine penetrated, and Carl looked up, puzzled, the words yet to leave his mouth. The whine turned to a shriek and a nearby display case exploded into white powder, its chain molecules disintegrating. A glittering wheel skimmed from the falling cloud, straight towards the autogun. It hit with a sound like a high-speed grinding wheel going through a tin can, and the autogun's body clattered to the floor, separated from its legs.

'What the—?' Carl began, as Cormac again turned to him.

Target.

The glittering wheel turned at right angles and shot towards

Carl. It came up from the floor, across him and beyond. He stood there, his expression still puzzled, then a red line appeared at a slant across his face from chin to temple. He staggered, and the upper part of his head above that line simply fell away, then he slumped to the floor, blood pumping into a spreading pool from the exposed face of his brain.

After a long pause, Cormac walked over and gazed down at him. That chunk of his skull had been chopped cleanly away like a lump of Chinese radish. Looking up, Cormac studied the thing that had done the deed, the thing hanging in mid-air and revolving slowly. Now he discerned that it possessed a small grey star-shaped body from which extended blades of some treated form of chainglass – it had to be a special glass to have gone through its case like that. He walked over to the destroyed display case and picked up the plaque lying in the chainglass dust: Shuriken throwing star with Tenkian micromind, microtok-powered and grav-capable.

In the dust also lay a holster with a small programming console inset in it. The strap, he realized, fitted perfectly around one wrist. He picked it up and put it on, then held up his arm. The throwing star flicked gore from its blades, retracted them and hummed down to the holster like a falcon returning to its master's arm. As he watched the shuriken slot itself home, Cormac felt the holster grow warm. There was much, he realized, that he must learn about this weapon. He suspected this was the beginning of a long association.

'My father did not die here,' Cormac repeated.

The drone sighed again, and again pulled itself down closer to the ground. This time it did not look so threatening, so much like a giant vicious arthropod, but weary – which was odd really, considering it ran on a fusion reactor.

'After we killed the second Prador adult, it was a hard fight getting out of there,' Amistad told him. 'David was captured, along with others, and taken offworld by one of the last Prador snatch squads to get away from here.'

'Snatch squad.' Cormac felt stupid. Was he just going to stand here repeating everything the drone was telling him?

'There was no time or resources to be spared to try and find those who were taken. I wanted to find him, but I could not be spared, and there were Prador to kill.'

A lengthy pause ensued, and Cormac gazed out across lands that had once seen such vicious conflict and horror. His father was taken by a snatch squad. He knew precisely what that meant, intellectually, but did not want to accept it on any other level.

'You would think that a machine mind is incapable of emotion,' the drone said.

Cormac had thought so, but the Golem Crean had disabused him of that notion.

Amistad continued, 'We are capable of emotion, and more, and when our minds are hurriedly put together under the exigencies of a fight for survival, we are also quite capable of going insane. This is what happened to me, this is why I felt sure I must find David Cormac's kin and tell them what had happened to him. Luckily the Tritonia AI intervened before I loaded that on your shoulders at such an early age. After I left Earth I searched for five years. I joined the police action against Jay Hoop's organization on Spatterjay. We found the camps and released those prisoners who had yet to be cored and thralled, while eliminating those who had ceased to be human. We checked what records we could find, and discovered how many millions had been processed. I know that millions will never be found, never be known about, but some could be traced and David was one of them.'

'What happened to him?'

'Surely you understand?'

'I'm not sure . . .'

'Your father was taken to Spatterjay where, from the bite of a leech, he was infected with the Spatterjay virus. When the virus had sufficiently changed his body, made it tough enough to withstand such abuse without dying, most of his brain was cut away and replaced with Prador thrall technology.'

There it was: the plain horrible truth. Cormac felt sick at the thought, but he also felt distanced. This was a father he could be proud of, a man to be admired who had met such a horrible end, but he was also a father Cormac could hardly remember.

'He became the property of a Prador captain called Enoloven, whose domain lies just inside the Prador Kingdom at the border, on the edge of the Graveyard. Enoloven was high in the hierarchy of the Second Kingdom, but when the old king was usurped – an event which led to the end of the war – Enoloven was not in favour with the new king, and had no place in the Third Kingdom. He was attacked and killed, his properties divided amidst the loyal and much sold off. Your father was one item sold to human criminals resident in the Graveyard.'

Cormac suddenly got the nasty idea that the human blank he himself had seen in the Graveyard had been his own father. No, that was madness.

'I found your father's new owner,' said Amistad as he snipped a claw at the air, probably in response to some strong memory, 'and his cohorts. They did not survive the meeting.'

'My father?'

'Used for display fighting against genetically modified beasts.'

'What did you do with him?'

'The only thing that could be done,' said the drone. 'Look down at where you stand.'

Cormac did so, and noted that just ahead of him was a clear rectangular section of stone set into the otherwise burnt and heat-glazed rock.

'I could not bury him complete because what he had become

was something that would never die easily. His ashes lie there, underneath that stone.'

Staring at his father's grave, Cormac tried to understand what he was feeling. He wanted to feel grief, but only because surely, that was what should be expected from him. He felt nothing like that. This place was a good and dramatic one. This was completion, an ending to a story and the beginning of another.

'Perhaps you would like me to cut some words into the stone?' the drone suggested.

'I feel no need for them, though perhaps my mother or my brothers . . .'

'If you will allow.'

Amistad loomed up beside Cormac and intense light flickered across the stone ahead, which crackled and smoked. As soon as this ceased, Cormac stepped up and gazed down at the perfectly incised shape of a scorpion cooling from red-heat.

'Yes, I think that's fine,' he said, and turned away to keep an appointment with the future.